# A Choice to Yield

## By

## Lonz Cook

ELEVATION
BOOK PUBLISHING

Copyright © 2009 by Lonz Cook

ISBN   978-1-943904-00-6

*Published by:*

BOOK PUBLISHING

*400 W Peachtree St NE*
*Suite 716*
*Atlanta, GA 30308*
*Printed in the United States of America*

*Published  September 2015*

# Dedication

To all those who endured the dynamics of the imagination and embraced the idea, this dedication goes to you. For invested hours and hair twisting pulls, the outcome of agony produced this book. It lives because of you!

My grateful admiration goes beyond, where the journey of the idea began, and paths wandered directionally awry, yet together intertwined a joyous end.

Thank you goes without word. My love travels with open arms embracing those who contributed. More than a dedication in words, you have my emotional gratitude, and as promised a just reward ventures to your hand.

Thank you all, my loving friends

# Chapter 1

Mark and Angela flew on the return flight to Atlanta in seats
23A & 23B. It marked the end of an amazing weekend.
Memorable events flashed through their minds, bringing
goodness to their hearts from sharing quality time. It was her
first trip with a man, a man she truly enjoyed, felt love from,
and adored. It was Mark being the perfect gentleman,
making the experience a standard, showing her what a
woman should know.

It started at the airport in South Florida. Mark had things
coordinated as the experienced traveler. They caught the
shuttle to a rental car company, took off in a convertible, and
drove to a lovely bed and breakfast. On the way, Angela
noticed how buildings were different in comparison to those
in Atlanta. The clay shingled roof structures were noticeably
bold with bright colors, and building windows were mirrors
from the dark tint reflecting the sun. Both the natural and
manicured landscapes were great with strong colored
vegetation, bold flowers, and green grass. The palm trees
were tripled in comparison to the number of Georgia pines,
and they were large enough to give shade along the byways.
Within two hours, they arrived at the wonderful bed and
breakfast, standing as a castle in the midst of giant hotels. A
building with character, reminiscent of the 19<sup>th</sup> century
which held it's own in class and style.

Friday night began with a walk along the beach which gave
view to the moonlit ocean, sparking the imagination of a path
to forever. Mark did everything imaginable to touch her soul.
He whispered sweet nothings, sweetly sang a love ballad
with the rhythm of the approaching waves, and held her as a
man on a mission. She never knew a man's skin could
glisten, reflecting the soft moonlight. Mark was truly

amazing. The night filled with dinner, wine, and dancing, setting the stage for a solemn calm, a cuddled slumber.

Saturday morning launched with breakfast on the balcony viewing the ocean. It was the taste of good coffee, a mixed bowl of tropical fruits, and the smell of fresh sea air giving her the spark of joyous intent. Mark lavished her with passion before leaving the hotel. He made love to her, taking her to heights of pleasure, repeatedly, until she broke tears. Angela never cried from a man's touch, experienced such passion, or lived through the extensive focus, and all from gentle hands. She cried before leaving the room that morning, and was thankful for each tear.

It was lovely jazz music from 10 am until 9 pm on Saturday. Sitting in the park at the jazz festival, enjoying the music, he made sure she had everything of comfort. When the music played, they danced to whatever moved them. Like any good people they mingled, shared in singing with the crowd, and laughed at themselves while searching for shade; dodging the bright sun. Though it was their first festival, they behaved with total comfort, seeking a closer connection. And like all other festival goers, they grooved with each act.

Saturday night ended with another love making session. Angela fell along the bed grasping for air, after Mark stopped moving with the sound of crashing waves, and finally released her from his tight embrace. They laid in silence and felt the cool ocean breeze. The French doors to the balcony were opened during the night so the air touched them before and after the heat of passion. Making love repeated in sessions until early morning hours.

Sunday morning they had coffee on the balcony watching the sun rise. They sat in silence and allowed the moment to embrace the ideas of tomorrow. It was their connection to nature, to a gift, and to life. It was a symphony of events to a new day and they experienced it like a gaze of years into the future. The Jazz Festival was shorter in length and started later in the day. They attended as planned but adjusted their seating location, hiding from direct sun rays during the concert. They decided to leave the festival a little earlier and enjoy the beach. On the beach, Angela and Mark conversed on everything and anything that came to mind. They shared in content the important things most people miss when blindly in love. They walked, laughed, and played into the evening. They relaxed until their early Monday morning flight.

Angela smiled at Mark, as she admired him having the energy as vibrant as the sun. She held Mark's arm and placed her head on his shoulder while the plane hurried down the runway. During the flight, she remembered Florida's white sands, ocean waves, and feeling the cool breeze while sitting in the warm Caribbean sun. It was the calm after a peaceful storm, the extenuation of Mark showing his true love. Mark smiled at Angela as if the moment was a confirmation of true love and celebration. His smile told her of his luck, his joy, and his excitement having her in his life. "Hey baby," he said, "I had a wonderful time. We should do it again?"

"When do we leave?" Angela whispered. Smiling, as she finally settled for the flight. She held onto his arm, closed her eyes, and reminisced to the phone call with Paula, just after meeting Mark earlier in the year.

"Paula, you're not going to believe this. I didn't think I'd ever cross the color line."

"What line are you talking about?" replied Paula

"I met a man."

"And surely a line you crossed? Aren't you heterosexual and attracted to men? I'd understand if you were with a woman."

"You don't get it; I met a very nice man."

"As I hope you'd meet a nice wonderful man. Why not? You deserve to meet one."

"And I met one. He is so handsome. He's intelligent, seems quite kind, very gentleman like, and those few hours were the best time. He is absolutely charming."

"Then why did you call me and talk about crossing a line?"

"He is a man of color."

"Oh, a man of color; you mean black?"

"Yes, he's a black man."

"Oh, oh my dear poor woman, you can't."

"Why the concern? Is it bad?"

"Oh, it's bad, have you heard what kind of men they are?"

"Yes, I've heard it all. I heard about the smell black people have, the bad behavior, the lack of respect for women, the lack of respect for authority, and how they can't communicate with the general public because of their Ebonics language. Yes, it's why my meeting him was so astonishing. I met one who relates to me and understands much more than the stereotype."

"How did you meet him?"


Winter months of 2006 Angela visited a Barnes and Noble bookstore, researching multiple interests, or purchasing novels. She frequently noticed a tall slender well-dressed African American male who periodically spoke to her. He greeted her with a "hello" or time of day with the kindest voice. His manner was normal for any American man. Very courteous, with a gentle demeanor, was his consistent impression. Angela never paid much attention to him, other than his entrance, as a habitual response to her surroundings, she was observant for security reasons, being a single woman one can't be too careful.


One particular Saturday afternoon, Angela passed the black man as he stood in a romance section of the store. She took the chance to speak first, remembering at any given time, the gentleman would speak to her. This time she broke the ice, "Hello," she said, "How are you?" Startled in response, "Hi," he replied with a smile. "It's nice seeing you."

Angela smiled and moved without replying. He continued to search shelves for an interesting book. Angela walked to the next aisle, and noticed the gentleman's head would periodically bob, as if he were hooked to a fishing line on the lake. With each bob, she'd wonder what book he chose. For some reason, she never recalled seeing him in the Romance section. Curiosity took control, as her intrigue to find what on earth he was looking for.

Angela maneuvered near the gentleman and observed his book selections. She watched each type of book he'd finger through and wondered of his motivation. "Is he trying to understand women?" she asked herself. She walked near him, within an arms reach, and selected the last book he returned to the shelf. "Interesting book," she thought after reading the back cover. "A romance novel, yet different from the general theme, woman desires man, man swoons woman, woman marries man, they live happy ever after. Not this book, differently so, the book is realistic in nature, man meets woman, together they fight controversy, find a better path, and return to reality." She thought to herself.

"I see you have similar interest," Mark said.

"Oh," Angela replied quite startled, "Yes, I do."

"I like reading the romantics, but not the feel good types."

"Feel good?"

"Yes, you know those happily-ever-after books are all based on fantasy."

"Yes, those Harlingen types. I read them from time to time, but they aren't my favorite selection."

"Allow me to introduce myself, I'm Mark. And your name is?" he asks, offering to shake her hand.

"Angela" she replied, reaching to accept the handshake.

"I see you here quite often. Well most times when I come in, I'm normally in the self-help or business sections."

"Yes, we've crossed paths in here quite often. Well don't let me stop you from finding a good romance novel."

"You weren't interrupting me at all. As a matter of fact, once I find one, would you like to know the title so we can later compare notes?"

"Sure, it's nice of you, but I have so many books to read at the moment. On second thought, maybe you can tell me about it one day when we cross paths."

"Sure, maybe over coffee. Great, here's my card. Call me."

"Sounds like something good to do, here is my card." Angela replied walking to another section. Angela never turned to see if Mark was looking, she didn't want to give off any vibe of interest. She thought he was a nice guy but not an interest to date. Mark watched Angela walk away before reaching for another book she'd spotted. "She is a very attractive woman," he thought. "I wonder if she'd…No, not quite, no way. Often times I can tell if a woman would have interest in me; especially a pretty woman, a Caucasian woman; probably not likely," and thought nothing more of it.

Angela returned searching for a particular book of interest. She settled in a comfy chair and started reading. "Chapter 1," she sighed, as if the introduction fed her intrigue. A quick glance above the book and passing her was Mark; not passing intentionally but on his way to the checkout. Mark glanced with a smile, a quick wave goodbye and moved right along to pay for his book. "He is really nice, and seems very polite," Angela thought. Returning to her book she read the first paragraph. Within minutes of reading, something bugged her about the earlier incident. Her mind boggled to why she agreed to have coffee and discuss his book. "You know, I don't normally agree to any interaction with men of color. It's not like me. I never thought conversing would be harmful, so why do I question it?"

Mark left the bookstore, got in his auto and drove back to his office. On the way, he recalled his few moments with Angela. "She was very nice to me in the bookstore. I'm sure her agreement to have coffee with me was a kind gesture. No way did I feel interest from her. If I see her again, we'll find out if it was kindness or not."

Mark grew up in a military family, attended high school on base where all the kids were practically the same. All of his friends were of multiple ethnicities, Arabic, Asian, Black, Caucasian, and Hispanic. Just like the military, the families mingled day in and day out. Dating anyone of interest was a normal occurrence. There were no concerns to him about race, until visiting his grandparents in the southern states of the U.S. Mark developed a liking for all people and never took those old stories of his grandparents to heart. He respected his history, but never allowed it to influence his decision about people. Well, not until it was time to attend college. Mark followed his parental influence and decided to attend a Historically Black College or University (HBCU). He left the all-equal military environment for a college in Tennessee. The four-year experience opened his eyes to his blackness. Yes, the experience was a revelation and there he realized how African-American he is. Those stories of his grandparents hit home, but Mark was strong in his conviction to believe what he saw growing up in military environments. All people were the same and to like whomever you wished.

Angela, born in a midsize Midwestern town to an upper-middle class family, attended high school where there were few minorities. She saw a small number of Hispanics and was rarely exposed to a Black family in town. However, Angela never interacted with anyone other than Caucasians. Her eye-opener was when she attended her state university. She met and interacted with a few African women, not African American, but from Ghana. Her exposure to the women was an interesting experience, but not dynamic enough to befriend them into her inner circle. Angela distantly observed African Americans but not really took the time to integrate any into her circle of friends. She didn't quite push them away but neither did she try to cross barriers of interaction. It wasn't her cup of tea at the time, nor did she have any interest or motivation to do so. Angela graduated college without ever getting close to one person of color. It wasn't that she made an effort to avoid creating friendships, but she had no interest to integrate her world. The same crew she finished college with the same inner circle of friends whom she began her adult transition.

Angela and Paula continued their phone conversation.

"Never, did I imagine my interest would take me to this experience," said Angela.

"Most things we never see. You shouldn't blame yourself, it just happened. What really happened?" replied Paula.

"Ah, where can I start? Many things happened and surprisingly so its nothing like one can expect."

"You expected something?"

"To be honest, I actually did because of known conceptions."

"Oh really, this guy made those multiple conceptions true? Then it's proven you shouldn't be saddened by your actions. You should be happy it's over and you've learned those perceptions are quite true."

"No, actually not one was true. Funny thing, it's actually better than I expected. Once I realized what to expect, of course."

"It's something you'll have to explain. I have all day," said Paula.

"Let me start by saying, its nice having a true gentlemen show so much respect. At the bookstore, we found ourselves having in depth conversations. Nothing demeaning about the subject or exchange, it was very interesting."

"I've seen where people wait for chairs and how they look at others. Did you have odd looks from the crowd?"

"I didn't notice anyone looking at the time, because it was very different. I mean, it wasn't like we were together. It was just two people conversing over books. Our seating was across from each other, not lateral as in most couples. Why would anyone notice us?"

8

"Because most people do, they notice but probably too shy to say anything."

"It could be they saw two interesting people in conversation. Anyway before you analyze my story, let me finish. We can talk about the social thing later."

"Angela, I have to go. Call me later - I want to hear it all."

"Ok, Paula, I'll call you when I get a chance to talk. Bye," Angela replied. "Weird," thought Angela. "I didn't think my best friend would…..no she isn't…., she wants to know it all. Yes, a know it all."

Mark grew wary of his conversation with Angela. "I haven't heard from her. Should I call her?" he pondered while dressing for Sunday evening. Mark thought of a great place for live entertainment. He recalled this swell place, jazzy, and contemporary with great meals. There's always a surprise artist-in-waiting who often joins the stage. You never know who'll show up and play with the band. Sometimes it's a popular professional, who recently finished a gig or is just passing the time between shows. I should call Angela and maybe she has nothing planned. Mark grabbed his cellular and called her. After two rings, Angela answered "Hello."

"Hi Angela, its Mark, I hope you don't mind me calling."

"No, I don't mind. I think it's kind of surprising really."

"Oh, well allow me to continue the surprise. What are you doing tonight? I don't want to make it seem like I'm forward, but I thought about you. Are you interested in going out for dinner and music?"

"I haven't anything planned. But, dinner and music sounds interesting. What kind of music?"

"Jazz."

"I don't think I like jazz. I mean I've heard it but its nothing I thought of actually listening too."

"You know you'll never find out what it's like if you never try. Come on, the food there is wonderful and the atmosphere is pretty interesting."

"Well, I'm not doing anything…. so."

"Good, what time do you think you'll be ready?"

"I think around eight."

"Ok, let's meet at the bookstore and drive together" Angela paused before she answered, thinking, "I have to trust this guy not only at the jazz place, but during the drive there and back. Oh, what if he doesn't take me where we agreed? What if he's a horrible driver? What if he's really a serial killer?"

Mark listened intently during the pause. He waited for an answer to their driving together and figured it wasn't her comfort zone. "Angela you can follow me there. Or better yet you can meet me at the place."

"I think meeting you is better," she replied.

"Ok, let me give you the address. It's the corner of Roswell Road and Hyman Place called Cafe 290. I'll wait for you in the parking lot and we can enter together. You have my cellular number right?"

"Got it, I'll see you at eight," sighed Angela with a sound of relief.

"Great, I'll talk to you soon." Mark replied and discon- nected the call. "She is not too trusting. I can understand why, it's a good thing she's driving. I know it's got to be a control thing, if she doesn't like it; she can leave at her own will. I can understand."

After preparing for the evening, Angela drove with caution to the location. She noticed the club wasn't in the city's best location; however the people going inside seemed pretty decent. "At least it isn't a hole in the wall kind of place," she thought as she parked. Her car was right in front so she could observe the place before walking in. She watched multiple ethnic groups enter the club. People from all lifestyles, dressed quite well, mostly in casual attire, went in. The median age of folks seemed around the mid 30's. She also noticed multiple expensive cars parked in the lot. "There is a serious clientele at this place, it can't be so bad."

Mark arrived five minutes before eight and scanned the parking lot. He didn't see Angela in any car. So, he decided to call her for a location check. Before dialing he noticed a missed call. It was a number from an old friend. "I'll call Angela first and return the other call," he thought. One ring Angela answered. "Hi, I'm nearly there," she said, sitting in the parking lot observing the surroundings.

"Great, let me know when you arrive. I'll go to the front so you'll see me. I'll wait for you there."

"Good, I'll see you there." She replied before disconnecting.

Mark returned to the cellular phone number dialing the missed call. One ring and Reid answered, "Hello Mark."

"Reid, it's amazing you called me. I'm where we use to hang out long ago. How are you?"

"Not bad, as a matter of fact, I'm doing well. So you're at the old stomping ground? Is there a good band playing tonight?"

"Glad you're doing Ok. No, nothing I know of tonight. I'm meeting this lovely lady as a matter of fact. What's on your mind my man?"

"I called to catch up. I hadn't talked to you since, oh..."

"...Months," answered Mark.

"Yes, months. Does this lady have a friend?"

"I'm sure she does, but right now Cafe 290 is new to her. I think new experiences can be fun, but sometimes they can be scary. It's exposing her to something quite different. You know, most new   friends aren't too accepting to different environments nor are they impressed very often."

"Her first time at Cafe 290, it's a place where many enjoy? Are you breaking the ice for her?"

"Breaking the ice? Well, in a way I am. Here she comes. I'll have to call you later or if you come I'll see you."

"Cool, be careful not to introduce too much at once. I know how overbearing you can get." Reid laughed.

Angela approached the front of Cafe 290. She is dressed quite nice, attractive as a fresh day in spring. "How lovely you are tonight." Mark complimented.

"Thank you," Angela smiled. "I haven't been here before, and as you know, it's quite interesting. I read about it in the weekly *What's Happening* paper. The place has rave reviews." Reaching to assist her up the stairs, Mark replied, "Yes, I told you it's awesome. There is always a very nice crowd and though it's not the best decorated place in town, it's inviting in atmosphere." They walked into the club, after Mark held the door for her. The first impression is the simple decorations, and the band not playing as expected, but soft music in the background. There are multiple couples sitting for dinner and people of different ethnicities all around the bar. "Is this the normal clientele?" asked Angela.

"Yes it is. The place is owned by an Italian guy. His clientele is any one who loves jazz."

"How nice this place seems."

"Were you expecting something different?"

"Well, I don't want to sound out of place or stereotypical, but yes I thought it would be more of a dark place."

"Oh, you mean mostly black people as the major clientele. Well, it's why I asked you to meet me. I'm glad you took the chance even though it's not quite what you expected. Is it not being darker a disappointment to you?"

"No, it's no disappointment. It's quite fine here. I just expected a little different."

"Thanks for your honest answer; I like a woman who shares her real thoughts."

The two walked to a table. Mark pulled out a chair for her and stepped aside, encouraging Angela to take a seat.

"The best table and seat in the place," he exclaimed.

"Why do you think it's the best?" asked Angela.

"It's out of the general path, easy to get to for the wait staff, and we have a great view to the entertainment. Best seats in the place."

A waiter appeared just as Mark sat across from Angela. "Hello I'm your waiter tonight. Can I take your drink orders?"

"Angela, I don't know what you like, but can I take a guess?" Mark stated.

"Sure, please do," Angela winked.

"She'll have an Apple Martini and I'll have a Black Russian to start."

"Great choices are you ready to order dinner or do you need a few minutes?" asked the waiter.

"We'll take a few minutes and look over the menus."

"I'll get these drink orders in and return for your dinner request."

"Thanks" Mark replied to the waiter.

"Apple Martini; what made you order it?" asked Angela

"A guess, it's sweet and sour to the taste, strong enough to say it's a drink, but smooth enough to sip and feel the effect of drinking."

"Oh, feel the effect of drinking. Are you trying to get me drunk?"

"Oh no, of course not; you asked why I chose the Apple Martini. I thought you'd enjoy it. Was I wrong?"

"No, it's a drink I've never had. Well, I've had martinis but not apple."

"Hopefully you'll like it. Are you hungry? There are great chefs here at Cafe 290."

"Yes, I am quite hungry. It was our plan to have dinner here right?"

"Yes it is. May I suggest a very fine dish for you?"

"Please do."

"There is this bourbon chicken dish to die for. It melts in your mouth, and the taste lingers with the veggies. It's my favorite. Then if chicken isn't your cup of tea, there's this lamb dish, exquisite to enjoy."

"Oh the chicken sounds lovely."

"Great. It's Bourbon Chicken for you. I'll have the lamb dish just to be different."

"Sounds great to me," answered Angela.

13

The waiter returned with drinks. Automatically Mark informed the waiter of their dinner orders. Angela noticed she didn't have to make her order. It was as if, well, it was quite different for her as it was a first time someone ordered for her; a little thing to notice.

"I understand this is a first for you."

"A first for you; what do you mean?"

"It means being across from a man of different color or ethnicity, in a very cultural place, having a great drink and hopefully enjoying a delicious dinner."

"Well, since you put it as such. Yes, it is a first for me. But I hadn't noticed you being different from others." As if, it was Angela's honest answer. It's the exact reason why she hesitated to enter the place with Mark.

"Hey, it's Ok to be afraid of change or something new. I don't mind exposing you to something different. I know you'll enjoy this. From our conversations in the bookstore I learned you'd enjoy the experience."

"What if I don't?"

"We simply don't return. But, I know you'll enjoy it or I wouldn't have asked you to meet me here."

"Ok, I'm open to see how it goes."

"Thanks for being open tonight and thanks for coming with me."

"What are your friends like?" asked Angela.

"My friends are all so different. I can't explain them in a general statement. "Do you have friends all alike?"

"No, I don't have cookie cutter people as friends. I guess my question was silly now thinking of it?"

"Actually it's a very good question. Most people gravitate to someone similar as a comfort zone, and we do the same in our social circle."

"True statement, very true. I think we like those we are comfortable with. And comfort goes with exposure."

"Yes it does, the greater your exposure, the better you learn more of your comfort zone." Mark reached for his drink as he finished his statement. Angela looked around to see whose watching. She observed the multiple tables of interracial people having dinner which sparked her curiosity. She noticed no one watched them as Paula asked earlier in the day. "You know, it's an inviting atmosphere."

"I'm glad you feel this way. It's an affirmation to my perception of things."

"So, why did you ask me here?"

"I wanted us to have dinner and enjoy the music together. Do you think there's another reason?"

"No, it's just out of the multiple places here in Atlanta to visit. I just wondered why here?"

"It's a great place, once you get over the entry. I think Atlanta is full of wonderful places, and my like for people fit just as well."

"I normally stay on the north side of town."

"We're on the north side, just a little further south than you're accustomed."

"Oh, I see, still north of the perimeter."

"Yup, and there's more to enjoy inside the perimeter if we get to another date."

"This is a date?"

"Well, not if you don't think so."

"No, I don't think it is. We're just two people having dinner in a jazz place."

"The explanation is good enough for me."

"Ok, I hope I didn't offend you by saying so."

"No offense taken.'

The music set started with a band. The music became much louder than the soft jazz during their earlier arrival. There was a five piece band who enjoyed playing their sound. One right after the other, music fans stopped to look at them as if they were waxed action figures.

"My, how much interest do they get?" Angela pointed to the band.

"You haven't any idea who they are?" Mark replied.

"No. I'm not much of a jazz connoisseur."

"The guy in front is one of the major Jazz Players in the nation; he comes here often, mostly unexpected and plays in a jam session. They aren't a complete band."

"You mean he plays here for free?"

"I don't know about him playing for free, but I do know if you saw him in concert, our tickets would cost more than $50 per person."

"Wow."

"Its part of what makes this place so awesome."

The waiter served the meals as the music drew a larger crowd. People in greater numbers stood around the bar, the tables filled, and the fact of having the best table in the house became evident. The dinners were excellent, just as Mark described. One bite and a burst of flavor exploded in her mouth. It was enough to make Angela smile. "I told you it was good," Mark commented.

"Oh, it's surprisingly good. I knew you spoke of having wonderful taste, but I had no idea how good this was going to be." Angela replied, taking another bite.

"My, at the rate you're eating, I'll have to protect my lamb," Mark laughed.

"If it's any thing like this chicken, you may have to," Angela responded with a giggle. She realized it's the first time she laughed or giggled tonight. It's amazing how a wonderful a meal can change the outlook on a place. She continued to observe, listen, and enjoy Club 290. "Paula would love coming here," she thought.

After dinner, drinks, and music, the night came tumbling to an end. Mark paid the waiter after receiving those last drinks for the night. Ending with the band's last set; they finished their drinks and realized it was quite late.

"How was your evening madam?" Mark asked.

"It was very good. I liked both the meal and music. Thank you," replied Angela.

"Are you open for a late night cup of coffee?"

"No, not tonight, but thanks for a lovely evening. It was quite nice."

"Are you ready to leave?"

"Actually, I am. I have plans for tomorrow."

"Great, I hope you enjoy your week. "

"Sure thing, I'll enjoy the week of work, this was a great start."

"Can I walk you to your car?"

"I don't mind," she answered. "I'm glad he offered because I didn't think it would be safe going to my car," she thought

"Please, after you," Mark stood and waved his hand for her to lead. They walked to the exit. Moving across the parking lot, the two strolled to the car.

Mark exclaimed, "This is one of the safest places in town. Not too many incidents occurred near Cafe 290. It has its own security throughout the parking lot, and it's well known as off-limits to thieves of Atlanta."

"It's nice to know," replied Angela.

"Nice it is, another reason I like to come here. Are you sure you enjoyed yourself?"

"Oh, I did for sure."

"Good," Mark replied, opening Angela's car door. Angela entered and started the engine. Mark closed the door and waved goodnight before he returned to the club entrance, walking without looking back. "I guess it was an experience for Angela," he thought. "How can I get to know her? I'll see her again at the bookstore next Tuesday."

Angela called Paula on her drive home

"Paula, am I too late for a chat?"

"No, of course not you go right ahead. How are you?"

"Oh, tonight was awesome."

"Oh really? How awesome was it?"

"It was pretty awesome for a first date."

"Did you say date?"

"Yes, I said date," answered Angela. It was amazingly interesting for one night of dinner and jazz."

"You went to a jazz club here in the city?"

"Yes, here in the city and it isn't far from my place. We should go there and make a girl's night of it."

"Are you serious?" asked Paula.

"Of course I am. Are you afraid to go?"

"Afraid is not what I'd say. I think challenging would be better."

"Challenging to you or me? I saw a mixture of people there and nothing seemed so challenging about it. The food was awesome, the music was great, and the artists were white."

"It isn't a color or race thing. What makes it challenging is it isn't my cup of tea. You know, it isn't my type of music."

"We can do another place of course, something into your type of music? You think it'll offer more enjoyment? I think a little Rock and Roll is in order. We can plan this weekend."

"Sure, it's awesome having a friend who can share it all," replied Paula

"You mean someone to keep you in the comfort zone of like people."

Angela found herself at bay, "What's the fear? It isn't like black folks will band together and run her out. I didn't see any such thing at all." Arriving home, Angela grabbed a bottle of wine, poured a glass, and moved to the living room. She lit a few candles, all in one swoop around the room. Sitting in the corner, with a remote in her hand, a click of the button and her favorite song filled the air.

"Wow, a relaxing song," she thought and pondered, "What happened tonight? When I dated the last guy, he didn't do things like Mark. The conversation itself was about me, his courtesies were gentlemanly, and respect was apparent; tonight was interesting. I don't know if I'll ever go out with Mark again, but he's impressive."

Mark returned to the bar, ordered a drink, and stood in observation of the diverse people in the club. Amazed at the numbers, he was surprised to realize the mixture was 7 to 1 black to white. For every large crowd of people, there was at least one white person and nothing odd being said. "I know Angela has never been exposed to such a location, and I hope she isn't ill with it. She didn't seem angry when she left," he thought. "After this drink, I'll leave."

As if the night ended on a bleak note, Mark arrived at his place, threw the keys in the normal spot, hit the shower, set his alarm for a 7 am and hit the bed. Within hours the alarm blared as it signaled the day beginning. Dress, coffee, a quick breakfast, and out the door to the job. Just as he entered the car, his phone rang.

"Hello," said Mark

"Hi Mark, its Angela."

"Wow, I didn't expect you to call me this morning. How are you?"

"Surprisingly well and why are you surprised?"

"I shouldn't be but I feel like I am. How was your night?"

"As if you didn't know"

"Is it a happy or a sarcastic answer?"

"Why would it be sarcastic?"

"Am I supposed to answer? It sounds like a set up." Mark replied and started driving his car towards his office.

"No, you don't have to answer, I'll just tell you. I had a wonderful time with you last night. Thank you."

"You're welcome. I'm happy you had a great time. Hopefully we can do it again soon."

"It's a possibility."

"Just a possibility?"

"Yes it's possible we can go out again."

"Did you think last night was a date?"

"No date, but an interesting time. As a matter of fact, it's why I called you. What do you have planned Wednesday?" Angela asked.

"Nothing much; just a quiet night at home and catching up on some sleep. You know we older guys need to bounce back after a long night out." Mark laughed.

"Oh bull crap, you're in great shape and I know a nap is all you need. I'm thinking of taking you to a place I know. Since you shared something with me, I'd like to share an experience with you."

"Ok, well, I'll follow your lead."

"I'll call you with the details at noon. Don't be afraid," Angela laughed.

"I won't, Angela. Talk to you later."

"What am I going to do?" Angela asked herself. "Why would I offer to take him out with no idea where to go?" Angela left the kitchen with a cup of coffee, and moved into the bedroom to finish dressing. "I know, we can go to Londzell's in Roswell and it will do the trick. There the numbers aren't anything like last night. It's a Wednesday night too. It truly makes it a bland night. I'd like to see how he operates in such environment. Yes, put him in an environment opposite to what I experienced."

Mark made it to the office just in time for the morning roll up. He answered those weekend dating inquires from office buddies and filled the guys in on last night's events.

"I think tonight will be very different," he tells Fred, a work companion from Wisconsin. "Where can she take me on a Wednesday night in Atlanta?"

"I think I have an idea, but you're not going to like it" replied Fred

"And why not?"

"It isn't dark at all, if you get my drift."

"I've never cared about specific patrons to a particular club."

"Then you'll like this place, at least I think you will. Didn't she say Roswell?"

"No, but I assumed it was Roswell."

"Mark, get ready for a surprise on Wednesday night."

"Are we watching baseball there?"

"No, not at all and it's not unlikely you'll hear bagpipes."

"Bagpipes on a Wednesday night? Are you serious?"

"No, I'm kidding" Fred snickered.

"I can't wait to see where she's taking me. Are you going to tell me?"

"No, it's a surprise and I want to hear all about it tomorrow."

"So you aren't going to tell me and get me prepared for whatever you think will surprise me?"

"Tell me your experience Thursday morning. I've got to run."

"I'll see you around Fred." Mark replied, while walking to his cubicle.

Angela headed to the bookstore, taking a break from her day. Paula was sitting at a table and waved her over, "Angela," she called.

"Hey, what are you doing here?" Angela asked.

"I wanted to get out of the house for a few. After last night I didn't want to call you but I'd hoped to catch you here."

"Oh really, I thought you'd call me this morning and tell me about the weekend plans." Angela sighed.

"What are you sighing about?"

"Nothing really, just thinking of Wednesday night with Mark."

"You're seeing him again? I thought it was a friendship and not dating. How could you want to see him again?"

"He's intriguing, different, mysterious, and interesting all in one."

"Sure, I bet he is. I mean different."

"What do you mean?"

"He's nothing like the guys you should go out with or is he anything like you, us, and you should think about your image."

"What's wrong with my image? I have a good image."

"Now you do, but what if people start seeing you more with Mark? It is his name right?"

"Yes it's Mark. And so what if they see Mark and I together more often? Do you honestly think people will change their thought of me just because Mark is a person of color?"

"Are you naive or did Mark give you drugs?" Smirking, Paula looked around the store and noticed a few people of color in the place. "See, there are people who make assumptions about women like you who would think of dating a person of color."

"And I make assumptions of those people too. Why are you so dead set against me having fun?" asked Angela.

"I'm not against you having fun. You don't even know Mark. Honestly, do you think it's safe to push it and be out with a black guy?"

"Safety is your concern?"

"Partially, and the other thing is people having negative thoughts about you and will attempt to cause you harm."

"This isn't the 20$^{th}$ century you know."

"No it isn't, but there are people with those thoughts."

"Ok, I'm not enjoying this conversation. Let me tell you, I appreciate your concern, but Mark is a very nice guy. Nothing like the guy who slapped me around or the one who ignored me except when he wanted something," Angela breathed as if irritated with her long time dearest friend. "Are you saying they were better because they looked like us?"

"I'm just explaining there are consequences. There were unacceptable attitudes with the others, but the public didn't see them like they will see you with Mark."

"Am I living for the public? Did you marry Ron for the public or was it for love?"

"What kind of question is that?" Paula replied with a heated look.

"It's the same shallow comments you're making." Angela grabbed her coffee and left the store. Not looking back at her friend, she entered her car and drove off wondering. "Was Paula right?"

# Chapter 2

Mark couldn't for the life of him figure out to what location Angela was referring. Especially on a Wednesday night, there wasn't much happening in the city or suburbs. The suburbs are much smaller; there can't be much happening where she'd like to go. There wasn't much happening in the city because each surrounding town has it own laws and policies on alcohol, dining, and entertainment. Not too much happens unless there is a private club or closed activity. Mark lived in Atlanta for years. He had a lot of exposure to so many things in the area.

Earlier times in Atlanta, clubs were active on any day of the week. It's amazing how much the city and surrounding areas have changed. Now, the city sidewalks roll up after midnight and liquor sales end until the next morning. Especially on a Wednesday night, the streets aren't even active for sporting events. "We'll have to wait and see when Wednesday comes," Mark thought.

Early Tuesday morning approached after a long Monday night slumber. Angela yawned, placed her feet in those worn slippers, rose to the beat of the radio and headed for the shower. She had the energy of an excited schoolchild heading out for a new school year. "Why am I so excited it's only a date," having those private thoughts. "It's not like there will be excitement but the place is going to be awesome. I know he'll like the location and the activity. Am I getting too involved or is this just excitement of him being of a different race? Whatever it is, I'm like a school kid." Angela smiled and continued the morning routine. "I want to relax this morning before heading to the office. I'll check out the bookstore on the way."

Mark, elated for a Tuesday, went with the flow of his work day, starting his morning early, and making deliveries on the way to the office. Account managers have to build and keep the rapport whenever they can. Excited for the day, Mark doubled with the fantasy of becoming a famous writer; he noticed nearly every detail of interaction between people. He also created story lines to support the activities he reviewed. Normally it was amazing how simple they were when he created every character and then wrote jokes and lines for them. Writing was an art and it was the reason he reviewed *"How To"* books on matters of *Publishing* and *Creative Writing*.

Mark left the last office on his route and landed right at the bookstore. Jumping at the opportunity to stop, he parked and headed into the store. He ordered coffee and noticed Angela, as she received her order.

"How lovely it is seeing you this morning." Mark commented.

"Oh, hi Mark." replied Angela.

Nice seeing you here. What a pleasurable coincidence."

"It's nice seeing you so early- Are we ready for tomorrow tonight?"

"Oh yes, wouldn't miss it for the world. I can't for the life of me figure out where you're taking me."

"Don't worry, you'll love it. Isn't that what you told me earlier, before going to Club 290?"

"Yes, it is. As a matter of fact I sound like you, don't I?"

"Isn't it early to switch places," Angela giggled.

"Switched places. I can understand, it sounds funny. Now I know how you felt the other night. The unknown is an amazing fear factor."

"What about the unknown? Are you afraid of a little mystery?"

Mark reached for his coffee as he responded, "Fear is fear itself. I fear nothing....well most nothing anyway."

"Macho man," Angela laughed

"Really sounded fearless didn't it," Mark laughed in reply.

They moved through the bookstore finding adjacent seats.

"What are you doing here so early?" asked Angela.

"I came in just for coffee. I didn't expect to see you or stay for awhile. I'm glad you stopped and we got a chance to chat this morning. It makes my day when I see a lovely woman."

"What a comment or compliment? Should I take the compliment as something personal or an attempt to get close to me? Or should I ignore it as simply his observation?" Angela thought before responding "Thank you. Your words are too kind. I'm not fixed up for a date now. And the morning is – well my quick mirror fix up for the day. Nothing special."

"Oh, you're special for sure." Mark smiled. Uncomfortable, Angela frowned, rose from her seat and said, "I thought we were going to be friends. I'm sorry but we'll have to cancel tomorrow night."

Angela left while Mark stood in amazement and thought, "Oh wow, my moving without thought. My brain on automatic pilot and not thinking of what I'm doing. Messed up a great time for Wednesday night; I'll call her and apologize."

"What a jerk! Thinking I'll let him get close to me. He's not even my type. I thought he was a nice guy. Turns out, he's no different from any other jerk I've met." Angela stormed to her car recalling her girl friend's advice. "Paula was right. They are so aggressive and so easy to read it's ridiculous." Angela tossed Mark's business card, got in her car, and drove to the job.

Still in shock, Mark couldn't believe Angela took his comment as a come on. "I honestly thought we were beyond breaking the ice and I wasn't showing her any aggression." thought Mark. "It's as if I'd have to walk on eggshells and really think of what not to say. It's a horrible way creating a friendship. Now I at least know my limitations with her. That is, if I see her again. I will call her about it tonight. It's against my better judgment, but you never know."

"Angela, I told you. Those guys are all alike, they want one thing, go after one thing, and it's conquering the chase. You can look at him and know its all in the color." Paula commented.

"I didn't want to believe you, but it looks so. Just as I thought it was comfortable, he goes and tells me I'm beautiful early in the morning." Angela boldly explained.

"So he didn't ask you to get in bed with him?"

"No, I told you he made me feel uncomfortable, like a piece of meat."

"Whatever he told you, is another ploy for sex. It's all those guys want and it's nothing different in their approach. I told you its better to stay with your kind."

"But it started out so well and interesting. How could anyone be so coy in their presentation and then make a 180 degree turn to aggression? I don't understand it."

"Again, let me remind you, you can't trust those people. And the men are only after one thing. I see it all the time when it happens. Every couple, the woman is demoralized, demonized, and mistreated to no end. They abuse the women not of their kind."

"I hear you. I don't think its all true. But, I can't believe he would do such a thing," Angela replied.

"Angela, you aren't listening to me. Allow this to be your one and only experience and one you should be happy to survive."

"Hey, I have another call…gotta go." Clicking the phone "Hello," Angela answered.

"I am so sorry I offended you this morning. Please accept my apology," Mark presented.

"Good-bye Mark. Never call me again," Angela disconnected the call. "How dare he call me knowing I don't want anything to do with him?" Angela thought.

Mark, surprised at Angela's response, looked to the calm of day and reached for wisdom in thought. He walked to his car and returned to his routine track to the office. "I cannot for the life of me understand why she's so angry at a compliment," baffled Mark. "I am sure Wednesday night is off. I'll let her cool off and maybe she'll call me one day."

"What an ass," Angela exclaimed. "You know I hate admitting it, but you were right, Paula."

Paula replied with a smile, "I told you. Proves I know best and you should listen to me more often. Now about Wednesday night; we can go out for a few drinks and maybe shoot pool."

"Sounds nice enough. What kind of guy is he, because I know you had someone in mind for me to go with?"

"Pretty nice, fair in looks, and seems like fun. I'll call him to confirm right after we hang up."

"Ok. I'll go - let me know where and when."

"Good, I'll get back to you soon."

Paula called her friend Bill and coordinated a date for Wednesday night. Paula remembered Bill being a blue collar worker with nice manners, which she only met twice. The first time was when she and Ron were out and about playing pool. Ron started the conversation with Bill at a billiards place near Jimmy Carter Boulevard. He impressed both Paula and Bill by being a down to earth guy. At the end of the night, Bill and Ron exchanged cellular numbers and since have kept in touch as they now attend pool tournaments though out the city. Since most of the pool tournaments are predominantly white, and since the city is pretty integrated, there's no pressure for playing with anyone you don't like. However, there's no harm in friendly competition; surely there is no pressure to socialize beyond the game. At the end of each tournament, Ron and Bill gathered with the teammates and entertained each other until the end of the night. Never did Bill and Ron welcome other people of color to join them; they kept their activities to a minimal for a show of social acceptance. With no expectations, it wasn't a fact Ron or Bill didn't like people of color, it was more of nothing in common. Bill consistently spoke on multiple issues when it came to African Americans. No comments were ever positive, as his belief was they received multiple breaks in life. Hatred spewed in such a manner there were deep dislikes, it was a general rule to his social upbringing.

"Bill - Hi darling man; how are you?" asked Paula, when Bill answered his phone.

"Doing well my friend. What are you and Ron up to today? Did I miss a tournament?" asked Bill.

"No, I'm not calling because of a tournament. I'm calling to see what your schedule is for Wednesday night?"

"I don't think I have anything planned. Maybe a pool game here or there but nothing in general."

"You should come with us. I have this friend who would love meeting you." Paula smiled.

"Oh is she pretty?" asked Bill.

"Would I invite you if she weren't?"

"I know how you ladies think all women are pretty and we guys define beauty differently." Bill replied, laughing.

"Not funny. I wouldn't get a horrible woman to meet such a nice man. Believe me I have great taste in people. And this woman has been my friend for years. She's darling and lots of fun. We went to college together and she attended my wedding. Oh, she's lovely for sure and takes good care of her health. You know, one of those pretty gym women."

"Nice to know. Ok, I'll be there on Wednesday. Where and when are we meeting or should I come to your place?"

"Let me talk to Ron and I'll call you back."

"Thanks for the invite, can't wait because I always have a great time with you two."

"Talk to you later, bye."

"Bye, darling lady."

Ron walked in the front door after Paula ended her conversation. "Hi love, home for lunch" he spoke.

"Hi babe. I talked to Bill on the phone earlier today."

"Oh really? What did he have to say?"

"I invited him out to meet Angela on Wednesday night." Ron replied with surprise, "What? Where are we going and what are we doing?"

"I'm playing a little match making. Some black guy made a move on my girl and I want her to remember where she belongs."

"Did she get upset about the guy?"

"Yes she did; after she went to dinner with him Sunday night."

"Oh she did! Was she out of her mind or doing the exploring thing as many white women do?"

"You honestly think white women explore across the tracks all the time?"

"Yes I actually do. Some of them get caught up on the thrill of rebelling and find themselves in a bind where no white man will take them back."

"Well its good we're stepping in to save Angela before it happens."

"OK, I'm in on whatever you want to do. Bill is a great guy so he'll sweep Angela off her feet in no time."

"I think he's nice, but Angela will be tougher than you think."

"Is she so against a good man?"

"No not at all," Paula hesitated in response, "she thinks men are challenging and in college she didn't jump to some of the best guys ever."

"College was good to you though, wasn't it?" Ron snickered, creating a sandwich.

"You want chips hon?" asked Paula.

"Dodging the question? I hit the nail on the head. Darling I loved you then and love you now. No worries from me, I know who the boss is in this house."

"You better," Paula laughed.

Mark ran behind schedule as he pursued his goal for the day. "Being an account manager is generally dependent upon successes of customer relationships," Mark thought. As dynamic and strategic as ever, Mark quickly made his customers feel great even though he arrived minutes late at every location. "It never fails. Every time I start making great sales and win commitments, there's a fall back in another area. I still think I did nothing wrong with Angela," reflecting in thought. Time and time again, Mark reviewed his morning actions. Step by step, word for word was analyzed to conjure up a response if the opportunity presented itself. "I can start by sending flowers." Mark said to himself. "A great idea, all women like flowers, but does it mean I'm being too forward? I'm starting to doubt this woman and I don't know what I've done to get such a response."

Paula called Angela on the cell, "When will you be here on Wednesday night?"

"What time is good? I get off the usual and normally hit the gym. But if I have to be there, I'll workout in the morning." replied Angela.

"You should workout in the morning because I want you here right after you're off."

"Ok I can get there. What are we doing?"

"I have someone for you to meet."

"No, I don't want to meet anyone."

"You should because it will help you get back to your roots."

"I left my roots?"

"Maybe not left, but ventured away. I just want to remind you what a good man has to offer. One who looks like your father, my father, and the type of people who doesn't cause any grief."

"All men cause grief and what makes you think I ventured away by just going to dinner and a jazz club?"

"Amazing! You don't even realize what you've done. Its Ok, we'll get you back."

"Listen Paula, you're starting to tick me off a little. I'm coming with you so don't push this guy on me to make you happy. I'm fine not meeting anyone."

"Angela, I'm just looking out for my best friend. I love you, always have and want you to be happy."

"I know you're thinking of me and want the best, but easy with the blind dates. I'll meet the guy, but not as a blind date. I see it as an introduction and nothing more. What kind of guy is he?" asked Angela.

"He's nice, really nice. I've never seen him with a woman, but I'm sure there were some in his past. He's always courteous and never seems like a jerk."

"Sounds nice, but it's what I fear Paula, the nice guy syndrome according to a friend."

"You trust me, don't you?"

"I trust you to a point - the same as you trust me."

The pickup pulled into Paula and Ron's drive way, stopping short of the family truck. A last look in the mirror, fingers through the hair, pulled the collar and buckled the pants. "Here," said Bill to himself, "good to go." Knocking on the front door Bill held one rose and one sunflower in his hand.

"Hi Bill," said Ron as he opened the front door.

"Howdy Dude," replied Bill.

"Come on in and settle in. Angela isn't here just yet but I heard she's on her way."

"No problem." Bill walked to the couch, took a seat, and sniffed the flowers. "I haven't any idea why women love these dang things. If you want a chance I'm told you've got to do it. Hasn't worked for me yet but I hear it's the way to go."

"It's a great idea. Ron laughed. It's much more for a first impression than for not having one."

"Yea, it's a first impression."

Angela knocked on the front door, waited for an answer while reaching for the door knob. Paula ran to the door from another room in the house. "Hi Bill," she spoke as she opened the door, just as Angela pushed it.

"I thought you'd just come in Angela," commented Paula.

"I was just opening the door and going to announce my arrival. Isn't it what I normally do?"

"Timing is everything," Paula responded with a smile. "Bill, this is Angela. Angela, meet Bill. You two get comfy while I finish getting ready."

Bill rose and reached for Angela's hand in his greeting. "I am so pleased to meet you. Paula mentioned you were pretty but I think gorgeous."

"Thank you for the compliment. I'd say you are quite a nice looking guy."

"Thank you," Bill said as he returned to his seat.

The room went silent. The ice breaker was just that, an ice breaker, as courtesy always called for. Angela waited for a comment from Bill. Bill waited for a comment from Angela. Neither of the two found enough interest to start a conversation while waiting for Ron and Paula. Both Ron and Paula entered one after the other. "Are you two ready?"

"Yes, I think so," replied Bill as he stood to leave. "Please," as he waved his hand towards Angela.

"He's such a gentleman," Paula commented.

The four entered two separate trucks. Angela jumped in Paula and Ron's vehicle as Bill moved his truck. "Why is he driving alone?" asked Paula.

"I thought we were going in one truck," replied Angela.

Ron answered, "No, he wanted to drive his truck as he's not coming back after dinner. Maybe you should ride with him."

"I'm not so sure of riding with him just yet. He's a looker but too quiet for me."

"You just met the guy and sometimes people take a minute to warm up." Paula responded.

"Well, you have a point." Angela opened the door and waved towards Bill.

"My goodness, is it hard to see I'm trying to match him with her?"

"No," replied Ron. "It's just you're trying to push something not so comfortable for her."

"But she can be comfortable with the black guy at dinner the other day."

"That may be a different situation."

"How different? She can do much better and here's her chance."

"Her chance to meet a nice guy; I see where you're going." Ron replied as he started driving down the street.

Angela smiled as she entered the truck. "I didn't know you were driving so I guess it's only fair I ride with you, if you don't mind?"

"Please, I'm glad you joined me; gives us time to chat before dinner."

"What kind of work do you do?"

"Oh, I'm a carpenter, have been for 25 years."

"Really, you seem so young to work for so long."

"I started working with my uncle and father during the summers when I was thirteen. I never stopped and when I graduated from high school, I went full time."

"So, you've lived in Atlanta all these years working in construction?"

"Yes, I'm a native, which are few and far between."

"You've seen much change in Atlanta over the years, I'm sure."

"Yes I have, as things change sometimes for the good, but not much for all people."

"Well, that's society; no changes are for all people even though the effort is for change. Someone will fall short of benefiting," replied Angela.

"Yes I grew up on the North end of Atlanta, near Alpharetta before the sprawl. It used to be country side and farmland. My family used to ride into downtown for events, and take 30 minutes to return. It was pretty nice in comparison to now. The city was full of life, as long as you stayed north of Auburn Street."

"Auburn Street?"

"Yes, it was where the majority of blacks lived and they were not so open to whites. Times changed and at least it's better in racial relations I think. I remember my school bussed in a few black kids. It was different; I didn't want to be one of those kids back in the day. But at least they got a good education."

"Yes, I heard of busing but I didn't get involved. There weren't many black people in my town. We had more Hispanics, mostly Mexicans."

"I'd guess it's not as bad or challenging with Mexicans. But I know watching the turn of power was mesmerizing for a lot of people here in Atlanta. I bet the Mexicans didn't become Mayor or create a powerful influence like here."

"No, I don't think so. But I'm not into politics."

"I can understand. I'm not into it, but you have to pay attention to things happening around you. It's why the North side of Atlanta has a smaller minority population. We banned many of them from entering the area for years and nothing changed until the late 80's."

"That explained the demographics."

"Yea, it's different now, but still keeping the numbers small keeps the value of the homes high. My folks always told me it's Ok to work around people of color, as they say today, but just don't live near them. Which, I can't for the life of me see the importance of so many people living near each other. I guess things are changing."

Silence fell as they turned into the restaurant's parking lot. "We're eating at the Golden Corral for dinner?" said Angela as she broke silence.

"Oh, I love this place. Ron likes it too. We normally come here before a tournament."

"I guess it will do."

"Oh, you don't want to eat here? Where else can we go satisfying everyone's taste?"

"As I said, it's Ok. Nothing fancy for breaking the ice between us," Angela sighed.

"I think we'll have a grand time and the cost isn't too expensive. I think we'll get drinks afterwards. Ron did mention heading to the billiards room for a bit. We can break the ice there. Don't you like to shoot pool?"

"At least we can have a drink or two, maybe we'll have a few laughs, and I'm not good at shooting pool." All the while Angela thought "I'm not too sure about this but I'll go along with it for awhile. Hopefully shooting pool will be much better than the ride over." She turned and smiled at Bill as she exited the truck. "He didn't get my door – am I being critical?"

Bill stepped lively to Ron as the four met at the restaurant's entrance. "I don't know if she's interested in me. I think it might be better if the girls drove to the pool hall and we chat." Bill proposed.

"We'll talk about it after dinner."

The four returned from the buffet line with a complete meal. "I love this place," remarked Ron.

"Yes, it's great with the number of items available. I'm already thinking of what to get next." replied Bill.

"Oh, I'm pretty happy with the fish and the desserts look great. I hope I have room left for the dessert bar." smiled Paula.

Angela scanned the people around the dining area and was silent in conversation. All the while she listened to them laugh and joke. Not even once did Bill try to get her involved or interested. "Bill, what books have you read lately?" asked Angela.

"Haven't had time to read lately. I'm normally on a site from sun up to sun down."

"Oh, I thought you'd find some time between tournaments. What kind of book interests you?"

"Not too sure."

"Oh, I know the answer," commented Paula, "those girly magazines men take to the bathroom are his type," she chuckled.

"Not even. But I do like <u>Xtreme Male</u>, and <u>Monster Truckin</u> magazines. Those two normally get my attention but I hardly purchase them. They are always around the work sites."

"Interesting" replied Angela. She thought "As if I expected something different in an answer. I guess if I don't try to talk to him, he'll not share anything at all with me." She tells Bill, "You have to come with me to the bookstore one day."

"That will be nice. Hopefully I'll find the time in between jobs. I can't promise I'll be able to go soon, but when the weather changes, I'll have more time."

"It's nice of you two to plan ahead. Ron and I used to plan before we got too busy. I think having some quality time between you will do a great deal for the relationship." Paula chimed in.

"See, there you go. Let it go without your input will you? If things work between them it's because of them and not your interjections. I'm sure Angela is a big girl and can handle Bill." Ron suggested.

"Yes, I'm a big girl and it's why I'm finished eating."

"You aren't having dessert?" asked Ron.

'No. I've had enough thank you."

"It's the best part. I'll save room for mine."

"Oh, I'm having a piece of chocolate cake," Paula commented.

"Ice cream seems to make it right for me," Ron said.

"You folks enjoy it. I'm going to wait for you." replied Angela, thinking, "As if I have other things going on while waiting or like I'm able to leave?"

While she observed the others finish dinner and taking little activity in the conversation, Angela felt a change of heart in going to the pool hall with the others. "I have to make the best of it and enjoy what I can with Paula tonight. I'm not so sure about Bill. It's something to do tonight if nothing else."

Back in the truck on the way to the Pool Place Billiards near Jimmy Carter and Peachtree Industrial, Bill and Angela rode listening to the radio. Bill was anxious to arrive at the joint so he could show off his skills to Angela. His first impression of her wasn't too great at the moment, but if he showed her how well he shot pool, he would gain her interest. "I better see if she's a competitor or if she can play," he thought.

"Didn't you like dinner or wasn't it your style?" asked Bill.

"No I enjoyed the dinner. It was interesting and you three are very comfortable with each other." Angela said.

"Oh, we hang out all quite well together. Wait until we get to the pool hall." Bill continued to drive in a rush to arrive.

"Are we teaming together when we play?" asked Angela.

"I'd think we can, but it depends on how you play. Have you played before?"

"I've played before. Not the greatest player compared to you and Ron, but I can hold my own for a girl."

"Oh, we'll see and play it by ear. I want you to know, I hate losing."

"Sure places pressure on me," replied Angela and thinking, "boy a lot of pressure on me…NOT!"

"Good, you should have pressure to play the best you can."

"We'll play, however it goes, it's Ok to just play and have fun."

"As long as we win, it's fun. I like winning. It's my competitive nature."

"It's not always winning; it's the fun in the game isn't it?" Angela responded. Her temperature boiled in her mind, as if she looked for a quick out in the game.

"Hog wash. I play to win, always have always will; it's my nature to be competitive and be the best at everything. Driven to succeed and beat the crap out of my competition."

"Wow, you take it so serious. How do you ever enjoy the game? It's not always about winning."

"It is where I come from. I play this way with every sport."

"Are you a sore loser?"

"Oh, not really, at least I don't think so."

Bill parked in front of the bar, The Pool Place Billiards. Angela didn't wait for Bill to open her door as she noticed him move to the front of the truck and head for the bar's entrance. Ron and Paula stood at the bar and ordered drinks. "I ordered beer for you Bill, and wine for Angela." Ron pointed as the bartender placed the orders on the bar. "We have the pool table in the center, first row. How are we going to do this?"

"I'd guess we can play teams as we begin and see where we go from there." replied Bill.

"I think it's a good idea," responded Paula. "Angela and I can team up against you guys the next game."

Angela grabbed a cue from the table and tested how straight it is by rolling it on the table. It's a practice most pool players do before a game and with a foreign pool cue. She then applied chalk to the cue's tip and placed a little powder on her hand. "I thought you didn't play pool much Angela?" Ron stated.

"I can hold my own. I told Bill on the way here, I played a little but nothing to the likes of you two."

Bill told Paula, "You can break," as he completed the rack and placed the rack guide back in the table slot. The four were ready to start the game and the three watched Paula prepare for the breaking shot. "Best two out of three," shouted Ron. "We'll change after the first session."

"Ok, sounds good to me," Bill responded.

Paula spread the table sinking the three-ball in the corner pocket. She scattered the table quite well and found multiple shots. She sank four, one after the other, and finally missed on the fifth shot. "I didn't know you shot so well since college. You've improved your game." Angela giggled.

"Ron and I play quite often these days. I get better all the time, just not quite like these pool hawks." Paula replied while walking towards Angela, "Your shot, Bill."

"I know," Bill replied as he bent over the table for a shot. One after another balls sank in various pockets. He got down to the 8 ball and had no clear shot, so he banked the cue ball and bounced the 8 ball open for Ron to finish. "There, I set you up for a great finish partner, if Angela leaves you with one shot."

"Oh, I don't know if I can sink the first ball, Bill. I haven't done this in a long time," Angela said, positioning herself for the shot. Bang, one after another, balls fell into the pockets. "8 ball corner pocket," Angela pointed with her cue to the exact pocket. She looked at Bill and Ron who stood near each other in observation. "You looked surprised. I said I can hold my own, but not as good as you two. It's luck since the balls were mostly ducks. Rack'em for game two," she said just as the 8 ball dropped in the pocket.

"Angela, you still have it." Paula raised her hand in the air for a high 5. "I remember suckering many guys in college for beer money and phone rights back in the dorms."

"So you can play," Bill smirked.

"I hold my own as I said earlier," replied Angela. "Don't be a sore loser Bill. It's just a game."

"I haven't lost yet. Remember its three games for the match."

"You can break now," Ron said after he had racked the balls.

Angela sipped from her wine glass, and positioned herself for the break. Bang, three balls fell in different pockets. She maneuvered herself around the table taking calculated shots; never stopping for a break she sank one after the other. "8 ball side pocket," she called.

"Amazing!" Bill shouted and spoke low to Ron in the next breath. "We were conned."

"I knew all the time she could play." Ron replied.

"Why didn't you say something buddy?"

"What was there to say? We play skilled people all the time. We seem to do well in tournaments."

"But this is different. I can't let her beat us like this."

"We can ask for a rematch and play the girls again. Think of it as a way for you to date Angela and get her involved in the tournaments. Then you and I will have needed support when we travel."

"Good idea. But I don't think Angela really likes me very much."

"If you just be cool, you'll win her over. Trust me and don't do anything silly."

"Silly? I'm much better with the ladies than you know."

"Ok," Ron responded thinking, "I hope you really are." He looked at Bill and said, "It's your turn to rack'em."

Angela placed her empty wine glass on the bar. She waved over the bartender and ordered a beer and another round for the others. She took a seat on the stool and waited for the round to arrive.

"You are a great shooter," the black gentleman sitting at the bar said to her.

"Thank you, but I'm not really good."

"I bet you are, but you play your skills down not to hurt their feelings."

Looking surprised, Angela responded "No feelings to hurt. I really don't play very well. I'm just lucky tonight."

"I sure wish I had your kind of luck all the time," the guy smiled.

Bill observed Angela in conversation with the black guy at the bar. "Does she talk to everyone?" He pointed to Angela so Ron noticed.

"No, not that I know of, I heard she's customarily friendly to people, but not to an extent of talking in depth."

"I hope not. I can't see us taking her out to some of those places where so many players are black. You know, they would love getting themselves with a pretty white woman.

Makes me ill when I see people do it. It ain't right you know."

"She's just talking or being courteous. I'm sure she's just being friendly within reason."

Angela returned with the drinks just as Paula made her strike. Bill and Ron walked over for their drinks from the far end of the table. "I saw you laughing over at the bar. Did you make a new friend?" asked Bill.

"No, just some guy telling me I shoot great."

"See, he's complimenting you so you can take interest in him. I don't get those guys. They think they can pick up any woman. Disrespectful, that's what they are and wanting our women, I can't believe them."

"Why are you getting growled up? It was only a comment and nothing to pick me up on. Besides, I can handle my own and if I need help, I can yell." Angela responded thinking "The guy did everything any other kind person would do. This guy has a serious racial problem."

"I hope you aren't like so many white women I see."

"I don't think you should even ask me such question."

"I'm not asking I'm making a comment."

"Ron, your shot," Paula yelled.

"Finally," he replied.

Paula walked over to Angela and speaks at a lower volume. "You have to be careful not to turn Bill off. I think he's a very nice man and good to people. He's just commenting on his belief and it isn't bad you know."

"I'm not worried about his belief; there is no concern from me. In my eyes it's hanging out with my best friend and her husband," Angela smiled as she replied.

"You know he likes you."

"Well, he's ok Paula, not impressively so, but ok."

"Be patient with him, good guys are hard to come by. He's generally a good guy so don't blow this. I know how you are with men."

"Yes, you don't have to remind me. I'm well aware of how I like my men."

"Let's let them win this one and call it a night. I think we can get them to do this again another night."

"I'm not sure if they'd want to stop now. Bill hates losing."

"Then, let them win the next set and we'll figure another night out."

Ron took his last shot sinking the 8 ball. "Game over ladies, it's your set. Your turn to rack 'em and Bill - you break."

"Sure thing, Ron," replied Bill as Angela racked.

"Ok, best two of three remember." Bill said breaking and sinking three balls. "I don't think the ladies will get to shoot this time."

"Sure, I bet you say that to all the girls," Paula snickered. The group watched Bill sink every ball as if the level of play is the same as in a tournament. One after one, he banked, doubled, and jumped the cue to clean the table. "Next!" Bill yelled as the 8 ball sank in the corner pocket. "That's one game and one to go. Rack 'em." he called out in a cocky tone.

"I'll rack'em," Angela said, placing her cue stick on another table. "It's your break, isn't it Ron?"

"Yup, sure is." Ron replied. Bang and four balls sank, including the 8 ball. "Game over! Are you ready to play the last set?"

"No, I'm not ready. Let's play another day for the last set. I'm ready to call it a night." Paula said to everyone.

"I like that idea," Angela interjected.
Bill chimed, "Good deal. I'm game for a next time." As if he's excited to get to know Angela more.

The four moved closer to leaving the table and walked past the black guy at the bar. "You folks sure know how to shoot pool. I enjoyed watching it."

"Thanks." Angela replied.

"You'll talk to anyone won't you?" Bill commented to Angela.

"The guy was being nice, why not?"

"There's no harm in being polite to anyone," responded Ron.

"He knows good skilled people when he sees them. He wants to be like us that's all." Paula giggled.

"Yea, they know whose better. Angela, are you riding with me to Ron's house or are you interested in a nightcap?" asked Bill.

"If I ride with Paula and Ron, you can head home. I'm not up to a nightcap. Can I take a rain check?"

"I'll take you back to Ron's, it's on the way. It'll give us some time to talk."

"I think we can call it a night here. I have your number."

"No, you should ride with Bill." Paula encouraged just as Angela wanted the night to end.

"Ok, I'll see you two at your place."

"Bill let's go."

"Angela, I'm so glad we got a chance to meet." Bill said as he opened the passenger door.

"It's nice to meet you too." Angela responded as the door closed. "I can't wait to get back," she thought.

"What do you have planned for the weekend?"

"I don't know yet."

"Do you think we can get together again?"

"I think it will be nice depending on what we'll do. Let me call you once I'm sure."

"You didn't have a good night?"

"It was ok. I'm not trying to discourage you." Angela responded thinking, "Gosh, I wish he'd just take the call later as his answer." She then said, "It's not a bad idea; it's that I do a number of things on the weekend."

"Then you should know where you can fit me in."

"Let me check and I'll get back to you. I think we can have fun together." Angela truly thought, "Right, in a million years."

"Good, then I'll pick you up on Friday. We'll do something different. Can I get your number when we get to Ron's?"

"Yes, I'll give you my cell number so you can catch me."

Silence fell in the cab, music played along with the sound of tires rolling - road roaring. Turn after turn the truck moved closer to Ron and Paula's house. "We aren't getting there fast enough," thought Angela. "Another turn and we're there and I can't wait to get out of this truck." Finally they arrived and Angela reached over to Bill and touched his arm saying, "Thanks for driving tonight and my number is 404-123-0400. We'll talk about Friday later Ok?"

"Yes, we can talk later." Bill responded as he wrote the number down. "Let me get your door."

"No that's ok. I'm heading home right now. You don't have to get out."

"No kiss good night?"

"Maybe next time."

"Ok, well maybe I'll kiss you next time."

"Good night Bill." Angela closed the door and walked to her car. "I hope he loses the number. I know he won't lose it but I wish he would."

# Chapter 3

"Finally home." sighed Angela. "I can't believe that guy," she thought as she prepared for bed. "He's very angry and believes he's so much better than people of color and so closed to even being friends with other nationalities. How awful? What an ass!"

The slumber was peaceful for Angela as the night moved to morning. Being the disciplined worker, she followed her routine. Coffee stop at the bookstore, and a peek at the latest release, she noticed the usual faces arriving. One particular guy caught her attention and she maneuvered for a better look. She moved to investigate his interest, and for a closer gander, making herself visible. "A cute guy for sure," she thought. "I like his features, his physical appearance, and he dresses well. He's obviously professional."

One peek beyond the book in his hand, Christopher noticed a gorgeous woman. "Wow, it would be nice meeting her one day." Christopher stopped at the bookstore to find a recommended read on *Executive Leadership* from the newly acclaimed expert. He stood at the first door display, a little off his travel path, always happy to see a lovely woman. Not that he's a lady's man; he is, of course, a man. "I'll break the ice with her," he thought, but doubted himself for fear of the response. "Why not say something to her? She'll either respond with a kind gesture, or be closed to my greeting."

He looked up from the book as if a military sniper looking for the best shot opportunity, Christopher perched for a close arrangement between them so others will not notice if there is rejection. Each move, with sly maneuvering, he found himself in Angela's sight every time she looked up. "Now," his mind told him, but his feet moved reluctantly closer. In a clumsy awkward moment, but still showing confidence in his swagger, he spoke. "Hi, how are you?" he asked.

"Hi, I'm fine thanks." Angela responded with quick eye contact and a dip back to the book in her hand.

"I hope I'm not interrupting, but you are a very lovely lady and I couldn't help but speak. My name is Christopher," he said reaching out his right hand.

"I'm Angela."

"You come here often? I'm sorry; it sounds like a pick-up line."

"That's funny. I actually come here quite often. It's easy to get here from my apartment and it's the fastest stop for morning coffee."

"I don't come here too often; actually it was important for me to do some research for business this morning. I didn't expect to get a chance to talk to a lovely lady."

"Thank you. You are very kind." Angela responded looking into Christopher's eyes. "What type of business are you in?"

"Financial Management." Christopher responded, pulling out a card. "I majored in finance in college and landed this job right away. I guess it was luck."

"Luck? I doubt it was luck. You seem quite the intelligent guy."

"Well, I graduated Summa Cum Laude from the University of Georgia. And I managed to have fun while doing so."

"Oh my, a really bright guy." Angela smiled thinking "What a change from last night." She then asked, "Where is your office - if you don't mind me asking?"

"It's not far from here. I can get there within 10 minutes, and in full traffic."

"Oh, my office is close too. It's nice not to fight traffic during the commute. It's an Atlanta dream not getting stuck commuting to work."

"I'm fortunate in that area. My home isn't far from my office either. I kind of planned it, couldn't afford losing the time."

"I know what you mean. There are so many other things you can do versus being stuck in a car for hours on end."

"I manage my time well, network when I can, and make sure I work out every day."

"What gym?" asked Angela while she hoped LA Fitness on the North end of town.

"I go to a little gym in Roswell. I like it there, not too fancy but it supports my effort. And it's right in the middle of my commuting path."

"It's nice knowing you're a man who looks out for his well being." He dressed nice too, even smelled really nice Angela noticed.

"I try. It seems you do the same. You work out often?"

"Yes, LA Fitness is my gym and I get there at least 4 times a week. Depending on what I have planned on Fridays."

"Fridays are sometimes hard to work out, but I seem to manage. Well, I have my book and I need to pay for it. Is there some way we can finish our conversation?"

"Sure – Please, I'd like to talk to you again."

"Here's my card, my cell number is on it. Please use it when you feel like calling. I'm sure to look for your call Angela. You aren't too old fashioned are you?"

"Old fashioned?"

"Yes, you know when someone gives you a number to call, you are afraid to call or wait until you see him to break the ice?"

"No. I like the fact you give me the choice of calling instead of me giving you my number. I'll call you."

"Please do," Christopher responded walking towards the cashier then turned saying, "Have a great day and I hope to hear from you soon." Christopher smiled.

"Oh, you will," Angela responded, placed the book on the table and left the bookstore. "I'm sure to call him, not too anxious but he seemed interesting as well as nice." Angela thought.

"I'm definitely going to get her call." Christopher thought as he watched Angela leave the bookstore. "Man is she a gorgeous woman, and bright too. Those qualities make it good for conversation and interaction. I just hope my impression is correct."

Angela made it to her office, started her day and at the first break she pulled Christopher's card for a look-see. Christopher Mulligan, Financial Management Analyst-the card read. She fingered the office number on her desk phone, as a way to remember the numbers. Not quite dialing it on a live line, she keyed it in for a redial just in case this becomes a serious thing. "Here I am jumping the gun again" she thought. "I don't want to jinx things, but it would be nice having an impressive man in my life." Her day continued as lunch came and went, the busy pace of her work found the day ending beyond her usual quitting time. The next move was her exercise class where she went due to the delay at the office. She found herself on a tough fitness effort to fulfill the compliments heard this morning. "I've got to work harder, push baby push," she thought and breathed while sprinting on the treadmill. Weight lifting, working multiple muscle groups - no routine or focus on one part, she pumped, creating a tough challenge to increase the muscle pain. "If a gorgeous man can pay me such compliment, I'd better at least work to maintain it. I want him to think the same the next time he sees me."

Christopher concluded his day following the normal routine. Earlier in the day, he commented to a co-worker about Angela and explained the chance meeting of a lifetime. At least it was his thought for the time being. Since he hadn't received a call from Angela and his day was ending, there's still hope for a chance meeting. "I'm sure she's going to call, it's just a matter of time and patience. If she doesn't call me within the week, it's no big deal. But to make sure I get a chance, I'll make sure to hit the Barnes and Noble Starbucks the day after tomorrow just to reinforce my intention. I don't want to seem anxious but it's my way of spending the effort." Christopher strategized his next move over and over to ensure he presented an opportunity to see Angela. "I'll have morning coffee making multiple visits to the bookstore and then visit LA Fitness near Old Milton in the evenings, with hopes of seeing her. I have her trail and can create multiple sightings and chances to reinforce her decision to call." Just as many games played before with other women, Christopher learned to create opportunities and allow the woman to make her move. He also understood the key to successful meetings and interaction is timing. Not to say Christopher had many women in the wings, but his dating experience started in high school. He dated the cheerleader even though he wasn't the jock. In college, he managed to maintain a serious relationship, but ended it after deciding it wasn't something for long term. He then randomly dated as needed, made friends, or just completely satisfied the need for sensible interaction. Staying focused on his studies, he managed to score well among friends, frat groups and sororities which dynamically kept him abreast of all campus events. He developed a classy style during college and came into a great job position where he was able to spend accordingly without worry.

"No call tonight," he thought as he planned the morning's route past the bookstore. "Just to sneak a peek upon this lovely woman; no expectation, just make sure I saw what I think I did." He crashed hard for the night after a hellacious workout and a simple dinner and subconsciously dreamed of his first date with Angela. Something most guys do when they want to impress during the first date.

The next morning Christopher placed his plan in motion. A fast trip to the Starbucks and hoped the timing is right. As Christopher made his entrance, Angela was two people in front of him. "Great timing," Christopher thought as he smiled. A quick reach beyond the two people to get Angela's attention, he lightly touched her shoulder and said "Excuse me," to the others. "Hi Angela," Christopher smiled.

"Good morning, Christopher," Angela replied. "Funny seeing you here; are you looking for another book after you get coffee?"

"No, I'm here for coffee and you."

"Me?"

"Yes. Not to be forward but I've wanted to talk to you since meeting you yesterday. I hope you don't mind."

"No, I was going to call you but wasn't quite sure when. You know a girl's prerogative." Angela turned and ordered her coffee and stepped aside to continue her conversation with Christopher. "I hope I didn't sound out of touch with women equality."

"No, it's a woman's prerogative for sure."

"Good. I'd hate to start on the wrong foot or with the wrong idea."

"I think we're starting out just fine. Do you have time for a chat or are you on your way? - I'll have a cappuccino please," Christopher ordered, "I'd love stealing a few minutes to get to know you."

"I think I can spare a few minutes," responded Angela.

"You look wonderful. Do you look this way every morning?" asked Christopher.

"He noticed," Angela thought, "Thank you. You're so kind."

"You're welcome and it's true. I only wonder if it's like this throughout the day or are you a morning person?"

"I'd like to think its all day," Angela blushed.

"I'm sure it is," Christopher responded as he waved to the table facing the window towards the front of the store. He and Angela moved towards the table and Christopher pulled out the chair for her. "Such a gentleman," Angela thought.

"I wonder what things you like; what's your favorite color, favorite music and if you'd like to have dinner with me?"

"Wow, I haven't heard anyone want so much so quickly."

"You know Angela, timing is everything and I'm pretty forward and quick to the point. I'd love to get to know you better and wouldn't mind having fun along the way. Are you game?"

"I think I can answer - red, all types, and having dinner could be fun," replied Angela.

"Oh, a quick response and direct; I like it," Christopher smiled.

"And I like Italian, Chinese, Japanese, and Mexican foods. However I'm not afraid of trying new and different things."

"Those things are great to know. Is there something else you'd like to share?"

"Well if I tell you everything now, we might not have much for a dinner conversation."

"I think we'll always have something to talk about. As I feel it's easy to converse with you now. Oh did you have breakfast? Am I interrupting the most important meal of the day?"

"I'm not big on breakfast, but I normally have a little something at the office."

"It's got to be part of your secret to looking so wonderful."

"Flattery will get you a lot of places," Angela giggled.

"I honestly find you very attractive. So here's the deal. I can pick you up or meet you someplace - whichever makes you feel comfortable, and have dinner, a movie or live music. How does that sound?"

"Sounds quite nice; how about Saturday night?" asked Angela.

"Saturday night is fine with me. Are you going to call me to make sure I have your number or may I take your phone number now?"

"Now is fine. 404-123-0400," Angela responded.

"Great," Christopher answered while placing her number in his cell phone. "I'll call you later today and we can coordinate the date. Is it ok with you?"

"Sounds like a plan," Angela responded thinking, "I like a man who plans the evening."

"I can't wait to see you soon," Christopher stood to pull Angela's chair as she rose, "I need to head to the office and I'm sure you need to go as well. Not as if I'm making the decision for you. I'm respecting your time."

"You're right. No worries as I need to leave and continue my day. I'll wait for your call."

"Allow me to walk you to your car."

"That's ok, I can get there. Thanks anyway."

"Ok, well expect my call later. I'll wait until either lunch or after the job; unless you don't mind me calling during the day."

"I don't mind, but we'll have a better chance to converse if you wait until after."

"I can wait until you are comfortable. No problem."

"Great, so I'll see you soon, ok?"

"Yes you will and you'll hear from me before then," Christopher smiled as he and Angela walked separate directions. "A great morning already," Christopher thought as he drove from the bookstore's parking lot.

Angela drove to the office thinking, "Christopher is interesting. I'm glad he came by this morning." The thought and possibility of having a date with Christopher was something to share with her best friend. Angela speed dialed Paula just as she arrived at her office parking lot. "Paula- Hey, what's up?"

"Hi Angela, I'm on my way out. What's up with you?" answered Paula.

"You aren't going to believe this. I met a nice looking guy the other day and he asked me out."

"Oh really? I thought you were going out with Bill."

"No, I don't think so. He's probably a nice guy in general but not my cup of tea."

"You know I have one question about the new guy."

"He's white, so don't go there."

"Just checking. You know it's better to keep you on the right path and with quality guys."

"Quality guys," Angela chuckled.

"Why are you laughing Angela?"

"We have different definitions of quality. Anyway, I don't have details about the date but Christopher is gorgeous and seems classy."

"What does he do for a living?"

"I'm not sure just yet, we haven't gotten there in conversation, but his dress is totally business professional. I'm sure he has a great job."

"Let's hope he's not the arrogant type. You know, some of those professional guys like trophy wives or girl friends."

"Why don't we take this one step at a time and not prejudge or assume anything. I like his style and it's all that matters. I'll find out more and you'll know the same, ok?"

"Don't get defensive - I'm just looking out for you."

"I've got to go in. I'll call you another time."

"Bye Angela," Paula disconnected the call. "At least Christopher isn't a man of color," she thought as she drove along her way.

Angela made her day periodically thinking when she'd hear from Christopher. "Should I call him?" she contemplated. "Well, why not? He came to me this morning but I don't want to seem too anxious." Just as she picked up Christopher's business card, her cell phone chimed with a text message. "Thinking of you and a fun date," the text read.

Smiling and with angst, Angela responded, "Fun thoughts we share. Would love to know what's planned.-want 2 tell?" Angela saved Christopher's phone number in her cell and made a note of his office phone as well. "I think he's a charmer. It's nice there are guys with class out there. At least he has a nice get to know you style with a simple interaction. Good touch."

Christopher smiled from the text reply. The day and business continued as usual. "No phone call or text message during the entire afternoon and its nice to know a woman appreciates not having pressure." Christopher actually liked his thought as he started thinking of what he should set up for the date. "Dinner, but where? How about the Village Tavern? Its close enough where we don't have to fight traffic and it's a very nice environment. Dancing? I'm not sure but there is a concert at the new amphitheater. No, a concert isn't good for a first date. I think maybe a movie is in order, and then drinks or dessert. If nothing else comes from our conversation, the saving grace is analyzing the movie. This subject is my fail-safe if our conversation goes dry. I'll call her to choose the movie." Christopher made it his plan and then called the Village Tavern for reservations. "Timing is everything. The average movie starts after 7 so I'll schedule dinner for 5:30 on Saturday. We can arrive early and have a couple drinks before seating." Christopher then text messaged Angela "Any movies of interest?" Waiting for Angela's response, he decided to find a coffee shop close to the area. "A nice coffee, wine, and pastry shop would do the trick." He thought aloud. "Good thing no one is in the office to hear it," he laughed.

Angela smiled at her phone chime as it received another text message. "I know its Christopher," as she read with excitement, "Any movies of interest? – At least he's asking for my input. I like such things about him," she thought. In her reply she chose two - an action/drama and the expected chick flick. But before she responded, she decided on the action as a guess he'd enjoy it much better, as most men do. "Action flick is Ok," she texted Christopher with a second line reading, "You choose the show time." Smiling, Angela completed her work then left for the gym.

Christopher made a rash decision to meet Angela at her gym just to observe. "I'm obsessed and don't even know why," he thought as he turned back to his car and headed to his own gym. Traffic is horrible as usual; however it's more important to complete the workout than to make excuses. Without a second thought, Christopher worked out harder than before and pushed his body to its limit. "I needed this to get my focus back and get real about Angela. I can call her instead of trying to see her so much."

"Pick up the phone Angela," Bill shouted.
"Hello," Angela replied.
"Hey Angela, how are you? This is Bill."
"Hi Bill, I'm fine but busy at the moment. I'm leaving my gym and need to get cleaned up."

"I only called to see if we can get together this weekend."

"I have plans but thanks for asking. Maybe another time."

"You mean you had another guy chasing you when we met?"

"No, I didn't actually. But I decided to take up an offer I got today."

"Well, why don't you cancel that one and take mine."

"I won't Bill. Not even with you for someone else. It's not right."

"Sure it is. It's right because you can make an excuse and go out with me. You know you want to."

"Actually, I don't want anything to do with going out with you."

"What?"

"Let's just say it was nice meeting you and leave it as is."

"And here Paula said you were a nice woman."

"Thanks for calling but please lose my number."

"Bitch-your numbers lost and don't ever ask about me." Bill shouted "Fucking Bitch!!!" in frustration.

Angela felt relieved but didn't like the fact Bill had her number. "I hope he doesn't call me again." Just as she thought of the recent phone conversation the cell chimed again. "Hello."

"Girl, what on earth are you doing?" asked Paula.

"I'm doing exactly as I want and need to. Bill was not my type."

"I can't believe you'd push him away, but date a black man. How dare you?"

"What the hell are you saying?"

"You sure know how to close a door. Bill is a great guy and you dumped him before starting. What kind of woman closes a door to a nice guy, a great white man?"

"A very smart one! Are you finished? I'd like to finish cleaning up."

"I'm finished. Call me later."

"When I get a chance I'll will. Bye." Angela made a second attempt to clean up from the gym. Her phone chimed just before getting close to the shower. "If this is Bill I don't want to talk to you," Angela said without reviewing the number while she answered.

"Wow, I'm glad I'm not Bill," replied Christopher.

"Oh, hi Christopher. Do you go by Chris? Or should I continue with Christopher?" asked Angela.

"Well, my friends call me Chris but we have to get to know each other better for you use it."

"So, Christopher is how it's going to be?"

"No, don't get mad I was joking."

"I'm not in the mood for joking. But it's nice you aren't Bill."

"Heck, from the tone of your voice its nice not being Bill. If you don't feel up to talking, I can call another time." Christopher insisted.

"Yes, why don't you let me clean up from the gym and I'll call you back."

"Please do. I'd love talking to you and filling you in for Saturday night."

"Ok, we can talk later. I'll call you when I'm finished and settled down."

"Great. Talk to you then. Bye," responded Christopher.


Angela finally settled in, finding herself engulfed in her nightly routine, and fortunately turned her phone off. "No talking to anyone else tonight," she thought as she reflected on her feelings. "All can wait for my response, and I know Christopher expects my return call but it's not the right mood for anyone. I'd hate turning him off," Angela pondered. Soon after reading a good chapter of her book she fell deep into a rest. Hours passed in slumber where comfort and relaxation applauded her body and imagination.

*"Hi Angela it's beautiful seeing you again," said Mark.*

*"It is quite nice. I really enjoyed out time together. I don't think I got the chance to thank you." replied Angela.*

*"Sure you did. It was in your smile and the laughter. I thought we'd have another time out together but it wasn't in the stars I guess."*

*"I think our time will come," replied Angela, as she jumped over a running stream where the lilies were in full bloom. The snowcapped mountains were a touch distance from the extension of her hand. There were winged lions soaring in the sky, and blue birds landing on the tree limb, right above Angela's head.*

*"I truly hope we get a chance to meet again," Mark shouted and waved as he walked along the snowy road.*

*"So do I," echoed Angela, "So do I."*

The morning alarm sounded and a jump from bed to start the routine. "Wow, Mark? I can't believe I thought of Mark. What a dream. What does it mean? Probably no meaning at all," Angel carried the conversation with herself. "Nothing at all."

No call from Angela by early morning. "No worries," Christopher thought. "I guess she was in a horrible mood. Or, maybe she changed her mind. I'll not bother her today and wait for her to contact me. Patience is always in my corner. I'll just plan the date."

Every moment in comparison to other dates in his past, Christopher eliminated the failed activities impressing other women. Even though each woman was not exactly alike, the activities he wanted to do were very similar. Dinner, movie, coffee or dessert are all exact or expected. "I need something more from a first date with Angela, then again maybe not. It is our first date and talking will do just fine," Christopher contemplated. "I'll contact her today and tell her of my idea. I'm sure she'll enjoy the night and come around to my influence. Most women do, even when they least expect to." Christopher left his place and drove directly to his office. Early arrival allowed him time to draft Angela an email. I'll text her for her email address and hope I get a chance to send it this morning." Christopher wrote:

Hi Angela,

Let's meet around 5:00 pm at the bookstore and drive together to the Village Tavern. We have 5:30 dinner/drinks reservations. We can take in the latest action movie (as you suggested) at Mansell Crossings. I do have plans for after the movie if you feel we're doing Ok☺ . Oh, my plans aren't forward, just fun as in dancing or coffee. Let me know if this works for you.

Call me when at lunch today or when you get a chance.

Can't wait to see you,

Christopher

Sometime during the morning, Christopher received the email address from Angela. Without delay Christopher sent the saved email and a copy to his home account. Feeling confident in the communication success, he settled in for the rest of his work day and smiled periodically as excitement built for Saturday night.

Angela appreciated the effort Christopher was making, and sent a second text "thanks for the effort," as a way of encouraging Christopher to follow through. Her response was remarkable as she felt exhilarated with butterfly emotions. Just the thought of Christopher making such an effort showed the quality in guys she should attract. "I should never allow anything less from a man," Angela pondered on her recent dating past. "I knew there were great guys out there for me."

Friday and girls' night out was the routine the two had at least since college. Once a month, the girls committed to spending one night for girl talk. It is what great friends do like sharing secrets or discussing concerns of their relationships. The two are like sisters when it comes to men. In college, they conversed about every date, on every guy, and often spilled their passionate secrets. Later in life, they never allowed distance or jobs get between them, as the friendship continued and their minds supported each other.

This Friday night was no different than any other girls' night out. Angela and Paula met for drinks and snacks, as eating dinner wasn't their main focus. "Ok girl, what's going on with you?" asked Paula.

"Oh, there is this guy I met. I told you about him. Remember?" answered Angela.

"Yes, the guy you met at the bookstore. You and that bookstore," Paula giggled.

"He's so impressive. He's doing all the right things."

"Like Ron did for me back when we first met? I was so swept away."

"I remember. You were in heaven from the attention and you almost didn't spend time with me."

"Don't you let it happen to me Angela, I don't know what I'd do not having you in my life."

"Oh, you don't have to worry. This guy is impressive but it's only a date. It's nice thinking of the future, but let's have one thing happen at a time."

"Wow, it really sounds funny coming from you, the dreamer. You've always jumped to conclusions about men. It's why I'm surprised you didn't fall for Bill."

"How dare you throw that guy into the conversation? He was an ass!"

"He's not different from those others you dated in college. Remember? I was there."

"I dated some quality guys then, didn't I?" Angela smirked.

"You dated a number of guys similar to Bill. The only difference at the time was they were in college. You were in tune with people like us. Now you seem changed."

The waitress appeared at the table just as Paula finished her sentence. "Can I interest you in another round of drinks? Or is there something I can get for you?" asked the waitress.

"No, nothing for me," answered Angela, "I haven't quite gotten to the middle of my drink, Paula how about you?"

Paula faced the waitress "Darling you can get me another beer. I'll be finished with this one by the time you return."

"I'll be right back with your beer," the waitress responded as she left the table.

"What were you saying about my changing attitude?" asked Angela.

"I didn't say attitude, I think it's your taste in men. Remember, I've known you for years. We've shared all our little secrets and now it's like you're on a different track. I'm somewhat concerned."

"You shouldn't be concerned. I'm the same Angela from years ago. You know we all go through a transition from time to time. Remember when I stopped dating jocks?"

"You only dated one jock in your life. It's not like you had a hand full of them."

"Yea, one was enough to make you hate them. Those guys were so...aargh, such assholes."

"Not all of them. I thought the one you dated was sweet." Paula winked and laughed because she knew the guy was a total bum.

"Are you kidding? You're kidding, right?"

"No, I'm not kidding. Just think. You could be his wife, have three little football muscle heads running around the house. No brains and total masculine hormones running amuck. Aren't you missing out on that scenario?"

"That's a far fetch on jocks. I didn't like there better-than-thou or every girl wants them attitude."

"I think it's more, the sex, the attention, the challenge, and the possibility of wealth that so many girls throw themselves on them," Paula winked just as she finished her beer before reaching for her new glass the waitress left.

"Either way, I'm not looking for a muscle head, even though many are smart. I've learned more of myself over the years."

"You have changed, and it bothers me."

"Paula, change is good. I have to change and develop." Angela looked puzzled, as if she's referring to Mark, thinking. "Why on earth was she jumping to a conclusion? Or am I jumping to the conclusion?"

"Oh, you're exploring more than ever. I still can't believe you pushed Bill away, he's a great guy."

"He was an ass."

"He was the same type you dated before."

"If you're referring to change, then I've changed for the better. It's why I like Christopher. Though we haven't had our date but I know he's going to be interesting. So change is good. There is a greater quality of men out there." Angela frowned as she enforced her thought to Paula. "You didn't settle for Ron. Why should I settle?"

"You're getting older and still single. Not to push you into a wedding gown, but time is flying."

"Oh, that's what you think? I'm fine being alone, but having a wonderful man in my life is worth shopping."

"I sound like your mother. I'm worried you'll find a bum out of desperation and not look at the total picture. You know, there is public opinion."

"What? Are you kidding me?"

"No, I'm not. As a matter of fact I have to remind you - the man you let in your life will be the image you display to the rest of the world."

"I know where you're going with this. I think you've had one too many. Should I call Ron to get you or can I take you home?"

"I'm not done yet."

"You act as if I don't have great taste in men. It's like if I don't follow what you want or think, I'm lost."

"I think, well, you need guidance and I'm here to keep you on the right path."

"I'm calling Ron. I can't take you home. I've had enough. I love you to death but this crap has to stop. I'm old enough to know what kind of man I want in my life. I don't need your approval, but whoever ends up in my life, you'll know to accept them." Angela dialed Ron and held the phone up to her ear. "Ron you need to pick up Paula. I'm leaving as she's had too much drink to drive and talking too much crap for me to listen. She's at Winners on Mansell and North Point Parkway." Angela gathered her things, looked at Paula, and said, "Ron is on his way. He didn't answer the phone but you don't need to drive. He'll be here like he always is. Here is $20 for my part of the tab. I'll catch you another time when you stop being such a bitch."

Saturday morning arrived as if the night shortened in time. Angela felt anger for Paula from the previous night's excursion. "I can't believe she has so much nerve. The thought of her being such an ass makes me feel incredibly mad- arrgh, damn her," Angela thought as she started her day. Saturdays were mostly set aside for maintenance between home, errands, and herself. First things first, clean the apartment. She rose to the occasion as she moved from room to room, wiping, spraying, polishing, and the like. She filled the apartment with music from the radio station 100.5 fm WKUF, sang a few tunes and went to the cleaners.

Errands were a different effort. After cleaning for most of the morning, Angela went to the closest discount department store. The store was normally busy with all types of people doing their weekly shopping. She liked the store because it offered a variety of things for a decent price. But like many other people, Angela shopped for quality as well and in her normal day she'd drop by Kroger for a few other items. In Kroger she noticed an interracial couple shopping and seemed to enjoy their time together. "No different than any couple," Angela thought. In a different aisle, Angela noticed another couple, interracial but more dynamic perhaps. This time it was a black man and a Hispanic woman. The woman was very light in complexion, as if she were Caucasian. Angela realized the woman being Latin by her comments to her husband or gentleman. He responded in Spanish which she had taken in college. "Wow, I knew there were mixtures of people with Latin descent, but I never gave it much attention," Angela pondered as she completed her shopping.

Christopher stepped out of the car in front of Kroger, on Old Alabama Road. He'd left the gym earlier and wanted to pick up a few things before heading home. Aisle after aisle Christopher grabbed a few items he knew were needed. The small basket started filling as if his shopping became spontaneous with unneeded goods. "They always say never shop hungry," Christopher laughed at himself. The next corner aisle, he noticed this lovely woman, and it took his mind away from the goods he thought were needed. With a quick step he explored the same aisle the woman went down. "It's Angela," Christopher smiled and quickly moved toward her. "Hey Angela," Christopher called.
Angela turned and recognized Christopher. She responded, "Hi Chris! - oh I meant Christopher".
    "Hey, what brings you here?"
    "The same thing you're doing here. It's a grocery store."
    "Yea right, duh," Christopher smiled thinking, "I could have at least said something clever."

Angela laughed with Christopher. "Hey, are you ready for tonight?"
    "I think I am. I'm looking forward to it. I have a few things I want to finish today, but you're definitely my plan."
    "Exactly what a girl likes to hear, being on someone's plan," Angela smiled.
    "Oh sure, you're on my plan and hopefully we'll have a great time. I'd like you on my plan in the future. You know, they say first impressions are only once and you've impressed me. I can't wait for tonight. I want to find out more."

"I do too. Well its 5:00, at the bookstore where we met right?" asked Angela.

"Yes and I'll be there waiting. It gives us four hours until we see each other again. But who's counting?" Christopher winked.

"Who's counting? I'd guess we both are," Angela smirked, "I'll see you later." Angela returned to shopping but with a smile in her heart. "He made my morning."

Christopher completed his shopping and left the store. "What an idiot? Sometimes I get caught up in trying to impress a woman. I'll do better tonight," Christopher pondered driving home.

Christopher parked his car right in front of the Barnes and Noble. It's 4:45 pm, and the weather is perfect for his evening with Angela. He'd dressed to impress, even in jeans. He knew the outfit fell into a little hip fashion, but also was sexy enough to turn heads, classy enough to impress, and accented for the very essence he was pursuing - Angela's affection.

Angela took her time getting ready for the date. She made her selection between a summer dress and jeans. The jeans won the contest because Angela wanted to impress, but not overdress. She selected the perfect blouse, which showed her girlish figure, and left room for a little imagination. Angela chose a nice summer heel shoe, about two inches. The shoes made her outfit exactly as she pictured. All matching with everything in the right place, and not too encouraging, but encouraging enough. All of her clothing colors accented her beautiful eyes, skin tone, and trumpeted her seductive figure. A few looks in the mirror at the hair, the make up, and the outfit, and off she went.

Angela arrived with fifteen minutes to spare and found Christopher seated outside the coffee shop, "Who's driving?" she asked.

"I'll drive. Park your car and let's take mine," responded Christopher.

"Ok." Angela replied and moved her car near a tree in the parking lot.

Christopher quickly got in his car and drove to Angela, stepped out of the car and opened the door for her. "The gentlemanly thing to do," thought Angela. "Every little thing counts," thought Christopher. Back in the car, Christopher asked, "What type of music do you enjoy listening to? I have a nice selection."

"I listen to the top 40 when I'm in the car. At home I have a collection of Rock, Country, some Country Rock and Classical. I'm flexible to anything you'd like."

"Sure is nice having varied taste. It means you're flexible to enjoy a number of clubs when we want to go dancing. You do dance right?"

"Yes, I'm flexible and dance to nearly anything. Though I don't think I'm the hottest dancer, but I enjoy it."

"I haven't met a woman yet who didn't enjoy dancing."

"Oh there are some, you know. I'm not one of them."

"Actually, I'm happy you aren't one of them. I enjoy dancing from time to time myself."

"A guy who likes to shake it," Angela smiled in her reply, as Christopher turned from North Point left onto Haynes Bridge. "Have you eaten at the Village Tavern before?" asked Christopher.

"No, I haven't. I've seen it a few times driving by and there is always a nice group of cars there. It seems nice from the outside."

"It's quite nice really. It offers a very relaxed atmosphere and the service is awesome. I think the food is just as good. If I were a critic I'd have to say three and a half stars, maybe four."

"Good, but are you an easy or hard critic?"

"I think I'm medium because I'm no expert on food."

"Oh you enjoy consuming it for sure I bet."

"You are right, there is nothing like a good meal." Christopher answered as they arrived. Quickly Christopher parked, exited and opened Angela's door. He held his arm out for Angela to grasp as they walked towards the entrance. "You look stunning," Christopher commented. "Thank you," Angela smiled with her response. "You aren't going to say anything about me?" asked Christopher.

"You're not going to give me a chance to really check you out? Ok, you're handsome and I love the way you're dressed."

"Thank you so much," Christopher replied as he opened the entrance door. "Hi, welcome to The Village Tavern," the receptionist spoke.

"Hi, I have reservations. The name is Mulligan," Christopher replied. "It will be a few minutes wait. Is it ok?" asked the receptionist.

"Sure, I don't mind." Christopher responded and turned to Angela asking, "You don't mind do you?"

"No I don't mind a little wait."

"I have to run to the men's room. I'll be right back." Christopher made his move towards the men's room. Angela took a seat on the cushioned bench. The receptionist smiled as Angela caught her eye and returned the smile. "You're a lucky woman," the receptionist commented.

"I think I am. Why do you think so?"

"You're with Christopher and he's a lovely guy. I hear he's a serious catch."

"You know him?"

"Not personally but I've heard good things about him from my girlfriend. They dated once or twice. She wanted him to get serious and he wouldn't for whatever reason. She didn't tell me exactly why but did say he's totally gorgeous. I sure hope it works for you. You two look marvelous together."

"Thanks, it's our first date." Angela responded with a puzzled look. Christopher returned, stood next to Angela and said, "I chose this place because of the variety on the menu. I knew you'd like a few things, but wasn't sure to be specific. I hope you don't mind."

"No I don't mind at all. It's a lovely place so far."

"Yes, it's charming and as a guy it isn't a masculine comment." Christopher laughed.

"No it isn't too guy-like, but that depends on the guy." Angela smiled in return.

The receptionist called "Mulligan". Both Angela and Christopher moved towards the podium for the escort to their table. "Please follow me," the waiter directed. As the two sat across from each other, the waiter asked, "Can I start you off with drinks?" as he handed them a menu.

"Yes I'd like a whisky sour," responded Christopher. "Are you thinking of something Angela?"

"I was thinking of something light. A glass of wine will be nice."

"We have a house Chablis or Zinfandel that goes with nearly any meal. Will they do?" asked the waiter.

"Zinfandel, white zinfandel will be perfect," responded Angela.

"Thank you and I'll be back with your drinks shortly," the waiter responded and left the table.

Looking over the menus, they both sat quietly for minutes. Periodically, Christopher peeked above the menu for any kind of opening to converse with Angela. "May I suggest something for you?" asked Christopher.

"Sure, please do." Angela responded holding the menu with a thought, "I hope he doesn't think I'll eat anything."

"I suggest the chicken dish. I think its one of the better prepared meals here. However they even serve pizza for those who want something different. And you can never go wrong with pizza."

"The chicken sounds lovely. I think I'll have it. What are you having?"

"I'll have the steak tonight. I had poultry last night and want to mix things up a little."

"Sounds good, which are you having, the Rib Eye or the New York Strip?"

"Yeah, red meat will do me well. I normally stick to fish and poultry, but tonight's special."

"Oh, you're so sweet."

"Yes I am, as a matter of fact, nothing like being sweet on the first date. Does it impress you?"

"Its nice hearing you have me in mind."

"Does every man have you in mind the first date?"

"The norm, isn't it? Every man wants to impress the first date, or I'd not go out with them if I didn't think he'd have me in mind."

"You have a good point."

"Did you decide?"

"Decide? You mean dinner. Yes, I'm having the strip. Are you having a salad first?" Christopher asked as he reviewed the menu again.

"Well, I think Chicken California will be just fine. It's more than enough and I doubt I will finish it." Angela took the wine from the waiter and sipped for taste. "Good selection goes well with poultry."

"Yes, I think it does." Christopher responded and said "Thank you." to the waiter.

"Are you ready to order?" asked the waiter.

"I'll have the NY strip, medium well," Christopher answered.

"And you madam?"

"The Chicken California," responded Angela.

"Excellent choice, is there anything special, as in appetizers?"

"No," answered Christopher.

"Thank you and I'll be back soon with your orders," chimed the waiter.

"Thanks," Christopher said with a smile. "Tell me more about yourself Angela."

"Oh, there isn't too much to tell. You know I'm a transplant, went to college, moved here with a girlfriend because she said Atlanta was very nice."

"You know I did the exact same thing. Except I didn't follow a friend, I was recruited for my job in Alpharetta. The company gave me an internship first, and then made an offer later."

"That took a lot of pressure off of you, didn't it?" asked Angela.

"It made it easy for my transition from college. After I graduated from the University of Georgia, it was a snap to find a great job."

"Oh, you're UGA alum. I hear UGA is a fantastic school."

"Yes it is, and a lot of fun too. The campus is not to far from the city and the town have similar big city amenities at your finger tips. Those years were a lot of fun - especially for a country guy from upstate NY."

"So you aren't a native."

"No, I'm from Albany and it's not the size of Atlanta. I love the weather here. No big winters."

"I love it here too. The weather isn't that bad."

"And the people seem really nice. Not to say folks up North aren't but there is truth to the Southern hospitality."

"You know, most people are nice, but some still hold onto the antics of the old South."

"Maybe some, but not all; I'm finding out most are transplants like me."

"Yes, I guess, but I ran into a few along the way."

"They weren't scary I hope. I came across some who still believe I was not worth their grain of salt, all because I'm a Yankee."

"I've heard that one." Angela smirked. "At the same time they think ...." Christopher jumped in "you're the dumbest person in the conversation. I normally ignore them and keep my smart remarks to myself as I figure out ways to make them eat their words without hurting their feelings."

"How do you manage?" asked Angela.

"Technique. One day I'll have to share it with you."

"What about your parents? Were they educated and from NY as well?"

"Yes, they both grew up in Albany. I think they're lovely, down to earth people. Dad is an accountant and mom, a local elementary school teacher."

"Sounds like a lovely couple. What did you do for fun?

"Besides winter games, I did the normal things. My activities were a balance between outdoor and indoor. Did the normal things kids do."

"I used to ice skate in the winter…" Angela was interrupted again as Christopher interjected, "on the frozen lake? I once skated on thin ice and it broke just as I crossed. I'm so glad I wasn't a heavy kid. Or I may not be here. You wouldn't like that now would you?"

"I think its nice having you here," answered Angela.

"I hope you actually believe it - in time. I'm sure you will."

"Maybe," Angela answered but thought, "He's really confident. I guess his job makes him that way."

"I usually find myself intrigued in the company of people who feel excited to be around me. I'm sure you'll join the band in time. You'll see."

"Did I say something making you skeptical?"

"No, but I can see it in your face. Most people don't believe me when I say things as such."

"I didn't say there isn't belief in it." Angela changed from a defensive nature and asked, "Tell me, what made you live in Alpharetta versus downtown?"

"The job is up here on the North side. I wanted to be close so I wouldn't have to commute."

"Oh you know, Atlanta traffic is…" Christopher jumped in, "hell on wheels? Yes, it's the worst. I'd rather drink than drive in the traffic. They say you can get used to it, but I don't believe many people do."

"Why didn't you take a job downtown?"

"I wasn't quite offered one there and decided here was a better place. Everything you want is within ten minutes, downtown is twenty plus, depending on the time of day, and this area is growing. Why would you want to live anyplace else?"

"Because there is more nightlife for youngsters like us?"

"This isn't a sleepy town. You just have to know where to go. And since you're out with me, I'll get to show you a few."

Silence fell at the table. Angela stopped trying to make small talk and decided to let Christopher take the lead. "My gosh, I'm starved and it's only 6:15. I hope dinner comes soon," said Christopher.

The waiter arrived with a dish on each arm. He placed the steak in front of Christopher and then served the chicken to Angela. "Will there be anything else? Sir, the steak sauce is there on the table. I can serve fresh pepper if either of you like. Is there anything else I can get you?"

"No, that's all thanks." responded Christopher.

"I'd like a refill of water if you don't mind." Angela blurted just before the waiter left the table.

"Oh sure, not a problem; and you sir, would you like a glass also?"

"No, I'm fine."

The waiter immediately responded to Angela's request. Christopher took the first bite of his steak. "Umm, good as usual," he said. "How's your chicken?"

"I haven't bitten into it yet, but I'm sure it's good. It smells..."

"..delicious," Christopher interrupted. "I know it's good. It's one of my favorites and also why I suggested it."

"Good choice," Angela commented after taking her first bite. The conversation died while both focused on the meal. Angela decided to break silence, "Are you a member of a fraternity?"

"Yes, as a matter of fact I am. It was the best thing in my life."

"Which fraternity?"

"You mean there's more than one?" Christopher answered with a smile. "I'm a brother of the best ever."

"Ok, and that is?"

"Sigma Omega Chi is there any other?"

"I don't know about fraternities but they were the guys who seemed really classy. I agree you are definitely a member."

"Acknowledge the brotherhood and what a compliment. I appreciate your view of me. I know you like the idea of being with a classy guy. I am no doubt probably the classiest guy you've ever known."

"I think you're assuming there aren't any other guys with class and substance interested in me." Angela placed her fork on the plate, stared into Christopher's eyes as if sending a message, "you insulted me asshole," and smiled. "You seem really nice to me Christopher, but I get the feeling."

"I'm the man for you? Sure I am. You'll realize it in no time. I'm sure of it."

The waiter arrived at the table, stood near Angela and asked, "Do you have room for dessert?"

"Oh no, no thank you," Angela replied.

"I don't think so but thanks for asking. Why don't you bring the check?" responded Christopher.

"I'll return with the check," the waiter replied and took Angela's dish. "Are you finished sir?"

"Yes I am thank you." The waiter took both plates from the table. "You know, Christopher I wasn't quite finished with dinner."

"You weren't? Oh I'll get the waiter."

"No, its too late I'll be ok," Angela frowned.

"Well the timing is good as we have a half hour for our show. If you're hungry after the movie we can have dessert."

"No I'm ok. I think I'll be fine. I had enough."

"Great, then I'll pay the check and we can head over to the theater." Christopher picked up the check and placed his credit card in the folder."

"Can I pick up the tip?" Angela asked as she picked up her purse.

"No way, I have it. Remember I'm the classy guy you've never had in your life."

Silence fell upon the table as the two waited until the credit card slip returned for signature. Angela looked more at the décor. Christopher eyed Angela as if to catch her attention.

Not once did Angela say anything as she contemplated the last nice dinner out with Mark. No comparison to the décor between the Village Tavern and the Club 290. The Club 290 being older and focused on jazz music didn't match up to the potential romantic environment and therefore wasn't quite comparable as apple to apple. But the comparison wasn't just the environment; it was a flash to Mark. "He didn't seem so self-indulged as Christopher," she thought, "I'll chalk it up to him trying to impress me."

The waiter returned the check for signature saying, "Thank you so much for coming and I hope you enjoyed your meal. I'd love seeing you again."

"You're welcome," replied Christopher as he signed the check slip. "I'm ready to leave. Angela, are you ready?"

Angela rose from the table with her purse and waited for Christopher to walk with her. "I'm ready Christopher."

"Great!" Christopher replied as he moved out of the booth and placed his hand at the small of Angela's back. "Did you truly like this place?"

"I sure did. It is very nice. Maybe next time we can sit and chat at the bar. I saw it when we entered."

"It's a nice bar. The place is really busy on certain nights," Christopher responded as they both walked to the car. "Sometimes there's music from a guitarist. And when the guitarist isn't inside, he's on the patio around back. It's an interesting place for sure and can be a lot of fun. I think we should return one day during the week so you can experience the fun."

"I think coming back will be nice."

"Good." Christopher opened the car door for Angela.

"Thank you," Angela replied and clicked the seat belt. Christopher climbed in, cranked up the car, and drove off to Mansell Theaters. "We are on time and I have tickets to the movie. You did say action right?"

"Yes, I suggested action. What are we watching?"

"*Love and World Exploration*. I hear it's a great movie. Action-filled with good reviews; I hope you like it."

"We'll see. I like action as well as romance but I figured action is best for the both of us. Most guys aren't into chick flicks," Angela explained.

"I'm into chick flicks, when the mood is right. Wow this place is crowded. You'd think this was the Oscars with so many people at the theater."

"You know it's always crowded on the weekend. I haven't seen one yet where movies aren't sold out." Angela replied.

"Even when there isn't a blockbuster show playing?"

"Its worse when it's a blockbuster playing."

"I'm glad I planned ahead and purchased the tickets earlier."

The two entered the theater and headed directly to theater three. It is the largest of the fourteen theaters available. They took upper seats near the middle of the screen for a perfect view of the show. Minutes before the previews people seated themselves near Angela and Christopher. "I used to date the girl walking by," Christopher pointed.

"Oh really?" asked Angela.

"Yes, she was interesting but we didn't make it because she wanted more. Most women know a good catch when they see one."

"You should speak to her."

"Why should I? It's over and I don't go back."

"I understand not going back, but what if she turned out to be the one worth having?"

"Are you saying you aren't?"

"No, but you actually know her and you're just learning things about me."

"I'd rather learn more of you than back track. She's nice but she wasn't my cup of tea. Not quite my style of a woman."

"I'm sure you have high standards and are you sure I can meet those high marks?"

"So far so good; you're on the right track to stardom."

"I'm not so sure that's a compliment."

The movie previews ran and both Christopher and Angela sat in silence. Focused on the show, each watched intently without a peep between them. Laughter erupted at various parts of the movie as if there were a symphony playing a chart of notes in crescendo and decrescendo in unison. Ninety minutes later, the movie ended when the credits rolled up the big screen. People started leaving, one after the other, they left their seats and advanced to the aisle which led to the exit. Christopher stood and reached for Angela's hand as if a guide to secure his guest. Nothing touched his hand as Angela went the opposite direction for the nearest stairs. Angela didn't turn around to see if Christopher followed; it was her natural thing to do, as most guys usually watched her action and responded. She thought Christopher would respond like any other man at her movement. Obviously a miscommunication on both parties, the show ended with the feeling of individuality setting in. They met just at the crossing of the stairs and the main passage to the exit hall. Again, Christopher reached for Angela's hand and this time she finally noticed. "Wow, what a disconnect?" Christopher thought as finally their hands were joined, finger to finger.

"How did you like the movie?" asked Angela.

"It was pretty funny at some points. Overall it was entertaining."

"I rather liked it, humor, a little romance, and action. What else can a girl ask for on a first date?" Angela giggled.

"The date isn't over. Let's see - we had dinner, a movie, and now dessert."

"You'd like dessert? Where do you have mind for dessert?"

"The Cheesecake Factory; its close by and we can be there in no time. Come on, the night's still young."

"Sure, we can have dessert. I kind of changed my mind. I'd like dessert." Angela responded and held his hand tighter.

"Cheesecake must be a favorite of yours. You know what they say 'Sweet things are a way to a girl's heart.' Is this true for you?"

"Sweet things are always a way to a girl's heart. It's the content of the sweet that counts."

"Am I getting sweet on you?"

"You may be, just may be."

Angela found a parking space exactly in front of the Cheesecake Factory doors. She decided to drive, as not to make a second trip for her car after dessert. Christopher parked two rows forward of Angela. He was fortunate to find a parking space so close to Angela as everyone in Alpharetta had the same idea. The restaurant was packed with customers and there was at a twenty minute waiting list.

"What would you like to do? Would you like to wait or have a seat at the bar?" Christopher asked.

"We're here for dessert. Why don't we order from the cheesecake bar and eat under the moonlight?" suggested Angela.

"A remarkable idea. Who says we have to sit inside to enjoy dessert?" Christopher responded and guided her inside to the cheesecake bar. He handed the menu to Angela and said, "You know the best cheesecake is anything with pralines. But it's nearly gone, how about the Oreo?"

"I'm not sure. If I'm going to have dessert for tonight, why not go all the way. I have to work it off tomorrow anyway. I like the Turtle."

"Are we going to share?"

"Sharing would be nice, saves me from working out so hard tomorrow. We can share." Angela smiled in her answer.

Christopher felt ecstatic to have her in the palm of his hand for the moment. Quick-witted, he comes up with, "Will we continue to share the rest of the night?"

"Share the rest of the night? Am I understanding? Are you alluding to us sharing the night together? You must be..."

"Crazy. Right I am crazy. Don't take it the wrong way. I'd love sharing the night with you. We can explore dreams, discuss fantasies, and find out more of our beliefs. How else can we get to know each other? We didn't have time to talk tonight."

Angela quickly agreed without saying, "We definitely didn't talk. He sure as heck did."

"Are you going to order or try to persuade me into a long talk?"

A bar table opened just as Christopher ordered. Angela quickly moved to take the seat as the waiter cleaned the surface. Once seated, Angela waved to catch Christopher's eyes and acknowledge they were sitting there. Christopher briskly walked over and asked, "I thought we would sit outside under the stars?"

"The timing was awesome. I grabbed the table, it's a good thing. We can order drinks from the bar and enjoy the dessert and conversation here."

"I thought it would be a better setting outside. At least there I'd have your total attention."

"You'll have my attention here as well. You'll just have to sit close enough so I can hear you."

"Close enough it is. There's our number I'll be right back. If a waiter comes, please order a Whisky Sour for me."

"Ok," responded Angela thinking, "I knew he wouldn't like us sitting here but it's a better move than to stay with him the rest of the night. Maybe the next date we'll talk."

Three bites into the cheese cake, Angela stopped eating. It wasn't the Turtle, it was the Oreo and of course not her favorite as she suggested. Christopher drank his Whiskey Sour and a glass of water. "Aren't you going to eat more?" Christopher asked.

"I've had enough. You go right ahead and enjoy it."

"I didn't know you'd stop eating it. I thought we were sharing but it seems I'm eating the most. Are you watching your beautiful figure and it's why you stopped?"

"Well, you know a woman must watch her intake as it's staying in shape for you guys that count," Angela smirked as if her comment was to cut like a knife.

"And you look marvelous. What time are we working out tomorrow?"

"We?"

"Yes, we. I thought it would be nice working out together."

"You know my workouts are serious and sharing - it is like someone calling you Chris."

"You can call me Chris," Christopher moved closer to kiss her cheek. Angela pushed back "Not so fast Christopher. You haven't crossed that bridge yet."

"Oh my, Angela, I thought we were hitting it off well."

"The night was interesting, but I'm not too quick to share the goods. I'd hate to pretend and mislead; maybe at the end of the next date, when we know each other better." Angela stood and grabbed her purse. "I'm tired. I'll call you. Better yet, call me when you can think of something fun to do. I'll be up to it." Christopher stood, grabbed her hand and kissed the back of it. "I know you'll love our next date, every woman always does." Christopher smiled just as Angela pulled away and leaves the restaurant.

"Maybe the next time is better." Angela thought. "He isn't a bad guy, just so many girls made his head pretty big. He seems a lot of fun if doing the right things and a charmer for sure. Yes, next time he calls I'll have to tell him what I like."

# Chapter 4

The sun woke Angela after a comforting slumber. "Last night was very interesting," Angela thought while reaching for her cellular, just as it rang. "Hello," Angela answered.

"Hey Angela, its Paula."

"Hi," Angela paused for Paula's response as she recalled their last encounter.

"I'm sorry for the other night. I know I can be a bitch at times but, I'm always looking out for your best interest."

"Yea, I hear your crap all the time. Remember when you jumped to conclusions in college? It always happens when I'm not doing things as you see fit."

"Don't go there, college was different. We aren't kids anymore and I worry about your future. I want you happy like I am. I have a wonderful man and you deserve one too."

"They say you have to kiss frogs to find the Prince. I'm still kissing frogs, well sort of."

"Was Bill a frog?"

"Yes, a crap of one at that. I found out without kissing him-thank goodness" Angela laughed.

"Oh I bet he isn't so bad. If Ron and I weren't together, I'd date him."

"Different strokes for all kinds of folks; as they say back home." Angela shook her head while moving around in the room.

"So, do you have company?"

"Should I have company?" asked Angela thinking, "I knew why she called this morning."

"Well, you were so excited about Christopher. Isn't that his name?"

"Yes, it's Christopher. He was ok but not one to bring home on a first date."

"The way you sounded earlier, I thought you were in lust."

"Paula, you know me much better than that. It takes more than someone showing interest for me to venture there. I'm content with myself and when the time comes, it will happen. No sooner. This isn't college anymore you know."

"I know, but it's been a while since you've shared your experience with me, and I live through you. Don't get me wrong, I love my Ron, but I like hearing what happened."

"Well, lately I haven't felt up to being with a man. The spark hadn't come across just yet. And besides, I live for me, so don't pressure me for your excitement."

"There's no pressure. I want to know, as I want you to be happy." Angela heard Paula snicker as she said, "When are you going to see Christopher again?"

"Last night didn't go well and I think he's a little arrogant. I mean, he's full of telling me everything about him, how he was the hot guy, and had the nerve to point out some girl he dated."

"Sounds like he was really trying to impress you, don't you think?"

"Impress me? Well maybe he was trying a little too hard. If he calls, I'll go just to see if he'll repeat the same thing. He does have potential, a good looking man and some class about him."

"He's from the right gene pool too. That's important for your future kids."

"How the hell would you know he's got perfect genes?"

"I'm paraphrasing the things you told me about him. I'm sure he's from the right gene pool. Look at how he's a really nice person, smart, aggressive, and confident. He's got to have the right stuff to accomplish so much. He's got a great job, makes a great living, and knows how to enjoy life."

"You got a lot from my description. I didn't know he has an idea how to enjoy life. We went on the first date. I didn't tell you all those things."

"Sure you did. I read between the lines. Trust me on this, I know men and he's probably the best one for you."

"I'll go out with him if he calls, to make sure I didn't misread his personality. But he does have a number of qualities. Not quite the type you're pushing, but nice qualities."

"I have to go Angela," Paula screamed "Hold on!" away from the phone's mouth piece. "Ron is waiting for me. Remember, I love my best friend and forgive me for being so pushy the other night. Gotta run."

"Bye," responded Angela and thought, "That woman has the nerve. I know what she's thinking, 'The right gene pool' – How dare she imply its better? Ever since Mark she's been acting really strange."

Sunday passed into night, not much going on and Angela became restless. The single life seems to offer times of restlessness, especially when there's nothing on television, no great books available, as she finished her last by the pool earlier. No movies as she just saw one yesterday and surely she didn't want to call anyone; especially Paula. No, not call her. "What did I do on a Sunday night in the past?" Angela asked herself. "I had friends I could hang with. I normally did multiple things during the day and then crashed from being exhausted. I had dinner with friends or cooked for a few. I curled up with a good book – that reminds me I need to pick up another one tomorrow. I called family, and then I found something interesting on television. What makes tonight so different?" Angela walked around the apartment for something to do, clean, or prepare for the coming week. She found nothing out of place, one thing here, another there, and it was the same as last week.

Finally she jumped in her car for a drive as it was a decision to find something to do. "It's not quite too late in the evening; maybe I'll grab a movie from Blockbuster." Angela headed to Blockbuster. On the way, she decided to detour and headed south towards the city. The building lights and the Perimeter skyline were just beautiful, as there was a pink glow on the King and Queen buildings. Angela turned right onto I-285 and found herself at the Roswell Road exit. She took the exit as it led north to her part of the city. It was as if a magnet drew her closer to Club 290. Just as she passed a few night club spots, she found herself driving slowly through the parking lot of The Punch Line and Club 290. She parked across the street from both locations in a strip mall lot. She sat there and observed people, thinking of last weekend how she enjoyed the jazz music and the company. "I should go in," Angela contemplated, "I'm alone. I don't go in places alone, it's not ladylike." She told herself. Watching person after person enter and exit the club, she noticed the mixture of people and how they seemed relaxed or involved. "I've seen enough, I should go."

Blockbuster was nearly empty as the hour was late in the evening. Angela noticed she observed Club 290 for nearly 30 minutes, with added drive time to her nearest store, placed her almost at closing time. Quickly Angela grabbed a romantic drama movie, paid, and returned home. Back in the apartment, she sat for a minute after grabbing tea from the kitchen and popped in the movie. Barely watching, she fell into a light sleep only to wake in the middle of the show. She pushed herself for bed without following the usual prep routine, and sleep finally overtook her.

Monday morning and Angela had no motivation for the office. She dragged around the apartment, like a teenager trying to cut school. "I'm just not up for work today," thought Angela. She decided to work from home and sent emails to her office, announcing her decision. She slowly set her day in motion, as there was no rush for anything, working from home allowed her to enjoy the morning and remain busy via the office VPN (Virtual Private Network). Quickly Angela settled in with activities, focusing on the daily work objectives. She grabbed a cup of coffee, a bagel, and returned to her desk for a conference call. Work continued through the morning until 10:30 am. Angela checked her schedule and decided to get out of the apartment and work in a different environment. She quickly dressed, packed her laptop, picked up her cellular, and found herself heading to the bookstore. Angela left just ahead of lunch traffic. North Point Parkway was horrible during lunch, the close proximity of corporate headquarters, the multiple restaurants, stores, and other businesses all seemed to filter into the roadway like ants on a mission. Her timing gave promise for a ten minute drive.

Angela found a great parking spot right in front of the bookstore. She grabbed her things from the car quickly and briskly set up her laptop in the store's Starbucks and ordered a latte. Grabbing the seat in the corner away from the main traffic, she settled online to complete her work. The excellent internet signal allowed the laptop to move with speed for the VPN connection. "Totally operational without problem," Angela smiled in thought, as it comforted her concern of being out of the office or being unavailable to whoever tried to communicate with her. "Great, no new email messages or IM's during my disconnect." Angela thought, following up from her previous communiqué.

Lunch time was apparent, as the number of patrons nearly tripled in Starbucks. Patrons passed her, like cars zipping by on GA 400. Others found comfort at tables near by, and particularly those who escaped the office wanted to continue working, powered their laptops making the location their break of sanity. From near silence before the bewitching hour came noise from conversations, key clatter, and occasional laughter, coupled with the service staff yelling orders in preparation and with delivery came interrupting roars. "I'm not sure this was a great idea," Angela thought, reading her last email, unable to focus because of the laughter across from her corner. "Next time I'll pick after lunch as a better time to work here." Angela continued to type away and fought not to stop and observe the activities around her. Every so often her concentration failed as the crowd became her entertainment. She sat there with the laptop stuck on her email, as if mesmerized by a channel of her mind, like the flashback of a horror movie, forcing her to pay attention or else. Angela decisively closed the laptop, as it would be a wasted effort to continue trying to focus. The crowd became full of life and a personality within itself. The variety of people stole her interest. Especially the guy sitting next to her, with all the entertainment of lunch time hustle and bustle, he continued to maintain focus in his laptop. Angela also observed the crowd's movement and decided it was time for a coffee refill, and maybe a snack. Moving around to order, she raised her coffee cup as if it meant a refill, just as she approached the cashier line. "Hey Gary, I'll have another," Angela said.

"Gotcha, Angela," responded Gary. As she moved closer to the cashier, she viewed the snack selection. Of all the cakes, muffins, and snacks, nothing seemed to appeal to her hunger.

"Is that all," asked the cashier.

"Well," Angela paused as she looked at the snack display, "Yes, I don't think I'll have anything else".

"Three –forty-five," the cashier spoke. Angela responded, giving the cashier four dollars and pointed to the change box. Quickly she moved back to her laptop, checking if anyone moved it or bothered it in any way. Validating it was safe, and after hearing Gary call her, she briskly stepped to retrieve her new latte. "Thank you," Angela told Gary and smiled a flirtatious grin.

"Anytime."

Settled again, Angela sat for a few minutes, still entertained by the crowd of patrons. She observed the laughter at other tables, a couple of girlfriends chatting away as she and Paula would when on better terms. There were guys finally finishing lunch, and others purchasing coffee to go. The crowd  dwindled and the sounds diminished to a level for controlled focus. Again across from her, there was still the guy who never stopped with the fingers clacking away, like a ferocious chipmunk snipping on a nut, his focus was admirable. "No more procrastinating," Angela said to herself, lifting the top of her laptop and pushed the 'on' button. Waiting for the laptop to boot up, Angela took in the last of the patron activity. The traffic moved from the bookstore to the coffee shop and traffic moved the opposite direction gave the last entertainment. "Finally," Angela excitedly clicked on the email icon and waited for a response. She waited as the hour glass spun, and spun for nearly two minutes. "This is really moving slow." In the office, she learned when machines move slow there is a quick-fix process to follow. As a soldier following orders, Angela concisely proceeded with the troubleshooting procedure. Minutes later, still nothing happened. Again, she followed the procedure as if her life depended on it. And again, nothing responded as expected. "Dang it- Just my luck my laptop goes on the blink; just when I have to send this email to my boss. Damn it!" Angela said quite loudly.

Eric, a computer programmer, heard Angela's disgust. How could he avoid hearing her when sitting across from her? Eric noticed Angela working on her laptop when he came in the coffee shop. Not quite Eric's routine to leave the office in the middle of the day. He ventured into the coffee shop to escape the horror of politics. Office politics were hell at times and drove even the most talented into a frenzy. "Do you mind if I take a look at your laptop?" asked Eric.

"Oh, I'm sorry I disturbed you," Angela responded with surprise.

"No problem, I've worked in louder situations." Eric moved from his table and turned Angela's laptop around. Quickly his fingers started the clacking noise, as if a pianist playing a fiery piece at a classical concert. Like the orchestra responding, the laptop flashed, as if the magical alliance had an agreement with the astrological stars. "I think that will do it. You can get to your email now," Eric directed as he turned the laptop around.

"Oh, thank you so much. I needed to get this email out before my boss left for Toronto. Thank you so much." Angela apologetically raised her hand while the other maneuvered the mouse over the screen. Without another word, Eric returned to his work, and Angela finalized the email. "Done," Angela said aloud with excitement.

"Good for you," Eric responded, as he momentarily stopped typing.

"I owe you."

"It's nothing, I had to make an adjustment on your program, open a portal to your internal network firewall, and ensure you had a connection. It was nothing."

"Doesn't sound like nothing. It was amazing. You know, it was magical to us who only key punch and surf. I owe you."

"Well, thank you but it was nothing. I'm sure any gentleman would do the same."

"No not really. Hey, it's lunch time, have you eaten?"

"No, I haven't, but I have to get this out and I'm on my last line of code. Thanks for the offer." Eric returned focus to his laptop and started coding again. Angela sat in silence and returned to her email account, focusing on another application and started her work. Her stomach growled from hunger as it hits hard from delayed feeding; which she thought of munching to satisfy earlier. "You have got to let me take you to lunch," Angela directed to Eric. Still typing Eric didn't budge and kept his focus on coding the last line. Moments later Eric ended the typing and looked back at Angela. "Ok, I just finished and since you insist, we can go."

"Awesome," Angela answered while turning off the laptop and packed it away. "Do you have any place in mind?"

"No, I'll let you decide."

"I think we can do Sweet Tomato."

"I like that place. Are you sure you want to go there? I get into the soups."

"Sure I like it too. I'm glad you agree. Should I drive?"

"If you want to, I don't mind. You are coming back right?"

"Sure, I'm coming back," answered Angela "as in - duh" she thought.

"Just checking, as I have another function to create." Eric responded while placing the laptop in the carrying case.

"Function?" Angela questioned as she led the way to her car.

"Oh it's a software activity for an application. When you want something to happen on the application, it's called a function. To act or react as in a response or initiation of an event. Function," Eric explained.

"I see. Then I guess our function is lunch," Angela laughed.

"I'm starved," she commented, while starting her car. Eric climbed in, secured his seat belt, and sat back in silence. "Where are you originally from Eric?"

"Oh, north of here."

"Cummings?" Angela replied. "I didn't hear an accent in your voice -well not a southern accent."

"I mean true north. It's considered Midwest, but true north by the map."

"True north?"

"Yes, almost to Canada."

"Its cold weather for sure up there. Do you miss it?"

"Sometimes," answered Eric as he looked out of the window.

"Your lane is empty on this side. We can get there faster if you come over here. I'm only suggesting it. You don't have to do it."

"I can take it. Thanks for looking out for me," responded Angela as she maneuvered the car over. "I moved here a few years ago. It's been interesting ever since. I meet great people, and a few others you'd not like, but in general, Atlanta is a nice city."

"I think so. I came because of the job."

"Really?"

"Yes. I worked with the company in college as an intern. I was offered a job after graduation. So I came and it's an interesting place."

"I think so too. Have you done many things since moving here?"

"Yes, but not too many. I focus on work mostly." Eric jumped out of the car just as Angela parked and quickly moved around to open her door.

"Thank you," Angela smiled thinking, "A gentleman from the true north. I don't even know his name. She then said,

"Since we're having lunch together, its funny I don't know your name."

"I don't know yours either. I'm Eric."

"Angela."

"Nice meeting you and I'd say I'm fortunate having you buy lunch too."

"For what you did, it's nothing at all."

"Great. How long do we have?"

"I usually take a full hour for lunch."

"I do too - so we'll be back at the bookstore before 2:00. I think I can handle the timing."

"Good for me too," Angela responded while filling her plate with veggies. Eric continued down the line behind Angela, selecting certain vegetables for his salad selection. They both arrived at the cashier, "What drink can I get for you?" asked Angela.

"Water is fine for me."

"Two waters," Angela told the cashier and pulled out her credit card.

"$17.82," the cashier said.

"You can find a seat and I'll catch up with you." Angela told Eric.

"No problem but let me at least take your tray." Eric grabbed the tray and went to a booth in the center aisle. He cleared both trays as if setting the table for dinner, like many times as a child, placed the empty trays on another table, and walked to the soup bar. Angela saw his actions, smiled and thought "How kind," then followed him to the soup bar.

"I love these soups," Eric hummed. "I like the bread," he hummed to himself as if happy thoughts ran through his mind, like a kid happy to eat. He turned and saw Angela two places behind. "Would you like a muffin," asked Eric.

"I'll be there in a minute," responded Angela.

"Ok."

Eric completed his selection and returned to the booth. He waited for Angela's return before taking a bite, as he was taught to do. As soon as Angela took her seat, he asked, "Did you find everything you like?"

"Yes, I did. It's why I love coming here so much. Everything in here is awesome. Even the pasta dishes are great. And I have to watch how much I consume."

"You are lovely," Eric said.

"Thank you Eric."

"No problem. I think its fortunate you wanted to bring me here. Thank you again for lunch."

"As you said no problem."

Silence fell on the table as neither one initiated a conversation. Minutes passed, and Eric glanced at Angela, "She's very pretty," he thought. Angela stopped eating, looked at Eric and said, "I'm so rude. I'm sorry I'm not talking. I was starved and now that something hit the spot, I can better focus on my behavior."

"It's Ok. I understand. People talk when they have a chance."

"Well, we don't have much time, but a little conversation will help pass the moments. You said you're from a northern state. Which state were you referring to?"

"Michigan. I grew up in Michigan, the Upper Peninsula."

"Really? I've never met anyone from there. I've never been there either. What's it like?"

"Well, pretty quiet, a little country side; people are very nice and simple living. Most people are truly hard working and enjoy nature. Are you a traveler?"

"I travel sometimes, but not to any foreign countries. Traveling abroad is surely my dream as I'd like traveling around the world one day. You know, seeing the wonders of the world, enjoying romance in Paris, dancing in Spain, or just sampling food in Italy. I'd love to experience the good things in life. How about you, is travel in your future?"

"I'd like to one day see Egypt."

"Now, there's another place I'm interested in visiting. I can imagine climbing to the top of a pyramid and picturing how they built the structure back in those days. You know they say it's a theory how they moved such large brick blocks. Some say aliens visited the earth and placed them there. I think it's amazing."

"Sure, it's amazing."

"Yes, it's like the gifts of the earth are so many and I have to see them. How do you like water sports? I like them a lot. I enjoy scuba diving, snorkeling, and body surfing. Have you been to a beach?"

"Well the Great Lakes have beach-like areas. But as for the ocean, I've never seen one."

"You haven't seen the ocean? Everyone should see the ocean at least once in life. You're so close to the Atlantic. Savannah is only three plus hours drive from Atlanta. That could be a fun trip too. Savannah is one of the oldest ports in America and it's settled by a large Irish population. So, March is an active month and offers all kinds of city events."

"Interesting," Eric commented and bit the top of a muffin.

"Yes, I truly think so. I went once, but didn't stay for all of the events. They have a riverfront full of quaint shops, very nice restaurants, and city entertainers. It's all by the Savannah River and there's even a river dinner cruise. Can be like a party boat. Savannah is quite the town."

"I didn't know there was so much to do outside of Atlanta."

"Since you're into nature, the Smokey Mountains are a couple hours drive. You can even hit Helen, Georgia and start in the foot hills. Why don't you get out more?"

"I kind of have hobbies taking up most of my time. I either work or stay involved in my hobbies."

"What kind of hobbies? If you don't mind me asking," Angela asked while picking up her plate for the busboy. "Thank you," she said to the busboy.

"I like to play Doom in my free time. It's fun and keeps you entrenched."

"Is that an online game you can play with anyone in the world? I've heard of it."

"Yes it is. But it's very deep and enjoyable. Once you play you're hooked." Eric smiled for the first time while Angela observed him.

"You have a lovely smile." Angela complimented.

"Thank you," Eric responded with a blush. "Oh, look at the time, I have to get back."

"Yes, we have to go." Angela grabbed her things and slid out of the booth. Eric stood and waited for her to lead the way out to her car. Eric managed to maneuver in front just to open the building's door and allow Angela to exit first. "He's such a gentleman," Angela thought then said, "Thank you," and pushed the electronic key to unlock the car doors. Eric entered and buckled up while Angela did the same on the driver's side. "I enjoyed lunch with you Eric. I think you'll have to share a contact number with me and let's do it again."

"I'd like that," Eric replied while grabbing a business card from his pocket. "I'll write my cell number on the back. The one on the card is my on-call number."

"I think we can handle having lunch. I'm thinking even getting together to hang out somewhere."

"I don't hang out much."

"You don't? I thought you had a hobby and met with other people."

"I do have a hobby, and my friends are all online."

"Is it because of distance or is it centered on the game?"

"It's the game. But sometimes I cook."

"As in becoming a chef or cook for a hobby?"

"I cook for a hobby, well sort of. I want to cook and develop it into a hobby."

"How do you plan to develop your hobby?"

"I signed up for a cooking class at Whole Foods."

"Oh really, when are they?"

"Saturday mornings. Some classes are during weekdays, but I can't get to those because they are too early during the day. I can get to the Saturday morning classes as long as I'm not on call."

"Saturday morning."

"Maybe you should tag along and see if you like learning how to cook?"

"You know, I just may."

Traffic was normal for 2:00 pm as the lunch rush quieted down. Angela and Eric returned to the bookstore but instead of parking the car, Angela pulled in front of the coffee shop.

"I'm going to spend the rest of my day working at my apartment. Thank you so much for your help. I had fun with you during lunch, it was an interesting conversation."

"You're welcome. If the laptop loses its connection again, just call me and I'll walk you through a different trouble-shooting process."

"Ok," Angela responded.

"And thank you for lunch. You can call me if you like." Eric said while grabbing his laptop and pausing to close the car door.

"Saturday cooking class, interesting; I'll call you." Angela said while grasping at the lock on the cracked door. "Have a great day," and waved farewell as her car door snaps into place. Eric stepped aside as the car pulled away. "She was nice," Eric thought.

Angela returned home and researched the game Doom. She Googled the title and read the Wikipedia description. She read it to be a subculture in gaming as multiple users can play simultaneously and from any internet connection. "And I suspect the culture is large enough to keep Eric really involved. I wonder what the game is and how it attracts." Angela asked herself. "I don't think it's important. It's not like I'm going to date him anyway. But he was interesting and was easy to talk to."

Eric returned to his work routine focused on writing code and developing those functions. He picked up where he left off as if lunch never happened. Traffic in the coffee shop returned to a snail's pace, and Eric managed to drink one cup of coffee all afternoon. Patter of fingers, nonstop and never a glance to view who or whom passed or bumped his table. Nothing seemed to startle him as his focus maintained on the laptop screen. "Dang it," Eric snapped above whisper. "I'm killed in this session. My day is over and its time to leave anyway. I can pickup where I left off after dinner," Eric thought as he packed his equipment for travel.

Christopher rarely chased a woman after the first date. For some reason Angela had been on his mind. "I'll call her Wednesday and ask her out. Well, maybe ask her out with Cedric and Margo. They'll break any anger she has. That is, if she'll go. Why wouldn't she?" Christopher asked himself. Automatically, Christopher recalled his actions on Saturday night and how it didn't end so well. Date after date, and with other women, Christopher remembered each step to which turned out well, and those that didn't. The failures were far and few between, because it seemed he could do nothing to push a woman away. Or, his success was greater than his effort, as when women normally chased him at every whim. It was Christopher's norm, to talk of himself and show little interest to the woman. Since men are creatures of habit, they fail to see every woman has a different concept to dating. The evening mattered to Christopher, as it was the first failure in many years when he didn't feel successful for a first date. "What have I done to not have Angela eating out of my hand?" Christopher thought as he searched for Cedric's contact information. Moments later Christopher managed to dial Cedric's number. "Hey guy," Christopher spoke.

"What's up Chris?" asked Cedric.

"Not much. I know you're busy as usual, so I'll get to the point. I'm trying to land this gorgeous woman."

"As usual, a woman is involved. And...?"

"She's quite a catch, and I can't seem to get her totally interested. It's nothing like other women I've dated."

"Look at the women you've dated Chris. How different is she from your norm?"

"I think she's just playing hard to get, as I don't think she's so different."

"What did you do? Did you two have a date or did you just meet her?"

"We went out last Saturday night. I did the usual thing and she pretty much pushed me away at the end of the night."

"Were you drinking?"

"I had two drinks the entire night."

"Did you talk a lot?" asked Cedric.

"The usual amount," baffled in his answer, Christopher added, "I don't think she would have said much had I not talked most of the night."

"Knowing you, she probably tried and you cut her off. Ok, so you need Margo and me to fix it for you. What do you have in mind?"

"You know, the norm, like Margo talking to Angela and the two of us playing off their conversation. It should show her how in sync I am with women."

"What night do you want to go out?"

"I'm thinking Saturday because she normally has a girls' night on Friday."

"I'll confirm with Margo, but I can answer you now. Make the date; Margo is game for anything I bring up to her. She's just great."

"See, Cedric you're a lucky guy. You better hang on to her."

"You better stop talking so much and you'll have the same thing." Cedric looked over his cubicle, "Gotta run, dude."

"Later guy," Christopher snapped his cell phone ending the call. "I've got to call Angela, but at a good time so not to seem like I'm begging her," Christopher contemplated. Waiting until Wednesday made it a perfect strategy for her to have enough time to say yes and adjust plans if needed. "It's Wednesday," Christopher decided.

Eric prepped for his next cooking class by creating a list of items needed for a global region. Each class took him to a country around the world with its eclectic taste, presentation, and style. Usually, Eric shopped midweek after reviewing the schedule, allowing him to enjoy his weekends for Doom. His habits allowed him to manage his priorities well, and kept him abreast of things outside of work and his game group. Because it was his nature, he shopped at the same Kroger near his apartment. He didn't purchase those items at Whole Foods, where the classes were held. Even though the store is awesome with its products being natural, he felt it was a little pricey. However, he did buy certain ingredients with the $10 coupon he received for participating in the cooking lessons. It was Wednesday evening and Eric followed his shopping routine. Arriving at Kroger, after 7 pm, he headed into the store and retrieved his list to decide what aisle to hit first. He pulled the cart behind him as if pulling the little red wagon as a child. One item, another, and another, the list is nearly complete when Angela appeared right in front of him. "Hi Eric," Angela said.

"Ah, hi Angela," Eric responded with surprise. "It's nice seeing you. How are you?"

"I'm ok. I need to pick up a few things and head home." Angela had recently left the gym and stopped at Kroger en route.

"I see. Did you have a great workout?"

"Yes, it was awesome. Do you workout?"

"Sometimes, but I'm inconsistent."

"Consistency is the key. And of course the diet."

"Diet? I eat whatever I feel like having. I guess I'm on the 'see food' diet." Eric smiled as he reached for tomato sauce.

"Tomato sauce? Are you cooking Italian?" Angela looked puzzled.

"No. Not Italian. Did you know tomatoes are used in a number of dishes around the world?"

"Well I heard there are numerous types of tomatoes. I'd guess a lot of countries use them in their diets."

"That's what fascinates me about the cooking class. I learn more of the world by food."

"Right, you're cooking this weekend. I think it's great. I said I'd drop by, if you don't mind."

"No, I don't mind."

"What time is the class? And isn't it Whole Foods?"

"Saturday morning around 8; it's early but leaves a lot of time for other things throughout the day."

"I should go with you and watch. Is it ok? You don't think I'm pushy, do you?"

"No you can come along. I don't mind."

"Great. I'll see you at the store at 7:45 or be in class at 8 at the latest."

"That's good if you want to see the entire dish being made. They start on time because of limitations."

"I'll be there, no problem. I want to see the class before joining. You know, take a sneak peek."

"Sure. Well I've got to finish my list," Eric moved forward and said, "Bye."

"Bye, see you Saturday," Angela responded.

Christopher paced looking at his watch, every four or so steps, he raised his arm. "She's nearly leaving the gym. I don't want to call while she's there because I don't want to interrupt her or leave a message." He thought as he paced four more steps. "It's time," Christopher said, as he punched Angela's number on his cellular. The phone rang on his end three times and no answer. The voice mail kicked on after the fourth ring and asked for a message. Christopher ended the call without leaving a message. "She must be working out a little longer tonight. I'm sure she's there." Minutes later, exploring the possibilities of missing her, Christopher settled for a second option, sending an email. Waiting a few additional minutes, his anxiety makes him feel as if time stood still or the second hand on his watch moved slower than usual. Avoiding the possibility of sounding too anxious, Christopher called a friend to make the time move faster.

Angela paid for her items and left the store. She'd left her cellular in the car, because it was a quick run in for specific things. The only reason she delayed was because of Eric. "It was nice seeing Eric and receiving more information on the cooking class." Angela thought while grabbing her cell from the car's middle console. "I missed a call from Christopher, should I call him back? Or should I wait for him to call again?" Angela imagined the last date and promised she'd accept another invitation if it ever came. She also wanted to validate if their last interaction was him being so anxious or trying too hard to impress. "Benefit of doubt gives way to a probable call. Isn't doubt the norm for a girl? Benefit of doubt." Angela pushed redial on her cellular as she arrived to the apartment. Christopher heard the signal for an incoming call while he talked to a friend to waste time. "Hey can I call you back later?" Christopher asked. And with a confirmation he clicked over to the oncoming call. "Hi," Christopher answered.

"Hi Christopher, I saw where you called," Angela responded.

"Yes, I called. I want to know if you'll have a second date with me. A couple friends and I are heading out Saturday night and I'd love you to come. I promise to behave better this time."

"Well, I think you were ok last time." Angela commented while thinking, "I'm making it seem encouraging to him. I hope I'm right."

"I think I can do better. I was shocked at the end, but I had a little too much to drink. I want you to know I'm really a gentleman and can show you a wonderful time. And to show you a better time, I want you to meet my friends. I know you will hit it off with them and it'll be awesome."

"Friends?"

"Yes, my best friend Cedric and his girlfriend Margo."

"I think it could be fun" – "if nothing else I can at least talk to Margo," Angela thought while responding.

"We plan on dinner and dancing. We will pick you up around 7 p.m. at your place or is meeting you at the bookstore better?"

"I guess picking me up with your friends is ok. How about picking me up at the apartment?"

"I'd like that."

"Good, email me your address and I'll validate the directions with you once I get them from Mapquest."

"I'll email the address to you. Talk to you soon and Saturday night 7 pm right?

"Yes. I'll pick you up."

"Bye Christopher," Angela snapped her phone shut just as Christopher said, "Bye."

Friday morning came like a whiz. Thursday was a flash, as Angela worked extra hours to meet a critical deadline. Leaving from the office late, she managed to get to the gym, work out, and avoided socializing. Fortunately the silence helped her with a peaceful night, which she often appreciated. Paula normally called to confirm their girl's night out, and there weren't any messages from her on Angela's cell. Eric did not call to inform her more on the cooking class for Saturday. One person called twice. Christopher left messages showing enthusiasm for Saturday night. A little much for one day, but he called to support his ego, and to ensure Angela didn't change her mind or reschedule. With Christopher, it was his normal effort as his job taught him to follow up on all appointments and dates. It worked on former dates as they really liked the attention. The first message was very direct: "Angela, I'm confirming our date for Saturday night 7pm. Give me a call and let me know if we're still on." Angela erased the message and moved on to the other; "Angela, I really need to know if you're still on. If not, I want to know so I can tell Cedric and Margo as soon as possible. Please confirm tonight." The message played an urgent signal just as Angela erased it. "He is a pain in the butt. I'll call him now but pushing me makes me want to say 'Screw you buddy, I'm not going'." With that thought, Angela grabbed the phone and redialed Christopher's number. Christopher answered the phone and before he could say anything, Angela spoke, "Chris, I'm still on for tomorrow night. Pick me up at the apartment. The address will be in the email. I'm looking forward to it." Angela ended the call and moved about the apartment following her normal routine – cleaning up, dinner, preparation for girls' night out. "I need to call Paula. We didn't say where we're going," Angela thought and dialed her number. "Hey Paula, what's going on?"

"Not much," replied Paula.

"Where are we going tonight?"

"Well, I didn't call you because Ron has a tournament and I want to support him. We leave around 8. Are you interested in going?"

"Will Bill be there?"

"Of course he's going to be there. He's Ron's partner. I spoke to him and he said if you come along, he'd behave."

"Behave. Are you serious? I think I'll pass tonight. You go ahead."

"But why not come along? We usually have girls' night, but going with Ron never interrupted us before. Why not come along?"

"I know we've gone to many of Ron's tournaments, but not with Bill. He's a pain in the ass and I don't want to deal with him. You have a great time. I can stay home and finish cleaning my apartment. I have to get up early tomorrow anyway."

"Why are you getting up early?"

"I have a lot going on. I have to workout in the morning; attend a cooking class with Eric, and a date with Christopher."

"You have a lot going on. Who is Eric? And where did you meet him? Is he nice? Is he…."

"White? Yes he is. I met him at the coffee shop. Look, you go ahead and I'll catch you Sunday." Angela ended the call frustrated and thought, "Aargh, why does she always ask that?"

Saturday morning Angela rose with enthusiasm to embark on her busy schedule. Like a recruit in training, she quickly dressed for the first event, grabbed clothes to change at the gym for the cooking class, and ensured she'd gotten everything needed to shower. With all items in the bag over her shoulder, she headed out on her quest. On the quick drive to the gym, Angela called Eric. "Hey, Eric."
Eric responded in a tired voice from playing Doom all night, "Hey Angela."

"You sound tired. Did you go out last night or did you sleep late?"

"Playing Doom and I actually won my session."

"Will you make it to the cooking class?"

"Wouldn't miss it for the world, I'll be there."

"Should I call you on the way so we can meet and go in together? This is my first time."

"You can call, but it's just as easy getting to the class. When you get there, go upstairs by the far cashier near the dining area."

"I'll remember that, it seems easy enough. I'm on my way to the gym and I'll see you at the store. Talk to you later."

"Sure, bye," Eric snapped his phone shut and headed to bed. During the night, he didn't sleep because the game took on a new personality. As it often does, the game intensity became challenging with each level and when there's a great opponent it gets better. Eric followed his pattern as usual, Friday night it's the game and Saturday, depending on the time he goes to bed, it's another session. The only time when he didn't focus on the game over the weekend, was during the cooking class. He never missed the class, as it was his second pleasure. Cooking was similar to an art. He was an artist in his profession; why not create something delicious at home? Cooking became more and more of a passion. Eric purchased additional pots and pans- top line brand, fancy knives, and pricey dishware to add to his collection of kitchenware. He also purchased plastic-ware, so he could save or freeze his fancy dishes for classes or co-worker samplings. The challenge Eric found with cooking was interference with his Doom game. While on-call for computer technical support, he paused the Doom game and resumed where he left off. He tried cooking while being on–call and worked on a technical issue. The issue took so much time, the ingredients spoiled, as he didn't think to refrigerate them, while he worked to solve the problem. And during the cooking class, he learned how to prep ingredients just before cooking, so the dish is fresh and the quality is right on. But he learned not to cook while on call as the chance for interference was too great. On any other off-call weekend, he'd fix new dishes and save them for the office. Any given

Monday, most of his co-workers always inquired to what type of food he learned to cook. The last time he took food into the office, he managed to share a fine Mexican cuisine. It took the office by storm and multiple requests followed as a favorite for any office occasion.

Eric napped before dressing for the cooking class. He grabbed his plastic-ware with the prepared foods, picked up a coupon for lunch, and took off for the store. He drove with ease because time didn't warrant a rush. Eric had his travel time down to a science; and even planned an alternate route in case of a traffic incident. Arriving with minutes to spare, he followed the sign in process, picked up a number, and headed to the kitchen on the second floor. There he glanced around for Angela, just in case she made it before him. With no sight of Angela, Eric continued his routine preparation and greeted his chef instructor, a couple regulars who he didn't know their names, and spoke to a new person lined to be his partner. Angela arrived seconds before the class began. She took a seat on the outside, as the room was a little crowded. She stationed herself with Eric and the kitchen in view, as if she was at an aquarium. Intently watching, she took notes of preparation, heating temperatures, and dish placement. Since the store's noise carried because of minimal acoustics, she couldn't hear everything the chef mentioned or explained. Periodically, she'd wave to Eric and show thumbs up. Forty minutes into the class and Eric finally waved to Angela with a smile. The cooking was nearly complete; Angela finally maneuvered closer taking a spot near the prep counter. "Hi Eric, you look great while you're cooking. I see how much you enjoy it."

"Yes, I love it. It's like a calling." Eric replied.

"I wonder, is this one of your favorite cuisines or do you have many?"

"I enjoy them all. Once I learn how to cook certain dishes, I get to add my own little twist without breaking the style. I guess, you'd say I don't paint the entire picture, just add a little piece to perfect from my standard."

"Do you only cook or can you bake?"

"You learn everything here. I bake as well. I was thinking of baking muffins in the morning."

"Really, what kind?"

"Whatever I feel like creating. I'll know when I purchase the ingredients. Did you have fun at the gym this morning?"

"Yes I did. It was a really good workout. I didn't think I had time for my normal routine so I pushed in different areas where I normally don't. It was awesome and I feel it."

"Your discipline shows. I'm sure all the guys here are paying attention." Eric smiled at Angela without expecting a response.

"Is he complimenting me?" Angela thought. "Thank you Eric, I think," Angela responded. "I guess this is the final part of the class. Is there a taste test?"

"Yes, don't go anywhere. Stay there so you can taste my dish."

"I'll stand here." Angela intently watched Eric in motion and observed everything the chef instructed. "This is going to be good." Angela thought, with a glance around the room, she noticed her thoughts aren't alone. Every other person in the room thought the same for sure as there was a motivation for everyone to become a taster. Fortunately for Angela, Eric reserved his sample for her first and then any others who'd like to try. Like clockwork, each cook pulled the dish from the industrial oven. Eric placed his on the corner then stepped away and returned with a digital camera. He normally took a picture of his product as a way to keep his cookbook together. At his home, he had a personal cookbook filled with favorite recipes, various types of dishes he'd learned to prepare, and some meals he totally created from imagination. Shot after shot he took a picture as a profes-sional photographer ensured every angle is covered and presentation was perfect. Like anything else Eric did, it was either damn near perfection, if not perfect. "Hey Angela, can you come over and hold this up a little? Grab the mitts so it doesn't burn you."

"Sure," Angela responded and followed his instruction.

"Right there, just a little higher on the edge," Eric snapped the picture. "No, hold it like the old cooking commercials; you know hold it around your mid-area and smile." Snap, snap, Eric captured the pictures. "Perfect. Thanks."

"No problem," Angela responded thinking, "That was interesting. He's flirting with me. I didn't think he liked me."

Eric finally carved his dish and placed portions on sample plates provided by the store. "Here you go Angela. You have the first bite as promised."

"Thanks." Angela grabbed a plastic fork as she accepted the plate from Eric. In a whisk she placed a small portion in her mouth. Eric waited for her response as he handed out other plates. "Wow Eric, this is awesome," Angela smiled. "It is really good, are you sure this is just a hobby of yours?"

"I love what I do. This is my peace of mind."

"You have a nice peace of mind skill for sure."

"I'm glad you like it. Go ahead, have a little more. I'm going to start getting my things together."

"Aren't you going to have any?"

"I will. There is always some left over and I end up taking it home. I have to gather my things and get back to crash. I have another challenger tonight with my game."

"What time?"

"We'll probably start around 8."

"How long is the game?"

"That depends on the level of my opponent. I'm pretty good and I read he's a serious competitor. We could end up playing until Sunday morning." Eric sighed as his body showed a downward turn of energy.

"Can I help you with cleaning up?"

"No, I'll be finished in a minute. Don't let me stop you from doing your things. Thanks for coming out."

"I enjoyed it. I'll start coming to class for sure. I like what I saw."

"You'll enjoy it, no doubt."

"I can imagine cooking all types of dishes. If I get in trouble will you help me? I know starting out I can use a personal guide. You are a nice guy and patient."

"Just call me. I'll see what I can do."

"Good. Thank you so much for allowing me to watch. Next time I'll be standing next to you." Angela discarded her plate and fork as she turned to leave.

"Don't forget to get a drink with the coupon," Eric reminded her.

Smiling, Angela waved as an indicator of understanding and kept moving as her mind entered her check list for the day. "Let's see, it's nearly noon. I have two errands and then home for the afternoon. I can relax before going out with Christopher. I hope his friends are interesting."

Paula and Ron were leaving Jay Christopher's Brunch Restaurant after having breakfast. Billiards tournaments normally last late in the night and especially if the location is far away from their home, it's a really early morning return. Since last night's tournament was on the other side of town, Paula and Ron didn't get home until 3 am. They crashed hard and rose to hunger. Since the morning was late when they finally got out of bed, Paula was not motivated to cook breakfast, so she persuaded Ron to go out for breakfast. Throughout breakfast and small talk, Paula thought of Angela and how it was the first Friday night in years they missed being together. Unless it was a family emergency and even then the girls would at least have a catch up conversation. This past Friday was different as Angela didn't want to accompany them. It was much out of the norm for Angela's behavior, even if she didn't like the guy it would have been ok. "Well, Bill isn't so bad he'd scare her away from me." Paula disclaimed as her thoughts challenged Angela's excuse not to come. "Ron, are we bad people?" asked Paula

"Bad people, I don't think so. Why do you ask?"

"Angela, she would always come with us on a Friday night. Even through college and throughout the years, we shared one night a week."

"Uh-huh. So you missed a night." Ron observed Paula's face when he responded. It didn't look as if she liked his answer. "You missed a night here and there before. Why does it worry you so much now?"

"Because of last weekend, we didn't leave on good terms. That bothers me. We never hold grudges or remain angry. It's not our nature."

"And didn't you girls talk this week? I thought you made up."

"We did, but it still isn't right."

"Don't worry, you two are so tied together, it will work itself out. Your friendship is too deep to fall apart."

"You really think so?"

"Yes, I do. You should call her," Ron suggested.

"I will on our way home."

Angela heard her phone chime just as she entered the car at the cleaners. "Hello," Angela answered.

"Hi. What are you up to?" Paula asked.

"Hi Paula, not much, just errands. I'm leaving the cleaners now and heading home for rest of the day. What are you doing?"

"I'm leaving Jay Christopher's with Ron. We had breakfast because I didn't feel like cooking."

"Late night?"

"Yes, we didn't get in until 3 this morning."

"How did the tourney go?"

"Ron won most of his matches, but overall they came in second. Not bad for a couple of country boys."

"Not bad at all." Angela replied and became silent as if waiting for the bomb to fall. "What are you doing the rest of the day?"

"Since we didn't have our usual girls' night, I wondered if you'd like to meet at the coffee shop for a few."

Angela thought before answering right away, "If I do, how long and will I be able to handle her comments before my date?" Angela replied, "We can but not for long because I want to nap before my date with Christopher tonight."

"Good let's be there at 3. Is it a good time for you?"

"Yes, 3 is fine. See you then." Angela ended her call without saying bye.

Paula is still holding the phone for a sign off or ending salute, then looked at Ron with disgust. "I told you things aren't fine with us still," she cringed.

"You two can work it out at 3. Don't let it boil into something. You two will be fine." Ron explained.

"I sure hope so," Paula said while snapping her cell phone shut and placing it in her purse. "I wonder what the hell is going on with her."

"Maybe she's going through changes and maybe she needs to cool down from last weekend. You are challenging at times you know."

"That's a heck of a thing to say Ron."

"I love you baby," Ron smiled.

"Sweet talk will get you anywhere you want to go." Paula blushed.

Angela arrived fifteen minutes early at the bookstore. She was meeting Paula in a few minutes and decided to see if there were new books of interest. She walked through the doors near the first shelf where new releases were displayed. Automatically she began her review and standing on the other side was Mark. Angela noticed how he seemed so interested in the book he was reviewing. "Should I speak or ignore him?" Angela asked herself. "If I say something will it place him back in my life or is it just a gesture of kindness?" Turning around after deciding to say nothing at all, Mark noticed her and caught her eye. "Hi Angela," Mark spoke.

"Hi Mark, how are you?"

"I'm well. How about you? I haven't seen you in a while now."

"I'm ok."

"That's nice. Don't let me stop you from looking, I'll see you around," Mark replied as he exited.

"Bye," Angela waved. "That was quick. Am I not his interest anymore? I shouldn't be anyway because he knows I won't go there with him. Nice guy but…."

"Hey Angela," Paula called as she approached.

"Hey," Angela responded and directed, "we can sit there. Are you interested in coffee or something?"

"I'll have a hot tea. Do you want something," Paula asked as they headed into the coffee shop.

"I'll have a latte, my usual."

"I'll order and be right back." Paula dropped her bag on the table while grabbing her purse and headed to the counter.

"I'll be here," Angela replied and found herself looking in the bookstore for a glimpse of Mark. It was as if subconsciously she wanted to talk to him more, maybe catch up on new books, or find out what was going on with him. She flashed to their past where they shared wonderful conversations to which no one had recently compared. She stared into the store in a mindless gaze like the thousand yard stare of a day dreamer.

Paula returned with a coupon in her hand, "they'll call us when it's ready."

"Thanks, I know the routine."

"Never said you didn't; why the tension between us?" asked Paula.

"I don't think there's tension; I think we aren't in sync at the moment. I hope I didn't say anything harmful just now."

"I think you did. You didn't have to respond with a smart remark. I'm sure you know the routine and didn't have to remind me on it."

"Are you PMS-ing?" asked Angela. "You seem to pick up the darndest things and jump all over them."

"Come on, we haven't shared time together and it bothers me."

"Doesn't mean you should get nitpicky with me. I'm doing fine and you should be too. Look, we've been friends for years. I'm not getting distant and there's no reason to be worried."

"I'm worried because it seems like you're not making the same effort as before."

"As if you are? Look, we've disagreed to disagree on things and it never bothered us before. I'm the same woman today as I was yesterday." Angela's response chimed just as the coffee maker announced their order was ready. Paula went to retrieve the order without first responding to Angela's comment. "Thank you," Paula told the clerk as she turned for the table. "Here."

"Thanks for the latte," Angela responded.

"No problem. But now you know we've been friends like you said for a long time. I missed you last night. It wasn't the same without you. I thought you like coming along with Ron and I."

"Well, before Bill, I enjoyed it, but not with him there. I don't like him and I'm sure he'd have said something or tried something offensive to me."

"You don't have to worry about him; he's dating a pretty brunette. She is charming and seems delightful."

"Then you had a great time."

"Still wasn't the same without you. I wanted my friend there and you weren't."

"Friend there? Why does it seem like I do all things to satisfy you?"

"It's the dynamic of our friendship. We've been this way all the time, remember?"

"I remember and that's it. Our friendship should be equal and not the way it's been for years. I think its time we started meeting each other, instead of you calling the shots."

"I don't call all of the shots. You have your own ideas of living and do your own thing. I just try to keep you on the right track."

"Right track?"

"Yes, every since you went to Club 290 it's been different."

"Oh please, go on."

"Well, if you must know, it's the influences you were around. It seems like you dislike Bill, when he was the type of guy you dated before. You're hard on Christopher and he sounds so charming. And I don't know about the recent guy…"

"…Eric."

"Eric, you haven't told me about him."

"And what's wrong with actually discovering my needs and fulfilling them as I see fit?"

"Nothing at all. I want you to know I'm here to support you just as we have in all the years before."

"You mean live your single life through me. Listen to me carefully; I love you as my best friend. I will not do anything to hurt you or cause you grief. However, I am a grown woman and will select and decide who'll be in my life. Don't do me anymore favors of blind dates. I can find my own guys. And treat my guy with the same respect as you treat Ron. Is that fair?"

"It's fair. But I get to hear all about them right? You're not going to stop sharing with me are you?"

"I'll share, but you can't comment or try to get me to do what makes you happy. As your best friend you should want me happy too."

"Best friends for life," Paula smiled, feeling better for meeting Angela.

"Best friends for life," Angela responded, lifting her latte in a toast agreement.

"Are you going to tell me about Eric?"

"Not now. I'm getting ready for a date with the charming guy Christopher. I'd like to keep my options with him because I want to go with an open mind. Remember he was a pain in the butt last time. You said he was trying too hard, I'll give him the benefit of doubt and try and have fun tonight."

"Has he told you what you're doing?"

"He said dinner and dancing."

"That should be fun. Do you know where?"

"Not yet, I think his friend picked out the location."

"Friend?"

"Yes, we're double dating instead of a one on one. I think it's good."

"Why would you think it's good?"

"If he becomes a pain in the butt again, I can at least talk to one of the others and try to enjoy the night."

"Good point. But what if you don't hit it off with his friends?"

"I don't quite know. I'll have to cross that bridge when I get there. So tell me what's happening with you."

"Oh, there's so much to tell. I went shopping the other day and found this lovely dress. It was adorable and I needed your opinion. We'll have to go back there a different day, as I know you don't have time today. My sister......" Paula went on and on about her week and events. Angela listened half heartedly, giving the temporary "uh-huh," and "oh really," responses as she tried to interact with Paula. "And so, do you think Ron will like going to Cancun for a vacation?"

"You two hardly go anywhere out of the states. Good luck getting him on a plane," Angela responded.

"Yes, you're right. I'll have to think about it a little more."

"Good. Listen its time I went home and took a nap. Will you call me next week?" Angela stood while waiting for a response.

"Sure." Paula stood and grabbed her purse. "Are we ok?"

"We're ok." Angela responded and opened her arms for a hug and said, "We're ok."

"Thanks, because if we weren't, I'd miss you in my life."

"I know. You'd be missed too." Angela broke the embrace and moved towards the door. Paula followed and once the two ladies were out front, they took separate paths to their cars. "Bye Paula." Angela waved.

"Bye. Call me tomorrow I want to hear everything." Paula responded while waving.

Angela noticed Mark's car parked next to hers. She peeped inside as she circled to her passenger door, so her snooping wasn't too noticeable. "What on earth am I doing?" she asked herself. She noticed a new book on the front seat but couldn't make out the name. Just as she turned around to walk to the driver's side, Mark appeared. "Hey again," Mark spoke.

"Hi. What a coincidence parking next to each other?"

"Yes," Mark replied while waiting to get in his car where Angela was blocking the entrance.

"I see you purchased a new book. What's it about?"

"It's a new author, so I can't really tell you. The description is pretty interesting. I'll have to tell you more about it after I read it."

"What's the title?"

"A Cyber Affair-The Good & the Bad, a fiction-reality type book. The description reads like a self help or self evaluation based on situations but focuses on internet dating."

"Sounds interesting; maybe we'll talk about it."

"Talking will be nice. Excuse me I have to get going."

"Oh I'm sorry, I'm blocking your way. I have to leave too." Angela moved to her car's driver side. Mark jumped in his car, clicked on the seatbelt, started his engine and backed out. Angela watched him leave as she entered her car. Just as she watched Mark, Paula observed her exchange with Mark before driving off. "I can't believe her!" Paula thought as she shook her head in disgust.

Angela finally settled in her apartment for a snooze. Before her nap, she selected her outfit, placed it on the foot of the bed, and returned to the living room. She found a cozy spot on the couch, turned on the television, and grabbed her favorite throw pillow. Quickly she fell asleep.

# Chapter 5

Christopher pulled out his blazer, selected a collarless shirt matching his eyes and sprayed it with cologne. "Not too much," he thought, placing the cap back on the bottle. He grabbed a pair of pants, placed them on the ironing board, and set up the iron for a quick press. "Everything has to be perfect," his thought concurred with his actions. Item after item, he checked for perfection, socks matched, shoes polished, blazer pressed, belt matching his shoes. He was being the total package tonight, as if attending the Academy Awards. His every move was to ensure there were no disqualifications with Angela on his appearance. After checking and rechecking his clothes, hair, face for a smooth shave, and cologne, Christopher dressed just as his cell phone rang. Not in haste does he answer, as he made sure his shirt was neat and in place as he hoped for perfection. Christopher answered just before the call went to voice mail, "Hello."

"Hey Chris, we're on our way," Cedric said.

"Great. I'll be ready by the time you arrive. How far out are you?"

"You aren't ready yet?"

"No, well almost, I'm putting on the final touches."

"She must really be important to you."

"She is, well, I want her to be. How far are you?"

"We have one more exit."

"That gives me ten minutes. Can we stop by a florist on the way to her apartment?"

"You're going to make me look bad with Margo, aren't you?"

"No man, you two have been together for sometime now. She won't mind will she?"

"No," Cedric answered and glanced at Margo and smiled.

"Ok, see you in a few." Christopher snapped the phone and returned to dressing.

Cedric took another glance at Margo as he drove down GA 400. "You're not going to believe Chris. He wants us to stop at the florist on the way to, um, Angela's place. I think that's her name."

"It's Angela. You told me the other night." Margo responded. "I think it's cute he wants to bring her flowers."

"You aren't jealous?"

"Why would I be jealous? You do so much more all the time and it's why I love you. Flowers now and then, as you do, are nice but I have the world of a man already." Margo replied, reaching over to gently run her fingers through Cedric's hair.

"I know sweetheart. You are the greatest." Cedric grabbed her hand and kissed the back of it.

"See, that's so sweet. Who needs flowers?" Margo smiled. "I hope Angela is a nice girl."

"I'm sure she is. It's Chris I worry about."

"He can be an arrogant ass sometimes. Let's hope he doesn't do the arrogant thing tonight."

"She's been out with him once. Like I told you, she slammed him at the end of their first date."

"This is a challenge for Chris. Oh my, I heard you earlier when we spoke on it, but I didn't realize this is the challenge woman for him. Let the games begin!" Margo laughed.

"Don't be hard on Chris. At least he's serious this time. He's putting in extra effort in dressing. He was just starting when I called."

"He dressed pretty nice anyway. I hope he didn't overdress as we aren't like black tie and gown."

"I doubt he's 007." Cedric and Margo laughed. Cedric took the exit and turned onto Haynes Bridge heading to Chris' apartment. Within a couple intersection lights, they would arrive at the apartment. Cedric called Chris on the cell, "Hey, we're here."

"Ok, be right down." Chris confirmed.

"We aren't there yet." Margo said as she pointed to the red light.

"I know but you know how long it takes him to come down? Remember the last time? We waited ten minutes."

"I remember."

"This way he'll at least be out front, if not on his way down."

"Good point. See, I knew I picked the right man for my heart," Margo said while smiling.

"Wow, how time flies," thought Angela. She rose from the couch, turned the television to a music channel and headed to the bathroom. "Shower," she thought while turning the knobs, undressed, and jumped in. Minutes later she was refreshed and started her preparation routine. Since she was wearing a dress, the process is shorter. Make-up, hair, moisturizers, perfume, all fell into place. She donned her fancy laced underwear, as if she expected a chance of exposure for a sensual event. Not her first thing in mind, but a possibility. She pulled her dress over her head and readjusted her hair to ensure it was still set as earlier. "I look marvelous," Angela smiled, looking in the mirror, spinning like a little girl. Finished dressing, Angela moved to the living room but first grabbed a drink from the kitchen and sat on her couch. She looked at her clock reading 6:45 pm. I have fifteen minutes and it's nice not to rush. Angela's cell phone chimed just as she settled to wait. "Hi," Angela told Paula.

"Have a great time tonight. And don't forget to tell me all about it tomorrow. Do you want me to call around 10, just in case it doesn't go well?" Paula did this for Angela giving her an excuse for escaping bad dates.

"No, I can handle this one. I'm better at ending things now. But thanks anyway," Angela responded.

"Call me tomorrow. I want to hear everything."

"I'll call you."

Taps on the door came just as Angela snapped her cell and placed it in her purse. Angela peeped through the peep hole and opened the door. "Hi Christopher, I'm glad you didn't get lost on the way."

"No way," Christopher smiled while handing her one yellow rose and one red rose, both touched with baby's breath and wrapped in soft paper.

"Thank you. You're so sweet." Angela grabbed the flowers and moved to the kitchen placing them in a vase. "Don't stand there; come on in while I put these in water."

"Sure, but we have to do it fast because Cedric and Margo are waiting in the car."

"That's right; it'll only be a minute." Angela finished running water in the vase and placed the flowers. "I'm ready." The two walked down the stairs hand in hand, as if they were a young couple heading off to the prom. "They look very nice together," Margo commented to Cedric. Cedric responded, "They do, don't they?"

Christopher opened the car door for Angela and then quickly ran to the other side. Once inside he introduced them, "Hey guys, this is Angela. Angela, this is Cedric and Margo."

"Hi," Angela spoke.

"Hi," Cedric and Margo answered in unison. "Where did you meet Chris?" asked Margo.

"We met at a bookstore one morning. I swear he followed me around the place, but he never admitted to it."

"Just like Chris, once he targets a lovely woman, he's on it."

Angela smiled, thinking, "I don't know if it's a compliment or a beware remark."

"You can't believe everything you hear." Christopher jumped in for his defense.

"You have a lovely dress," Margo said, "Where did you find it?"

"I think one of the chain stores at the mall."

"It's very nice and you fit it so well."

"We're going to VIII Fifty, right?" Cedric asked Christopher.

"Yes, that's the plan. Did you think of something different?"

"No, it's a very nice place. Have you been there before Angela?"

"No I haven't. I've never heard of it. Where is it?"

"It's on Holcomb Bridge."

"That's pretty close. I'm glad we don't have to fight downtown traffic."

Christopher spoke while staring at Angela, "Exactly why I chose it; it's convenient and offers the environment and class I want to share with you."

Cedric quickly glanced at Margo and smirked as if silently saying "He's laying it on heavy." Margo laughed.

"What's funny?" asked Angela

"Cedric making faces at me; he's always doing something silly."

"Really?" Angela quickly responded and thought, "I will be nice tonight. It can work, it can work."

Silence fell in the car as Cedric drove to the restaurant – dance club. Once in the parking lot, Cedric parked at a decent space and exited the car heading to open Margo's door. Christopher jumped out about the same time as Cedric, opened Angela's door, and reached for her hand to assist her exit. Just as Angela stood next to Christopher, his arm settled around her as a claim of poetic impressions for others to understand. "Christopher is really trying," Angela thought while walking in stride with Christopher.

"Welcome, the Maitre d'," greeted as the four entered the restaurant.

"Reservations for four – Mulligan," Christopher announced.

"I have it here. Please follow me." The four followed the maitre d' to their table. Christopher pulled Angela's chair out for her. Cedric did the same for Margo and then took a seat on the right of Angela and had arm's reach to Christopher. Margo sat across from Cedric so she could converse directly with Angela without interference from the guys. "This is a nice place," Angela blurted.

"Yes, I think so too," Margo added.

"Chris, you made a very nice selection." Cedric commented.

"I'm glad you like it. I came here once and it impressed me. The food is good, the environment was classy, and the great thing is Friday and Saturday nights, after 10 it becomes a dance club and bar; its dinner and dancing in one location."

"Is it usually crowded?" asked Margo, noticing the restaurant is about 70% full and more people were arriving. Some of the folks had reservations and others seemed to wait.

"We're here early. This place loads up after 10:30."

"Why did we come so early?" asked Cedric.

"Dinner is awesome and I didn't want us to wait so late. We can always move to the bar for drinks and conversation after dinner."

"That isn't a bad idea," Angela added.

"No it isn't," Margo agreed.

The waiter arrived and welcomed the four to VIII Fifty, presented the specialty and encouraged them to try the best of the house. Each person took a menu and read it as new students in college reviewing a syllabus. The waiter asked, "Can I get you something from the bar or would you like to order a beverage?"

"I'd like a whiskey sour and a glass of water," Christopher answered.

"Margo, would you like your usual?" Cedric lowered the menu and waited for her response.

"Yes, the usual sounds fine right now."

"She'll have a long island ice tea and a glass of water. I'll have an iced tea. Thank you." Christopher didn't ask Angela nor looked in her direction. Cedric nudged Christopher as a reminder to think of Angela. "Oh, Angela you're not going to order?"

"I'll have a glass of wine. White Zinfandel thanks," Angela told the waiter.

"I'll return shortly with your drinks."

"Everything on the menu sounds great. I'm thinking Roasted Wild-Caught Salmon. What about you Angela?" Christopher asked and lowered his menu again waiting for her response. Impatient, he asked, "Would you like me to order for you?"

"Chris," Cedric whispered. "Give her a minute."

"Can I suggest something instead? I remember you had chicken the last time we were out. Since you're into great health and watching that fantastic figure of yours, why don't you try the Spring Pea Risotto? It falls right in line with your diet, doesn't it?"

"No, actually it doesn't. I'm having lamb. I feel like something different," Angela answered and laid down her menu. "Excuse me; I need to visit the ladies room."
Margo placed her menu down, stood, and said, "I'll go with you. Cedric you know what I like."

"I'll order it for you," Cedric replied as he stood when the ladies left the table. "What the hell were you thinking Chris?"

"What?"

"I don't have to tell you it's not working with Angela"

"She'll come around."

"If you don't stop being so arrogant, she won't. If you were like this last time I can see why she didn't want anything to do with you. What happened to the gentleman I used to hang out with?"

"I haven't changed. She's playing hard to get so I thought I'd not chase her but give her a little of my charm."

"If you think you're showing her charm, you're going home alone."

"I won't be alone tonight buddy. She'll be with me and I'll call you Sunday morning to prove it."

"Almost sounds like a wager."

"No wager, it's a promise." Christopher smiled and patted Cedric on the shoulder as a sign of confidence. The waiter appeared with their drinks and said, "I'll return for your dinner order when the ladies are back."

"No, we know what they'd like. You can take the order now," Cedric said while lifting the menu for reading. "She," Cedric pointed to Margo's seat, "will have the Traditional Caesar salad and the Grilled Lemon Fish. I'm having the Filet Mignon, and we'll start with the Kobe Beef Sliders."

"And you, sir?"

"Angela wants the Lamb and I'll have the Salmon. Add Calamari for the appetizer."

"Very well." The waiter acknowledged the order and left the table.

The ladies looked themselves over in the mirror right after Angela washed her hands. "Is he always so sure of himself Margo?"

"No, I think he's trying. He likes you. He told Cedric you're the first woman who didn't just fall in line and puppy dog him."

"Puppy dog? That's a new one. What does it mean?"

"You know, just yes him to death and laugh at anything he says, accept him as a great catch and just do whatever it takes for him to give you attention."

"I see. I'm not following the rules of dating Christopher. I don't think I'm going to and if he asks, you can tell him what an ass he is."

"He's not an ass; he doesn't know what to do. He's out of his element. Most women are all over him by now and you haven't given him 50% of what he's accustomed to."

"I'll not give him that."

"Just give him a chance. He likes you or he wouldn't have had us come along. He's a very good guy and a damn good friend. Especially a great friend to Cedric, they do a lot of things together. As a matter of fact, they were together when Cedric and I met."

"It must have been a nice evening for the three of you."

"It was four. Christopher did have a girl friend at the time but it didn't work out for them. I believe they went their separate ways because she grew up."

"You mean she left him?"

"It's what I understand."

"No wonder he's the way he is. It's always a downer to get your heart broken."

"Who said she broke his heart? She grew up, no more games and wanted something serious. He didn't want the same. I'm not saying he won't get serious for the right girl."

"You don't have to worry about me getting serious with Christopher. I don't think I can take his arrogance. I feel like I give him the benefit of doubt and he goes the opposite direction."

"Don't worry, the night will get better. Give him a chance."

"It's why I'm here on a second date, giving him a chance."

The girls took their seats at the table and smiled at the guys just as they replaced their napkins in their laps. "How was the discussion?" Christopher asked.

"It was girl talk and it's not your business," Margo replied.

"I didn't want it to be my business; I just wondered how the conversation went."

"Well enough to keep us here," smiled Angela.

"I didn't think you'd leave without eating," laughed Cedric. "I know how a meal is important, especially since we're sharing." Cedric smiled at Margo and affectionately touched her shoulder.

Margo looked at Angela, "We always share our meals. Either its half and half or a bite of each, or just share one meal order depending on how hungry we are."

"That's very nice."

"You want to share?" asked Christopher.

"No, I don't think so. I'm still calling you Christopher, remember?"

"That's right. You can call me Chris now. It is our second date."

"Everyone should call you Chris," Cedric commented "It's not like your name means anything different."

"No, I like Christopher in general but my friends call me Chris."

"I get it, so who isn't a friend here at the table?"

"I said she can call me Chris now. I don't mind, actually never minded if she called me Chris. It would be nice if she created a pet name for me instead."

Angela whispered to Margo, "Pet name huh? I can think of one right about now." The girls laughed.

"What's so funny?" Christopher and Cedric asked.

"Nothing, it's a girl's thing." The girls winked at each other as Margo answered, then asked, "This drink is great. How is yours dear?"

"Oh I'm drinking tea remember" Cedric pointed at his glass. "How about yours, Chris? Is it awesome or what"

"I think it's good. The bartender made it pretty good."

"I sipped mine and it seems nice," added Angela. "Margo, what do you do outside of Cedric?"

"I do a number of things. I have this girl friend who is a lot of fun. We find interesting crafts to share, shop from time to time, and attend the gym together. She's funny and fabulous; and what an interior decorator too."

"She sounds fun. I have a friend who is interesting as well. Where did you find your outfit?"

"My friend Karen and I were walking through North Point mall and came across this specialty shop. We walked in and started shopping. Next thing you know I came out with this. It feels great, just as it looks."

"It does look nice. I heard you're a gym member, what gym?"

"New Life Fitness. It's really nice there and offers a lot of activities to help you stay fit. You look really in shape yourself. What gym do you go to?"

"LA Fitness. I've been with them since its opening. I enjoy what they offer."

"My girlfriend is in such great shape. She's like a trainer and I tend to workout extra hard. I don't do as much but I seem to maintain."

"You look great and I'm sure Cedric appreciates everything you put into it."

"Yes, he does. He tells me how lovely I am all the time and he gets the reward too."

"And it's how things are supposed to be. I'll have a man one day that loves me for all the quality I bring to the table."

Christopher butts into the conversation, "Are you talking about me?"

"Who knows Chris?" Margo responded. "I'm sure Angela will make that decision when the time is right."

"The time is right for me. The question is, are you ready Angela?"

Cedric tapped Chris on the shoulder "What kind of question is that Chris? Why put pressure on the lady in front of us?"

"Where did you meet Cedric?" Angela asked Chris.

"We met while he attended UGA."

"I was in Georgia State at the time. We met at a profession-al basketball game. Had seats next to each other and started talking." Cedric added.

"Cedric seemed pretty interesting, so we left there and went to midtown and next thing you know, it was morning."

"Yea, most of the night he doesn't remember; I had to drag him to my dorm and his frat brothers were surprised."

"You mean they didn't accept you as looking out for him?"

"No, they were surprised he'd gotten slammed drunk. It was his first time."

"I remember the morning after," Christopher laughed. "It was a tough morning as I had a quiz. Thank goodness I recalled everything while having a headache. I fell asleep just after finishing the exam back in Athens. The professor woke me at the end of class."

"Why do you drink now? Wouldn't that incident stop you from drinking?" Angela picked up her wine for a sip, waiting for Christopher's answer.

"It was the beginning. Cedric tell her how many beers I had."

"He had two beers. He was a virgin," laughed Cedric and Margo. "We tease him about Cedric taking his virginity."

"That's not funny," Christopher chided.

Two of the wait staff appeared with their meals. They served dinner as ordered and all seemed exactly right. Cedric ordered another round of drinks for all, and Christopher raised his glass for a toast. "Let's make a toast; to wonderful friends and a lovely beginning."
They clinked glasses and took the last sip finishing their drinks. "A lovely beginning; I'd like to believe this," thought Angela as she ate her meal. You can tell it was time for dinner, as each person didn't say much. After five minutes of munching, Margo broke silence. "Wow, were we hungry or what? Where's our manner?"

"Gone with the wind," responded Christopher.

"You're right Margo, we need to slow down. It's healthier to eat slow and savor each bite," Angela said as she placed her fork down after taking a bite.

"How's your meal?" asked Cedric looking directly at Margo.

"Wonderful," Margo and Christopher answered in unison. Christopher looked up and observed Cedric looking at Margo, "Oh, I'm sorry. I thought you were talking to me."

"Well, no, but I intended on asking you too."

"It's great." Christopher looked at Angela, "How's your meal?"

"Superb. You can tell I was pretty famished."

"I think we all were" Cedric interjected.

"Yes, we usually share but this time I kind of got carried away," Margo smiled, "I'm sorry, honey."

"No problems. I didn't give you a chance either."

Small talk continued throughout dinner, with Christopher still trying hard to impress Angela. Margo and Cedric covered most of Christopher's ill comments by creating a reaction joke, adding in scenarios where it made sense to Angela. Throughout dinner, Angela and Margo seemed to find more and more in common. From dancing interest to movies, the two girls were practically entertaining each other. Cedric and Christopher didn't mind talking about sports, stocks, and of course the girls.

"Margo is helping you big time."

"I see. I love your girl friend. She's the best."

"She is great. But you shouldn't mess this up, dude. Remember to relax and enjoy. Be yourself. You aren't a bad guy."

"I am relaxed and no problems. Let's see if the girls want dessert."

"Good idea. Excuse me ladies, are you interested in dessert?"

"No," the girls responded and giggled. "I think we're full," answered Margo.

"Yes, we are totally stuffed," Angela added.

"Dude, I guess that's it. Call the waiter for the check." Cedric looked to find a waiter. He raised his hand as soon as he gained eye contact. The waiter walked towards the kitchen just as he saw Cedric's hand. Cedric commented, "He left. It's always hard to get a waiter when you want one."

"I bet he went to tell the one whose table this is," Angela suggested.

"Probably so."

The table waiter came to the table. "Can I get you anything?"

"Yes, the check please," Cedric ordered.

"Sure," the waiter responded while taking some of the dinner plates. "I'll be right back."

Minutes later the waiter returned with the check. Cedric took it and said, "Thank you," as he read it, while Christopher peeped by leaning towards him. "I have this, Chris," Cedric pulled away from Chris's attempt to see the check. "At least allow me to split it with you," Chris insisted.

"If you insist, but you purchased the last time we went out."

"Yea, I forgot about the time we last went out. Go ahead I'll get the first round of drinks at the bar."

"Good deal!"

After Cedric finished paying the check, the four moved their activities to the bar area. They found a tall table and continued their conversations. Margo and Angela discovered more in common, like two middle school girls meeting at the beginning of a school year. The commonality wasn't just interest, but experiences during those teen years, parents' involvement with similar actions, and even having favorite dolls. They were truly establishing interest for future interactions to the point of exchanging telephone numbers, email addresses, and discussing habitual schedules.

The guys observed the girls getting along. "Chris you need to watch yourself. I think Angela is a very nice woman. She seems like a great find. You should try to get serious, and stay focused on her."

"Are you serious?" Chris replied while looking away from Angela to avoid her over hearing his comment. "I think she wants to be chased. I don't chase women. Either they meet me halfway or chase me."

"You have got to be kidding, right? The girl is really nice. She's trying and I believe if it weren't for Margo, she'd have left already."

"No woman walks out on me. It never happens."

"Let me remind you, she left the other weekend. Remember?"

"The date was over; I didn't pursue her to take me home. Well, not really pursue her."

"Ok, just take heed to my advice," Cedric sighed as he knew Chris wasn't listening.

"I'll take your advice."

Finally the music started playing just after 10:00 pm. The DJ hit hard with likeable music which invited a few dancers to the floor. Giving observation, the four decided to move closer to the dance floor and maybe grab a transitioned dinner table. "Is this ok?" asked Cedric.

"I think we should stand for a few," Angela responded as she looked around.

"We need to work off that great dinner anyway, standing for a few won't kill us," Margo agreed.

The four stood closer to the dance floor and watched as the number of dancers increased. Another song and Margo placed her drink on a table and grabbed Cedric. "Let's go"

"Sure," Cedric quickly said and followed Margo to the dance floor. Angela looked at Christopher and encouraged him to ask her to dance by saying "It's a nice song. Makes you want to move." Before Christopher answered, a woman tapped him on the shoulder and in a quick draw, he turned giving her attention. Angela waited and observed Christopher's behavior, "Will he introduce us, or will he ignore me standing here?" she wondered. No response from Christopher as he continually chatted with the girl he seemed to know. A minute later, Christopher was on the dance floor with his old friend. He was dancing and never looked at Angela. He danced a distance away from Margo and Cedric. Margo, being the observer, noticed Angela still standing in the very spot they left and no Christopher. She scanned the dance floor and found Christopher dancing with someone they had dinner with in the past. Margo pointed in the direction beyond Cedric's shoulder, "Look," she directed Cedric.

"You have got to be kidding right? Out of all the times for Betty to show; I'll be danged."

"You better get him before Angela leaves."

"If she leaves, it's on him. I told him earlier to behave and be respectful."

Angela continued to observe Christopher dancing. A gentleman approached her commenting, "I saw you four come to the bar. Did you have dinner here?"

"Yes we did," Angela responded.

"I bet it was really good. I hear this place is awesome."

"I think it is."

"Is that your guy out there on the dance floor without you?"

"He's not my guy, but he's supposed to be my date."

"Some date. Would you like to dance?"

Angela, being the lady, thought heavily on dancing with this gentleman. She hesitated before answering, "No thank you".

"You shouldn't let a jerk ruin your fun," the gentleman commented just before leaving.

Margo grabbed Cedric after observing Angela talking to a gentleman. "Hey, we should get her out here on the dance floor."

"I think we should. I don't think Betty will let Christopher go until the song ends."

"What a dork." Margo signaled let's go and Cedric followed. "Hey, come out with us and dance."

"No, that's ok; I want a word with Christopher." Angela told Margo, while steaming.

"He's in his own world and anger isn't going to do anything but push him away." Margo said and signaled her to come out. "Cedric, stand this one out. Angela and I are going out there."

"Sure babe."

The girls danced a few songs as Christopher finally returned to stand next to Cedric while the girls were still on the floor. "Can you believe Betty being here?" Christopher asked Cedric.

"Are you crazy or just insane?"

"What? I only danced with Betty. Angela will understand."

"I only thought you were crazy, now I know you're insane."

"If she's mad, she'll get over it."

"You are definitely insane. Remember I told you to cool it earlier? You're cool dude, really cool." Cedric shook his head side to side, disgusted with Chris' behavior. "Dude, don't you know one in the hand is better than three in the bush?"

"I know three is more fun than her."

"Then why did you ask her out?"

"To get her back from the last time; no woman plays a game like she did on me."

"I don't think it was a game, Chris. I think she came to give you a fair chance. What changed?"

"Betty changed. As you said, one in the hand is better than one in the bush."

"How are you going to get rid of Angela if you do this?"

"Well, I'll call her a cab. Tell her I changed my mind with her."

"That sucks, man."

"No, what sucks is her not trying to get to me. I have a woman who wants me. She's here but not really into me. At least I don't think so. Why not send her home?"

"Look, since you are going home with Betty, why don't Margo and I call it a night and drop Angela off."

"Great plan. You sure it's ok?"

"Dude, don't call me with another double date. This is the last time. We'll meet you some place next time." Cedric waved for Margo to come over. Margo grabbed Angela to head back to Cedric. Arriving to the guys Margo asked, "What's up?"

"We're leaving," Cedric frowned.

"Angela, I guess we'll see you later," Margo said while grabbing her drink to finish it.

"She's coming with us."

"Am I?" asked Angela to Christopher.

"I think it's best for you to leave. I'm going to stay with Betty."

"What? You brought me here and now you're sending me home so you can stay with another woman?"

"Uh huh, it's exactly what I'm doing."

"Asshole!!!" Angela shouted in anger and walked away with her bag in hand. "What a freaking asshole! I should've followed my initial instinct not to ever come out with him again." Angela thought as she walked to the exit. Margo walked behind her an arms distance away and just as they get to a point where one doesn't need to shout said, "He's an ass."

"Yes he is. You are so lucky to have Cedric."

"I love my guy. There are great guys out here, but Chris isn't one of them. Maybe this is a blessing in disguise."

"Maybe so" Angela thought and admitted to herself the hurt of being dumped for another woman. "It's the first time in her life a guy pushed her away so abruptly and without respect."

Cedric touched her shoulder and said "We'll drop you off on the way home," and they all entered his car.

"Thank you. I'll be ok," Angela said softly "I am so embarrassed."

"You shouldn't be," Margo encouraged with a positive voice. "At least we met and that's a great thing."

"Yes, so there's some good out of tonight; don't forget about Friday nights being girls' night out. I'd love you to meet Paula."

"I think I can make it. Right, hun?"

"You can make it. I'll find something to entertain me while you're out."

"What about Karen? Can I bring my best friend too?"

"Sure, I don't see why not."

"Thank goodness you're close." Cedric referred to the quick drive to Angela's apartment.

"It's what I love about living in this part of town." Angela stepped out of the car saying, "Dinner and drinks with you two was very nice. I look forward to seeing you again Margo. Take care, Cedric." Angela waved goodbye, watching the car drive away. "What a night!" Angela thought as she recapped the events. Furious as hell, the thought of being so disrespected boiled her with get-even emotions. "He doesn't know what he's missing-damn it!" Angela allowed her emotions to get the better of her, and since it wasn't late she thought of doing something more. It was only 11:30 and early enough to go out again or maybe call a friend. "Should I call Paula or Eric?" she asked herself as if one of them would actually make her feel better. "I don't want to call Paula as she'll say I'm too picky and make me seem like the bad one. If I call Eric, we may have fun but he's probably playing Doom." Angela finally entered her apartment, still deciding who to call. Finally she realized the demand for someone, someone who gave her undivided attention. Someone who would listen no matter what and someone who treated her with the respect she deserved. Angela dialed Eric on her cell.

"Hi Angela, I thought you were on your date."

"Hi Eric, it ended early. What are you up to?"

"I'm finishing my last game for tonight. I'm planning to bake those muffins I told you about and hit the bed."

"Bake this time of night?"

"Sure, baking is soothing and fun anytime you have the energy. You mean you've never baked cookies late nights?"

"I've baked cookies, but not muffins."

"So why not bake muffins? It's the same principle and it satisfies the need to create."

"You don't mind if I help do you?"

"No, I don't mind but I haven't anything to drink if you want something special."

"I'll bring the drinks, if it's ok."

"Bring the drinks. I don't mind. You know where?"

"No, I don't."

"I'm in the apartments off of Old Milton just east of the Arby's. Call me when you get to the intersection. I'll gather all the ingredients and get my recipe."

"I'll call you and do you have a specific type of wine or beer you want?"

"Anything, as I don't drink too much, so I couldn't tell you."

"I'll bring wine. Talk to you soon and Eric."

130

"Yes."

"Thanks." Angela smiled as she waited for an answer.

"No problem." Eric ended his call, finished his game and did exactly as he described to Angela. "Game over." Eric thought to himself. "Now, where is my recipe book?" Eric moved about the apartment to tidy up and search for his recipe book. He had the book after class and didn't place it in the kitchen as he recalled. "It's not good for a girl to see a messy apartment." Every thing has a place as Eric created and it was easy for the apartment to tidy up. One thing after another, jacket, shirt, dirty dish, and dirty cup, all had its place and Eric found his book while picking up each item. He found himself excited to see Angela for the first time. As if, well, the idea of enjoying a woman's company took over him. No woman visited him in this apartment, and it's been a full year since he'd entertained the idea of dating, or becoming involved. "Angela seemed really nice. She's beautiful, exciting, and smart enough," Eric contended, "and I love the fact I don't have to try and entertain her. Another good quality is she likes my playing Doom and she talks, without me trying to start conversations." The apartment is completely presentable, well to Eric's standard, and kitchen preparations became his focus.

Angela grabbed wine-coolers for Eric. She decided wine wasn't appropriate, and beer was just as inappropriate for baking. During the drive, Angela had the feeling of joy, as she knew Eric was much better than Christopher. "Eric wouldn't treat a woman like that asshole Chris, that's right freaking Chris not Christopher, asshole." Still fuming from earlier tonight, she imagined Eric's lair to be romantic, maybe a computer in the living room, couch, chair, coffee table, and a few knick-knacks of his game collection. "Who knows, Eric may have great taste?" she asked herself while approaching the intersection light where she agreed to call Eric. Grabbing her cell, Angela pressed enter to redial the last number.

"Hey," Eric answered.

"I'm at the light turning onto your street."

"Great. I have the ingredients out for the muffins. So your timing is good. When you get to the gate, I'll let you in. Just tell me when you get there."

"Ok. Are you sure you don't need anything else?"

"I'm sure. I have everything."

"I'm at the gate," Angela waited for a response. Eric pressed the control for the gate. "Is it opening?" asked Eric.

"Yes."

"Good. Drive to the second street on the right, take it and park on the third building on the left. I'm 311. I'll unlock the door for you so come on in."

"Ok, I'll be there."

Eric took another look around with excitement- he was finally having a guest. He contemplated if he should play music or let her make a selection. "I'm not sure what to do, but the best thing is to let her select a radio station and listen to anything she likes."

Eric unlocked the door, cracked it, and stepped back to the kitchen for the mixing bowls, and mixer. Angela knocked hard enough that the door opened when her hand hit the wood. "Eric," Angela called.

"Come on in."

"Hey," Angela greeted, "you have a nice apartment. It's pretty much as I expected; a neat man. I like neat."

"I try," Eric responded, "I didn't know what type of music you like, so I waited for you to make a selection. I can listen to anything."

"How nice of you to think of me. Where is your system?"

"Oh, I have an online station that's awesome. You tell me what your favorite band is and I'll create a channel for you."

"Is it like XM radio?" Angela asked, as she'd never heard of an internet radio station allowing a self genre. "It must be a geek thing knowing so much about web pages."

"I guess you can say so. I've been a geek as long as I can remember. Geeks are cool," Eric smiled after replying.

"I'm learning they are really cool," Angela blushed as she thought, "much better than the asshole."

"We've always been cool. It's others who don't realize how good we are until later in life. Well, after they go after the cool guys with no substance." Eric stopped talking and thought "I'd better stop plugging about the cool guys she'd dated." Eric continued to get the measuring cups, spoons, and other baking items, as he waited to hear Angela tell him what type of music she liked.

"I'm thinking about love ballads, from singers like Luther Vandross, or Gerald Levert."

"I thought you were more rock and roll. You're surprising."

"I'm not in the mood and those guys are pretty mellow."

"I should introduce you to another singer who's similar and upbeat with a mixture of music. He isn't as popular as those guys you've mentioned but, I'd say he's pretty talented."

"Is he a new singer?"

"No, he's been in the business for over 20 years. Just hasn't gotten the breaks from a big label."

"What's his name?"

"Vikter Duplaix. I'll play a sample for you. You tell me if you think this helps your mood." Eric moved to his desktop and selected the website. He created a channel as suggested on one tag, and played Vikter's song on YouTube. "Here it is. What do you think?"

Angela intently listened and ended up swaying; she grabbed Eric to slow dance, embracing him, holding him tight, as if he were a sailor leaving on deployment. For the first time, she made a move for affection, a move as aggressive or daring without fear of rejection. It was her first time, her very first out of many years of dating, or relationships, where she had no control. She wanted this, to soothe the agony from earlier, a kind touch, a gentle embrace, and Eric not being the aggressor, played right into her mind. Her exploding desire to be held became a reality. Angela pulled Eric tighter and placed her head on his shoulder, as if being held was a life line. She kissed Eric on the neck, gently, small touch, and a second time moving closer to his ear. She kissed his cheek. Eric, confused but happy responded by just dancing. He did not make a quick movement, but a move to encourage her actions. "I'm not sure if I should kiss her back or just let her...." Eric thought while holding her close and feeling the excitement rise. Angela continued her sweet and gentle kisses; she landed a soft seductive kiss on the lips, and pulled Eric as close as possible. Eric, finally, understood it was his turn to respond, especially if he wanted this to continue, and he did. He held her tight and returned the kiss, a full French kiss, gentle as she expected. He moved his body, his groin in motion, to connect, as if following the seductive dirty dancing movie he watched many times. Angela responded, with more kissing, more grinding, more touching. She broke the embrace and guided Eric to the couch, directed him to lay first and she climbed upon him. She continued to kiss, and caress, as Eric caressed her back and bottom. Still, Eric was trying to grind as the pressure to get out of his clothes increased. He pulled her and continued to place his erection where ever she wanted. It was the only thing he could do to continue as Angela stayed in control. Angela, stopped, stood, and grabbed Eric to rise, stripped off his clothes and blinked at Eric's erection, in a moment, it was back on the couch and Angela grabbed her purse and rolled a condom over the very erection she wanted inside her. She lifted her dress, dropped her panties and straddled Eric for quick entry. She rode Eric without thinking of who he was, she rode him like a revenge on Christopher, "See what you've missed asshole," she thought with her eyes closed and allowed herself to reach a climatic point. Eric held on, with both hands, watching her move, feeling her ride him as if he were a horse of a different race. Eric noticed the lovely laced bra, and the smooth skin, and the body of a goddess. Eric exploded just before Angela finally reached her climax.

Heavy breathing and music filled the room as they lay entangled on the couch. "No words could explain the quick satisfaction you gave me," Angela savored while laying there embraced by Eric. "I can really enjoy this."

"Thank you," Eric broke the silence.

"Why are you thanking me?"

"Well, because you are a dream come true."

"That's sweet, Eric. I felt a need for affection and you are a very nice man. I hope I didn't interfere with a girlfriend you have. Like now is a good time to ask."

"No girl friend. As you can see, this is really a bachelor's apartment."

"You know, I hadn't really noticed. But I do see the decorations are simple."

"I don't have great taste, or a desire for fancy. I think comfortable is my take."

"You know, I could put a woman's touch in the apartment. I can change the color scheme to match, add a few items here and there, and fix up the kitchen a little."

"Kitchen," Eric asked. "Are you serious? You can do the other things but I have two areas you can't touch; kitchen and desk. The kitchen is where I know things are and I enjoy cooking and creating great dishes, computer is where I enjoy spending my time on my game and working when needed. If you can stay away from those two, we have a deal." Eric smiled and thought, "I need a woman's touch in here and she's perfect."

"Why are you smiling?"

"I like the idea."

"Great, then I'll start tomorrow."

"What about tonight? Are you staying so we can bake muffins?"

"Do you still want to make muffins tonight?" Angela asked while laying another deep seductive kiss on him.

"Uh, I guess we can bake muffins in the morning." They rose and headed to the bedroom and found themselves engaged in another session of much needed and intense sex. Hours of rest and cuddle, Angela felt contentment, the kind of contentment where no pressure, no worries, nothing but herself to think of, and best of all, she realized she set no expectations on Eric. Out of a deep sleep, Angela heard a beeping sound, because it was not her apartment and out of her element, she nudged Eric. "Eric," she whispered.

"Huh," Eric sleepily responded.

"There's a beeping sound. Did you leave something on? Did you forget to turn something off?" The beep sounded again. "There it is. Don't you hear it?"

"That's my computer calling. What time is it?"

"It's six."

"Six! I'm missing my game. That's my partner calling me online." Eric jumped out of bed, put on shorts and left the bedroom for the computer. He sat at the desk and started key punching and mouse moving. "Oh, you can stay in bed if you like. Just close the door and I'll try to be quiet," he yelled.

"You can't tell him you'll play later? What about the muffins?"

"You can make the muffins or I can after this round." Eric thought, "I knew this would happen."

"How about coffee? Don't you have coffee in the mornings?"

"I do but I overslept. You can make a pot if you like, or head to the corner coffee shop. Leave the door unlocked when you go."

Angela, now out of bed, walked out partially nude into the living room, picked up her dress and panties and went into the bathroom. She noticed, not once did Eric move from the computer or take a peep at her walking in the room. "He loves that game," Angela thought as she cleaned up and dressed. "Eric, I'm going to my apartment. Call me when you get done with your session."

"Cool. I'll call you." Eric responded without missing a key stroke or taking focus off of his game.

Angela left the apartment and drove directly to a coffee shop just outside the apartment complex. Just as Angela arrived at the coffee shop drive thru, her phone rang and it was Paula. "Hi Paula, 7 am call on a Sunday? What's going on?"

"I couldn't sleep in this morning and I wanted to wake you so you could join me. Just joking, how did it go last night?"

"The date with Christopher?"

"Yes, the date. How did it go?" asked Paula

"It stunk. I couldn't believe the asshole."

"Did you say asshole? What happened?"

"Let me order my coffee and I'll tell you."

"You aren't home? Why are you out this morning?"

"I'm leaving Eric's house," she responded to Paula and then ordered, "I'll have a Grande Latte please." The clerk responded, "$4.53 please." Angela paid the clerk while listening to Paula.

"You spent the night with Eric?"

"Well, if you must know, yes I did and he's a perfect gentleman. Not like the asshole."

"Christopher must have been really bad for you to end up with Eric in the same night."

"He was nothing like he presented himself the first time we met. I got a chance to see his real personality. Let me tell you, it sucks and I'm glad I didn't give chase after him. He left with another woman right in front of me."

"What did you do?"

"Why do you think I did anything?"

"No man dumps a lovely woman and runs off with another the same night unless one did something negative." Paula explained.

"I did nothing negative. As a matter of fact I met a lovely lady and I'd love you to meet her. She called him an ass too."

"An interesting night for sure, two women called one man an asshole. I believe he was surely an ass. Why didn't you make him feel like he was the one?"

"Come on Paula. When did I ever make a man feel like he were a dream?"

"I remember you always got your man. Even when they were jerks. You didn't let that bother you. You did what you had to do."

137

Angela parked her car in front of her apartment, stepped out, climbed the stairs and said, "I'm not the same woman as then. It's not a game anymore. I want a guy to just enjoy me and the things I offer. Christopher wanted me to chase after him and accept the crap he pushed. Margo can tell you, it wasn't pretty."

"Margo?"

"The nice lady I mentioned earlier. I met her last night. She dates Cedric, Christopher's best friend."

"What about Eric?"

In her apartment, Angela went to the bathroom and started water for a hot bath. "He is the sweetest guy and it just seemed right to be with him."

"No you didn't!" Paula sounded surprised as she made the assumption Angela had slept with the guy.

"You know I don't kiss and tell, but it was so sweet. No pressure and I felt totally content."

"You did. What do you know about Eric?"

"Enough to be comfortable; he's a sweet guy, very attentive, and no challenges or conceit. He's totally different from the asshole Christopher."

"I bet he is, especially since you spent the night with him."

"Don't judge me. Eric is a sweetheart; he's a great listener, fun to be around, active where he includes me in his cooking, and smart. I know he's pretty stable and not a womanizer."

"Sounds like a great guy. Are you going to get serious with him?"

"I'm not sure, but I'll redecorate his apartment. We made an agreement last night. What are you doing later today? I was thinking of shopping for items to decorate with."

"What time do you have in mind?"

"Let's say 1:00 or so. Come here and we'll drive together."

"I'll be there. Let me tell Ron what's going on. If I don't call you before 1:00 everything is ok and I'll be there. I'll call you if I can't make it."

"The usual, talk to you soon, bye"

"Bye." Paula ended the call. "What is going on with Angela? I'll get more from her later today."

Angela settled into her bubble bath, latte in hand and thought of last night. "I really enjoyed Eric. He's sweet, kind, gentle, and takes no effort to entertain. We can do this, we can make it, he'll see right after I redecorate his apartment. I'm sure he'll love it. I'm sure he'll want me to do more with him. I just know it."

# Chapter 6

Paula and Angela walked into The Garden Ridge store, which sells goods from patio furniture and gardening items to artificial plants and picture frames, as well as furniture and party supplies. It also sells a wide selection of seasonal, holiday, and home decorating merchandise, and discounted clothing, shoes, and handbags. Once around the first turn, Angela spotted Margo, and with excitement tapped Paula on the arm saying, "There's Margo. The woman I told you about from last night."

"She really looks nice; a happy looking woman." Paula replied as she followed Angela at a hastened pace.

"Margo, I'm surprised seeing you here." Angela reached out to hug her.

"Oh, my friend Karen and I are shopping for some supplies. She loves this store. It helps her with her profession."

"Where is she?"

"She's around. I came over here to find a flower vase to match one Cedric broke."

"Accidents happen," Paula chimed.

"Let me introduce you to my best friend. This is Paula. Paula this is Margo. We met last night."

"You're the one supporting Angela's assertion on Christopher." In unison Angela and Margo responded, "What an asshole."

Paula laughed, "That's funny. It was that bad?"

"Was it ever? I'm glad you aren't bailing Angela from jail. I'd have hurt him some kind of way."

"I told you it was horrible," Angela added.

"It didn't turn out too bad for you Angela," Paula pointed out.

Angela frowned at Paula as if her comment was too forthcoming. To deter her from going further, Angela said, "It wasn't. I let it go and moved on. Just that fast."

"Good for you," Margo smiled. "You should never let a man treat you such a way. He's a friend, but he's an ass."

"I agree."

"Well I should try to find Karen. Nice meeting you Paula, I like your outfit. Nice colors and looks great next to your skin." Margo left searching for Karen.

"Thank you," Paula responded as Margo walked away. "You are right, she seems really nice. Calls it like it is."

"She's nice. You'll find out more when you get a chance to just talk to her."

"I'm already impressed." Paula turned, "Look at this. It's lovely," she exclaimed at the vase.

"It'll go well with my idea for Eric's place."

"Who is Karen?" asked Paula.

"Margo's friend, she's a professional decorator."

"If she shops here, she must be pretty cheap."

"I wouldn't say so; the items here are nice and reasonable in price. I guess it keeps her overhead down."

"Either way, this is a discount store. She could do better at another location."

"Business is business and she does quite well, or at least it's what Margo leads one to believe."

"It could be a nice thing depending on her clients. I'd bet to say her clients aren't rich," Paula said while replacing a rock item.

"I still say it's great for her profession. I would love to be a decorator. It seems fun and I can't wait to finish Eric's apartment. I know he's going to love it."

"You're excited, almost a little too excited. Tell me how you ended up spending the night with Eric again? Is he…?" Paula being inquisitive looking for detail in Angela's explanation, she walked abreast with Angela as they shopped, not to miss a word.

"It was a very nice situation. He didn't push, he didn't ask, he didn't do anything annoying. As a matter of fact, he was getting things together to bake muffins." Angela explained.

"Bake muffins. That's how he turned you on?"

"No, it wasn't the muffins; it was the way he danced with me when he turned on a nice song. It was the way he didn't pressure me when we were close. I knew it wasn't him being aggressive, it was me being needy. And especially since the asshole pissed me off. Eric was a nice soothing change."

"You went from one guy who pissed you off to another who treated you nice."

"Yes, that's it. Eric is a sweetheart. I feel he's pretty interesting and there's a certain depth to his character. I haven't learned it just yet, but I will." Angela replaced a pillow on the shelf and selected a different color. "This will match his couch and coffee table," she pointed out to Paula.

"You don't feel funny sleeping with Eric?"

"Why should I feel funny? We used protection and he's a nice guy, and the mood was right. Why feel funny?"

"Well, you used him."

"As if you never used a man before? I recall in college, you used one guy to make another jealous. And you used the jealous one to get you into football games for free."

"It was a different situation. We weren't adults just yet and now we know better."

"I know better, but I didn't use him; just made it a better scenario for us. I figured he was alone and uninvolved, I wanted affection, and he provided the opportunity. What is so bad for two consenting adults?"

"Nothing of course, you just used the man."

"I don't understand your definition of using him. He enjoyed me just as much as I enjoyed him. Nothing more or less, just pure enjoyment and I get to decorate his place. As a matter of fact, I get the better end of the deal."

"If you say so," Paula sighed. "I like this," she said while showing a trinket box.

"It's nice, very nice and I know where he can use it." Angela took the trinket and placed it in her buggy. The two continued through the store selecting decoration and storage items. Every item matched Eric's enthusiasm for computers and cooking, many storage items were for the kitchen and his desk, where Angela noticed an overflow of CDs and

SanDisks, all to support whatever he did. The other items were pillows, trinkets, towels, curtains, covers, candles, new kitchen measuring cups, pillow cases, pictures, and a banana rack. Angela spent well into $450.00 for the goods. Paula couldn't believe how much she was investing in Eric. Just meeting the guy he must be one dynamic screw or she finally figure Angela was reaching to satisfy her need for attention.

Eric finished his game after playing for six hours. He finally broke away to satisfy his hunger pains. Grabbing a banana, he consumed it on the way to the bathroom for a quick shower, and shave. He finished the day's hygiene by brushing his teeth. It was normally a morning hygiene routine, but since waking late and jumping on the game, his process was out of order. "I guess it's time to bake," he thought as he pulled a t-shirt over his head. "What did I tell Angela last night? I told her she could decorate my apartment," he thought while looking around his place. "It could use a woman's touch. Besides, it seemed like it would make her happy." In the kitchen, he noticed a number of items were out overnight. He did everything to ensure all ingredients for the muffins were good. Nothing spoiled or went bad. He sniffed the items, tasted the butter, touched the flour, and nibbled on the nuts. "There isn't a thing I need to replace," he thought. Eric continued to add, pour, and place items in the bowl, mixing the muffin batter. He followed the recipe as far as planned and added another item changing the taste of the muffins, just enough to exert flavor. He added a special type of flavor keen to his personal taste. "If Angela comes in time, she'll probably love my muffins. I hope she gets here just as they come out of the oven." Right after completing the batter, Eric prepared the muffin pan, as if it too were an art. He peeled the baking paper out of the box, and placed the paper in the indentations. Eric loved his baking hobby, as it gave him satisfaction, just like playing doom. Baking was surely not quite the same level as doom, yet he contributed just enough to enjoy the baked goods.

Margo left Garden Ridge following Karen to her next job. Karen landed a big job on the north side of town, a newly built corporate office complex. It was her niche, just as decorating a house, the ideas she presented helped a positive Chi[1] environment. As well, the colors and décor always impressed clients so greatly that her work became the focus of multiple magazines. Some big name magazines would use her office décor as back drops, or filming stages for television. She transitioned her niche into her life by making it her career, and creating financial stability. Margo followed Karen with the new accessories to the 5th floor. Karen, being the experienced one, kept a portable cart in her SUV so trips were minimal. "Can you get the door?" asked Karen.

"Sure, hold on," Margo responded as she maneuvered to the front.

"Thanks." Karen pushed and positioned the cart in the middle of the passage way. "Do you recognize any of these paintings?" Margo looked at the first, the second, and then the third and smiled." I can't believe you put these here."

"Why not? I always say your work is awesome. Even when you don't think so."

"And the owners like these?"

"Only one has seen them. The final review is tomorrow. Why, are you afraid?"

"I'm not afraid, but they look funny on the wall outside of my studio room."

"They are gorgeous and I told you I'd use them one day."

"You sure did. When did Cedric give them to you?" Margo frowned. Her paintings were precious and always in her control. She hardly allowed her work to be seen by the

---

[1] Chi – the circulating life energy that in Chinese philosophy is thought to be inherent in all things; in traditional Chinese medicine that balance of negative and positive forms in the body is believed to be essential for good health [syn: gi].

public. Rarely did Margo enter in an art contest since painting was her hobby.

"Cedric gave them to me Saturday before your double date with Christopher.

"I'm in shock. He'll hear something from me when I get back."

"Come on, the guy sees your work just as I do and he's really proud of you. The reason I had you come with me was to see how they fit in the decoration scheme. They are the exact things needed to pull the area together. The main decision maker is asking for your portfolio." Karen smiled as she knew Margo didn't make an effort to sell her paintings.

"Sure, I'll think about it. Damn that Cedric. And damn you, Karen." Margo smiled as she knew only a true friend would get her things sold.

"I'll have your check the following Monday. Would you say $3,000.00 will do for the three?"

"Paid from a hobby? Why not? You know I don't have a portfolio."

"If you want more exposure, I think it would be wise putting one together. At least if you're interested in selling more paintings."

"I'll think about it. I'm not sure I want my paintings out in public. The option is nice, really nice, but not quite what I thought of doing."

"Trust yourself, Margo. You have talent. We didn't just graduate from SCAD (Savannah College of Art and Design) to support a hobby. I'd hope we would continue in a profession." Karen pushed the cart further into the office environment as she spoke. "You know, when I moved from Philadelphia to Atlanta I had no idea I'd follow a dream. Remember when we met during out first semester?"

"I remember. You were this suit-wearing career woman, working for a top consulting firm. You looked totally out of place."

"Funny, I thought the same thing when I walked into the first class."

"Everyone thought you were a faculty staff member evaluating the professor."

"I didn't want to believe I couldn't fit. I mean, I graduated from Syracuse, was recruited by the firm, and got the chance to see the corporate world. Yet I couldn't quite get myself away from my creative passion. Every office I visited motivated me to create a different environment and increase the workflow. Instead of accounting and business processing, I looked at the décor and thought how I'd change it."

"It was your passion sending you to school," exclaimed Margo as she placed an item off the cart onto a desk-following Karen's lead.

"Yes, exactly. I couldn't keep going so I ventured and wanted to make sure my ideas were exactly in line with money making business concepts."

"It worked, because you're here and have a lot of clients."

"It's working for sure. I can get your products in too. If you let me; it's what friends do for each other, open doors you know."

"I'll think about it. It's not that I'm not appreciative, I don't think I can keep up with a demanding pace." Margo turned to see a poster of one of her paintings she did in SCAD. "When did you copy this?" Margo pointed. Karen stopped to look at the print Margo referenced. "Oh, I had this for a long time and it's another product you'll get paid for. I push it as a poster. It's my first time using it and people love it. If you don't want me to use them, just say so."

"I should be pissed at you right now." Margo frowned as she slammed the paper weight on the desk. "How could you just push these out without my approval?"

"Margo, don't be mad. I'm a friend who admires your work and wants you to know how wonderfully you paint. I love your paintings and so many others do too. I wanted to show you first. I only have one poster and that's it." Karen moved to hug Margo. "Friends push each other when they have such a talent. You have a talent for everyone to see. Cedric believes it too. You should let me push it for you. Continue to paint as you need and enjoy the money you'll make."

"I'll think about it. I know you mean well. Just like Cedric means well. But it's my decision."

"I know, I know, and I want it for you. If you don't want me to use your paintings then say so. We can take these down and return them to your apartment."

Angela picked up shopping bags outside of Eric's apartment. She struggled to lift them from the car when Mark reached out a hand and pulled the bag freeing it from a snag. "Here you go," Mark said as he smiled at Angela. "I didn't know we lived in the same townhouse complex?"

"No, I don't live here. I'm visiting a friend. He wants me to decorate his place and I thought it was a good idea." Angela smiled as she walked towards the building.

"Lucky man," Mark commented as he got into his car and watched her walk away.

Angela neared the front door of the townhouse when she smelled something good. "Eric baked the muffins," she thought as she knocked on his door.

"Hi Angela," Eric smiled as he opened his front door. "Here let me help" and grabbed one of the bags from Angela's hand.

"I should have called so you could've helped with the bags. I didn't because I thought you were still playing your game."

"I finished the game a couple hours ago." Eric placed one bag on the floor near the coffee table, and moved to the kitchen. "You should try one of these," he suggested while grabbing the dish of muffins and returning to the living room.

"I can but first let me take this bag to the bedroom."

"Just drop it there and taste this. I want to know your thoughts on how they taste."

"Ok," Angela responded and grabbed a muffin. She took the first nibble, holding her finger towards Eric; she took a bite, smiled and said, "These are awesome. What is it I taste different for coffee chocolate chip muffins? There is something else and I can't place it."

"It's my secret ingredient. You like them?"

"I love them. You have a knack for baking."

"Wait until I cook." Eric sat the plate on the counter and returned focus on Angela. "What did you get from…," he paused, looked at the bag, and then said, "…Garden Ridge?"

"A lot of decorating items," Angela responded while picking up items from the bag to show Eric. She sat a little statue on the coffee table as a center piece. "Since you play Doom a lot, I thought this piece was best as the motivating factor." Angela smiled and waited for Eric to respond. Eric stared at the statue for a moment and looked about the room. "I gave her free reign when I agreed, so if I renege, it's not right. If I say yes, I probably can adjust, and she'll be happy," he thought and then said, "Angela, I think it's very nice but not quite a Doom character."

"Either way, it's great for the centerpiece. Why don't you like it?"

"I didn't say it's not likeable, it's just not a Doom character piece. It is a good centerpiece for the coffee table."

"I'll use it anyway. What are you planning for dinner?" Angela changed the subject and focused on his cooking.

"I planned my meals. I didn't think you'd be here, so my amount is much smaller. I think I can throw something together. I guess this means you're staying?"

"I thought we'd spend some time together while I decorated."

"I get it. Sure why not? I can help. Just tell me what you want me to do."

"We can start with your bedroom. I bought a comforter, sheets, and pillow cases. I left a painting in the car which goes well with this set. It's not feminine; it's masculine, but eye-soothing. Your stuff isn't bad, it's just not as inviting."

"Ok," Eric responded and questioned himself about his actions from last night. "Did I open a door to hell or am I really impressed because I slept with her?"

"Can you get the painting from my car? I can start changing the bed." Angela took charge and started setting things in the townhouse. She pulled sheets, pushed the bed around, changed the dresser location, and rearranged the nightstands. "There, that's better," she thought. Eric returned with the painting and watched as she moved item after item. He didn't assist unless directed by Angela. She moved most of the furniture herself, as she noticed Eric wasn't much of a muscle guy. She only asked for his help when it was a little awkward to move or push heavier items. "Eric, can you get a hammer or something to place the painting here?"

"Sure," he responded, leaving the room. Just as Eric got near his computer, his alarm went off as time for another Doom session. He quickly grabbed the hammer, ran it back to Angela, sat it on the dresser and returned to his computer. Angela turned, grabbed the hammer and started tapping on the wall as she figured the perfect spot. Eric was totally involved in his first session playing the game. It was as if Angela was a ghost moving around the room and changing things around. Angela didn't touch him, move him, or bother him playing his game. She moved about the room changing this, throwing that, or just adjusting. "Three hours of changing items around and not one peep from Eric," she thought. "How amazing! I can't believe anyone can be so caught up with a game." Finally completing the change, Angela felt hunger pains and started grabbing items in the kitchen. She started dinner from all the refrigerated elements. Eric turned once to see what she's doing, but still didn't leave the game. She ended up cooking dinner for them both and as she announced dinner is ready, Eric yelled, "Yoo-hoo, we beat level 7."

"I guess that means you're good." Angela commented while she placed dinner on the table.

"Yes and I get better every time my partner 'The Midget' plays with me," Eric answered while moving to the kitchen for drinks. "I have a bottle of wine. Would you like some?"

"What kind is it? Anything red will go well with dinner."

"Burgundy it is. I have it and a great taste too." He opened the bottle, grabbed a couple wine glasses, and returned to the table. As he poured the wine, he told Angela, "Thank you for cooking."

"I saw you were busy, so I hope you didn't mind."

"Not at all, the timing was great because I have one hour before the next session."

"Is this all you do on the weekends?"

"Like I told you before, I play Doom and attend cooking classes. I don't do much else, unless it's work."

"You know, there is so much more to Atlanta."

"I'm sure it is. I'll get out there one day and do the tourist thing, but now I'm pretty content with my life."

"You should get out Eric. I know a little about Atlanta and we should check it out. At least go to a sports bar or something."

"Nice of you to offer but I think I enjoy my life at the moment. Cooking is great, playing Doom is awesome, and my job is exactly as I like it. What else is there to do in Atlanta? I don't like to mingle with people too much, I get my exercise by walking."

"…you go walking?" asked Angela.

"Yes I walk around the park and on the path on Haynes Bridge Road, but again, it's just walking around and not running like some people. I get my nature intake by doing so. If there's a concert at the Amphitheatre, I open my windows and listen as the sound travels here. And, I order in when there's nothing to cook. So, life to me is really good. I limit my miles on the car; catch the MARTA (Metro Atlanta Rapid Transit Authority) train to the airport when I travel home to Michigan, keeping my life simple. My friends are my Doom partners and a few other people I talk to. You are one of the few people I mingle with."

"Eric, you're a nice person. Why won't you let people get to know you?"

"I do, didn't you hear me. I'm happy with the way I am."

"Ok, I got the point. You're happy and life's good." Angela responded and thought, "Where can I fit in? Oh, I can get him out to see what he's missing."

Three weeks after Angela decided to get Eric out, it dawned on him that he should stop accepting calls from her. The first week she got Eric to attend a public concert at the Encore

Amphitheater. The experience was nice as he sat there in silence. They didn't talk much or watch too many people. The second outing was a public jazz concert in Suwanee. The music was good, made Eric smile, and the people were more relaxed. He saw an office acquaintance, and it eased him, but still he worried about missing Doom sessions with his online buddies. The cooking classes continued, Angela showed up as a member this time and there was where they found themselves deeply involved. Angela tried to compete with Eric on preparing multiple types of meals. Eric enjoyed the competition, as he loved cooking, but only showed enthusiasm for Angela at the class. They went out to dinner once in three weeks, Angela spent Saturday nights with him but never crossed the intimate line again, and Eric never pushed the desire. They talked over the phone, where Eric listened as Angela talked like a canary bird singing day in and day out. She called him everyday just before he'd settle for playing Doom. She picked up the game schedule and actually mastered not interrupting Eric's focus. It was Angela who purchased tickets, books, and music for the townhouse. Grateful, Eric offered to reimburse Angela for her spending, but she was so happy to do so, it was nothing he could do. However, he purchased her cooking classes for the coming sessions.

Friday of week four was upon them and no plans for the two other than cooking classes. Angela called and got Eric's voice mail, "I'm going out with Paula as usual. I hope to see you in class tomorrow morning. Have fun playing Doom."

Paula showed for girls' night like clock work. She couldn't wait to catch up with Angela as it had been three weeks with Eric. Paula wanted to know where it was going and if it was really what Angela wanted. Knowing her for years, Paula understood Angela's need as it pertained to men. This time they had drinks lined up at Stage on Haynes Bridge Road. This was another classy restaurant with a fair group of patrons. When she entered the bar area, she saw Angela sitting next to a gentleman. "How could she bring Eric to dinner with us?" she thought while moving closer to Angela. However, Angela wasn't talking to anyone and ordered her drink which set in front of an empty stool. "Hi," Paula spoke.

"I knew you'd be here soon so I ordered your drink. The usual, right?"

"Yes and thanks. I thought you were talking to the guy next to you. Is that Eric?"

"Oh heck no, not that he isn't cute, but I take our night for us. Eric is a nice guy and he's playing Doom right now."

"Still, as much as you guys go out, he's still playing a game?"

"He loves the game. He's fun when he's out, but his focus is the game, oh and cooking."

"I get the cooking, but I don't get the game. You gave up Bill and Chris for Eric. I don't understand."

"You know the answer and Eric isn't bad. He lets me be me and I like that in a guy."

"I don't want you hurt, but are you sure?"

"I'm sure so far." Angela answered and changed the subject. "I heard from Margo yesterday."

"Oh really, who's Margo?"

"You remember, the lady I introduced you to at Garden Ridge with the professional decorator friend?"

Paula sipped her drink and paused before answering, to recall her memory of meeting Margo. She flashed back to the trinkets Margo's friend selected and told Angela, "I remember the lady with the friend buying the cheap trinkets. I remember."

"Well, her friend sold three paintings."

"She's an artist?"

"Yes and a real good one. I didn't know it before, but her friend set her up with a number of customers. Now she's thinking of doing it full time."

"What does she do now?"

"She is an executive assistant for a large company here in Alpharetta."

"Being an Executive Assistant isn't a bad job. She has her benefits from working there and of course it's consistent."

"But it's not her dream."

"Not many people can follow their dream, you know."

"I know, but here's her opportunity and with her friend pushing her work with numerous clients, she's bound to sell more of her work. Just imagine, a lady who enjoys her hobby and gets paid for it. That's the American dream."

"It surely is a dream. I just don't get how her friend can push her work out there when she was buying cheap things from the store."

"I guess it's her way of breaking even. Maybe she charges well for the paintings and offset the desk décor with cheaper items. Who knows? It's her business and it seems to be working."

"I guess." Paula fell into silence and observed a guy really eyeing Angela. "You have an admirer."

"Huh, I do?"

"Yes, it's the guy over there at the corner of the bar. I caught him staring at you twice now."

"He looks nice. I'm not into it right now."

"You mean you're into Eric right now."

"Well yes, he lets me be me and I like that about him."

"You've invested time with him but you don't seem really excited like you are when there's a consistent guy in your life. What gives? Go ahead, spit it out."

"Nothing," Angela sipped her drink and looked at the guy again. "He is handsome."

"Don't avoid the question. What gives?"

"As I said earlier, nothing gives. He is who he is and I enjoy the simplistic things we do."

"Ok, don't get angry with me but tell me more about Eric." Paula insisted on proving a point she knew of her long time friend.

"Well, he likes to play Doom. He likes to cook. He's from Michigan and has a Masters degree. He moved to Atlanta for the job and works in software. I know he loves his job, which is always good, and he's a great listener."

"And?" Paula faced Angela to tell her more.

"And what?" Angela replied as if she explained all about Eric.

"You mean to tell me that's it about a guy you've spent three weeks with. Are you honestly satisfied with this bland guy? Has he romanced you at all?"

"I, well, no he hasn't romanced me. As a matter of fact, I've been the catalyst to every outing. Some of which he didn't care for. And there was one he enjoyed, but that was because of some guy he works with. I can't say he's tried to kiss me since we spent the night together."

"What? No affection at all?" Paula frowned at Angela as if she'd settled just to have someone in her life.

"No, there's affection, just not from his initiation."

"So you've slept with him again during the three weeks?"

"No I haven't," Angela responded with an angered look. "As a matter of fact, I haven't had the desire to. He's more of a special project than a relationship."

"Are you listening to yourself?"

"You know, I am. What the hell am I doing?"

"I'm your best friend and I know you pretty damn good. You have to let this one go. You aren't attracted to him at all and there's nothing keeping you interested. So why not entertain the admirer?" Paula nodded to the handsome guy at the end of the bar.

"Because his girlfriend just arrived," Angela pointed towards the woman who waved at the guy and as he responded. "I guess he wasn't admiring me after all. He was looking for her arrival."

"You're probably right. At least you know Eric is not worth investing more time. You do realize it, right?"

"Yes I do. He doesn't talk to me much anymore anyway. It's been like he's dodging my calls. So, I honestly guess you're right."

"As usual," Paula smiled. "Let me tell you what's happening in my life this week..." Paula went on and on with her and Ron's life, highlighting their events. The usual conversation about family, friends, work, and dreams; she carried this conversation for hours as Angela was accustomed to listening. Angela usually had her interjections, gave a little advice, and commented on Paula's life. But this time, instead of really paying attention, Angela fell into thought about her situation with Eric. She really honed in on the comments Paula made on how she accepted Eric with no real interest. "She's right about Eric. He isn't my type, he has no outside drive other than cooking, and he doesn't show interest in me at all other than during cooking class. I thought he was a good listener and all the time it has been about me just yakking away. I've been really stupid on this one." Angela frowned and interrupted Paula right in the middle of her sentence, "You are right!"

"...huh" Paula responded and asked, "Right about what?"

"Eric. I know nothing about Eric. I don't know what he likes, other than Doom and cooking. I decorated the townhouse and he steps around things as if it doesn't invite him. He changed the comforter back to his original. He didn't try to invite me out, not once. He'd leave for the game as if it was his lifeline and no one can interrupt him. Sex is not an option to him unless I throw myself on him, so there's no interest. And I'm, well, really pissed at going to the extreme to prove a point."

"I'm glad you came to your senses," Paula smiled as she leaned over to hug Angela. "Realizing it is half the battle and you're going to be fine."

"What are you doing?" Angela pushed back from the hug. "It isn't that serious. I'm no lost cause or in need of your sympathy."

"I'm here for you. You'll make a better decision with a guy soon. I know. I can always call Bill. He'd always take you back."

"Don't you dare bring up that redneck asshole. If you like him so much, divorce Ron and you get him. Geez!"

"It isn't like that at all, Angela. I'm looking out for you. The kind of men you've selected lately weren't the best quality."

"Bull. I choose great guys. And don't be condescending to me. I know what I'm doing with my life Paula. Back off with the guy bullshit."

"I would but you seem to…" Just as Paula nearly finished her sentence, Angela got up and walked out thinking, "that bitch. She's really becoming a true redneck bitch."

Saturday morning and Angela was back at her routine, workout, errands, and cooking class. She liked not following Eric at the end of class. The situation with Eric turned out to be just what the doctor ordered; it was as if nothing happened between them. A few laughs while cooking and life went on. After cooking, Eric waved goodbye and headed to his Doom game, and Angela headed to her apartment. Angela had no guy to focus on, and it was a change of effort. Angela continued to draw a conclusion on men in general. "Either its bad luck or I'm making horrible selections," she thought while driving home. "One of the guys in my future will be a total package." It was her wish, her dream, and her claim of thought.

Margo called Angela during the afternoon with hopes of planning an evening out. All of her other friends and Cedric had plans. Karen, her best friend, was out with her guy for their anniversary. Cedric was out with Christopher until Sunday, kayaking in the mountains. She thought of Angela as an opportunity to get better acquainted. "We had such a great time that Saturday night. I hope she has nothing on her schedule," Margo pondered while waiting for Angela to answer her cell.

"Hi, this is Angela," Angela answered because she didn't recognize the number.

"Hi Angela, its Margo"

"Hey, what are you up to?"

"Not too much. I'm calling to see if you have plans this evening."

"No, I don't. As a matter of fact, I'm wide open. I thought about renting a movie and staying in."

"Sounds nice, but I thought maybe we could do something."

"Sure, what do you have in mind?"

"How about going to Atlantic Station to the sushi bar or The Grape?"

"I haven't been to Atlantic Station. What's it like?"

"It's an interesting environment and a pretty nice place. Shops, apartments, and a movie theater are all available in walking distance for the people living in the vicinity. It's a pretty nice set up. There's even a gym available."

"Seems interesting enough, what's the Grape?"

"It's a wine bar, you run into interesting people and normally end up with dynamic conversations."

"What time do you think we'll leave?"

"How about 6 and we'll include dinner or tapas?"

"Good, who's driving, me or you?"

"I'll drive since you haven't been there. I'll be out front of your apartment at 6. See you soon."

"Looking forward to it; bye Margo," Angela waited for a reply before ending the call.

"Bye," Margo responded, smiling as her night just changed from the walls caving in on her.

# Chapter 7

Margo opened the door to The Grape and walked to an available table. The Grape was a wine bar, totally embracing with racks of wine bottles as part of its décor; it was quaint in comparison to larger establishments, but cozy, where people easily mingled while exploring flavors of wines. Angela, excited to explore with her new friend, followed without a word and noticed the patronage. A diverse crowd all mingled together, talking to one another, separate parties inviting each other to their conversations. "What a different bar environment," Angela thought as she took her seat next to Margo. "Is it always like this?" asked Angela.

"Like what?" Margo responded as if it were not an appealing place for Angela.

"People talking to each other as if everyone know one another."

"You mean warm and inviting? Yes, it's like this all the time." Margo passed the menu. "They serve tapas here too. In case you're hungry or just feel like snacking with your wine."

"I can get into this." Angela smiled while reading the menu, "I like the positive vibe here."

"I'm glad you like it," Margo replied. "It seems like a nice crowd tonight. I expected such, but not as many this early in the evening. Normally it's not as crowded, but still nice. Its fortunate we got a table."

"It's because this is my first time coming and I'm suppose to have a positive experience."

"Sure." Margo smirked before laughing.

"Really. You know if things work out easily, it's meant to be. This is easy so… you get the conclusion."

"I sure do and you're right. This is lucky for us."

"What do you suggest for wine tonight?" Angela pointed to the multiple bottles on the wall rack.

"You like white Zinfandel, why not stick with it for starters. I'm going to try the Shiraz. I'll let you taste and if you like it, I'll order it for your second glass," Margo said as she left for the bar as planned.

"Sounds good," Angela said to Margo just as she passed the table. She looked at the people involved in all sorts of conversations. The main thing she observed was how people talked without hesitation to the person next to them. Normally, there was such a concern to interacting with strangers, but here it seemed so normal. It was like everyone was interested in all and there's no hang up on race, gender, or sexual preference. Angela sat waiting for Margo to return with her wine and found herself making a comparison to her experience with Mark. "People at Club 290 were just as free in conversation," she thought while observing. The place is very active, surely a hot spot, and a great environment. Smiling at the thought of enjoying this in the future, she turned to see all the smiles on the people surrounding her. With one particular guy on her right she spoke, "Hi."

"Well hello lovely lady," the gentleman replied. "I haven't seen you here before."

"It's my first time. I came with my friend Margo."

"Welcome to The Grape," he tipped his glass of wine towards her as a toast.

"Thank you," Angela replied and looked for Margo's return.

"Oh, Margo will be back in a minute."

"You know her?"

"Of course I do. She and I went to school together. We graduated from SCAD the same year."

"Cool. This is the normal location your class meets. How nice?"

"No, not our class meeting, but we know quite a few people in the city, and it just so happens, Margo and I come here from time to time."

"This was a planned night for you two?"

"No, it's a hit or miss, but we always have great conversations when we do end up here. It's the type of place where everyone is everyone and no one person is ever alone."

"I gathered that. It is nice knowing you can go someplace where you are totally welcome; even if no one knows your name or who you are," Angela smiled, but not flirtatiously.

The gentleman giggled in response, "You almost said a line from the sitcom Cheers."

Margo returned to the table with the wine. "I see you've met Lance."

"No, not actually, we were just chatting," Angela responded as she took her wine for a quick sip.

"He and I..."

"Graduated from SCAD."

"He told you." Margo turned to Lance, "Good boy, Lance. Nice making Angela feel at home."

"Sure. You know it's what we do here."

"It's why I brought her. I know it's a great environment and the people are awesome."

"Yes, we are," Lance responded.

"Lance, this is Angela. Angela, this is Lance."

"Nice meeting you, Lance." Angela extended her hand for a handshake.

Lance took her hand. "The pleasure's mine. Any friend of Margo's is a friend of mine. No questions asked."

"You're kind."

"No, I'm real. Margo is the same way. As we all are here."

"Such a nice environment," Angela looked around the room and all others were still in their conversations, drinking wine, and snacking. The music was soft and upbeat.

"Lance," Margo called out, "Did you get the gig you wanted?"

"No, unfortunately I didn't. It seems all the new buildings downtown have large contracts with big firms. I can't even get into a subcontract with them."

"You remember Karen?" Margo asked.

"Yes, I heard she's doing great in Alpharetta."

"That is a fact and she did me a favor."

"Yea, what favor?"

"She sold three of my paintings." Margo lifted her glass with a smile as a toast of accomplishment. Angela and Lance followed suit and the three clinked glasses.

"I think it's awesome. I know a professional artist." Angela found it amusing she'd just extended her social circle to creative people.

"Yes, you do," Lance chimed in. "I told you your work is awesome. I'm glad she did it."

"Thank you," Margo responded. "Now I have to get serious with my painting. I'd hate to have the pressure of creating so much so quickly."

"No, you don't have to do it so quickly," Angela responded with a frown, as if she knew the business.

"Angela dear, we were taught not to be stagnant in our work. It's why I didn't like the idea of selling my work. I could work at my pace and not have the pressure of deadlines. Now, it depends on how Karen presents me in her sales pitch."

"I get it. But don't you have other paintings in storage or at your studio? This is the first you've sold."

Lance jumped in, "No way. Margo sold a few others while still attending SCAD."

"And you didn't follow through with it?" A baffled look appeared on Angela's face.

"I didn't want the pressure."

"Oh, I get it." Angela sipped more of her wine while Lance looked at Margo, "I get it. Honestly I do. If I had your talent, I'd have my own studio."

"See, a lot of responsibility, instead of creativity being my driver."

"I get it," Angela replied and said, "All you need is a business manager and you can do what you like."

"It just may work," Margo contemplated as she considered Cedric as a business manager.

"You know, I wouldn't mind doing it," Angela offered.

"See what wine does for you?" Lance laughed, "Drink wine, become thinkers, and start a partnership. Who can beat it?"

Margo and Angela looked at Lance with smiles and changed the subject to something less serious. They conversed about weather, music, Atlanta happenings, the theater, and new television shows. Time passed as if the clock was on a speed walk amongst the Smoky Mountain foot hills. On their fourth glass of wine, Margo left for the ladies room. She stumbled as she walked; a sure indicator of having a little more to drink than usual. Angela noticed and wondered if she would be able to drive home. "Without a doubt she can't drive," Angela thought as she decided Margo had enough wine. She asked, "Lance is there a coffee shop around?"

"Yes, it's the next block over, right on the corner."

"Do you think it's still open?"

"It should be. Its only 10:30," Lance replied as he looked at his watch. "I'm sure it is."

"Good. We've got to get Margo over there. I don't want her to drive and I'm not sure I can at the moment."

"I admire you're a responsible woman who looks out for her friend. I like it."

"Thank you. But I'm not looking for compliments; I need to get some coffee in her to help sober her up."

"It's a nice coffee shop. Similar to this wine bar and it serves drinks. Do you mind if I come along?"

"Of course not, my new friend is always welcome to come with us."

Margo returned and finished her last bit of wine. "We should order one more round."

"I think we've had enough. Why don't we hit the coffee shop?" suggested Angela

"Yes, good idea. I think she has it right. We should have coffee and get ourselves together before driving." Lance jumped right in, supporting Angela.

"Ah, I guess so," Margo agreed.

"Good it's settled." Angela stood and grabbed her purse. She moved aside to let Margo out and gave a nod to Lance as a silent 'let's go.'

"I'm right behind you girls." Lance interjected as he finished his wine.

The trio walked two blocks and observed the active street life. They watched as people enter and exit establishments, cars driving slowly on the streets, and looked above at the building lights reflecting life; both work and play. As they arrived to the coffee shop, Karen met them at the door. "I saw you coming this way. I didn't know you were coming here tonight, Margo. I'm glad to see you."

"Hi, Karen," Margo smiled with her greeting. "I didn't expect you to be here either. I thought you were out with your guy."

"He's here in the booth. Care to join us?"

"We couldn't, it's your anniversary."

"Come on, the night is still young and we've had dinner. This is a kill-time spot before dancing," Karen insisted they come to her table.

"It's ok with me," Margo answered, "but what about Angela?"

"What kind of question is that? You know, we include everyone you're with. Hi Lance, long time no see."

"Hey, Karen," Lance kissed Karen on the cheek, "it's been a while. This is Angela."

"Nice finally meeting you. I didn't know you were dating Lance."

"We're not dating, we just met."

"At The Grape."

"Yes, exactly. No offense intended, Lance."

"None taken," Lance answered as the three finally settled at the table. "It's nice seeing you again." Margo extended her hand to Phillip, Karen's boyfriend.

"I've heard news about you," Phillip responded with a handshake.

"I hope it's all good."

"It is, without a doubt. You're a talented woman."

"Thanks – this is Lance and Angela," Margo introduced the two as if they were a couple.

"We aren't dating, we just met," Angela pointed out.

"Yes, we were drinking at The Grape and next thing you know, Margo is too tipsy to drive. Angela is a responsible lady. She looks out for her friends."

"You are very kind in doing so," Margo winked at Angela. "Karen how was dinner?"

"We had a lovely time."

"I hear you're doing great in decorating," Lance commented.

"I'm doing ok," Karen responded.

"I like what you did with Margo's paintings," Angela added to the conversation.

"I'm not sure she likes it. Do you, Margo?"

"I love it. I'm just afraid I have to force myself to paint more than when it comes naturally."

"You're talented and if it stinks at the time, we can survive on prints."

"I can print multiple paintings," Phillip suggested.

"He owns his own print shop," Karen explained.

"Are you looking for help these days?" Lance asked.

"Yes I can use some help. Are you in the market Lance?"

"Yes, everything downtown seems to be slow unless you're with a big firm."

"Call me next week," Karen responded and handed him a card after digging it from her purse.

"Thanks."

"We can discuss terms next week. Don't forget to call and remember my contracts are all in Alpharetta or above the perimeter."

"No problem," Lance stood and looked at the ladies, "well ladies, it's my cue to leave you in capable hands. I bid you good night. Nice meeting you Angela."

Angela waved and responded, "Nice meeting you too. Drive safe, Lance."

"Kisses, Lance!" Margo shouted as he moved though the coffee shop. "He's such a nice guy."

"He's talented too. It's why I want his help. I'm glad he asked," Karen admitted.

"Did the three of you graduate together?" Angela asked.

"We staggered in years during school. Margo and I graduated together and Lance was a year behind but we shared a few classes."

"That's how you know each other. I'm impressed you still network together."

"It's what friends do, Angela. We look out for each other when we can."

"My friend Paula and I are similar, but mostly when it comes to guys for me, especially since I'm single."

"Karen and I mingle and seem to find other things more important. I guess since we have guys in our lives, we don't go there. Or did we?" Margo looked at Karen who's snuggled with Phillip.

"No, we didn't. I've been with Phillip the entire time and you found Cedric before graduating."

"Yes I did." Margo turned to Angela, "We don't set each other up, but I will tell you this, we'll help you find a guy if you'd like."

"Me find a guy? I don't think so."

"You should let us help," commented Phillip.

"I'm sure he has a few friends he can introduce you to." Karen added.

"No, I'm ok."

"At least tell us what you have in mind for a guy."

"Well," Angela hesitated in response, "of course handsome."

"There you go; half the guys I know are out." Phillip responded and they all laughed.

"Any of them would beat that asshole Chris." Margo reminded Angela of her last date.

"But my friend Paula thought it was me being the hard one and not him."

"Obviously she didn't understand Chris. He is an ass, a pompous ass."

"He sounds awful and you deserve better," Karen suggested.

"I think so too." Angela agreed and decided to change the subject. "Tell me about the new building you're decorating."

"It's a whopper of a deal. It was the right job to get Margo's work in a variety of buildings. The customer has a network of building owners and management companies where they reach out to decorators and architects. I impressed the main guy and he's introduced me to a number of his counterparts."

"Sounds exciting."

"It is, no doubt really exciting and of course it's business. I love running my business."

"She is a dynamic woman," Phillip commented and smiled. "She surely has a keen business sense. It's partly why I love her so much."

"Those are nice words, baby, I love you too." Karen quickly kissed Phillip. "I'm a lucky woman to have such a supportive man in my life."

"Yes you are. Happy Anniversary," Margo chimed.

"Thank you," Karen and Phillip replied in unison.
A waiter appeared with two cups of coffee. "The guy who left ordered these for the ladies."

"Thanks." Angela and Margo both replied. "Just like Lance; he's a sweetheart of a man."

"You should date Lance, Angela," Margo suggested.

"No, I'm not quite sure about him."

"Good because he'd not be interested in you."

"Why not?"

"He's gay. Did you not notice?"

"No, I didn't. I'd never have known unless you told me." Surprised at her newly found information, Angela fumbled in her statement, "I haven't been exposed to so much before."

"What do you mean so much?" asked Margo.

"I haven't been to the city and where I grew up and in college, my exposure to such diversity was limited."

"No black folks in your part of the country?" Karen asked.

"No, not at all."

"I think you'll find more of us leading you from the stereotypes you've heard; if you've heard anything at all."

"Well, I've heard a few things from my friend and grew up understanding there are limitations."

"Now is not the time to discuss this," Margo interrupted. "How about we girls have this discussion another time? Right now, you have a date with Phillip to finish."

"You are actually right. We can finish this later. I like the idea of just us ladies discussing it. Then I can tell you about the men," Karen added.

"No way I can represent myself there?" Phillip asked.

"Sorry babe, girls only."

Monday came like a speeding train hauling supplies for the United States' western territory. The work week took the lives of Karen, Margo, and Angela by storm. Each carried their responsibilities to the utmost professional expectations laid upon a person. Karen landed another contract and hired Lance to support her efforts. He came in handy as she led other junior designers to the new contracts. Lance filled in like a champ on the most important building where Margo's work displayed like Viking ships anchored ashore on foreign land during a winter storm. Margo fought diligently on not quitting her job and committing herself full time to her painting. She kept in line with corporate America, commuting every day for a dead end position. Yet she found motivation to paint and managed time to win the support of Cedric. Like anything else, Margo and Cedric's lives were a partnership and it worked best as they supported each other. Angela worked her heart out. She continued to pursue excellence in her profession, kept a strict workout regimen, and didn't once buckle to visit Eric. She called Paula once in three days, which was practically unheard of since college. There was a sense of change for Angela; she started recognizing the diversity of people around her more often.

Not a dramatic change, but just an eye-opener as she learned more of people.

Thursday arrived, and Angela found a free moment at noon to call Margo and invited her to the gym. They discussed working out together the Saturday night of the dreaded double date when she and Christopher finally called it quits. "What an asshole," Angela remembered and vowed never to allow another man to treat her in such a fashion. Finally Margo answered her cellular. "Hi, Angela."

"I guess I'm special now - you have caller ID for me. It's nice," Angela smiled while responding.

"Of course, what's up?"

"I've been exercising like a storm. I think I may have burned myself out. I need a push. Are you interested in working out with me today?"

"I think I can manage. I need a partner who'll push me too. I get to these walls and nothing I do gets me over."

"I know the feeling. Which gym would be best?"

"Let's use yours this time and next time we'll try mine. How's 5:30?"

Angela's evening workout was 5:00, yet she compromised meeting Margo's time being a half an hour later. But traffic considerations make it perfect for the both of them. Angela answered, "Perfect. I'll meet you in the parking lot."

"Good. See you there."

"Bye, Margo."

Angela arrived at the gym exactly at 5:15. Leaving her car, she walked to the front entrance waiting to see Margo. While waiting, she observed several people entering the gym and some actually were courteous enough to speak. Angela, being the new southerner, spoke regularly to people as they spoke to her. Hardly, before moving to Atlanta, did she speak first unless she knew the person. Now, it was almost habitual to greet strangers. "It's become a habit," she thought comparing herself from past to present.

Margo pulled her car to the sidewalk where Angela is waiting. She yelled, "I'll be right there," and drove to park her car. "It took me forever to get here," Margo shared with Angela as she approached.

"You're right on time, I barely waited ten minutes." Angela held the door for her new friend to enter. The desk clerk asked, "Do you have your badge or membership card?"

"Yes and this is my guest," Angela responded while showing the card and signing the guest sheet for Margo.

"Is she looking for a membership?" asked the clerk.

"No, she's visiting, thank you," replied Angela as she directed Margo to follow to the locker room.

"Every gym is the same." Margo commented.

"Yes, it's a business. They have to get members and sometimes I think they push a little too hard."

"Like you said, it's a business and they have to make a profit."

"As long as they don't throw it on people, it isn't such a turnoff."

"Nice gym. I was here long ago, but never took the full tour. It was too far for me to travel when I moved. This is really a nice locker room."

"I like it. Do you have a lock?"

"No, I didn't bring one."

"You can take a chance by leaving your things in an unsecured locker. I do it sometimes, but not often. Or you can put your things in my locker and I'll secure them."

"I can, sure will. What are you planning to do today for a workout?"

"I think, well my legs are so sore, so I'm not sure. What do you feel like?"

"I need cardio and I saw a number of treadmills and cross trainers. I may just walk on a treadmill for ten minutes and run for thirty."

"I guess running the soreness out of my legs is something I should do. I can walk and run with you. It'll be a nice time to chat the ten minutes or if we run slowly, we can talk for the entire time." Angela rubbed her legs with muscle cream. "This stuff stinks but it works."

"Girl, you're aging!" Margo laughed.

"No, not aging, not that!" They both laughed at Angela's remark. "I'm ready. Let's go find a couple of treadmills close together."

"I'm right behind you." Margo grabbed her towel and stepped lively following Angela. She noticed the number of people arriving and how many people were already there. "Is this the busiest time of day?"

"It can be at times. I see two open, but we have to move before someone grabs them." Angela nearly sprinted to the stairs to ensure she grabbed two treadmills. Margo quickly followed, as if the sprint was her warm up. "It's not that serious is it?" she asked, huffing.

"Sure it is. It's our plan and we agreed to do cardio. I need it after a day like today. And the week so far has been hectic. It's the first day I arrived at the gym at a decent time."

"This is decent? You can't take off a little earlier to get here when things are more available?"

"This is decent, the crowd is larger Monday thru Wednesday and it decreases on Thursdays. Fridays it's like a skeleton."

"Only the serious workout on Fridays; it's generally the same I've noticed at all gyms. The muscle heads are here all the time."

"They are coming. I like to watch them while I do cardio. I try not to be so obvious, but my goodness, those guys are…" Angela fanned her face while talking about the weight lifters.

"…fine?" Margo finished the sentence and looked down. "You are so right, my goodness."

"Are you seriously considering painting fulltime?"

"Yes, I am seriously considering it. I spoke with Karen and she thinks I have a chance to really make an impact on the market."

"Karen is awesome. I wish I had a friend who was in a good position to help me with my talent. Unfortunately I haven't a talent," Angela giggled. "Well not the type of talent you can sell."

"What are you talking about?" Margo gave a grinning puzzled look.

"Oh no, I mean sewing or writing, maybe crocheting."

"Sure, and I thought you were out for fun."

"Don't get me wrong, if the right guy comes in my life…"

"Like the guy over there, on the seated chest machine."

"Maybe, if he were a lighter complexion."

"Angela, you have specific taste in men. I can accept your taste. I'd date him if I didn't have my Cedric."

"Are you serious?"

"Sure, why not? He's a gorgeous man and fine. Look at the body, and you're going to tell me he's not attractive."

"I never said he wasn't attractive, he's just not my cup of tea."

"And you've never been interested in someone like him?"

"I can't say; well I went out with a guy who was similar."

"As a date, you went out with him?"

"No as friends. He was really interesting, sweet, kind, attentive, and well my friend Paula didn't approve."

"Why not? He sounds very nice."

"She didn't like the idea of my crossing into their world."

"Tell me, did he treat you well? Did you enjoy the places he took you? Did you enjoy the conversation?"

"I did. All of the above."

"But your friend didn't approve. I understand peer pressure. It's the same reason I'm starting to take my painting seriously."

"I see. You have public influence. This is different."

"Not really."

"How can it not? Some people will not like it and I'm not sure if I like or can handle the public pressures." Angela looked down as if she wasn't happy with her comment.

"Darling, it's the craziest thought you could have. Are you living or are you limiting yourself to life?"

"Right now, I'm not doing much of either. Just working, and working hard."

Margo took in the conversation and breathed while running the last ten minutes of her run. She peeked at Angela who'd stretched out and increased her pace. She couldn't talk at such speed, and the girl was moving as a long distance runner finally getting to the finish line. While watching Angela, Margo couldn't help but ponder on her fear of seeing other types of people. "It's not like I'm dating a black guy now, but at least I have in the past. I met Cedric and he just had it all for me. He's a really great guy. Had he not come in my life, I surely would be with Mark. He was such a darling man. I chose Cedric because he was open to a long-term relationship and I fell for him. Mark, well he wasn't ready for a commitment then - I bet he is now. No, don't do it, not yet. Let's get Angela to open the door first, before we go there." Margo kept up her pace, not quite as fast as Angela, but surely a strong finish. "What's next?" Margo asked.

"I think we can do a circuit and include abs. Is that ok?"

"Sure. I need to start a serious program with weights. I normally hit body sculpting and other classes."

"I do too at times, but other times I like to lift with the machines."

"Good, I'll follow you." Margo followed right after they'd wiped the machines. She watched guys and gals work out, mingled with a few, and played the baiting game to catch a date with eye candy. The weight machines were pretty active as many people were involved in pushing, pulling, lifting, and pressing with various exercises. The two started on a vacant machine, taking turns, Angela led the way with serious focus and Margo followed with a strong effort. In-between sets, Margo would point out different people she knew. Though she'd just wave, she didn't want to interrupt her workout. She kept focus on the time because after the work out she had to drive a little distance for dinner with Cedric.

Angela pushed Margo during her turns. She had it in her mind working hard was the way to a better body. Margo followed but extended her effort just to show her sincerity to Angela, even though her workouts weren't as intense. "My goodness, Angela, this circuit is tiring me out. I didn't think the weight lifting would hurt so soon."

"It normally doesn't unless you don't push to this level all the time."

"That was my message. I don't; not this hard anyways. I'm not trying to gain mass. I like toning."

"Hang in there with me, it's the last set and we're done." Angela wiped her sweat off the machine's seat. Margo sat and started the set without changing the weight selection. "Aaaugh," Margo exerted as she pushed.

"Too much weight. Why don't you stop and reduce the amount."

"No just one more," Margo responded while pushing with every last bit of effort and energy.

"That's it, you've got it. Push!" Angela shouted.

Margo completed the set and rose shaking her arms. "It was tough. I kind of liked it, but not for a routine. Maybe once a week."

"You'll feel it tomorrow, if not sooner," Angela responded while they walked to the locker room.

"Back to the routine, I have to fix dinner once I'm home. Cedric cooks on the other nights. We alternate nights."

"That's nice. I like a man who cooks. You're lucky. I met one guy who enjoyed cooking but that's nearly all he liked, besides a computer game." Angela spoke while opening the lock on the locker.

"I guess since it's the norm for me, I need to remember I am lucky. Thanks." Margo smiled as she retrieved her gym bag.

Angela arrived at her apartment within minutes of leaving the gym. She jumped in the shower, cleaned up, and dressed comfortably to relax. She cooked a quick meal, very light as usual, and then settled with a glass of red wine. Her phone chimed with the special ring tone for Paula. "Hi, Paula," Angela answered.

"Hey, I have got some news for you."

"What news?"

"Ron, Bill, Amy and I are heading to Jamaica for two weeks. We leave in the morning and we'll return Thursday afternoon the following week. I'm so excited."

"Wow, such short notice and Jamaica? I thought you were planning a trip in the spring for Cancun? How did you manage to get a trip so soon?"

"Ron and Bill won a pool tournament. It was the number one prize, and listen to this -we get $2,000 spending money too. Bill and Ron are sharing it 50/50. It doesn't matter how they share it, as long as we're going."

"Great. I hope you have a wonderful time. It's a place you've always wanted to go," Angela commented as she recalled a time they spoke on travel.

"Yes it is, and the only problem is, you aren't going. I told you Bill was someone to hang on to."

"Are you out of your mind? I wouldn't hang onto a guy like that if my life depended on it. Trip or no trip; hell how's he going to handle all the black people in Jamaica? You know it's a dark country."

"I bet he isn't worried about it. I figured a few on the resort, but as long as we do the private thing we'll be ok. If he doesn't adjust, Amy will have to deal with it."

"I'm so glad it's Amy going and not me. You four have a great time. Think of me when you're shopping for souvenirs."

"I'll be glad to pick you up something. Have anything in mind?" asked Paula as she attempted to minimize the shopping for Angela experience.

"Yes, I want the coffee. The famous mountain coffee should be awesome. I think it's the only thing I want from there. I'll have to get there myself one day to shop."

"Oh, you could have been coming, if you weren't so harsh on Bill."

"Listen, drop it and enjoy. I'll see you when you return." Angela thought but wanted to extend the conversation to see if Paula at least investigated the sites in Jamaica. "Where in Jamaica are you going?"

"Ocho Rios. It's a five star resort and the pamphlet says there is a lot to do."

"Like?"

"Well, Dunn River Falls, the lighted canoe river ride, the beaches, bicycle the Blue Mountains, hit the hot tubs, and all the other water sports. Ron is excited about drinking the entire time. I haven't talked in depth with Bill."

"I see you've read about it. Glad you're informed of what's there. I want you to have a wonderful time and take lots of pictures."

"Are you going to be ok without me?" asked Paula as if her input into Angela's life was the sustaining force to normalcy.

"I'll be fine," Angela answered with sarcasm in her voice.

"Don't forget I'll miss you on our girls' night out. Don't do anything crazy without me. And we'll catch up when I return."

"Go and have a wonderful time. You need to pack, so go pack. I'll be fine and can't wait to hear about your experience." Angela ended her call wondering why Paula insisted on mentioning Bill.

Friday afternoon, just after lunch, Margo and Karen talked about the weekend. They both happened to have free time from their guys. Cedric was heading out with Christopher to a hard rock concert, of which Margo wasn't too interested in hearing. Cedric enjoys his rock and understood Margo's dislike for the hard, really hard stuff. Margo insisted he take Christopher instead, to which he obliged. Karen's guy, Phillip, had classmates visiting and a few fraternity brothers in town for their annual get-together. Phillip was a Naval Academy graduate and also a Kappa Alpha Psi. Fortunate for Phillip, all of his friends got along and they had so much in common, it's as if the group should have their own fraternity. When they visited Atlanta, none of the wives, girlfriends, or partners accompanied them. They truly let their hair down and get absolutely wild. One year, one of the friends got totally wasted and danced on stage with nude dancers, landing him in jail for fighting the bouncer. Another year, they played poker throughout the weekend non-stop, didn't sleep at all. This year they had a ball game, a party scheduled at a popular dance club and a theater show to attend. Karen accompanied them one year, it wasn't the best time for her, and Phillip kept apologizing for his friends, and sometimes for his behavior. She decided at least once a year, Phillip can be one of the boys. They, *the boys,* assisted each other whenever they could throughout the year, and if it was trouble one is going through, the group stand tight in response. They grouped together as most military people when supporting each other.

Margo asked, "What do you want to do tonight?"

"I have an idea if you're up to it. How about we go to The Fox Theater? I can get tickets. After the Fox, let's hit Bell Bottoms for dancing."

"You know, I haven't been to either of those places for some time. I worked out with Angela yesterday and the girl tried to kill me."

"You need the workout just like I do," Karen snickered.

"Are you trying to call me fat?" Margo's resentment came through the phone to Karen.

"No, don't take it as an insult. Remember we used to workout together. I know how you've slacked off."

"You're right, I don't workout as hard anymore. Unlike you, who wakes at 4:30 a.m., run six miles, then does yoga before going to work, I'm not as dedicated to the fitness thing."

"I'm jealous of you, because you still look great without working hard."

"Making up, huh?" Margo giggled. "Let me call Angela and see if she'll come with us. I don't think she has anything going on. I remember her having a friend on Friday nights and maybe she can come along too. It can be the four of us. Do you mind?"

"No, it's a fine idea. The more the merrier. Just let me know how many tickets I have to reserve."

"I'll call you right back." Margo switched her phone to dial Angela. Within four rings Angela answered. "Hi, Margo"

"Hey, what do you have planned tonight?"

"Nothing at the moment; my best girl friend is heading to Jamaica for two weeks. Since she's gone, I haven't planned anything in place of the time."

"You should come with Karen and me. We are heading to the Fox Theater and then we'll go dancing at Bell Bottoms."

"I don't want to be the fifth wheel. I don't think so. Maybe when I get a date I'll hang with you guys."

"No, the guys aren't coming. It's a girls' night out. Are you interested?"

"Yes, if that's the case. What time?"

"Let's meet at 6 for the 8:00 show. I'll call Karen and let her know it's the two of us."

"Ok, are you coming to my place or do you want me at yours?"

"We'll pick you up," Margo insisted since Karen had the farthest to drive and with the most free time.

"See you at 6." Angela ended the call. Margo called Karen and provided information for tickets and let her know Angela was the only one coming with them. She also informed Karen of Paula's trip to Jamaica without Angela.

The ladies made it near the Fox Theater in one piece. Any given Friday, Atlanta had a steady flow of bumper to bumper traffic. Karen showed her super-maneuvering skills as they drove to the city. Extremely scaring Angela, Karen consoled her by saying, "It's not my normal way of driving."

"Thank goodness!" Margo replied.

"Amen to that!" Angela, Margo, and Karen all laughed as she parked at a perfect location. They walked across the street to the ticket office's will call window. The three entered the theater and found their seats, just in time for the opening act. They enjoyed the show as expected. Intermission fell upon them and when the theater lights came on, the three stood and headed for the ladies' room, as if they were commanded. While washing her hands, Karen broke the ice, asking Margo, "Is it wine time yet?"

"I could use a glass," answered Margo. "How about you?"

"I'm game," answered Karen. "Angela, so far, what did you think of the show?"

"It was really nice. I'm following it. I forgot how great it is watching live talent."

"The only way to watch good entertainment is live." Margo jumped in to comment.

"Yes, it's the only way to go. At least in my book; are you up for wine too?" asked Karen.

"Sure, I'm game. As a matter of fact, let me buy the first round," Angela insisted.

"Ok, I'll get the next. It's the least we can do for the drivester."

"We made it, didn't we?" Karen smirked.

"Yes we did," both Angela and Margo responded in unison.

The three walked to the wine bar and ordered. Just as promised, Angela paid the cashier and followed the crowd back to their seats. The rest of the show ended in a bang of applause. "It was awesome." Angela spoke.

"I'd watch it again," Margo said and smiled. "I may do just that with Cedric. He needs more art in his life. I mean besides my paintings."

"I thought you two got around to all types of events."

"We do, but not this type. Not as if I'm complaining."

"You get out quite often. If Phillip and I could find the time, we'd enjoy more of Atlanta and its night life."

"At least you two have someone to enjoy things with." Angela said, feeling left out, not being in a relationship.

"Don't worry, you'll find the right guy," Margo pointed out. "I'd like to introduce you to a guy I have in mind."

"Don't do it," Karen advised. "I remember you sending someone on a blind date. The guy was so bad the girl went blind."

"That isn't funny."

"Yes it is," Angela laughed. "The last time I went on a blind date was horrible. The guy was a jerk and now he's in Jamaica."

"You missed a trip to Jamaica?" Karen asked.

"I'd rather go with an ape than to have gone with him."

"That bad!"

"Yes, well actually worse."

"Worse than Chris?" Margo inquired.

"Pretty bad, but, well," Angela paused before finishing, "equally bad; just different bad, if that makes sense?"

"It makes sense."


The three continued their conversation about Angela's dating experience all the way to their next location – Bell Bottoms. Just arriving Angela noticed the diverse people in line. "Is it always like this?" Angela pointed to the people in line.

"Most times it is. I haven't seen it with a smaller crowd. Not on a Friday night," Karen answered.

"We loved coming here back in college. It was our escape for a Friday night and cheap as the cover charge was $5 then. Now I'd guess its $10. The music is fun as it focused on 70's, 80's and early 90's music. Old school jams and everyone dances with everyone. It's what I like about it. No pressures to be seen with someone or anyone. Just dance your heart away," Margo explained as they parked and walked to the club entrance.

"It's not the best looking place in Buck Head." Angela pointed out. "But it sure is popular, look at the cars around the place."

"It's popular and a lot of people come here, especially a more mature crowd."

"Anything like VIII Fifty in Roswell?" Angela asked Margo.

"No, not quite. I think this one is a stand alone and can't be compared," Margo answered as they got in line. Waiting for their turn to enter, the three ladies noticed private parties inside and most got through the door without paying. The girls quickly followed the last person in line and the cashier allowed them inside as party members. The girls heard a great up beat song and went directly to the dance floor without ordering drinks. The three danced together for a half hour before stopping for a breather. Laughing at the surroundings, Angela realized she danced with various people because the floor was so crowded. One person would face you, dance, laugh, and move on as if it were a circuit of people moving about the floor. There were couples dancing together and there were singles dancing with anyone available. As well, groups would dance as if they were the focus of the entire floor. Everyone in the club seemed to dance at one time or another. Some were engrossed in conversations near the bar, or near the patio. Angela noticed a number of people walk out to the patio just to cool off from dancing at length. When she took a chance to walk out for cooler air, she noticed people from all walks embracing as lovers, some matched by skin color and others mix matched. Her observation became apparent that people here had no concern of what most others did. She remembered what Paula influenced, as well as her limited exposure to people of color. "How different," Angela mused, nonchalantly observing. One drink and another one and a half hours of dancing, talking, and people watching, the girls finally decided to call it quits. They left the club smiling about what they observed, the dancing they enjoyed, and the money saved for the night. Heading north, they decided to stop at a convenient store gas station for coffee just before entering GA 400. Instead of all three entering the store, Angela volunteered. She purchased three black coffees and quickly returned; handing two coffees to Margo, she jumped in the back seat and was now ready to leave. Angela always looked around the location out of habit. She recognized a car from earlier in her life, and someone whom she couldn't place a

finger on owned it. "Who drives that car?" she pounded her memory trying to recall. "I know the car and I know who owns it. I just can't remember." Angela thumped her head while thinking and Margo took notice asking,
"Why on earth are you thumping your head?"
　"I'm trying to remember," she replied.
　"Remember what?"
　"That car at the convenient store; I know that car but can't remember where I saw it."
　"You know a car?" Karen jumped in.
　"I know the car and who owns it. I'm sure of it."
　"There are a lot of cars like that here in Atlanta."
　"I'm sure, but it's so familiar," Angela explained, "You know when something sparks your memory? That car sparked something that either I was in it or someone I know drives it."
　"It will come to you in time," Margo insisted. "Let it go, it'll come back."

The girls made it to Angela's apartment while continuing the small talk about their night. They added subjects exploring more of relationships, clothing styles, shoes, furniture, travel, and of course men and how different they are. Angela ran inside her apartment and prepped for bed, the coffee did nothing to impact her slumber. She instantly fell asleep as her head hit the pillow. Karen and Margo continued their conversation and included how nice Angela seemed to accent their group. They both enjoyed her personality, and how eager she was to have fun and enjoy life. They agreed to reach out and include her in everything they do, even if she was the fifth wheel. Margo had plans to make it three couples for sure, especially since she had a perfect guy for her. Karen insisted on Angela coming over to her home the next weekend. She planned a dinner for all of her close friends and a few employees. The rest of the weekend Margo decided to invite Angela on a picnic and other events her and Cedric planned.

Saturday came in easy but fast as Angela jumped out of bed and realized she had little time to get to her cooking class. She zoomed through her preparation, dressed, and left for class. She barely snatched her cell phone as she got it off the charger. Angela raced to class and arrived just as it started. She maneuvered into her usual spot without breaking her quick pace. She bypassed Eric without speaking or acknowledging his existence. Class started and Angela fell right into the routine of learning. She truly enjoyed learning how to make so many different foods. It was her personal investment as life continued to change and new friends were on the horizon. After completing class Angela ran errands like grocery shopping, stopped at the cleaners, got an oil change for her car, and cleaned her apartment. The day flew as no moment was left to do anything for pure enjoyment. Since last night's events went into the wee morning hours, she didn't mind relaxing with a book and a bottle of wine for the evening. It was the first Saturday in ages where she missed working out and for the same reason, she felt tired and yet, she felt lonely as if not having a special someone haunted her. The loneliness lurked in the shadows from behind the walls of her apartment. She sat in silence, without movement, still as if she were a mummy, to ensure her mind didn't play tricks. Angela didn't move for minutes, she thought of her last months living in the city. She compared all of her dates, her events, and what she most enjoyed. She recalled the unusual location where she met so many people. "Life is changing with every new event and things are opening to a different world. It is really different from what I grew up understanding and even living here for a couple years, it's changed. It surely is different." Angela pondered more on the excitement of men she'd met, the fun she had, and the disappointments she endured. She compared every account from beginning to end, and remembered the best time she had with a man since being in Alpharetta was with Mark. She thought of how comfortable she was just being in conversation, she thought of his gentle mannerisms, it was his encouragement self identity and enjoyment without expecting something from any event. "Why did I push him away? Was it Paula's acceptance, or was it fear? I don't know for sure. I don't ….." Angela fell asleep while trying to understand her thoughts.

Sunday morning and Angela woke exactly in the same position as the night before. It wasn't unusual to do so, but leaving the reading light on, the wine out of the fridge, and never drinking the first glass, was not her normal activity. At least in the past she'd put up the wine if nothing else. Her book had fallen on the floor and she was surprised the thump didn't cause a stir. She started her Sunday morning routine as every move accomplished something around the apartment. She wanted to attend Mass at nine, so getting ready was her effort. Just as she finished dressing and was preparing to leave, Margo gave her a ring.

"Hi," Angela answered.

"Hey, did you sleep well?"

"I did. I fell asleep in my chair and never made it to bed."

"You were tired. We must have kept you out too late," Margo giggled.

"No, not really, but I enjoyed it."

"I'm glad. Listen, I don't want to take up too much time of your morning, but Cedric and I are heading out for a picnic this afternoon. Are you interested?"

"I'll be the third wheel. I'm not so sure I'd feel comfortable with you and Cedric on a romantic picnic."

"You will not interrupt anything; it's our way of enjoying a lovely day. You should come. We'll meet at the park on Kimball Bridge. You and I can walk the path and get back to nature. If you're worried about Chris coming, he isn't and Cedric will bring a book as usual. I'd love you being there." Margo insisted.

"Ok, I'll be there after Mass. I'm heading out to the church now and I'll meet you around 1. Is that ok?"

"It's fine. Don't worry, we'll have fun." Margo ended the call and smiled as she knew it would be a wonderful time. "She's a doll," she told Cedric.

"Are you scheming?" asked Cedric.

"No, not even."

"Babe, I know you. I know you so well. What gives?"

"I'm just happy to have a new friend."

"Sure, sure you are," Cedric laughed. "I remember the last new friend you had and lost playing Cupid."

"You and Karen say the same thing."

"Maybe we're trying to tell you something." Cedric sighed. "Poor Angela."

After Mass, Angela returned home to change from her nice outfit and headed out to the park. She called Margo to ensure things were still happening as planned. She decided to stop and pick up a salad for the picnic, just not to show up empty-handed. Knowing she probably didn't need to, as she'd learned Margo was organized and fun to be around, it was still the courteous thing to do. At the Kroger, she observed Mark shopping, but didn't say anything to him. She didn't think he noticed her as he faced the products and she had a chance to really look at his features. "He is a very handsome guy." she thought. Then she flashed back to the conversation with Margo at the gym. "Why don't I want to go out with him?" she asked herself. "What was my reason?" As she left Kroger for her car, she recognized the car she saw Friday night. "Oh my goodness, it's the car I couldn't place. It's Mark's. What a coincidence!"

Mark continued shopping and admitted later that he saw her. He followed his routine of Sunday grocery shopping. He liked Sundays as Saturdays were so busy and hectic, especially at Wal-Mart but this time his list wasn't huge, it was quick and easy. He decided to hit the closest Kroger. Earlier in the day he'd heard from Margo, a friend whom he dated, but never got serious. She invited him to a picnic today, but since he had earlier plans, he couldn't make it. "She sounded really sad I couldn't get there," he thought as he wandered the last aisle. "I know she and Cedric are doing great. He loves her and I know how she feels about him, it's a match made in heaven. They are such great people. I wonder…NO, not again," as he recalled being the object of a blind introduction to another of Margo's friends. "She's always up to something," he chuckled. "I'm glad I'm not going. I'll have to catch her and Cedric another time. Knowing how it went in the past, not going is a damn good thing."

Angela made it around 1 and Margo waved as she pulled in to park the car. Sitting at the covered park picnic tables, they had everything out and ready. Cedric opened a bottle of sparking cider, and poured three glasses just as Angela arrived to the table. "Here you go." Cedric greeted Angela with a glass of cider.

"Thanks," Angela said as she took the glass, and then commented, "I thought you couldn't drink alcohol in the park."

"Taste it. its cider," Cedric suggested as he waited for an answer.

"It is cider. I thought for sure it was wine or champagne."

"Looks are deceiving, aren't they?"

"Yes they can be."

Margo pointed to the different types of food she prepared for the picnic. She had a specialty dish for dessert so Angela could eat freely.

"See, I have fruit, pretzels dipped in semi-sweet chocolate, and salads. I hope you brought your hunger with you."

"Everything looks wonderful. What do you want me to do with this salad I brought?"

"I'll place it in the cooler just in case you decide to take it home. I have practically everything else for us."

"I see, and the cider is good too. Thanks for inviting me out today. I'm not sure what I'd have done today. It's been a busy week and Friday night was totally enjoyable."

"I'm glad you came," Cedric spoke as he raised his glass of cider.

"Are you ready to eat?" Margo asked and admitted, "I'm starved."

The three grabbed plates and created master pieces for their meals. They talked while eating and laughed at a few of Cedric's explanations of his adventure with Christopher the past Friday night. They enjoyed being in the park on a Sunday afternoon, as if this outing was a family routine. They all told stories of their past and how it seemed they grew up on the same block, even though their hometowns were at least two thousand miles apart. It had to be the same era of parents who grew up in mainstream America. Baffled at the commonality, Angela became curious as to how Margo and Cedric were exposed to so much diversity and understood how to fit in and relax. She pondered on the thought as Margo asked if she'd like to take a walk along the paved path. The path led into the wooded area where nature presented a picture of beauty. Many people either rode bicycles, roller bladed, or walked on the pathway as it stretched for a few miles. Runners enjoyed it because it shaded them from the sun and kept them off the street. Lovers enjoyed the path because it provided scenery for romantic interludes. Margo enjoyed the path as it gave peace of mind, while she could drill Angela for information. "Are you ready?" Margo asked Angela.

"Sure. Are you coming Cedric?" Angela asked as she noticed Cedric didn't get up to walk with them.

"No, you girls go ahead. I think you can talk freely without me."

"Oh, its one of those talks, huh?" Angela asked Margo with a look of question. "Is there anything serious you want to talk about?"

"No, just girl talk, that's it," Margo answered as they took to the path. Cedric took out his book and started reading as the girls cornered into the wooded area. "I wanted to just chat, nothing serious or even focused in an area. It's getting to know you better," Margo explained to Angela the conversation and walk without Cedric.

"I can go for this. I enjoy you guys. You're a funny couple."

"I'm glad you like us. We like you too. I'm even happy you get along with Karen and Phillip. They are awesome people. Are you coming to Karen's dinner party?"

"She insisted I attend." Angela had no idea to the type of party Karen gives.

Margo explained Karen's parties. "I know you'll enjoy all the people around. It normally is a few of her closest friends and those top people in her firm. She gives the nicest dinner parties. And you'll enjoy her place. It's lovely."

"I don't mind going. It could be fun," Angela added.

"You should come for sure."

"I bet. Karen seems to have things quite nicely together. I wouldn't expect her home to be anything but well decorated."

"Trust me, it's a lovely home." Margo stepped around the curve and pointed out a lovely nature sight full of green shrubs, wild flowers, and a creek, that would make a beautiful painting.

"Will you look at this?"

"It's lovely. I didn't think things here were so beautiful."

"Nature's always beautiful. Just like you. It's why I wanted to talk to you away from Cedric. I'd like you to pose for me."

"Pose? Nude!" Angela gave a puzzled look as her imagination only saw her nude in a picture.

"No silly, I don't do nude paintings. I want to do a portrait and I'd like you to be my model."

"If that's the case, I'd like too. When do you think we need to get started?"

"I'll let you know, but I chose you because you have such lovely features which I can easily blend with my style of art."

"Thank you for the compliment."

"You are so welcome," Margo answered and thought, "It'll be one half of her wedding gift. Now to get the other half, once she meets him."

"Is there a deadline you have to meet with this portrait?"

"No, it's an idea at the moment," Margo answered as she walked and Angela followed beside her. "It's just an idea I know you'll like and if you like it, you can be part of the royalties."

"You mean you've decided to sell your artwork?"

"Yes, Karen and I came to terms. But my work is still kind of my work, so to say. She sells nothing I disapprove and we agreed she'll not push the pieces I want to keep to myself. It's on my terms and my terms only."

"Karen agreed to them without an argument or discussion?"

"There was a discussion, but she agreed. I know she has my best interest at heart."

"It's still business you know. She'll push you for the good stuff," Angela warned as if she knew Karen's motives for business.

"Not Karen, she'll stick to our agreement and she places friendship first and foremost. She's not a business cutthroat."

"How does she do it? How does she stay in business and not practice the killer attitude most people employ?"

"She's a great woman and believes in relationships being her model of success. I'll let you talk to her about that one. I can't quite answer it right. I will tell you this, she's surely a great lady and smart too."

"I know she's smart. I gathered her wit from those times we were together. And she wants me in her home?"

"Yes, at the dinner party. You'll love it, trust me." Margo explained how to get to Karen's as they started their tracks back to Cedric. "Keep our agreement in mind, remember the portrait is our secret and we'll start soon. I have to get focused on my painting again and get a routine together. The only way I can start painting until Karen sells a few more is working my full-time job. When I get myself back on a creative schedule, I'll call you and we'll coordinate a time. Ok?"

"Sure, just let me know and I'll work around your schedule," Angela agreed.

"Hey, how was the walk on the trail?" asked Cedric

"Pretty nice," the girls answered. "It was pretty nice."

# Chapter 8

Thursday came like a hurricane hitting the Floridian coast. It crashed and made its way into the night. Karen called Angela just after she settled in. "Hey girl, what's up?" Karen asked.

"Not much. I'm just about to relax before going to bed" Angela replied. "How are you?"

"I've been busy as usual and doing pretty good actually. I'm not going to keep you up late, but what are you doing for lunch tomorrow?"

"I haven't a thing planned. I'm open, actually, the entire afternoon."

"Good, then let's have lunch tomorrow. Let's say 12:30 at the Cheesecake Factory?"

"Sure, I'll be there."

"Great, I have lots to share with you and since you're on your way to bed, I'll not keep you up. See you soon."

"Sure, I'm glad you called," Angela smiled, as a flashback from high school days when a cool kid invited you to a party.

"Me too, have a great night and see you tomorrow. Bye." Karen disconnected her call. She turned to Phillip and watched him prepare for the evening, changing from his working attire into something comfortable. "Why are you watching me?" he asked.

"Just admiring my man as a woman should."

"Oh yeah?" he answered moving closer to Karen and grabbed her for a tight embrace. "Here's a closer look."

"I see." Karen spoke with a softer voice, her knees weakened and her body slightly shivered. In the instance of the kiss, the seductive gentle touch of lips, Phillips strong body coaxed Karen into a position where she felt his every muscle, and the pressure of his embrace aligned with her sensitive zone, bringing her to arousal. He lifted her and Karen fell limp into his arms, as if she were a maiden finally taken to bed. Karen laid back in anticipation, as her imagination led him down a path to her convulsions;

touching those erotic points of pure delight, gentle kisses upon the smooth skin, and his gentle massage sending nerve tingles, like a brisk wind touching her uncovered body on a summer's day. Phillip indulged himself to his loving woman; he climbed upon her in a natural state between those inviting legs, his passion trying to escape the clothes he recently put on. His lips still exploring and moist, kissed her body until reaching Karen's neck, to tease her to the point of turning her into the aggressor, and inspiring her to moan for more. Phillip followed Karen's lead, as she undressed him upon the bed, and then grabbed the lifeline of his manhood, as if pulling a tug rope, leading him to a position to enjoy. She engulfed him like a candy sucker, and tickled the top of the loin, which always drove Phillip crazy and mad with desire. Karen made her moves as she envisioned and practiced in her mind at those free moments throughout the day. She made Phillip squirm to nearly exploding. It was right where she wanted him, hot, bothered and ready to erupt, before climbing aboard for the ride. Yes, she rode him like a wild buck, placing herself in proper form for them both to climax. Phillip held her hips and pushed for the life of him, as she tugged and rocked to her point, pulling him close to her breast by his ears just as she exploded, and shivered from ecstasy. Phillip joined her; he'd never miss the opportunity to join his love, his woman, his life. They lay entangled, savoring the moment in heart and mind, and Phillip stroked Karen's back, his hand like a feather. She laid in silence, accepting his caress and recalled the buildup of desire, the love she wanted and received, and smiled as she realized how lucky in love she was.

Angela was elated about Karen's lunch invitation. Her admiration for Karen grew with greater exposure. As Angela discovered Karen's successes, she realized the dynamics of Karen. A woman running a successful business spoke volumes to Karen's strengths, her fun personality was magnetic, and the way she exuded respect from people left many with immediate admiration. Angela wanted to learn how she did it. She saw an opportunity for Karen to become her mentor in business. Friday afternoon couldn't arrive fast enough. Angela knew she had to achieve a specific deadline to free up her lunchtime, as Karen dedicated part of her afternoon. She didn't want to upset the chance for that one-on-one opportunity to ask for mentorship.

Angela completed her work from the night before and found her plan executed quite nicely, freeing the entire afternoon. Karen scheduled reviews for acceptance with a couple of clients, as two of her major buildings were complete. It was her last step in the process before final invoicing. Both jobs were successful and it gave Karen the entire afternoon to do other things. She showed up 11:30 at the Cheesecake Factory and decided to get a table and wait for Angela. It gave her time to recap on her last projects while reviewing the activities for the current buildings. Besides, it was Friday and normally the place was packed by 11:45, the beginning of the lunch rush, and on Fridays it could take on the early behavior of happy hour. Angela scanned the restaurant and walked towards the rear when Karen stood and waved for her. Just as she approached, Karen spoke, "Hey, glad you could make it."

"Me too. I left early trying to beat the lunch rush" Angela replied.

"I did the same thing and came right over as my last appointment finished early. I know this place gets crazy, but I enjoy the food."

"So do I." Angela sat opposite and finally got comfortable just as the waiter arrived. "Can I get you something to drink while you review the menus?" asked the waiter.

"Sure," Karen spoke, "I'll have a glass of water with lemon."

"And I'll have the same," Angela ordered.

"Thanks and I'll be right back with your drinks." The waiter responded and left the table.

"I know we don't have too much time. Well, I have my afternoon open at the moment but I can get some things done after lunch," Karen admitted.

"I have the entire afternoon, as I'm ahead of schedule. I might go workout early today and not return to the office."

"What do you think you'll have for lunch?" Karen held the menu as she spoke.

"I was thinking of the Turkey BLT with no fries."

"You know a BLT doesn't sound bad, but I need roughage. I'll have a chicken salad."

"I see you eat pretty healthy."

Karen smiled with her response, "I have to. I'm aging you know."

Angela giggled with her answer. "Yeah, sure you are. We all are aging. I think you know you're older when your boobs touch your navel. Everything before then is adjusting and not aging." Karen giggled with her and got serious. "Let me get to why I wanted to have lunch with you."

Angela braced herself as Karen's tone quickly changed from laughter, "Ok," she replied in a doubtful tone as suspecting something awful.

"I must have you attend my dinner party on Saturday night."

"A must?" Angela asked while thinking, "Why is it so important?" without asking aloud.

"I need you because I hear you're taking cooking lessons. I need a partner in the kitchen with me to set this up."

"You want to hire me?"

"No silly, I want to show off your skills and I enjoy you so much as a person that you must come and have my friends see you as I do."

"You sounded so serious with your must and tone. I almost didn't understand."

"Forgive me, I get serious sometimes. But it's something you'll probably get used to as we interact more. You do want to come, don't you?"

"Not if I'm working," Angela replied while shaking her head at the seriousness of Karen's explanation.

"No, not working, I want you having fun with me. See, I enjoy cooking too and thought you and I could throw a heck of a party. Every time I have a party, I get to show off a few of my cooking skills from some class I took."

"You took cooking classes?" Angela asked in surprise.

"Yes, I did. I took a few at the same place you are taking them, and I took a trip to Italy to learn more of Italian dishes."

"You are serious about your cooking if you went to Italy."

"It was a vacation package, and girl, the wine and the countryside were awesome."

"So it must have been expensive to go."

"No, not at the time, but it was fun. I have to say so. And the guys, well I shouldn't go there, but be sure it was fun."

"You went before Phillip?"

"Yes, it was before Phillip, even though he enjoys my Italian cooking, I don't dare explain how I learned it."

"Oh that's funny."


The waiter returned and took their orders. The two sat in silence for a moment. Karen thought, "My invitation didn't come across the right way." And Angela thought, "I surely don't want to work for her in the kitchen, even though she thinks I'm ok with helping her cook."

"Ok, I didn't come off right in the beginning." Karen reflected her earlier comment to Angela. "I should first apologize at my direct approach as a business person and not a friend." Karen paused before saying, "Angela, will you come to my dinner party and assist me in cooking? I'd love sharing my kitchen with you and I think we'd have so much fun together. You enjoy cooking and so do I, so why not share a few tricks we've learned?"

"You know, Karen, I was thinking the same thing. I'm glad you clarified the dinner party and my being there. I'd love to come, as I find you and Margo so much fun and interesting."

"Good, it's settled. What can we prepare for this party Saturday night?"

"It's a great idea. I don't mind helping at all. As a matter of fact, it'll be the first time I cooked for other people since those classes."

"Are you nervous about doing it?"

"No, not at all. I want to, as I haven't had a date come over where I can cook for him. I'm ready though, girl, am I ever ready."

"You'll have your chance cooking for a guy, probably sooner than you think."

"Do you think?"

"You're gorgeous, funny, a great personality, and lovely character. Sure, he's right outside waiting to discover you."

"I'll believe it when I see it," Angela commented, and then changed the subject. "What do you have in mind for the dinner?"

"What's your best dish?" Karen asked.

"Well, since you know Italian and I've learned a few dishes in Italian and Mexican, why don't we combine the two?"

"Italian-Mexican dinner party, I like the theme."

The waiter returned with their lunch orders and the girls kept discussing the dinner party menu to create a combination showing the bridge between the two cooking styles and created a common theme for the décor. The lunch became a partnership in planning and ideas. Karen was so energetic taking in Angela's suggestions, she practically agreed to every one of her ideas. Angela felt different since the beginning of the conversation and agreed to the idea; she threw everything into the planning discussion. She and Karen talked for an hour longer on the decor and menu. They finally agreed to a menu that they both felt comfortable cooking.

"Will you purchase the ingredients for twenty people on your dish?" asked Karen.

"Twenty people? It's going to be a large party."

"Yes, twenty people. I give a large party once a year for my closest friends and business partners. Some are the same, but you get the idea right?"

"I get it. I'll be happy to."

"Keep your receipts, so I know how much to reimburse you," Karen suggested, as she didn't feel comfortable asking Angela to spend her money for the dinner party. The shopping receipts and business partners attending will help her accounting section use a portion for business expense.

"I'll keep the receipts. What time do you want to start?" asked Angela.

"The dinner party actually starts around 5:00 but I like to serve around 6:00. Most people will be there by 6:00. You and I can start at 1:00 or so. Is 1:00 ok or is it too early?"

"I think 1 is perfect. I've never cooked for twenty before, so I need all the prep time I can get.

"Great then I'll see you at 1," Karen said, paying the waiter who returned with the check.

"I'll get the tip." Angela offered.

"No, don't you dare. I have this. We'll have so much fun tomorrow. I'm so excited to have you in my kitchen. You know, I love Margo, but she isn't into cooking and we tried it one year and it was a disaster. It's why I encourage her to paint." Karen laughed.

"I understand. I like her paintings and I enjoy her so much."

"We both do, trust me. She's been my best friend for years."

"Nice, really nice, best friends who can talk about each other and not have a concern about feelings."

"Don't get us wrong, we are honest with each other and still respect feelings, but honesty is our policy. We can get over the hurt, as we agreed years ago to hold no grudges."

"Paula and I can get there but it's not quite the same. She's been really hitting me hard with her actions."

"Paula? Is she your best friend?"

"Yes, she is."

"Ask her to come with you I don't mind. Let her bring a date too."

"That's nice of you, but she's in Jamaica and won't be back until next Friday."

"If she's a friend of yours, she's a friend of mine. Just let me know when you can get us together. I'm there."

"Great. I think we all can have a good girl's group." Angela smiled while thinking, "Karen is so cool."

"I'm glad we had lunch together," Karen said, rising out of the booth.

"Me too. I'll call you tomorrow. I'll be there around 1 after shopping."

"Great. I can't wait to get started; it's going to be so much fun."

Angela smiled, saying, "I'm going to enjoy doing this."

The girls made it to their cars and headed in separate directions. Angela returned to the office to check in for any new requirements on her work. Karen met a prospective client after receiving a call as she entered North Point Parkway. Both ladies knew they had to shop for ingredients, as they worked the rest of Friday and planned going to a grocer at the end of the day. Angela worked her schedule to support her new objective. She thought her luncheon would last longer. As usual, since most people take off early on Fridays, she found the chance to do the exact same and of course, Paula wasn't here for their girls' night out. "This weekend is going to be a lot of fun," Angela thought as she left her office and headed to the Farmer's Market in Roswell. She wanted the freshest ingredients and after reviewing her list, realized a chain grocery store may not have the items for most of the recipes.

Karen ended her day with a new client. She enjoyed running her firm as well as being so active in sales. She took personal pride in developing a lucrative organization and bringing on Lance made her time available for business development. Yet, cooking was her passion and finally having someone with equal passion in her kitchen tomorrow excited her to no end. After the meeting with the new client, Karen found herself driving to the International Farmer's Market in Atlanta. Traffic was hideous but she fought it like a great boxing champion fighting his way through the fifth round after a standing eight count. She took on shopping as if it were a tied bout leading to the twelfth and final round.

Saturday morning arrived with smiles from Angela as she rose for the day. She planned her activities for the dinner party. First thing was of course, the workout and she actually made it a hard one, as she expected to enjoy the coming meal. Second, she returned to the Farmer's Market to ensure everything needed was purchased. She checked the list twice for accuracy and the amount estimated was supported as she never cooked for such a large number of people. "Karen must have huge cooking pots." Angela thought as she pushed the cart down the aisle and doubled the amount of items she needs. Cooking was always fun for Angela, since she continued to develop her skill with each class, and practiced to improve. She recalled cooking with Eric and how her meals, if not equally good, were better in most cases. Every item she chose had to be perfect, so the selection process took a little longer with her attentive process. She sniffed, tapped, squeezed, and shook vegetable after vegetable, fruit after fruit, until her senses approved the item. Before long, the cart was full as if she was cooking for an Army. "Wow!" she thought as she headed to the cashier. "I may have overdone it. I'll just ask Karen for half and keep the rest for my apartment." she contemplated, placing items on the conveyor belt at the cashier station. It was nearly 12:30 pm and she promised Karen she'd be there by 1:00. Angela was unsure of Margo's directions to so she called Karen for directions. After two rings, Karen answered, "Hi, Angela."

"Hey, I didn't get your address yesterday. I have all these items and I'm making sure of Margo's directions to your house."

"Margo has been here a number of times, but just in case, I'll give you directions. Where are you?" Karen asked.

"I'm at the Farmer's Market on Houzer in Alpharetta. Can you direct me from here?"

"First, let me give you my address. Better yet, let me tell you where it is. Much easier for you so there's no map involved. Do you know where Country Club of the South is by chance?"

"Yes, I've passed it on Old Alabama."

"Yes, go to that gate then to the first stop sign. Turn right and I'm the fourth house on the right."

"Simple enough," Angela admitted and thought. "Wow Country Club of the South is a high end neighborhood."

"I'll have the gate security guard expecting you. Just give him your name when you arrive and he'll give you the same directions again. Ok?"

"Yes, you made them easy. I'm on my way," Angela said while loading her car.

"Are you bringing a change of clothes? I normally don't cook in what I'm wearing for dinner."

"I thought of it and my dress is in the car."

"Great, you can dress in one of the guest rooms."

"I'll be there."

It took twenty minutes just to get to the other side of Alpharetta because of Saturday traffic. "Only when you want to get somewhere was there ever traffic," thought Angela. With two turns and three lights, she finally drove on Old Alabama Road. Following Karen's directions, she pulled up to the gate, "I'm here for Karen Cox and my name is Angela Bainbridge."

The security guard answered, "Yes. Ms. Cox told me to give you directions. Go to this corner and turn right. It's the fourth house on the right."

"Thank you," Angela said while pulling away.

"You're welcome," The guard answered and waved as he watched Angela drive on as directed.

The houses were mansions on a lovely golf course. Angela drove slow to take in the size of each home. She figured each house was at least 6,000 square feet and most were designed to die for. Every house was crazy gorgeous and had to be immaculate. The landscape was beyond manicured; it was actually works of art. Angela drove slowly and since turning she only passed the third house. "Wow!" Angela thought as she pulled up to Karen's home. "It's beautiful." She pulled into the driveway. "Amazing place!" She finally came to a complete stop and hesitated getting out of the car. "Karen can't live here; she doesn't seem like the type." Angela thought, doubting Karen's instructions. "She didn't give me an address and the security guard could only know my arrival if Karen told him. Wow, what a house!" Angela took in a final look before exiting the car. The house was brick, four car garage, large windows, a big crystal chandelier seen through the center window, see-through double doors at the front entrance, and French doors at the dining entrance were all noticeable from the outside porch. The architecture was splendid. After looking, she finally decided to trust her instructions and started unpacking the car. Karen appeared out of the front door, "Let me help you." Karen insisted.

"Sure, no problem," Angela answered. "You have a lovely home."

"Thank you. We like it here, so we decided to actually go for it."

"There's a lot of room for two people."

"It's cozy," Karen answered and focused on getting the veggies out of the car. "Follow me to the kitchen."

"All right," Angela responded as she carefully took each step behind Karen observing the home décor. "Wow, Karen has really great taste!" she pondered. They arrived to the kitchen and Angela noticed the size was larger than her apartment's living room and kitchen combined. Pots aligned along the ceiling fan over an island stove; the marble counter made its way around the walls and over lower cabinets, and the cherry wood color cabinets accented the color of the kitchen. The refrigerator and freezer were stainless steel, it had enough counter space for a breakfast nook and the tall chairs were matching cherry. The kitchen flowed with the décor, as one would assume the rest of the house's theme decoration. "The place is totally awesome and huge, just plain huge!" Angela thought as she continued placing bags on the counter. "I'll head out for the other bags," Karen said. "Why don't you start pulling things out and I'll show you around the kitchen when I return."

"Ok I will," Angela responded while pulling items out from the bag and placing them on the counter. Some items required refrigerating and she placed them on a shelf of the fridge. "What a nice refrigerator." Angela thought as she took in every aspect of Karen's kitchen. "This is going to be fun. I can just tell." There are knives, spatulas, pans, dishes, and every kitchen tool imaginable a chef would use. "Karen really gets into cooking."

Karen returned with the final bags of groceries. She handed one to Angela and started unloading to review her purchase. "You brought a lot of good stuff. I like everything I've seen so far. You're a woman who knows how to shop for fresh vegetables. I like that about you. Did you learn this when you started cooking class or is it something you grew up doing?"

"Thanks, I think it's a combination of class training and growing up watching my mother. I used to shop with her for fresh vegetables at the farmer's market back home."

"You picked up a great skill. You know, the meals are not only a reflection of cooking, but their greatness is with the fresh selection of ingredients. You did a great job. I know we'll make a fantastic meal." Karen smiled as she continued pulling items from each bag.

"I sure hope we do. I'm so excited to start cooking." Angela pulled a cutting board from the counter and grabbed an expensive cutting knife. "Is there a bathroom nearby?" Angela asked as she moved away from the kitchen into the hallway.

"Sure, it's to the right as you walk towards the den. Before we start cooking, can I suggest something?"

"Yes please do," Angela paused, waiting for Karen's suggestion.

"Can you take your dress up stairs to the guest room before we start cooking?"

"You know, that's a great idea," Angela responded while heading to the half bath. "She makes so much sense." Angela thought while she was in the half bathroom. After washing her hands, Angela headed to her car for the dress and an overnight bag. Returning into the house, she stopped at the double staircase heading to the second floor. Without knowing the exact room, Angela was hesitant to explore the house looking for the guest room Karen wanted her to use. She headed back to the Kitchen holding her dress and bag. "Which room would you like me to use?"

"Top of the stairs to the left, second room down the hallway," Karen answered while pulling out mixing bowls.

"I'll be right back," Angela walked as directed. "Wow this house is huge, and my God, it's so beautiful," she thought as every step showed more detail of the house decoration and design. At the top of the stairs was a sitting room/ library and it overlooked the backyard pool. Its décor is with 17th century furnishings, as if Queen Elizabeth visited and the bookshelves were built into the wall. Every space seemed well tailored and designed to be useful, yet it allowed natural light from the big French windows or, "are they doors?" Angela pondered as she continued her journey to the guest room. The open door to the first room on the left allowed Angela to peek. It had a canopy 18th century brass bed well decorated with silk pillows in bright colors. The furniture matched in gold trim, with cream-colored fabric. The wall colors were neutral against the gold accented room and the bed was the total focal point. As not to take long, Angela moved along the hallway and noticed the room on the right being decorated as another guest room, well decorated in modern 20th century style. The next room Angela opened the door and it was the room to which Karen directed her. "Oh My Goodness!" Angela smiled and dropped her bag right in the doorway. "This is lovely, totally awesome!" she thought while finally walking into the room. The decoration was all-Arabian, marble tops on the furniture, a round bed with a soft chiffon canopy, a big window with silk and chiffon curtains, brightly colored as one could imagine. There was a full bathroom, the size of her apartment's bedroom. The tub was high and sunken. The shower was glass and marbled tile. The twin sinks matched in marble, and the fixtures were pure gold. There were flat screen televisions, one next to the mirror and the other just past the privacy toilet with a bidet next to it. "This is surely a palace," Angela thought as she found the closet to hang her dress. A quick feel for the bed's comfort and she left for the kitchen.

Karen chopped vegetables on the cutting board when Angela arrived. "Oh my goodness, your house is gorgeous," Angela smiled with an impressionable look on her face.

"Thank you." Karen responded. "We found it and fell in love with it. Phillip was so particular about the location and the comforts he wanted. He grew up in a house similar to this."

"You mean Phillip is from a wealthy family?" Angela thought about the question as being too nosey, "I mean, is he an heir to a big business?"

"No, this is Phillip and I working together. He grew up with his father working as a chauffeur for a wealthy family. Phillip and I worked hard to get here. No inheritance whatsoever, just pure hard work and good financial planning"

"Your home is totally awesome." Angela moved closer to the far counter, picked up her knife and asked, "Are there additional bowls I can use?"

"Sure, let me show you around." Karen moved towards the bottom cabinets and opened one door after another showing Angela where things were stored. In a few minutes Karen explained the entire kitchen organization. "Don't ask for anything, just move as if it was your kitchen."

"I can do this. Really, I can do this." Angela smiled and grabbed a couple bowls, some oil, and pulled out the corn meal.

"Hey, I have a bottle of wine, would you like a glass?" Karen asked.

"Sure, it would be quite nice to have one while cooking."

"You can handle it while you're cooking right?"

"Yes, no doubt. And I promise not to overdo it with the meals. It's how I get into a great cooking mood. You know, drinking wine and being creative."

"You have any recipes with you?"

"No, I remember what I've rehearsed so many times before."

"I was just saying as there's a book holder over in the corner. Just in case you decide you want one."

"What about music?" asked Angela.

"Any kind in particular?" Karen opened a drawer and retrieved a remote, pressed a button and country music filled the air.

Surprised Angela said, "That's country music. I didn't know you like country."

"I grew up visiting my grandparents here in Georgia. They loved country music. It grew on me as a child, and though it's not my favorite, it's the music I listened to while cooking with my grandmother. So whenever I get the urge to be creative in cooking, I play country music; some oldies and some current."

"You are so neat." Angela smiled as she remembered the song playing.

"You never told me where you grew up."

"I'm from the Midwest. Not a large town and not a lot of diversity. You know not a lot of different ethnic groups in my town."

"Really?" Karen wasn't too surprised, as she had traveled to Midwestern towns with her accounting job. "I've been to places as such."

"So you understand."

"Understand?"

"This is really exciting to me. I've never been in a house like this and ..."

Karen finished her sentence "...never thought black people lived like this right?"

"I hate to say it but no, not at all."

"One day I'll give you a history about black people, but I'll save it for another time." Karen poured a glass of wine from the bottle she opened. "Don't let the stereotype or myths fool you. A number of blacks around the world live this way. And some are really successful."

"I know the music guys and sport players." Angela admitted her understanding as she took the glass of wine.

"Yes those too, but they weren't the first or the only."

"Really?"

"Yes, really. You were really sheltered, weren't you?"

"To other types of people, yes."

"I'm glad you're coming out of your shell, you'll see more here in Atlanta. You'll see more diversity tonight at dinner. We have all types of people coming, and they'll love your cooking, I just know it."

"Yeah, you think so?" Angela asked while mixing. Karen sipped her wine and said, "I'm sure of it. I assume you're as passionate about your cooking as you are about other things. As Margo explained, you have passion about your job and when you find the right guy, it'll be with him too. It's why I invited you to cook with me, and you know how hard it is to find someone who can cook with equal passion?"

"Oh, it's what I enjoyed about Eric. We cooked together and even competed."

"Why didn't you invite him?"

"We aren't together. It was a mistake." Angela sipped her wine and pulled out wax paper from the cabinet. "I went from one extreme to the other when I met Eric."

"It happens, you know. We do things we often don't understand."

"You are so right. But in this case, I at least learned to cook. I love the classes and I see him every cooking class. The difference is I keep my distance now."

"You aren't awkward at all?"

"No, not at all; I even slept with the guy and there's no awkward feeling."

"What?" Karen answered surprised. "You did what? Don't answer."

"I don't mind. It wasn't his idea. He was in the right place at the right time."

"One of those; it happens to the best of us."

"Did you fall for someone for comfort?"

"A long time ago and nothing I'm at ease to tell. But let me tell you, I remember," Karen laughed.

"That good?"

"Yes, that good." Karen turned around and looked for anyone close as she didn't want her next comment to get out. "Nothing like Phillip, trust me; I'm so glad we're together. Angela, you can't tell Phillip I admitted it." Karen giggled as if it were a huge secret.

"Mum's the word," Angela answered while rolling and flattening the recently made bread dough.

Karen pulled a large saucepan from her hanging rack, placed it on a burner, and lit the flame really low. She poured multiple contents into the saucepan and grabbed a spoon to mix the ingredients. "Yea, if you tell him his ego will explode. I don't think I could handle him then."

"He has an ego the size of Texas."

"When it comes to me, yes he does. He claims I'm his best catch."

"You two aren't married are you?"

"Not by his choice. It's my choice, but to me we don't need a piece of paper to claim each other. I mean, I will marry him in time but right now I want to explore business options and focus on the success I can build. He'll be here when I'm ready."

"And he understands your drive without complaining or pressure?"

"He understands, as a matter of fact, he encourages me to reach every goal. We have a partnership in the relationship and in business. He's my greatest advisor."

"I thought you were the brain behind everything."

"I am, but remember, you need someone to bounce ideas and situations off of and expect totally honest answers. Oh, and don't forget business savvy too." Karen stirred the sauce ingredients,  and then turned to grab other items on the counter to prep. Angela continued her plan to make enchiladas and grabbed a square pan from a cabinet. "You mean, you base your relationship on business and not love? How did you get to such understanding?"

"Who says it's not love?"

"I assume you meant Phillip is your business partner and a boyfriend; but not the boyfriend first and then the partner."

"No, I mean yes, but both. He is my lover, my best friend, and my business partner. We do nothing unless it's an agreement or joint decision. And when he or I need to make a rush decision we make it and talk about it later. A method we live by. I think it's something he learned while in the Navy."

"I like the idea. I mean it works if you trust each other enough to be a real partner."

"It works, trust me." Karen grabbed flour and olive oil with other ingredients to make fresh pasta.

"You learned to make fresh pasta? I'm impressed."

"You get what your money's worth, when you pay attention," Karen giggled.

"Can I ask you a personal question?" Angela hesitated, waiting for a response.

"Sure, go ahead."

"If you two are doing so well, why don't you have a house staff?"

"Who says I don't?"

"I thought since we're cooking you didn't have any staff. A house like this surely would at least have a butler."

"Fairy tales must run through your blood," Karen laughed. "No, I have house help when I need it, but in general, we manage well. I enjoy cooking and so do my friends. Like I told you before, I love cooking and would never cater."

"I see. I don't mean to offend you."

"You didn't." Karen drank more of her wine then asked, "Would you like a refill?"

"Sure." Angela finished her wine and passed the glass to Karen. "I'll have to slow down on the second glass. I need to remember my other dishes."

"I'm sure you will."

Karen and Angela continued preparing dinner, one dish at a time, each tasting sauces from each other's creations. Karen's Italian cuisine turned out very different from local restaurants. Angela's favorites turned out lovely as each pot filled an authentic Mexican aroma, and spicy enough without burning the liver or lung. Karen loved the taste and applauded Angela. Before the evening, both girls were laughing and hugging from the conversation and secrets they shared. "Remember, Angela, men are awesome creatures. When you find the right one, it will hit you like a ton of bricks; especially when there's one who doesn't fit the bill you had in mind."

"I'll remember."

"Good. Look at the time-we have to start getting ready! Why don't we set the table and then get cleaned up."

"That's a plan." Angela moved to the cabinets for the dishes she saw.

"No, not those, we're using the china out in the dining room."

"I'll follow you." Angela stepped lively and quickly grabbed multiple plates for the dining room. The décor followed the impressive theme of the house, and so did the humongous dinning room. It was nearly as large as a dining hall in someone's palace. It was easy to set a table for twenty, and then add a few more. Angela was amazed at the house size.

"There are towels in the bathroom and you're welcome to everything in the room. Make yourself at home."

"Thanks I will. What time do you want me down?"

"I think 6:45 at the latest. It's when I'll be down."

"Will Phillip be here then as well?" Angela asked so she didn't feel like a third wheel.

"Did someone call my name?" Phillip entered asking.

"Hi, Phillip," Angela greeted him with a smile.

"Hi, Angela. Hey, baby," Phillip moved to kiss Karen. "It smells great in here. I know you ladies did an awesome job. I'm starved." Phillip moved to the kitchen.

"Don't you dare!" Karen pointed a finger, "You can wait a little longer."

"I'll wait," Phillip responded as if they were orders from a ship's skipper.

Angela left the dining area and headed to the guest room. She followed Karen's instructions and took a long Jacuzzi bath, with oils and bubbles, watched television and relaxed for nearly a half hour. She nearly fell asleep if it were not for the television announcing the time. She jumped out of the Jacuzzi and rushed to dress for the evening. "You know, I can really get used to this," Angela thought as she brushed her hair in the final process of her preparation. The doorbell rang and a few guests arrived just as Angela walked down stairs, like a debutante descending to meet her date. Two friends of Phillip stopped and observed her descent to the bottom and without hesitation moved to the end of the stairs with their hands out to introduce themselves. "Hi I'm Sammy. My, you look wonderful." Angela smiled "Thank you, Sammy"

"I'm Louis. You can call me Lou."

"Hi, Lou. Nice meeting you both." Again Angela smiled.

"Wow, if you two don't behave tonight," Phillip laughed. "You two sailors, Angela watch yourself, the wolves are howling."

"I can handle them, Phillip." Angela said.

"A confident woman - very nice," Lou commented.

"And don't forget lovely too," Sammy added.

Blushing from the attention, Angela led the three to the kitchen but the men turned into the den, as if they knew where to go. Just as she checked on the meals and readied for the final touch, Margo and Karen walked in giggling.

"Hi, Angela," Margo smiled and moved closer for a hug.

"Hi. I didn't know you were here."

"I came just before those other guys. Watch out for Sammy, he's a serious flirt."

"They both are, but Lou is a little sly with his actions." Karen added.

"I can handle a little flirting. I thought there were only couples coming."

"Oh no, we'll have a combination of twenty people, including you. Don't worry about pairing up with anyone, be yourself." Karen moved to pour a glass of wine for Angela. Margo observed while tasting the hors-d'oeuvres. "Wow, Karen, you really made these great this time."

"It wasn't me alone. Angela made everything Mexican and I made Italian. It works."

"I know everyone is going to love it."

"Where's Cedric?" Angela asked.

"He's in the den with the others," Margo answered.

"The guys go in there to talk sports and business or whatever. We'll move in there as soon as a few others arrive." Karen moved towards the den with a bottle of whiskey in hand. She knew which one to take as Phillip always enjoyed serving a special type to his guests. "Here, darling," Karen said while passing the bottle to Phillip.

"Thank you, baby." Phillip smiled and leaned giving a gentle kiss to his lady.

"I've come here for years and you two still have the same spark," Sammy complimented.

Lou perked in and added. "They do and it's fortunate for someone to find such a love; especially when your job kept you traveling. With the invention you made for the Navy, I'd retire early and just enjoy life."

"What I know of you Phillip, retiring would never happen," Cedric added.

"You're right, he is a workaholic," chimed Lou.

"You guys talk as if I'm not standing here."

"It's respect bro, its respect and admiration." Sammy raised his glass for another shot of whiskey, which Phillip poured.

"I didn't know you invented something for the Navy. What was it?" asked Cedric.

"I never told you and rarely talked about it. But since Lou bought it up, I'll explain. It is a tool for engines, making the sailor's job easier. Nothing fancy, just a simple tool allowing a sailor to squeeze between a tight spot and still repair an item without overhauling the engine. It was more of a common sense tool than anything else."

"It saved the Navy millions by keeping the ships out of port when they needed to repair an engine. Phillip was smart about it the way he got it into the system. He patented the tool, found a manufacturer, and had a company present it to the Navy. When the Navy bought the tool, he silently left the seas and became a landlubber."

"You mean a returning land lover," Phillip smiled and sipped from his glass.

"So you made your money on designing a tool," Cedric said and sipped a little more than usual, surprised. This story is new to him as he thought Phillip was a retired injured athlete and worked for a large engineering firm and owned the print shop.

"Well, the engineering degree does come in handy," Phillip smiled.

"I have the same degree and saw some of the exact problems. You have a niche for solutions. I have to hand it to you." Sammy raised his glass as if a salute.

"I agree," Lou added, "It's always a lesson of new reasoning on every project with you. I learn so much."

"Guys, this is a dinner party, not an awards ceremony." Phillip eased the comments as he headed to the front door to invite more guests inside.

"Is it true?" asked Cedric.

"Every bit of it and then some," Lou answered.

"Wow, no wonder he's so energetic and focused."

"No, it's not him alone. Karen is truly a businesswoman. She has her interest in this too."

"I know about Karen. I didn't think she was the major breadwinner though."

"My man, you're in for a surprise. Wait until you learn more about the two." Sammy smiled as if there was a mystery to the money trail.

Margo, Karen, and Angela all played hostess to the arriving guest. Karen introduced each person to Angela. With open arms, every person was warm and inviting, courteous and extremely polite. No one asked about professions or seemed interested in business. Every conversation seemed to be about kids, travel, decorating, or sports. Angela noticed the diversity of the group as she stood in the den or parlor. She noticed people of different nationalities, ethnic groups, and complexions, and yet not one seemed uncomfortable or on edge. She noticed there was a monetary divide as well, and yet it didn't matter. "I thought it would really be different than this. In the movies you'd never see such a group together and I had no idea people were so easy to enjoy one another. Even though there's a divide. Interesting," she pondered.

Dinner went without a glitch, as everyone commented on the variety and the cuisine differences and similarities. Karen talked business a little and then spoke on current events around the world. Margo and Cedric talked to a few people who loved to travel and owned a yacht docked in Savannah. Sammy and Lou were hilariously funny as every time she observed them, someone around them was laughing. Other guests were just as interesting in their behavior, even Lance seemed to fit right in. At the end of the dinner, while most were leaving, people started helping with the table as if they knew Karen had no staff; which seemed out of the ordinary for wealthy people. Karen insisted everyone leave things on the table and she'd get them. Angela and Margo moved leftover food to the kitchen in the midst of the crowd. "What a weird scene." Angela thought. "It is so different than what I expected."

Karen and Margo knew the routine. The leftover food became quick lunch snacks for the week and often served as dinner. The kitchen was a mess and Sunday morning was surely a day of cleaning. Margo volunteered to return and help but Karen wouldn't have it. Angela offered, and was denied as well. However, Karen did offer breakfast, if the three decided to sleep over for the night. "Karen, this mess is huge, are you sure you don't need help?" Angela asked.

"I have a system. It'll be clean in no time." Karen answered. "Besides, it's something Phillip and I do together and talk about the night."

"Oh, you mean Phillip is going to help you?"

"Yes, he doesn't mind. Do you honey?"
Phillip answered, "No. I'm ready to start," as he brought in plates from the dining room.

"You two are such a team," Angela commented.

"You're welcome to stay the night and you know where to go. It's pretty late and I'd love you to stay."

"I think we'll pass," Cedric answered while Margo nudged him in the side. "Um, second thought we'll be here."
Out of observation, Angela answered, "Only if you let me help with the dishes."

"What do you think Phillip?" asked Karen.

"It's not necessary, but if she wants to I don't mind. We could get a process flow like station assignments."

"I knew it. You'd surely coordinate anyone assisting us." Margo and Cedric looked at each other and nodded their heads as in "why not?" They both moved to the kitchen, one over the sink and the other over the dishwasher. "We're ready," they laughed.

"I'll bring the plates in to you Angela; you scrape the leftovers into the garbage and pass to Margo. Margo rinsed the heavy stuff off and passed it to Cedric. Cedric loaded the dishwasher and started the cycle."

"What will you two do?" asked Angela.

"We'll watch!" Phillip started laughing. "No, we'll clear the table and tidy the area."

"You were surely in the Navy."

"Coordination works wonders."

"Yes it does," Karen added. "Let's get started."

The five worked as assigned, talked, and laughed as the night slid into early morning. Not one found themselves off to bed, after cleaning the kitchen, den, and dining room, the conversation continued and the time flew, as if the night just started moments ago. "Anybody for a cup of coffee?" asked Karen

"Not for me. Wow, we talked all night." Margo noticed.

"I never knew how much fun you guys were. I'm happy you invited me," Angela publicly admitted.

"She's tired, poor thing," Margo joked.

"No I'm…well I am, but that's not the reason I said it."

"See, I told you." The group laughed. "Don't worry." Karen hugged Angela with one arm from the side saying, "We enjoyed you too. Next time you should bring your friend Paula and her husband. We'd love to meet them." Angela hesitated in her reply, as if questioning Paula's attitude or beliefs. She knew it would be a hard sell to get them here. "We'll have to let you decide on inviting them. You'll have to meet her and make the invitation. I'm not comfortable inviting other people to your home."

"A friend of yours is surely nice. Look at you; you're one of the nicest people around. You know, birds of a feather flock together."

"That is what they say," Angela responded thinking, "It is what they say, but I don't believe it of people like Paula. She would have a fit coming here." Angela spoke again, "We'll see when they return from Jamaica."

"When do they get back?" asked Margo.

"Thursday night."

"Then why not the four of us go out on Friday, isn't it your normal girls' night out?"

"Yes, but." Angela hesitated because she knew what may happen and didn't want to hurt anyone's feelings.

"No buts about it," Margo chimed. "We'll do it. Right Cedric?"

214

"I'm not getting set up on this one," Cedric responded.

"I'm with you." Phillip agreed. The guys walked into the den and turned on the television to the sports network as the girls continued their conversation.

"I think we'll have fun. It will be nice getting out without the guys next weekend. I need the time again." Karen admitted. "I had such a good time with you two last weekend. I wouldn't mind doing it again."

"Let's do it. I know Cedric wouldn't mind."

"Well, I'd say ok, but I have to check with Paula to make sure she's up to it," Angela responded knowing Paula will want to catch up after her trip.

"Good, then let us know when and where. I'll clean up my calendar," Karen said while moving to the coffee maker.

"I'm open. Just tell me whenever and I'm there." Margo added.

"I'll call you two as soon as I confirm with Paula." Angela smirked, as she knew not to be totally upfront with Paula about Karen being there.

The three ladies settled and tired feelings overwhelmed them. Margo moved sitting closer to sleeping Cedric in the den. Karen walked to the dazed Phillip and encouraged him to relocate upstairs for bed. Angela took the path right to the guest room for a nap. She fell into the lovely bed, like a princess. The five ended up sleeping the rest of Sunday morning.

# Chapter 9

Thursday arrived and like clockwork, Angela anticipated Paula's call. As the working professional, she carried her routine. Periodically during the day, she recalled her weekend experience and what she'd learned. "If I knew things were this way, I'd have enjoyed Mark when I had the chance, and not listened to Paula." Bewildered while writing a memo to herself, she multi-tasked in thought. "Why did I reject him when all he'd shown was pure gentleman activities? I'm so silly. Imagine, having a guy who'd actually listen to me, engaged in my mind as well as enjoying me, and without me giving an effort to impress. How lovely is that? Look at what I closed the door to; Christopher a self-indulged person, Eric a self-entertained guy – nice, but no effort towards me, and Bill, a total ass. All because I wanted to be accepted by my friend and the general public who could care less about what I'm doing. Wow, amazing realization." Angela paused in her thought to answer the desk phone. In an instant, her mind evolved strictly to business as her day continued. Lunch passed and no call from Paula. With nervous twitching,   Angela pondered on the potential conversation with Paula. Angela anticipated losing her best friend in the world by introducing Karen during tomorrow night's dinner. "It's a rock and a hard place." she thought as every moment alluded to a minute closer to Paula's return. "Maybe I can build Karen up. It's not like she doesn't know of her being Margo's friend, and she met Margo at the Garden Ridge. I'll tell Margo and Karen tomorrow night isn't good and the following week is better. This will give me time to sell Karen to Paula and maybe she'll accept her. It might work. I don't want to lose my best friend, but I like the doors opening to me now."

Paula arrived late in the afternoon. The trip went so well and she couldn't believe how much fun she had on the island.

She and Ron did so much sightseeing, relaxing, fishing, drinking, dancing, and shopping all over the place. They spent time on secluded beaches, watched the sun rise and set, and would stroll the beach, sending them back to their younger years; dating for the first time. It was an amazing experience even though the locals would beg or push their goods on the tourist. Once the four got the hang of it, they realized how to avoid confrontation from the locals. Bill, especially, had to adjust to the local crowds. He couldn't believe how underdeveloped the country seemed, seeing how gorgeous the resorts were. He didn't speak much to the local people, other than the hired help, and most times he managed to limit his interaction with them, unless it was someone from England or the UK who worked at the resort. If he really wanted something, or had an interest in exploring, he took the major tours with the largest number of Caucasian people in a group. Or he had his girlfriend Amy set things up for them so again he'd limit his interactions. Confident in his Atlanta surroundings, he felt insecure outside of them, even though Paula and Ron reinforced no one cared about him personally. Paula and Ron got to a point of ignoring his concerns and just went for the fun. They actually left Bill and Amy a couple times when Bill hemmed and hawed about going out in public. It became a challenge for the four, yet Bill figured he'd be ok at the resort. On a couple occasions, Amy left Bill back at the resort to go shopping. She didn't realize the depth of his concern until a week into the vacation. Yet she understood and did everything in her power to make it comfortable for him. Paula was glad the trip with him was over and actually took the MARTA north to the North Springs station. She called Angela just as they boarded the North Springs train. "Hey, girl, we're back." Paula told Angela.

"How was it?"

"It was awesome. Can you do us a favor and pick Ron and me up at the North Springs MARTA station?"

"Sure. No problem. What happened to your car? Didn't it start or is the battery dead?"

"We drove with Bill on the way down. He and Amy are driving from the airport. Ron and I got enough of the nonsense and decided to take the city train. We'll be there in forty-five minutes."

"I'll be waiting."

"Thanks and I can't wait to tell you about Jamaica."

"All ears." Angela snapped the cellular and finished the last email. "I wonder what happened so badly they didn't want to ride with Bill. Maybe she'll be open to Karen after all." Angela thought as she knew Karen joining the social circle would be challenging with Paula. Yet, she still didn't want to lose her best friend. The two were inseparable in and after college, as the only times they weren't together is when Paula married Ron. The relationship took on a new dimension; however, it still didn't break or diminish. "If I can do it, so can she," Angela thought as she gathered her things ending the work day. "There's got to be a way, there just has to."

Paula and Ron walked out to the kiss and drive lane of the city train station. Angela flashed her lights and got out of the car to open its trunk. "Hey," Angela spoke as the two walked closer.

"It's so nice seeing you," Paula smiled and hugged Angela.

"Nice seeing you too." Angela responded with smile and said, "You surely got some sun. How was it?"

"It was great." Paula said while holding her arms for viewing. "Ron burned about day three and before you knew it, he started tanning like crazy. It's the first time I've seen him so dark. I tease him as if he had an ancestor in the woodpile."

"No, I've told you. I doubt it very much," Ron responded, but irritated with Paula's teasing, then addressed Angela, "Hey, Angela," but stopped her from hugging him due to the sunburn.

"You really got burned."

"I tanned, but it hurts some."

"What happened there? Was it fun?" Angela asked. "I'll hear what Paula thinks, but I want to hear your side too."

"It was nice, very nice and interesting. I'd return for sure."

"You liked the people, didn't you?" Angela asked as in testing the water for Karen's introduction to Paula later tomorrow night or next week. They all entered the car and drove off.

"The people were actually nice. You had to get around them being third world. Other than that, it was an awesome place. And the scenery was really good. Just plain beautiful."

"Would you recommend it to someone else?"

"Without hesitation; just make a mind of who's going with you. I didn't believe it then, but now I honestly believe the saying – 'be careful who you travel with'. It makes a world of difference."

"Sounds pretty harsh." Angela answered she changed lanes on GA 400.

"Harsh it was," Ron explained.

"Amy was fun though," Paula added. "She and I talked a lot and found we three have so much in common."

"Funny you mention someone else. I met Margo's friend Karen and we had a great time. You'd enjoy them." Angela presented as she thought, "That was an easy introduction".

"I'm glad you had a wonderful time. We should all get together on a girls' night out."

"I told them we would," Angela admitted "but not this weekend, since it's your first weekend home from traveling."

"That was kind of you. I invited Amy to come with us the next time. You'll enjoy her."

"I hope so." Angela crossed her fingers, "I truly hope she likes Karen too."

The three arrived at Paula and Ron's home. They unpacked the car and headed into the house. Ron checked for any sign of intruders or robbery and walked into every room. Paula moved into the kitchen and asked, "Angela, are you staying for awhile?"

"I can. I'd love hearing more of what you guys did there."

"Would you like a drink?" Paula poured two glasses of whiskey after Angela's reply.

"Well, if it's alcohol, I only want wine, if not how about ice tea?" Angela's request startled Paula as she knew Angela would drink whiskey. She recalled Angela only drinking wine during dinner and at restaurants. "I don't have ice tea or a cold bottle of wine. I have whiskey and coke." Paula pushed as she poured the coke for the mixer.

"No thanks, it's too much to burn off," Angela admitted, as her first thought was to her weight and how last weekend she'd gotten off her routine.

"You can come in and get a bottle of water whenever. You know where everything is, so make yourself at home. Nothing's changed." Paula left the drinks on the counter and went into the bedroom with a suitcase. Ron pulled clothes out of the suitcase and put a few in the hamper deciding which others should go to the cleaners. "You are not going to believe this, but Angela stopped drinking." Paula shared her assumption with Ron.

"She has a good idea Paula. I think we may need to cut back ourselves. Did you see how much we put away in the last two weeks?" Ron replied and pointed out the room invoice on the bed.
"We put a lot of alcohol away, and I don't think we've ever drank so much in two weeks."

"We were on vacation and it was four of us. Don't you remember we ordered for other people too and let the trip pay for them?"

"Yes, I do and still, when you deduct the amount we ordered for others, it comes up to more than we drink in three months."

"I made you a drink in the kitchen." Paula grabbed her camera and returned to the living room. She stopped in the kitchen along the way for her whisky and coke. She sat next to Angela, who retrieved a bottle of water earlier. "Here, check these out." Paula pointed to her digital camera. She snapped it in a displayer and turned on the television. Immediately the camera displayed pictures of Jamaica. Both

Angela and Paula sat watching the automatic slide show of all the pictures. Paula explained certain pictures as they came up. She pointed out Amy in a few pictures when Ron entered the room. "She was a lot of fun," Ron added to Paula's explanation.

"I'm glad you guys enjoyed her," Angela commented as supporting their new friendship.

"Not quite as much fun as if you'd gone but I don't think much would have changed if you were there."

"You're referring to Bill's attitude."

"Yes, he surely was a pain in the rear. And Amy did everything in her power to make it less noticeable," Ron explained while Paula nodded in agreement.

"He surely didn't make the trip pleasant. I never thought he'd be afraid, or try to be so superior to those people." Paula nearly became angry at the thought of Bill.

"I wondered how he would survive going to a dark island," Angela said.

"You travel with a guy for a few days and think he'll be fine in any environment. I didn't know it was going to be so challenging. If I'd known, we would have gone alone," Ron admitted to his poor judgment.

"You didn't know and it's hard judging people by color." Angela added.

"What does color add to this?" asked Paula.

"I thought only people of color would act so horrible. Isn't it what you normally preach Paula?"

"No, not at all. I preach they should stay in their world and we stay in ours. I mean in our social circle. It's ok to know people from a distance, but not up close and personal."

"I see your view," Angela responded but thought, "it's going to be hard introducing Karen to her. I'll have to think of another point to make her open up or change her idea."

"I had such a great time. Look at me walking up Dunn River Falls," Ron pointed. "It was such an experience."

"If you had to do it again, what would you change; besides going with Bill and Amy?"

"I think just being with my wife is what I'd change," Ron answered and pulled Paula close in a hug.

"Ok, that's my signal to leave," Angela stood, grabbed her purse, and walked towards the door.

"Are you going out tomorrow night?" asked Paula.

"I think you can answer that one. I'm available, but let me know what you decide."

"I'll call you in the morning," Paula said while following Angela to the front door. "Thanks for the ride. I know I can always count on you."

"What are friends for?"

"Friends are people you can count on. Next time you should come with us on our vacation. We've always enjoyed you. Just find a partner soon, will you?"

"Sure, I enjoy you guys too, but I'll be fine with or without the partner. I'm learning so much these days."

"Oh?"

"We can talk about it later. I want to get to the gym. Relax and enjoy being home, we can talk tomorrow."

"Have a great workout and thanks again," Paula waved as Angela drove away.

Paula and Angela didn't talk for the next three days. Angela spoke to Margo, went shopping with Karen, and had brunch on Sunday with both of them. They chattered like schoolgirls on subjects from guys to travel. Angela told Margo and Karen of Paula's horrible trip traveling with the wrong people. She explained Bill's attitude about people of color and worried how in the world would he think of enjoying Jamaica? They laughed and joked at the idea of Bill being around so many people of color for nearly an hour. It wasn't until Margo said something really serious forcing them to stop laughing so hard. Margo asked Angela, "Are you planning to go away with them in the future?" Angela paused before answering as to understand Margo's question. "Are you insinuating I accept Bill's beliefs?"

"No, I want you to take a camera and record every event so we can make a comedy documentary." Margo laughed again. "I know you don't think as he or they do for that matter."

"I thought you were serious."

"Of course not. I just can't believe this guy being from Georgia with such attitudes and beliefs going to Jamaica for two weeks. What the hell was he thinking?"

"You know, there are so many people like him in the United States holding on to so many crazy beliefs." Karen added. "Those ideas and beliefs keep them so far away from the truth that it's sickening. Serves Bill's ass right."

"I think you would know more about it than Margo and I," Angela highlighted.

"Actually you're wrong," Margo added to the discussion. "It's out in the open and all we have to do is open our eyes. People show us all the time what they believe and some don't even hide it very well."

"I can see your point. But when does a person recognize it?"

"It becomes evident in a number of ways. Looks for instance, people will look at others in a certain way as in disbelief if they show opposite of what's taught. They end up staring and making those faces."

"Don't forget mumbling under their breaths too," Karen explained. "It's as if people want to tell you something and then aren't brave enough to really say it loud enough for others to hear it. It's the funniest thing."

"And then there are the confronters; people who say something sly while you're in the bathroom or away from a crowd. They try to either warn you or blast you as in being shameful or curse you for taking away something they never owned." Margo commented as she shared her experience dating people of different nationalities.

"Wow. I never knew," Angela surprisingly admitted.

"You knew, but it had no impact on you so it's normal for people not to pay attention. And I can prove a point, if you play along with me."

223

"Don't do it Angela, she'll trick you into admitting you peed in your underwear," Karen laughed.

"No I won't," Margo swore. "Have you ever found yourself interested in someone and never thought about dating him?"

Angela hesitated to answer while the first person came in mind was Mark. She didn't want to admit being attracted to Mark to Margo or Karen at the moment. "Yes, but it wasn't from race."

"It doesn't have to be race. It can be for any reason. What made you realize he was interesting but not enough to date?"

"The guy was nice, but man was he unattractive."

"I agree. You can't go out with a butt ugly guy. How would your kids look?" Karen giggled.

"Yea, it's bad," Margo added but continued, "See you support my point. You worried what others said about his appearance and didn't allow yourself to find out what kind of guy he was."

"He was butt ugly. Why go further?" Karen interjected. "I'm with you Angela on this one, it doesn't matter the race if a man is butt ugly, you run."

"Karen, stop kidding. I'm making a point," Margo sighed. "Come on, you get my point, Angela. I'm sharing this from my experience."

"And mine, too," Karen added. "Yes I've dated across racial lines. And when I saw people for people, Phillip walked into my life."

"Just as Cedric came into mine, but listen you have to be honest with yourself and not let others dictate who or what you should have as a partner."

Angela didn't respond but pondered on Margo's and Karen's explanation. "It's nice they felt comfortable enough sharing such insight," then responded, "I'm surprised at you both. I'd never known you were so open to dating different people." Margo exclaimed, "People bring different things to the table, even in one race, as you very well know."

"I know this for a fact. There were differences in Bill, Eric, and the asshole Christopher."

"Exactly, and people of color just add to the multiple flavors. Even though you find assholes in all of them, one way or another, and one is no greater than the other, but it depends on the man and his social upbringing." Karen added as she further explained, "A man in England is not quite like the man in Australia, even though their cultures are similar, the attitudes towards women are different. Like African Americans and Ethiopians or South Africans, their attitudes towards women are different. It's a social explanation and behavior development."

"So, you're telling me to be open and get away from the stereotypes, and follow my gut feeling on men."

"Yes," Margo and Karen answered in unison.

"I get it. And to be honest with you two, I have a guy in mind but I'm not sure he's interested in me anymore."

"Where did you meet him?"

"At the Barnes and Noble on North Point," Angela answered as she recalled Mark's features. "He's a handsome man too; very intelligent, well mannered, nice and fun."

"Fun?" asked Margo. "How did you get all that from a conversation?"

"We did more than talk, we hung out once and it was fun. It was before I met you two."

"You didn't know?"

"Didn't know what?"

"You're a pro now, you've been exposed."

"No way, it was only once."

"But you were swept away in conversations, more than once and he charmed you. Now you're thinking more about him, aren't you?"

"Well," Angela paused while self admitting, "yes, I have been thinking more of him." Then answered, "Yes I have or guessing it's him I think of."

"There you go, doubting your mind because it's against what you've learned. Be yourself for a change, will you? Just close your mind and think of the things you like in a person.

Don't put a picture with it; just think of character and how you wish to be treated," Karen suggested.

Angela closed her eyes and thought as Karen directed. "I like charming, courteous, a conversationalist, intelligent, respectful, spontaneous, and well-manners. You know, a guy who has great table manners and can go out anywhere without a chance of embarrassment."

"Sounds wonderful. Who do you know like this?" asked Margo.

"I have an idea." Angela answered.

"Put the most important things in looks, besides hair color, from 1-10," Margo suggested.

"Great body, awesome smile, impeccable dress, gentle and manly, and a fantastic voice are what I choose."

"Did Phillip walk in?" asked Karen as she turned to view the restaurant patrons, and laughed.

"Or Cedric, for that matter?" Margo giggled.

"I get it. You two found your Mister Right without focusing on race and ethnicity."

"My gosh, I think she's growing!" Margo said while winking at Karen.

"The baby is graduating." Karen commented. "We aren't saying to go on a search mission to find a man of color. We're saying start looking for qualities of a person without focusing on everyone else. Focus on you."

"You know, I can. It makes perfectly good sense." Angela replied but knew, "Paula won't go for it and as soon as I go with a non-Caucasian she'll have a fit. She isn't my mother; heck, mom will have a fit too." Angela looked at her new friends and asked, "How did you two get beyond parental concerns?"

Margo jumped right to answer, "In the beginning it wasn't anything for me because I wasn't serious enough to introduce any guy I dated."

"It was hell for me. My father was so hard in the beginning, I told him to get out of the old century or I'm gone." Karen recalled in her mind the harsh conversation with her dad.

"He wanted to punish me and cut off his support for my tuition. I had to remind him of the way he raised me, to be open to all people, to be fair, and be a person of strong character. And then I told him I'll get a damn loan for school and go ahead and cut me off."

"I bet telling him was hard."

"No, mom was in my corner and we worked on him. From there forward, once mom put her foot down and reminded him love is blind, he accepted anyone I introduced. And did I start introducing everyone! One guy from Minneapolis impressed dad so much, he pushed to keep me in the relationship when I wanted to get out. It broke off, but to this day, I'm sure dad would have enjoyed having him in the family."

"See it's different for everyone Angela. Family will have an impact, but my suggestion is to find the person for you and not them." Margo insisted.

Thursday morning at the bookstore's coffee shop, Angela found herself being extra observant. As if she was looking for a special someone to appear. She grabbed her coffee from the attendant and walked into the bookstore, like many times before, in hopes of crossing Mark's path. She walked to the normal areas, looking at books and looking up for passersby. When she got to the seated area, her mind flashed to a time where she held so many conversations, enjoyed the companionship, and dazed at how people were reading and conversing as she had. No one seemed to catch her eye while strolling the store aisles. She walked around bargain sales, the teen section, and the periodicals like a lioness on the prowl. Walking to the parking lot, to continue her commute to work, Angela scanned for a familiar car, where luck just may open a door. Disappointed, she continued her day driving to the office.

Paula talked to Amy about Friday night. She explained how Angela would enjoy meeting her and how the two would hit it off. There were no questions to their common account of dating Bill. Even though Angela didn't care for him, Paula stressed the common core as Bill being a great catch for either of them. The conversation led to Paula giving advice on how to keep a man. She stressed keeping Bill in his environment or similar environments would help their relationship. She then pushed and applauded the idea of having a good man in Amy's life, just as she pushed on Angela. She said, "Even if there were disagreements in the relationship, there are things one can work through." But in general, Paula pushed Amy to forgive Bill's way with people and accept him on a different scale. Amy went right along with Paula's suggestion, informing Paula of their plans to move in together. Paula ended up pushing harder to meet Angela since she noticed how happy Amy was with Bill. She appreciated how someone agreed with her and believe it or not, couldn't wait to rub in her selection with Angela.

Friday morning came in like a lightning flash from a summer's thunderstorm. It caught Angela on edge, as she hadn't heard from Paula since driving her and Ron home. The morning routine at the coffee shop didn't bring the results her heart desired. She continued along her day pondering on the conversation with Margo and Karen, and without imagining things, she recalled having Mark's cellular phone number from a service bill. She and Mark talked by cell a few times before going out. "Should I call?" she asked as if there were someone in her office cubicle to answer, while searching for the month she and Mark spoke. Nothing jumped out at her, as a recognizable phone number nor did one seem different. She remembered calling him once or twice but pushed redial instead of saving the number. Her records indicated multiple calls to new numbers because she used her cell for business as well as pleasure. Something she didn't do today since having a company Blackberry. "Picking one number I called twice will take nearly a day of dialing, and what am I going to say when he answers?" Angela didn't think of what to do beyond finding Mark. Just the thought of him not being available, not here, nor interested, frustrated her to no end. Yet, Angela maintained focus for business in the cubicle and seemed to get through the morning without an emotional interruption. It was near the end of the day when Paula called. "Hey, are we on for tonight?" she asked.

"I hope we are. I need a drink to take the edge off." Angela told Paula with enthusiasm to hide the frustration.

"Great. I have a guest. So, we'll meet you at Bahama Breeze on North Point."

"The usual time?" asked Angela.

"Yes, the usual time."

"Who is your guest?"

"Amy, I'm bringing Amy. She's a nice girl and I want her to have a drink with us. Does she make you uncomfortable since she dates Bill?"

"No. I don't mind her dating Bill, so bring her. I'll invite a couple of my friends too."

"A couple of your friends, I thought I was the only one."

"Are you serious? You don't listen to me. Remember I told you about Margo and Karen?"

"Oh yes, those two; the cheap decorator and her counterpart."

"They are really nice people Paula. I didn't say anything bad about Amy."

"You can't because she has good taste in men. Bill is her guy now; don't push him in the picture."

"What on earth do you mean?"

"Look, invite your friends and I'll bring Amy. We'll just have drinks and chat, ok?"

"I'll call the ladies and since its short notice, I'm not sure either will come. But since you offered, I'll do my best to get them there."

Paula frowned while responding, "They are your friends, so get them there; friend!"

Angela paused while looking up Margo's cell number on her phone. "What a bitch Paula is." She thought. "I was going to wait and ease Karen into the picture. The bitch can take it as it is. She won't take it too well, and now I'd love to rub her face in it. I can't wait to tell Margo what I'm thinking." The phone rang as Angela waited to spill her version of tonight's happy hour. "Margo, it's me, Angela."

"Hi, Angela, what's up?"

"Tonight. Remember when I told you about every Friday night being girls' night out with Paula?"

"I remember but I thought she wanted to stay in until next weekend."

"Well, she's ready to meet you two. Can you get in touch with Karen and meet me at Bahama Breeze around 6 or 6:15?"

"I can make it, but I'm not sure about Karen. You know how busy she gets and there's no telling what plans she and Phillip have."

"I know," Angela paused for silence thinking on this order, "Just call her and I'll keep my fingers crossed."

"Why so important for tonight?" Margo sensed hostility in Angela's voice.

"To be honest, Paula the bitch is finished. I'm finishing her off tonight and I'd love you two to be there."

"I'll call her and get back to you." Margo ended her call and sent a text to Karen and waited for a return call. It's Margo's way to reach Karen without interrupting business. It was an agreement the two ladies had, recalling earlier times when the cell phone rang a hundred times a day; especially from a friend. They decided the best way to chat was to text and then follow up with a call. Margo followed the agreement to a tee. "Do you have plans tonight?" asked Margo.

"Not really. I was going to find a good book to cuddle with. What's on your mind?"

"Having a girls' night out with Angela; she and her friend Paula are meeting at Bahama Breeze on North Point around 6:00 pm. Do you think you can make it?"

"I'm there. I need a girls' night because things this week were so dang hectic, but not at 6:00. I'll be there by 7:00 to 7:15."

"That's fine, I'll be there waiting for you. I'll call Angela and let her know." Margo ended the call with Karen and texted Angela with, *we'll be there. Karen will arrive a little later but I'll be there at 6:00.*

Angela smiled after reading her text. The idea of Margo and Karen attending made it easy and exciting to show Paula her life changes. And the idea of Karen coming later than everyone agreed made it better as a surprise visitor. "I'm mean, aren't I?" Angela thought as she imagined the look on Paula's face when Karen arrived. "It's time to show her she's idiotic for believing such crap. I fell for it with her years ago but now, it's so different. I feel alive, as there is so much to living and so many gifts to enjoy. I can't wait for 6:00 to get here."

The workday ended just as quickly as it began. Angela drove directly to the strip mall on the way to Bahama Breeze where everyone was meeting. She walked the strip mall while window-shopping. She walked into the Crate and Barrel store, wasting time and not particularly looking for anything. Wandering though the goods, she observed a furniture piece grabbing her interest. While approaching the piece, she noticed a shadow of a person just left of the building pillar. Not a clear shot or vision to the person, Angela moved for a better look. "Is it him?" Angela pondered. "It would be nice if I ran into him." She moved around to capture a better view. From behind, the guy looked similar to Mark. Angela moved quickly for a different angle, and observed the gentleman talking to a lady in the store. Still curious, to make sure it was him; she walked up to question a nearby sales person. Angela got the full view of his face, realized it wasn't Mark, and moved away from the salesperson without a word. Disappointed, she left the store and decided to head to Bahama Breeze and reserve a large table. Her drive to the restaurant was only a few blocks away. Angela walked into Bahama Breeze and explained her seating desires to the hostess. Angela sat at the bar waiting for the table and ordered a drink. "Why not, it's what we'll do when the others arrive," she thought, while watching the bartender prepare her glass of wine.

"Will this be all?" asked the Bartender.

"Yes for now. How much do I owe you?" Angela asked.

"Are you waiting for a table?"

"Yes I am."

"I can give this charge to your waiter or waitress and add it to your check."

"We can do that. Thank you." Angela smiled and turned towards the door, observing who entered. From behind her she heard a voice she recognized as someone she either dated or met. "Hi, Angela," Christopher greeted her. Turning around, and with a smirk of disappointment, she replied, "Hi."

"Funny seeing you here," Chris commented.

"I'm meeting some friends and hopefully they'll show in a few minutes," Angela responded while looking at her watch.

"How's life been these days?"

"Interesting, I find this can be a great place depending on the people in your social circle."

"It's always the case, everywhere."

"Maybe, but it also depends on what you define as good people too. It's all in the definition."

"You're probably right. Who are you dating now?"

"Why do you ask?"

"I wanted to know, as I'm pretty free these days. What are you doing later tonight?"

Angela turned to Chris and gave him a dirty, downright disgusting look as she recalled him being the asshole of the earth before responding, "No way in hell will I ever go anywhere with you."

"Why are you angry? We had a great time. Face it, you weren't interested in me and I did what any good-looking guy would do. It was your choice and now I'm offering a second chance."

"This conversation is over."

"It's not over, until you realize how men have the upper hand on women."

"What an asshole?" Angela said louder, "Go away Chris."

"I'll leave." Chris walked to the other side of the bar.

"Everything ok?" asked a gentleman with a sensual voice. A voice she truly recognized and immediately sparked images of multiple conversations. "No, it isn't him; I made the same mistake earlier," Angela thought before turning to answer. "I'm fine." When her eye fell upon the person she realized her fluttered feeling was correct. Mark stood next to her with his strong presence, smelling great, looking very clean and well put together. "I'm glad you're fine," Mark replied with a smile

"I am," Angela smiled in reply and silence fell because her desire to talk more and what to say both flustered her into a ball of nerves.

"If you need me for anything I'll be over there. Just yell or wave," Mark offered.

"Uh hm," answered Angela, "Why can't I respond, damn it." she thought, watching Mark walk away. Minutes passed as the number of bar patrons increased. Conversations were blaring and still Angela didn't make her move to talk to Mark. She finally got up the nerve to speak and Paula arrived. "Hey, girl!" Paula said.

"Hey," Angela sighed.

"You don't seem happy to see me."

"It's not you. I was thinking of doing something," Angela replied while she looked at Mark.

"Is he bothering you?" Paula asked.

"No, not at all."

"Good. Is this where we'll sit?" Paula pointed at the bar stool as Amy looked on without saying a word.

"Hi, Angela," Amy finally spoke.

"Hi Amy, right?"

"Where are my manners?" Paula turned and made introductions. "Did you reserve a table?" Paula asked while the buzzer went off.

"Good timing," Angela turned to the bartender and asked to take the check to the waiter.

"It's settled," the bartender explained.

"Who paid for it?" Angela asked.

"The gentleman standing there," he pointed.

"Thanks. I'll send him a note. Do you have a pen?"

"Sorry, I don't have one at the moment. When a waitress comes, she can let you borrow hers."

"Paula, why don't you get the table? I'll be right there."

Paula looked around the vicinity and where Angela was heading. "Be careful," she said, as if the group of guys would assault her in a public restaurant. Angela waved at Paula as if saying, "Mind your business." Amy followed Paula like a shadow, and in silence they tailed the hostess to a large table for six. Angela approached Mark with a smile, reached to touch his arm saying, "Thank you."

"You're welcome. I'm glad you're smiling now. I hope you have a great night and one day we'll catch up at the bookstore."

"I'd like to," Angela replied and asked, "Why don't you give me your cell number again? I lost it."

"Here, take my card. Call me and we'll get together, whenever you're ready." Mark passed the card and winked as if it were a pass for affection.

"Thanks and thanks again for the drink. I have to get to my girls."

"Have fun." Mark smiled, watching her return. "Wow, she is fine as ever," he thought as the group of guys surrounding him watched in agreement. Happy with her action, Angela now had a subtle bounce in her step to the table. "Who was he?" asked Paula as she approached the table.

"A kind man who bought my drink," Angela replied.

"You better be careful of guys who do want something in return."

"I actually hope so this time." Angela smiled.

"You have to be kidding, right?"

"No, I'm not." Angela frowned as if she can't believe how Paula was trying so hard to push her beliefs again.

"Some people are just nice. Doesn't matter where they're from or how they look." Amy added to ease the tension she felt between Angela and Paula

"Yes, they are." Angela agreed. "How was Jamaica, Amy?"

"I had fun. I enjoyed it and the island was beautiful."

"I told you we had a good time," Paula added.

"From your view Paula, maybe Amy has a different take on it."

"I enjoyed it, especially the shopping. I spent a little too much, but came home with a few nice things. It was my first time outside of the United States, and people were so different. They live with different values."

"I agree," Paula added to the conversation "We live with different values here too."

"You know those values are relevant to the surroundings." Angela opened as a point she was trying to make.

"Their surroundings weren't the same as being in the States."

"No," Amy confirmed. "It was like a third world country in some places and really nice in others. What extremes within a block of each other."

"I gather you had an eye opening experience on your visit, Amy," Angela said.

The waitress appeared for their drink and hor d'ouerves order. The three ladies ordered one glass of wine and two Margaritas, then decided not to order any food until Margo and Karen arrived. The waitress left as Margo arrived and greeted everyone, "Hello, ladies."

"You missed the waitress. I'll catch her." Angela moved.

"Hi Paula, nice seeing you again," Margo said while taking a seat next to Angela's spot.

"This is Amy," Paula introduced her to Margo.

"Nice meeting you Amy. I heard about your trip to Jamaica. Isn't it a grand island?"

"It is, and lots of fun and sun."

"How long did you stay?" Margo asked.

"Two weeks," Paula and Amy answered in unison. "I wouldn't stay so long the next time," Amy admitted the length being a little long.

"I can understand as it's a long time to be a tourist."

"Right, two weeks is harsh and it depends on the people you're with. No offense intended, Amy." Paula commented.

"No offense taken. I know who you're talking about."

"I think whomever you travel with, it's an experience." Margo tried to settle the conversation, as she hadn't heard the entire explanation to their comments. Angela returned with the waitress. Margo ordered her drink and announced Karen wouldn't be there for a while. The four broke into a general conversation about traveling abroad, people they saw in third world countries and experiences they shared in common. Shopping was the main subject and finding those great deals. Paula made a comment about meeting Margo in the Garden Ridge. "Your friend Karen must be really frugal with her decorating. I saw you two in Garden Ridge buying accessories, and I thought for sure she could have expanded a few dollars more."

"You don't think Garden Ridge has nice items?"

"Nice but inexpensive and I think unprofessional."

"You shouldn't go there, Paula," Angela suggested.

"I'll let her tell Karen about her cheap purchases when she arrives. But let me tell you, Karen is a dynamic decorator and knows her business. She works wonders with those inexpensive items and of course she's a hoot too. She loves to laugh, knows how to treat people, and pretty savvy. If I had her brains, I'd do exactly as she does. Did Angela tell you about her dinner party?"

"No," Paula turned to Angela. "You didn't tell me about the party weekend."

"Haven't had the chance, we haven't talked - besides you wouldn't be interested in it. Trust me."

"Why would you say such a thing?" asked Paula. "How was it?"

"It was awesome," Margo answered. "Angela and Karen cooked and the meal was exquisite. They really did a great job. The people were fun, the place was fantastic, and Karen can really host a party."

"What kind of people were there?" Amy's curiosity opened the door so Angela could explain who she met.

"Let's see, there were some very wealthy people there, a gay couple, world travelers, and all types of ethnic groups. There were Margo and Cedric, Karen and her guy Phillip, some business friends and their neighbors."

"Where was it?" Paula first thought it was at a rental location.

"We had dinner at Karen's home in the Country Club of the South."

"Those are some expensive homes. Are you saying Karen is rich?"

"I'm not saying she's rich, but she and Phillip do pretty well together."

"So, her business in decorating makes that kind of money? I bet she is smart for buying things cheaper but why wouldn't she purchase from a wholesaler vice a retailer?" asked Amy.

"She knows her business, trust me," Angela added.

"I can't wait to meet her, she sounds very intelligent and a lot of fun."

"Do you think Bill will like her?" Paula asked Amy.

"If she's from Georgia and doesn't go anywhere he's uncomfortable, he'll like anyone," Amy answered.

"He won't like Karen," Angela said.

"Karen is liked by everyone," Margo defended her friend. "Why would you say something like that? Oh right, I forgot."

"You remember why," Angela suggested changing the subject, and asked Margo, "Remember that guy I told you about. The one I had in mind?"

"What guy?" Paula asked.

"There's this guy who is witty, looks great, has a great conversation, and is totally awesome. We went out once and I didn't notice his qualities then."

237

"You mean Christopher? Sounds just like him," Paula guessed.

"Not that asshole," Margo said, "No way."

"No, not Christopher nor Eric, it's someone earlier."

"I can't remember someone you went out with earlier than Bill, oh my goodness you still have it for Bill. How could you?"

"You dated Bill?" asked Amy.

"It was a blind date and the only date. I never called him again or wanted to go out with him. I'm sure he's for you, Amy."

"Ok, it didn't work out. I'm glad, because I'd never gone to Jamaica if it had." Amy said acknowledging how it didn't matter to her Angela once went out with Bill.

"Then who is it?" asked Paula.
Angela spoke, "It's …" just as Karen approached the table "Hi, folks".

"Hi!" Margo said. "Pull up a chair. You can sit here between Angela and me."

"Glad you could make it," Angela smiled at Karen. Paula and Amy sat in shock as if they'd seen a ghost. "Oh, let me introduce you to Karen," Angela pointed to Paula and Amy. Karen reached to shake hands and Amy accepted but Paula stood. "You didn't tell me she was black!"
Karen looked at her hand and smiled, "Isn't it lovely?"

"What's wrong with you?" asked Amy. "You were in Jamaica for two weeks and it didn't bother you there. Why does it bother you here?"

"Shut up. I'm leaving." Paula grabbed her purse and headed out. "Are you coming?" she asked Amy. "Angela, you're a traitor. I don't know what happened to you!"

"Bitch!" Angela shouted in disgust and with a tear she added, "Lose my number. I'm so tired of your prejudice crap and I was so stupid to try and please you. And for what? A selfish friendship and be partial to the 'in' crowd. What the hell was I thinking when the world is so much greater than you and your kind? How appalling you are, and I now realize the size of your mind. Here is a woman of color who does more with her life than we can ever imagine and you think she's below you? What a stupid little person you've become. Leave and forget me as your friend!"

"You are just an ass."

Margo stood next to Karen as in a defensive stance preparing for that word of degradation. "Go ahead and say it," Margo challenged Paula, "Give me a reason."

"Come on Amy."

"Can one of you girls give me a ride?" Amy asked.

"Sure, I don't mind," Angela answered.

"I'm staying," Amy told Paula. "I may go along with it, but I don't believe it as I don't judge people the same way. I forgive those who do, but I'm not on board believing the crap and I need to clean up my act by standing up for what's right. Sorry, you're alone in this one."

Paula stormed out of the restaurant in disgust. She left in a hurry to return to her world of segregation. Angela sat with mixed feelings. She was happy it was over with Paula, but sad it ended this way. The girls sat in silence for a few minutes when a round of drinks arrived at the table. The waitress placed the drinks on the table and said, "It's from a gentleman from the bar."

"Which gentleman if I may ask?"

"The guy raising his drink."

"Well son of a bitch, it's Mark," Margo pointed as she moved to the bar.

"Hold your horses, missy," Karen said. "Remember you're with Cedric."

"He and I know this. I want to introduce him to Angela. Angela, this is the guy I was talking about."

"Are you kidding?" Angela responded with a smile. "He's the guy I was keeping secret as the one I'd like to date. We went out once and he's who I described the other day."

"Small world, huh?" Amy added.

"Interesting world," Karen laughed. "Go get him, Margo. If he comes, we'll say thanks. I don't think we all should go to the bar. It would scare the daylights out of him," she laughed.

"I agree," Amy said and added, "but it might make his day." The girls laughed as they watched Margo head to the bar. They observed Margo talk to Mark and pointed at the table as in directing him to come over. Margo returned with a huge smile, followed by two guys, one of them Mark. "Here's Angela, Amy, and Karen," Margo introduced to Mark.

"Nice seeing you again Angela and Karen, it's been a long time," Mark replied. "Nice meeting you, Amy." he ended.

"I didn't think you'd remember me, Mark," Karen said, "It's been a while since school."

"Yes it has. But I keep up with your business effort as I knew you'd be the one making it."

"I can't believe you went out with Angela," Margo jumped to make a point.

"It wasn't a date; it was just going out and sharing an experience together. Oh this is Henry, ladies."

"Hi, how are you lovely ladies tonight?" asked Henry.

"Nice meeting you. We're fine now and thanks for the drinks," Amy answered.

"You're welcome," Henry responded and stood by Mark.

"Don't let us stop you from your lady's night out. Henry and I have plans for the evening. Margo it was nice seeing you again. Angela, you have my card, give me a call sometime." Mark and Henry left the table for the door."

"Thanks again," the ladies shouted as they left.

"You better call him Angela," Margo instructed, "he's a great guy and I'll vouch for him."

"Oh really, how well can you vouch?" Angela asked.

"Pretty well, she dated him before meeting Cedric. But it didn't get as close as you think."

"You mean she didn't sleep with him," Amy commented.

"You'll have to ask Margo if she did. I haven't an idea." Karen admitted not knowing the answer.

"I'll never kiss and tell," Margo laughed. "Take it this way, he is truly a gentleman and if he had been ready to be deeply involved back then, he'd be with me."

"You don't think he's ready to settle down?" asked Angela.

"It was years ago, Angela. I don't know anymore. Do not make your decision on me, he's a catch. You're interested in him anyway and if I were you, I'd not let his past stop you," Margo explained.

"I don't think it will, I really don't think it will. Who's drinking the extra Margarita?"

# Chapter 10

Mark left Bahama Breeze ecstatic after meeting Angela and
Margo. Still unsure about the new friendship between the
two ladies, he questioned Margo's push for Angela to meet
him. "Man that cannot be good?" Mark thought as he moved
to his car. His companion, Henry - an old friend, admitted a
girlfriend will push a guy on another girlfriend and it's quite
common; especially if there's true friendship between them.
"Just think of this," he explained, "she's building you up by
telling her a few of those fun moments you shared together.
It's not bad, it's a good thing."

"What about the pressure of maintaining the same level? I
was such a jerk with Margo. We'd be together today if I
hadn't been so afraid of commitment."

"Evidently, Margo isn't worried about it. You had good
times with her and why sweat it if she's a friend of Angela's.
She's not going to push a bad person on a friend. So you're
in good standing partner."

"I see your point," Mark acknowledged. "How about I get
her out tomorrow? You know what they say - get'em while
they're hot."

"Didn't you try before and she pushed you back?"

"I told you our story?"

"Yes, you did. How would you call her anyway? You
didn't get her number."

"I saved it from months ago." Mark paused and considered
his action and desired to call. It was Mark who enjoyed the
chance meetings, those sneak peaks at Kroger, deliberately
parking next to her at the bookstore, or seeing her at his
townhouse complex. As a guy who never gives up for an
awesome girl, he recalled the very reason Angela stayed on
his mind and motivated him to keep hope burning. "I better
let her call me. I've waited this long, another day or so will
not hurt, and I don't want to scare her off again."

"You've got it in the bag, don't worry about it. She'll call, trust me."

Saturday made its way as Angela followed her routine after a rough Friday night. The girls ended up drinking way too much, especially after the drama with Paula.
"Amy ended up being a nice girl, even though she's dating Bill. Karen and Margo were just as silly as ever, what a couple those two make. They feed off of each other's jokes and comments." Angela pondered while running on the treadmill. "I think I'll call Mark today. Maybe tomorrow, as I don't want to seem overly anxious and I want to call him. It's not like I hadn't called him in the past. He's such a nice guy, and I know we should have kept going from the beginning. But no, I had to listen to Paula. Thank goodness she's on her way out. She won't call me for days, or if she calls at all." Angela continued her run trying for a great workout, really sweating to get those bad calories out of her body. "I still can't believe I let so many people influence me. Here I am, enjoying life and it could have been better or like this long ago? If I had been open back in college, life would be different. I could have met some good people back then, and had fun at social functions, instead of working at the library.   I wonder what types of guys could have come in my life." Thoughts of her past ran with times, places, people, and events, to a point where she finally understood why she didn't.

Angela continued her workout, going strong, and in between machines, she took greater notice to men, all types, as Margo influenced when they worked out together. This time Angela took a full look at every guy. Unlike before, she noticed every man of color, their looks and features, the multiple complexions - all were so vivid to her now. She noticed how each carried himself, so differently and yet they were so similar. Not to say they were different from Caucasian men to a distinctive point, but different in the way they displayed confidence and individuality. She also noticed how they communicated with each other, even in passing, like having a natural bond. Angela recalled going out with Mark to Club 290 and how everyone spoke to each other in that environment. She realized now, those people didn't know each other, but were courteous, as if they'd known one another for years.

Nearly completing her workout, Angela figured it was time to contact Mark. "The sooner the better," she thought, "time is of the essence and now is a great time." At the end of her workout, she ensured her day became a first step to Mark. She wanted to reach out to Mark after cooking class, which she eagerly attended. Her inattention to the time caused a schedule lapse. Rushing to get changed, she zipped to the locker room for a quick shower and dressed. She rushed to her cooking class. Her thoughts were not exactly gathered and she didn't speak to Eric during class. Yet every empty moment not focusing on class was spent on what to say to Mark. "Shall I open with an invitation, apologize for being so harsh when he was just being a gentleman, or ask him about his last read?" Angela mulled it over as she continued thinking of Mark in between cooking a new dish. "I can invite him over. No, an invitation may be too forward and send the wrong signal. How about calling him and letting him decide? No, calling might be too much of a chance. Or, maybe not, as I don't think he'll reject me. He was too nice yesterday, unless he has someone in his life. Damn, I may have missed the opportunity. He didn't say so yesterday to Margo, so …." Angela paused to check her dish… "he has to be available. He's got to be available. I'll call him before I start thinking and make sure he's available before moving on. Damn I hope he's available, I really hope he's available."

Mark looked at his watch while rising out of bed. Saturdays were just as important to his life as any other day, but particularly for a single guy, it was demanding. He dressed for chores. The normal vacuuming, cleaning, washing clothes, dusting, and creating a shopping list as most bachelors tend to do. He noticed the blinking message light on his cell phone while writing his list. "Did she call?" he excitedly thought before picking up the cell and dialing for voicemail. Just as the service connected, he disconnected the call. "What if she wants to go out tonight? What do I have going on?" he pondered. "It's not like I can't cancel. Or what if she decided to come here? Nah, it's not likely. What if she…" The cell rings for an incoming call.

"Hello," Mark answered, not recognizing the number.

"Hi, Mark." A familiar voice on the other end greeted him.

"Oh, hi," Mark responded with a little disappointment but happy it wasn't Angela.

"You better not mess over my girl," Margo said with vigor. Mark responded since he recognized the voice, "Come on Margo. You know I'm not the type to hurt your girl. Didn't you call earlier and left a message?"

"Yes, it's why I called again. It was important you knew my feelings, but it was better I told you. Angela's a sweetheart. When I first met her, and she said she wanted to meet a nice guy, I thought of you. I sure hope you two hit it off."

"I know she's truly a sweetheart. I didn't think she was open to me when I tried dating her earlier."

"She's open to you. Why wouldn't she be open to you?"

"Margo, we don't have to explain the why as you and I both know it takes a woman with strong convictions and self assurance to step out on something new."

"No, that's not it. She finally understands people so you better look out for her or…"

"You'll hurt me. Yes, I know." Mark laughed. "How's Cedric?"

"He's fine; he said hello and you guys should hang out in the future."

"Great, we should. I'm glad you two are making it. Tell him I'll be happy to hang out and hopefully the four of us can one day."

"I don't think we'll have a problem hanging out. He likes Angela too and you guys are ok with each other so, it's an idea in the making. You make sure you do nothing to discourage her."

"Don't worry. I actually tried getting to know her earlier, probably before she met you."

"Whatever. You get the message, right?" Margo reiterated in her serious tone.

"I get the message Margo, I get the message," Mark answered and ended the call.

Angela completed her class and ran to her car, with anxiety leading her to make the call. With the card Mark gave her, she dialed the cell number. Still nervous in what to say, she waited for an answer. "Hi, Mark, it's Angela," just as simple as that Angela thought while waiting for him to answer. His voicemail recording answered instead. "….please leave a message"… beep. Angela sighed in disappointment as the recorder began, "Mark, its Angela," she spoke and paused. Silence fell as she thought of something else to add "give me a call at…." beep, the voicemail ended without her leaving a number. "Oh crap. I can't believe I didn't leave my number." She redialed hoping for the voicemail. "Hello," this voice, so recognizable, strong but soft, melodic in tone, came across the speaker.

"Mark." Angela called.

"Yes. This is…" Mark responded in hope it was Angela but didn't want to seem overly anxious as it would be embarrassing if it weren't.

"It's Angela. How are you?"

"I'm glad you called," Mark admitted, "I'm fine. I hope you are too."

"I am. I'm calling to catch up, or maybe just chat. I mean, I'd love seeing you soon."

"I'm thinking the same. I wouldn't mind seeing you. As a matter of fact, I was on my way to the cleaners and we could meet someplace. Ah, if you aren't busy?"

"No, I just finished my cooking class. I'm pretty free. Where do you suggest we meet?" asked Angela as she crossed her fingers and thought, "Please don't say your place or mine…please don't ask."

"I know a place on Holcomb Bridge Road called Cafe Au Lait. It's in a small strip mall. If we can meet there in thirty minutes…?"

"There should work. Should I meet you inside or wait in the car?"

"Inside, of course, it's not like we don't know each other. I wouldn't want you sitting in the car. Waiting in a box isn't nice."

"I'll be there," Angela smiled in response.

"Great. I'll see you soon. I'll call if something happens."

"I'll do the same, talk to you soon." The two ended the call and headed to their destinies. Angela knew the café's vicinity, however she had never entered. Mark knew everything of this café, because he frequented it often enough. It became his leisure location since Angela rejected his advancement; he chose this location so it did not seem like he was applying pressure. Besides, it was convenient to them both. Mark recalled a message on his cellular and redialed voicemail. He listened and deleted it as quickly as he heard Margo's voice. "I took her call."

Angela, ecstatic and eager to see Mark, decided to pause and think why. Once more she realized Mark was exceptional and she didn't want to be overly excited. "Why do I want this so bad?" She pondered recalling the qualities she wanted in a man, the same checklist she told Karen and Margo. "Why am I hesitant?" she asked, "I was never hesitant before with a guy who seemed to have those qualities. Why am I hesitating?" It was as if the question eluded her while she drove to meet Mark. Every other red light stopped Angela on the way. It seemed she'd be a few minutes late. She didn't want to call Mark and inform him, but called Margo instead. "Hi Margo, its happening I'm going to meet Mark."

"Great! I know you'll have a good time. Where are you going?" Margo inquired.

"A café he knows close by."

"I'm glad it's on neutral ground."

"I thought the same. It's like I know better than to be alone with him, yet it's like I want to be, so no one will dislike us."

"Aren't you jumping to conclusions on being with him?"

"What do you mean?"

"Are you so worried about being with him to the extent someone would care who you're with? If you are, then you'll have to learn to let go. Boy, Paula and crew did a job on you. Don't doubt yourself, just see him and enjoy the company. What happens when people look at you? They look at you. It's no different from you wearing an awesome dress or when you have a blemish on your face, they look. What do they do? They do nothing but look."

"I'm not worried about them looking; I worry about what I think of them looking. I realize this is the first time I've really cared, because I like him."

"Then, you'll have to get used to people looking and it's just they are looking. But remember, we don't live our lives for them, we live for ourselves. Now have a great time and go talk to him. Let him know what's on your mind." Margo waited for her reply and thought, "It's a good thing I called Mark. She has challenges waiting." Finally Angela replied, "I will Margo, I will."

"Good. Call me when it's over, ok?" Margo instructed.

"I'll ring you. Talk to you later, bye." Angela ended her conversation as she pulled into the café's parking lot. Mark arrived minutes earlier and stood by the door observing Angela. "Wow, she still has a heck of an effect on me. I remember taking her to Club 290 and my counterparts thought she was really a beautiful woman. I remember talking to her nearly every morning for a week or so, and still to this day, she has a butterfly effect. Wow." Mark stood in amazement. "I don't want to blow this. I really don't want to blow this," he repeated to understand the importance of his statement and be conscious of his actions. "I'm not going to blow this," he said once more just as he opened the door for Angela's entry. "Hi," Mark greeted and smiled as she entered.

"Hi, Mark. Nice seeing you," Angela responded with a nervous tilt in her voice.

"Are you hungry for anything?" asked Mark.

"No, well, yes, something small maybe."

"Here's a menu," Mark said while handing Angela the menu as they stood at the counter. He then spoke, "let me tell you about the café. It's really cozy and offers deli type sandwiches, and there's a grill. The coffee is pretty good and the people are, well, you'll see in a minute." Mark ended his description as a waitress/cashier appeared. "Can I help you?" she asked.

"Do you have anything in mind Angela?" Mark asked.

"Not yet." Angela responded.

"How about coffee and we'll take a look at the menu for a while, and then decide?" Mark asked Angela.

"I think it's a good idea," Angela responded and waited for a table.

"It's open seating," the waitress informed Angela.

"Thank you," Angela replied while heading to a table near the front window.

"We'll have two regular coffees, and please bring cream with the order. Thank you." Mark ordered and thought, "I can't remember if she likes cream or not; better safe than sorry." He  walked towards Angela and commented with a smile, "Great spot. I love the view."

"I like looking out too."

"I think more of you these days," Mark said. "You're beautiful, and haven't changed since the first time I saw you."

"Thanks Mark, you're too kind. You know it's only been a few months at best since we first met. I couldn't have changed so much," Angela smirked with thought – "as if that line will work."

"I'm sorry." Mark noticed his honesty didn't go over well with her. "I mean, you are a beautiful woman, have great features, and I admire the way you take care of yourself."

"Thanks again, but you don't have to compliment me. I'm ok with you."

"Ok with me?"

"Look Mark, I like you but…." Angela stopped in the middle of the sentence thinking, "I like this guy. What on earth am I doing?"

"But… Are you going to finish your comment?" Mark asked with skepticism.

"Sure…we've already broken the ice and you don't have to sweet-talk me," Angela responded admitting to herself, "Good recovery."

"I know, but you're a lovely woman and I don't mind saying so. I appreciate your modesty, and I get to have an opinion, right?"

"It's not as if I don't appreciate it, its just we're starting as friends and hopefully we can continue without pressures."

"Friends first, I've got it." Mark sat back in his chair and looked out the window pulling his thoughts together. "How can I do this and not be overly pushy or drive her away again. Friends she wants, then being a friend is what I'll do…stay friends."

"Are you ok?" asked Angela as the waitress approached with their coffee. "Can I take your orders," the waitress asked.

"Sure." Angela made her sandwich order, and Mark followed with a brunch order.

"I'm not sure how to move forward, so I have to be honest with you." Mark's statement caught Angela's attention as she looked into his eyes. "I like you, liked you from the very beginning. We started as friends the time we talked about books we've read, our ideas on life, current events, and gave opinions on different subjects. We went out, not on a date, but as friends and had a great time; at least I thought so, and the reason we're here is because you did not want me to back off. So when you agreed to meet here today, I thought your mind was open to trying something more than friends."

Angela didn't respond, knowing he was right, then said, "I…, well I don't know what's gotten into me. I came here with the same idea as you. I think we'll have a great time together. I don't want to rush though, because there are some adjustments I have to make or get used to."

"That's it. I've got it, the reason for your hesitation." Mark understanding her message made him lean forward and sip his coffee. He stared into the blue for a moment with thought, "I have to get this out early or we're not going to work." He told Angela, "Here it goes, I like you and it's mutual. If we're going to do this, I'm willing to take one step at a time until you're totally comfortable with us, being an 'us.' I mean, this is a change for you, probably a big change and even though you have supporting friends, it's still a transition. I'm no different outside of my outer shell; well I hope I'm different to a point," Mark smiled, "but not really. If people see us, it's because most times they're curious, other times it's a disagreement, and at times a compliment. Everyone doesn't see us the same."

"I'm nervous, Mark, and I know these things. It's not like I haven't seen an interracial couple before, it's that I've not been the focus of being part of one."

"What did you think when you saw one?" Mark asked to pinpoint her fear, and to address her challenges.

"I really don't know. I thought it was interesting, more than intriguing, maybe why would she or instead of how could she or him."

"Have you figured why you would? Why did you come knowing I am excited to see you?"

"Because I felt, feel the same way. I just don't know how to handle the difference."

"Look at me and tell me what you like about me." Mark sat straight and focused his eyes on her. He noticed the sincerity in her look, her speech, and the nervous twitch in her voice as she answered.

"I like your mind; you're courteous, and genuinely kind. I like your attitude towards living, your carry of confidence, your sweet demeanor…"

"Don't say it too loud, they may think I'm soft." Mark laughed to break Angela's serious tone so she has ease in sharing.

Angela giggled, "I enjoy your humor, you're such a gentleman, and of course your masculine body. These are some of the things I like about you."

"Sounds normal doesn't it?"

"Sure it does, but...."

"It's still difficult for you. Ok, let's do this. We'll be friends and work on your perception of things. Now, you have to define friends."

"Friends? You know the usual get together and share things, talk, laugh, hang out, and get to know each other."

"What about dating other people?" Mark asked pointedly. Angela stopped in her thought as it didn't occur to her it would surface. She sat in silence and drank her coffee, took a deep breath and answered, "I. Well, I never really thought of it with a dating guideline. If you want to, it's a choice you'll have to make." Angela paused for a reply, knowingly it's not a choice she wanted, however if he chose to date someone else, it would not be the ideal situation or the one envisioned.

"I wanted clarification. I think, if not mistaken, you are serious about being friends and whatever happens right? Or am I guessing?" Mark asked, knowing her response was loaded as in 'damn if you do, or damn if you don't.'

"I didn't say whatever happens. But if you wish to date other women, it's up to you. I'll have to keep your dating them in mind while we're friends."

"Keep it in mind while we're friends? I'm, ok, not confused but starting to understand. It's your way out just in case you feel uncomfortable with the social pressure."

"Way out? I don't get your response."

"Yes, see if things go well, you become happy with the ease into a relationship as long as there's no confrontations of feeling threatened or frightened."

"I'm not afraid of anyone."

"Let me finish before you get defensive. I think your outlook and acceptance is changing and I think you want to, but just aren't sure how you'd handle being in the public's eye. Or if someone at the office whispered about you being involved with me, the black man. Am I on the right track?"

"I can't honestly put my finger on it, but it sounds right."

"Then you should think about it a little more, even as friends. Think, even if a person sees you with me as your friend, there are assumptions. When they ask you about the black guy with you, they'll ply you with snide remarks. Some will shy away from you, or treat you differently than before. Some will, well attempt to place you in a different category, as if you forfeit your privileges."

"You have a point. I don't understand how someone can change when they know me. What privilege? I'm not privileged, not rich, not better than anyone, I'm just Angela." Angela frowned in her response as if feeling racially insulted, by the guy she thought was so sharp, open, and confident.

"People change when they see something different. Look, I'll tell you what, let's do this friend thing and I can show you what I'm trying to explain. And the privilege thing, well I can show you that too. I mean, you are not rich; you're not a movie star even though you look like one, nor are you a snob. I'm highlighting a realistic social omen which lives with us. It's just fact and I'll expose you to a little of it. But first, let me show you who I am. Get to know me. Know me as you mentioned, and allow me to prove your thoughts." Mark waited for an answer just as the waitress brought food to the table. The waitress placed the sandwich in front of Angela and the breakfast on Mark's part of the table.

"Thank you," Angela told the waitress.

"Would you like me to warm your coffee?" asked the waitress.

"Yes, thank you and a glass of water for us both, please," Mark ordered.

"I'll be right back," said the kind waitress.
Mark made an observation about the waitress he surely could use to reinforce his point. "Angela, did you notice our waitress?" Mark asked.

"Yes, she's a sweet girl. I think sixteen years old."

"Yes and did you notice her ethnicity?"

"Asian. I noticed."

"Good, how did you see her?" Mark asked, making a point to her defining people. Angela bit the sandwich and pondered his question as if it was a quiz and her answer would make him understand it means nothing. "Well to be honest, she's just a girl. Smart for sure," responded Angela.

"Exactly what I mean," Mark pointed.

"What? I said she's a girl and smart."

"And I meant exactly as I pointed. Why do you say smart? Not saying she isn't but how would you know so quickly? We haven't talked to her, we hadn't asked her about her education, we hadn't asked about her views on life. What makes her smart?"

Angela stopped eating for a minute and really pondered his point before making a serious well thought response. "I see it's an assumption as we're taught to believe."

"Exactly, I think you're starting to hear what you're saying and understand what you're seeing. Can you honestly see your fear?"

"I'm not afraid. Honestly, I like you and it's not I don't see the social challenges we'll face. I see the challenges I would face," Angela admitted. Before desiring Mark, she never gave deep thought to the challenges of dating him. When Margo and Karen talked to her last Friday, their comments didn't quite sink in. Yet she admitted having doubts when facing her own reality. "It's a greater step than just going for it," she thought while looking at Mark.

"Here's what I'm willing to do," Mark added after thinking about her response. "I'll take one day at a time with you, point out things I see, and show you a difference in social events. I'll show you a bit of black culture as well as how all of us fit in our great country. If and only if you admit you want me," Mark laughed.

"Are you serious?" laughed Angela.

"Yes, I'm serious. I want to know if you want me as a friend, a future companion, and one day - a partner."

"A friend yes, and even…." Angela stopped as she found herself admitting Mark being a lover.

"Lover," Mark finished her comment. "Is that right?"

"Eventually, I'd like a great lover. Don't all women?"

"I'd hope so. Let me tell you what I heard. You want me, as a friend to build a strong foundation for other things to grow. Let me tell you, up front and direct. There's going to be times you're angered by other people, sympathetic at their response, and on the other hand, elated because you've learned so much about yourself and history."

"Am I back in college or being tested for a life challenge?"

"Actually, both; it starts with you. I'm willing to put my best foot forward and enjoy life with you. It's because…" Mark placed his hand on top of hers on the table, "…I'm so into you. I want this because you're witty, fun, and intriguing. I like your habits, and what I've seen of your style, I like it too. I enjoy you and will not date anyone during our friendship. I really like you and want you to at least meet me halfway. I don't dare date anyone outside of us; I'd hope you do the same." Mark looked for Angela's reaction.

"Well, you said a mouth full," Angela responded. "I like the idea of building a friendship and not dating outside of us. I'm open to learning new things, but don't expect me to immediately understand it right away. My views are still changing."

"We can do this Angela," Mark smiled, "we can do this. I have an idea, since we're on the same page. I think we'll enjoy having fun tonight. What do you feel like tonight - dancing, live music, movies?"

Angela sat for a moment before responding and observed people outside of the café. They took a peep at the two of them through the large-paned window. The stare wasn't bad; it was more inquisitive at best. "I remember wanting to take you someplace before we decided to stop talking."

"You mean before kicking me to the curb?" Mark laughed.

"I didn't kick you to the curb; it wasn't time for us."

"Now you're saying it's our time? I like your statement."

"Let me get back to tonight. I think we can go to Londzell's. It's right around the corner."

"Oh, I like that place."

"You've been there?"

"Yes I have. Recently though, long after our disconnect."

"Would you like to go?"

"Hell, yeah!" Mark laughed. "I'd love going there. Do you want me to pick you up or should we meet?"

"I'll pick you up. I know where you live and I'll call you before I leave my apartment."

"Changing roles; Ok, I'll enjoy you picking me up and driving. You're really cool," Mark admitted but thought, "control man, control is the key to helping her understand."

"How about 9, as I have to cook and eat dinner at home? I have to cook before throwing out some groceries."

"Great time; I look forward to it."


Meeting Mark was surely an eye-opener for Angela. She admitted while driving home, it was totally different being part of it instead of being the observer. She could not believe her own actions or how surprising the responses were to Mark when she actually liked him. "At least I think I like him," her mind admitted to confusion for a moment. "I told Margo and Karen what I like in a guy. When we talked about the man, I thought of Mark. Now, here he is right in the palm of my hand and I'm in doubt. Why?" Angela turned into her apartment complex just as the cellular phone rang. Without looking at the caller identification, she answered, "Hello".

"Hey, Angela," Margo spoke, "what on earth are you doing?"

"I have no idea. I honestly have no idea."

"Listen, I know what you're going through. I'm coming over. Got any wine?"

"I have a couple bottles. But I need to think on this, without anyone's input."

"I," Margo paused while responding, "I get it, but I want to share something with you and then you can think. We'll share one glass of wine and I'll give you a little insight to the bigger picture. Don't we need information to make an informed decision?"

"Yes, we do. I need more, but I think it's internal."

256

"Of course it's internal. It always is. See, I understand and I'll be there in an hour. Chill the wine glasses." Margo ended her call with Angela, pressing the issue to see her in person. Margo knew the challenges Angela was going through. Years ago, Mark was her idea of the perfect guy. Different from Angela, Margo knew the challenges of being involved in an interracial couple, especially since she wanted a serious monogamous relationship. Mark was perfect in her eyes. He gave the utmost respect, treated a woman like gold, and totally connected on the emotional level. And most of all, he was a terrific lover, extremely romantic, and amazingly smart. The only problem between Margo and Mark was the serious nature of the relationship. He was not ready to make the commitment, and Margo figured then was the time. When she pressed the issue, Mark bailed and ended the relationship leaving Margo devastated. During her low time was when she met Cedric. Showing her the patience and understanding, establishing the partnership and sharing strengths, Cedric quickly filled the void Margo thought she had. If it weren't for Cedric, Margo swore life would be horrible.

Mark parked his car in the garage and headed inside. He stopped after dropping his keys and thought of his conversation with Angela. "Man, I thought…" Mark searched his mind for an analogy and couldn't bring one to the surface. "Damn, here I go again. Why is it in this country we, I, have to go through this over and over again? Why do I have to be the one teaching instead of just enjoying, encouraging to make me look like a man? I know who and what I am, why can't others see me as such? If you do all the right things, go to school, make good money, equal in appearance, have strong character, you still have to prove yourself worthy. Why am I not given the benefit of doubt?" Mark found himself sitting in the darkened room, silent, with just enough light for his eyes to focus on things around him. He listened to silence as if searching for an answer or something to give a sign of change. "Change," he whispered with a masculine voice as if passing a message to soldiers on a defensive line in a war zone. "Change," he whispered as if voiced at a greater dimension had impact and could direct his thoughts. "Change," he whispers to God, as if praying to be seen as a man, instead of a man of color.

Margo arrived as Angela stood in the kitchen prepping her dinner. She rang the door bell and listened for Angela, but instead heard music from the apartment. Margo knocked and waited a moment to knock harder a second time to get Angela's attention and answer the door. Finally, Angela opened her door, "Why didn't you ring the bell?" she asked.

"Your music was too loud to hear it. I rang the bell first."

"I'm sorry. It's how I get lost in my thoughts sometimes. I drown my environment with loud music."

"College trick, huh?"

"Yes, I used to study this way; drove my roommate crazy," Angela laughed.

"I know what you're thinking and it's why I'm here. Where are those wine glasses?"

"In the fridge; help yourself," Angela directed while she continued to prepare dinner. Margo followed suit and did exactly as Angela instructed. After pouring two glasses, she passed one to Angela and asked, "Can I turn the music down?"

"Sure. The remote is on the coffee table."

"Thanks. Now!" Margo pushed buttons while speaking, "you know I need to share a few things with you. I don't want you to think I'm pushing you into something, nor leading you down a path. Everything I'm telling you is pure information and my experience," Margo explained and waited for acknowledgement before moving forward.

"Uh huh. I know it's your experience."

"Yes, mine and mine alone; however there are situations applied to every woman who crosses the line. You know those who decide to date interracially."

"Margo, you mean family consideration; kids, if things accidentally happen, having horrid sex, and being accepted by the public. Or what about not being supported, being left alone later in the relationship, being beaten and abused, and opening a door to drugs. It sounds so stupid but I'm actually thinking these things."

"You have it bad," Margo frowned then sipped her wine. "All the things you've heard to stereotype Mark are running through your mind. Let me throw something at you to reflect what I hear. So, Mark has to consider you being trailer trash, a druggie, a gold digger, a pacifist, a liar, a thief, a con artist, an elitist, and out of reach."

"Why on earth would you say such things?" Angela asked with surprise, not understanding where Margo was going with her comment.

"You're thinking of Mark, not as a single man, but as a race of men. He can do the same with you as a race of women. For instance, didn't you hear of white women who lied about being with black men to cover up their adultery or incest? Haven't you questioned history and wondered how we got so much and others didn't. How we took the land from black farmers in the 1600's and made them slaves. Haven't you heard of the Klan during its heyday hanging black men who just looked at a white woman, and women who defied them when they were rejected? Those events aren't made up, they are true. So, think about the little bit I've shared, why on earth would Mark want to date you?"

"I guess he's just as scared," Angela admitted it's fear to her seeing Mark.

"Being afraid of what? Being shot or being accepted by others? Did you know he has just as much to risk? Yet he likes you and doesn't matter what others think as he's dealt with it before. So, your hang-ups are strictly holding you back. If you're not going to do it, then make sure he knows; the sooner the better." Margo pressed as she finished her wine. "I think I've said my piece. You need to think about it and do the right thing, for you both." Margo left the apartment.

Angela sipped her wine and watched Margo leave. "I can't believe how she spoke of those horrible things. No one thinks that way today. At least not the women, or do they?" Angela stopped cooking, took her wine with her to the couch, and sat listening to music. She became overwhelmed with emotions while holding her glass next to her face. "How is it I can think of Mark being so great and then when it's time to try, I'm afraid? Why?" Sitting there she recalled her thoughts of being involved with other men. Just as Margo pointed in her visit, there is bad and good in all races of people. Mark is a good person, and I like his character, charm, how he's attentive, and handsome. I went out with him once, why can't I go as his date, instead of friends? I went out with Eric, Christopher, and Bill with less concern and they weren't as nice. The major physical difference is race. Wow, am I...no way. I actually like Mark. For months, I thought of him, when running into him I had schoolgirl feelings, I looked for him more often, he was sweet when he offered to help with bags at Eric's. He was courteous at the bookstore. Today, he was quick to understand me. He is the one, and I want him." Angela finally placed her wine glass on the coffee table and fell into a slumber. Her eyes closed and mind relaxed, she dreamed of:

*Mark embracing her, so close so strong, the brown skin, smooth, and his brown eyes reading deep into her soul, she held him, trying to feel the warmth, as if he were a blanket on a winter's day. Seeing the dynamic in skin contrast excited her. Behind them, she saw her mother, weeping with her hands over her face, like those disappointing looks she had given Angela when she was a child. "Why are you weeping?" Angela asked her mother. "I've been a good girl," she explained.*

*"You are, but I'm so afraid for you. If you go through with this, what will they think?" Mom responded.*

*"Mom, things have changed. I really like him and he's the nicest sweetest man. Why not?"*

*"Because he's black," mom scorned Angela. "He's going to give you a rough life."*

*"Because he's black? How can you say such a thing? I know some white men can and will do worse. Is his skin color the only reason? How dare you mother?"* Angela *returned holding Mark's hand, walking down the street. She stared at the window of a large department store pointing to a dress. She saw their image and smiled, as the contrast really showed how they actually matched, like designer clothes displayed on a mannequin. Happy with her selection and moving along, she sidestepped her mother, her friend Paula, and other people who were blocking their path.*

Her dream darkened and her mind went blank as she slept. One hour, two hours, three hours she slept as if she'd forgotten the date.

Mark waited for Angela after cleaning up and getting things together for tonight. He pondered how he'd get Angela to accept his intent of her becoming his girl. He thought of a mental plan to indirectly discuss and identify the advantages of following your heart instead of playing into fear. Time steamrolled to 9:00 pm, and waiting wasn't long. "Should I call her or what? Did she change her mind? Damn, fear strikes again. No I bet something happened. She forgot where I live, no that can't be it. She changed her mind. I knew it. Maybe not, maybe something happened and she's late. I'll let her call me, it will seem like I'm too aggressive if I call her. I'll give her a few." Mark turned his television on and scanned channels for something to watch. Rolling through the channel guide, he decided if shows were interesting and non-interesting, and reluctant to get involved in a television show, hoping Angela would show or call. He landed on a show of interest and watched it after all. Thirty minutes passed and no sign of Angela, he looked for a phone call or text message on his cellular which was totally blank. "Did she cancel without telling me? I'm going to be pissed! Don't jump to conclusions," he told himself. Another portion of the show and he decided it was not going to happen. 10:00

and the show went off, Mark placed a call to his friend he normally went out with. "Hey guy, what's up?"

"Man, I thought you were busy tonight."

"No, well yes I think I got stood up. It's a first time in a long year of dating. I've had cancellations before, but man, is this something or what?"

"It happens. Don't take it personal, something came up. Give her a call and see."

"I want to, but after our lunch conversation, I knew she would not make it."

"Then if you knew, why are you sweating it?"

"Because, dude, the woman is awesome and she's surely an angel. She's fine, witty, professional, fun to be around, sparkles in darkness, and straight up a take home to mama type."

"Remember, you shouldn't chase a woman who doesn't want you."

"I think she does. It's her first time dating a black guy."

"Then, there you go, she's not ready. When it happens to me, either they are eager right off the bat and excited to explore the opportunities, or discouraged and cancel. Some call, some don't, when they decide against it. I think she's not coming. If I were you, I'd call and just see where you stand. I bet she makes an excuse on why she can't make it, or she won't answer the phone."

"I'll call. Or better yet, I'll call our common friend Margo."

"She may give you some insight Mark. But, call somebody and get out, go somewhere. The night is still young."

"Cool advice, later, dude."

"Later," the friend ended the call. Mark did exactly as his friend directed, he made his first call to Margo. "Hi Margo, its Mark".

"Hi."

"I hope I'm not interrupting anything."

"No, you aren't. We're watching movies tonight. Cedric and I decided once a month we're not going anywhere and spend time with each other. Your timing is good. What's going on?" Margo asked.

"Did you talk to Angela today?"

"Yes, I did. I gather she didn't make the date you two were supposed to go on."

"Well, it's not supposed to be a date; however we were going to hang out tonight. Did she tell you something different? Or did she say she made other plans?'

"When I left her, she was in between going or not. It's a big step for her. I can't tell you if she's afraid or not. But it's not easy for her, no way, so you'll have to push if you want her to go with you."

"It's the last thing I want to do. Push a woman to change. She's got to change on her own. I can't force her to go out with me, as friends or a couple."

"I agree, but you've got to ease her into it. Listen, she likes you a lot. She's got cold feet for some reason. If I were you, I'd call. Just call and see if she's changed her mind." Margo suggested.

"I'll call, but it's …well, it's hard to, since she's so skeptical."

"Your choice Mark, it's your choice. I have to get back to the movie. Let me know tomorrow what happens, ok?"

"I'll let you know." Mark ended the call and sat for a moment allowing Margo's comments to sink in. "I can't believe she's teetering on me. What the hell? It's the norm and here I thought she was ready. So why worry about it? She is a gorgeous woman and not the only one out there. I can find another woman just as fast. But wow, I don't know if I want to go through the process of finding a new person. I'm kind of tired of it right now. I really like Angela, her mind is really my motivating factor." Mark dialed Angela's number against his better judgment. Angela answered in a sleepy voice, "Hello."

"Hey Angela, its Mark."

"Yes," Angela answered while waking from her deep slumber.

"I guess you either cancelled on me or the way it sounds, you fell asleep."

"Sleep, you woke me."

"I can tell. Go back to sleep, I'll catch you another time or better yet, you catch me, if you're ever interested." Mark ended his call in frustration thinking, "It really excited her to go out with me tonight."

Angela looked at her cell phone just as she stood to move to her bedroom. She moved to her kitchen to drink water and looked at the wall clock. "I can't believe I fell asleep," she thought and realized it was after 10:00 pm. "Oh My Goodness!!! I missed Mark's call." Angela redialed her last call hoping to catch Mark. "Hey, I thought you were going to sleep the rest of the night."

"I am so sorry. Please forgive me for falling asleep. I really want to go. Are you up to it?" Angela asked.

"I'm waiting for you. I don't think we'll get good seats arriving this late, but if you still want to go, we can. I can come for you while you get ready, if you don't mind?"

"I think it's a great idea. Come to…" Angela gave her address and directions while she ran the shower water. She did her quick dress routine and grabbed an outfit ready for the night. Just as she finished dressing, she sat at the end of her bed and recalled her dream. "I wonder why mom was crying. I'll have to call her. I hope Mark isn't mad for my falling asleep. I really like him and want to at least go out and see what fun we can have."

Mark called Angela announcing his arrival. She didn't let him come to the door; instead she rushed out to the car. "I'm so sorry Mark, I didn't want to seem like I'm putting you off. I honestly fell asleep. It must be from last night. We stayed out so late and I woke up so early. Please forgive me."

"No problem. The important thing is we're together heading out. Let's just have a great time tonight. Things happen," Mark responded but thought, "things really happen for a reason and I'm not sure she has the right reason." Silence fell on them as Mark drove off to Londzell's. With a little music in the background, Angela broke their silence in the middle of the song "Are you upset?" she asked.

"It happened and I'm glad you are here. I'm not upset really," Mark answered.

"Then I've never experienced such silence from you."

"We haven't been together. I'm hoping the silent treatment changes so you can get to know me."

"I'll get to know you. I think time is on our side. You know, with us being friends we'll find a lot of us time."

"Yes, being friends is the way to go. I agree, without a doubt."

"We have to build this friendship, don't we? I mean we need time to learn things about each other."

"Why? Why can't we enjoy being who we are and not put goals or ideas on us? It's like there is a different standard for dating me."

Angela fell silent as Mark parked near the club. He stepped out of the car, took a breath, and smiled, "I can have fun tonight," he thought before opening Angela's door. "Are you ready to have fun?" Mark asked Angela, as she exited the car.

"Yes, I think so."

"Glad to hear it." Mark smiled and walked behind Angela as they approached the club entrance. "This place is pretty crowded. I think there's a spot at the bar." Mark directed Angela as they walked through the entryway.

Angela said, "You lead, I'll follow."

The club's patrons were a reflection of Atlanta's diversity. Even the band reflected how talented people joined to make awesome music. There were all types of people sharing tables; couples, singles, unisex, and surely love birds. The club scene supported people of all walks enjoying the sound of jazz. "Music is so universal," Angela spoke.

"That's so cliché," Mark laughed.

"What do you mean? I wasn't trying to be funny."

"I know, but it sounded like a television commercial for the United Nations."

"Oh, I get it." Angela sighed. "It's going to be one of those nights. Everything I say will be analyzed to death?"

"No, it's not happening. Lighten up. We're supposed to be enjoying the place." Mark smiled at Angela while waving for the bartender.

"What would you like to drink tonight, Angela?" Mark asked.

"I'm thinking about a fruity drink. Whatever is fruity is fine with me."

"Ok." Mark acknowledged and instructed the bartender on the order. "I hope you like it," he told Angela, "I picked this up from Jamaica."

"I probably will. I remember your drink from the last time being out with you."

"You remember that far back?" Mark smiled, reaching in his pocket to pay the bartender. "It wasn't so long ago." Angela looked around the room and observed active patrons. She noticed how laughter seemed to fill the room, and people danced in the aisles. "I didn't know you had such a memory."

"Are you kidding me? How can a guy not remember a very impressive woman?"

"Impressive? Flattery is a good move. I thought you were still angry from my oversleeping."

"No, it's water under the bridge. I'm here with a woman, who is my friend." Mark smiled and raised his drink to tap Angela's. "Here's to our friendship."

Angela showed Mark a smirk just as she tapped Mark's glass. She turned back to the music and continued observing the diversity of the club's patrons. She then commented, "This looks like Karen's dinner party. The only thing different is a live band." She smiled.

"Would you like to dance?" asked Mark.

"There's no place to dance, unless we dance in the aisle."

"Well?" Mark reached to Angela as to guide her into the aisle for a dance. She stepped forward grabbing his hand and in an instant she forgot her worries and reluctance. His warmth and offer to partner was so different from dating the others. His kind, gentlemanly gesture reignited a spark of what took her the first time. Angela danced, as if the room started to empty. She allowed her natural state of mind lead to a mood of total enjoyment. No questions asked to where or why, or even the fact of being with a man of color, or the fact she feared Mark. Angela smiled when she looked at Mark dancing in front of her. "He is adorable." she thought while dancing. Mark didn't see her smile as he himself danced as in a groove, with his eyes closed allowing the music to move his body. Perfect in his mind, he didn't worry too much trying to figure out Angela. Instead Mark found a comfort in the music, the positive environment, and the idea of this gorgeous woman in front of him. At the end of the song, both Angela and Mark found themselves looking at each other, standing close enough to embrace, but hesitant in the fear of one making the wrong move towards the other. A patron pushed Mark while trying to get by saying "excuse me" and without resistance Mark moved closer and Angela responded. It was the embrace, the full connection they both fought, and without words they knew it was the moment to feel connected. It was the first, the very first time, either touched the other so closely. With arms around one another, Angela allowed a tear to fall down her cheek as if it were a cue for the band to play a love ballad. Automatically they moved and fought letting go. They swayed to the rhythm, lost in a trance, holding each other as if dear life depended on the outcome. One step over the other, one gentle sway and they connected, fitting perfectly. They danced as long as the song played. Mark smiled from joy, feeling the comfort Angela allowed. He felt the accomplishment, and wanted to acknowledge his victory in a special way. "Are you sure you want to be friends?" he whispered in Angela's ear as they danced. His voice sounded smooth to Angela. She nearly forgot there was a band playing; she forgot they were dancing in the aisle; she forgot the people around her. "No," she responded, "I'm sure I don't want that."

"Neither do I." Mark held her a little tighter. "I want to enjoy you and venture into us; as a path building a destiny, working on a journey of tomorrow. Do you think you can partner with me?"

Angela backed from Mark's embrace just enough to look into his eyes. "I'd like to, I'd really like to." She answered and placed her head on his shoulder.

Mark felt her discomfort practically escape the moment. He knew there was a sense she had to get through. Instead of making a point pushing for a commitment, or an agreement, he pulled her closer and held on for the entire song. Without a word, he strongly gestured his intent. "I hope she understands," he thought as he gently caressed Angela's back. Angela responded as her nerve endings sent messages to her brain, "I want to." The words were loud in her mind, "I really want to."

The night continued without Mark asking another relationship question. He entertained her and created moments to remember, while showing his intent to open a door to his life, and eventually to his heart. Angela followed suit, not pressing the issue, even though she wanted to tell Mark 'yes,' and force herself beyond the strong wall of doubt in her mind. She wanted to get beyond the urge to go against one stronghold and face the last mechanism antagonizing her decision. Her body desired Mark as a mission to survive, yet her mind fought with fervor to stand strong. Angela looked at Mark; recognizing his smile, the muscular body, the charismatic confidence, the well-groomed appearance, and validated all the things on her check list. Just as she realized her approval, her mind flashed to her mother's tears from her earlier dream. It was as if a child knew the decision would cause pain for her mother. "What pain?" she pondered while gazing at this gorgeous man.

Mark walked in stride with Angela while holding her hand. He lost concentration on making her his woman and companion, as a sense of comfort fell upon him. His night changed, the dance, the laughter, the shared signals making them so in tune, so connected, and sending the exact message of hope. He now smiled internally and followed his initial thought of building a relationship with Angela. Angela followed suit for a change as she walked, with disregard to observers, or picturing a negative image of Mark being next to her. The fear of being a subject didn't seem to be harsh or tough. It actually felt wonderful and the reflection was beyond friendship. "Such a connection," she pondered, taking a seat in the car as Mark held the door open. "Thank you," Angela smiled.

"You are so welcome," Mark replied and headed to the driver's seat. "I'm happy you enjoyed the night," he commented while settling in the car.

"I did. It turned out great. The band was awesome and the dance, well you know."

"I know, because I feel the same. So, I know you're probably tired since its 2:30 in the morning."

"Is it that late? I'm not tired, but you probably are. I'm game for going home or what's open? I'd love spending more time with you."

Mark, surprised in her answer, was struck with an empty thought. "Um, I know there's a breakfast place for coffee, but there isn't an after hour club on this side of town. How about coffee? We can go to the Waffle House if you'd like."

"I, well, better not. I think we can call it a night. Don't get me wrong, I was thinking of not letting the night end, but, on second thought it's better to head home." Angela changed her mind as she wanted a more personal moment with Mark. She realized he didn't want to push the issue and offer his home or her apartment as an option keeping the night active. Actually, she enjoyed the fact he didn't offer either of her thoughts because at the moment, she was unsure of what she'd do behind closed doors.

"I understand," Mark said while driving onto Holcomb Bridge Road. He played a CD for mellow music to soothe the drive. He said little or nothing, waiting for Angela to open an idea for conversation. Instead of leading a thought for quiet moments, Mark wished for a more receptive time when neither felt resentful. "It's not like I wouldn't, but if opportunity knocks, I don't think I'd take it," Mark thought while getting closer to Angela's apartment.

"I guess you've decided it's quits for us tonight," Angela broke silence with a surprise. She really didn't want to go home but considering there weren't too many places to go keeping them in public.

"Yes, we should call it a night. I'd love seeing you again."

"You mean sometime today?"

"Yes, today, maybe more like afternoon after I crash for a bit."

"The baby's tired."

"Hey, you took a nap. I didn't and now I'm feeling tired."

"I have an idea, why don't you come over and I can cook dinner for us. It'll give us time to really get to know each other without interruption."

"I'd like to. Let's say 7:00. Is it a good time for you?" Mark asked.

"Seven, is great. Is there any foods you don't like"

"No, not really, if I don't like it, I'll learn to deal with it. I'm open to new things. Or should I say new things to me."

"I like your being open to try different foods. Some men are so finicky."

"Not me, I grew up in a household willing to try anything and everything the family cooked. We traveled to different countries with Dad."

"You did? I wondered how you were so receptive to people."

"It's being open as you learn. There are great and awful people in every group. Yet you find them by interacting and not totally in observation." Mark pulled his car into the parking spot in front of her apartment. "We're here. I'll walk you to your door."

"You don't have to."

"I wouldn't be a gentleman if I didn't," Mark said while opening his door headed for Angela's. "Thank you," Angela said exiting the car.

"No problem." Mark held his hand to grasp hers while they walked along the sidewalk to her apartment door. "I really enjoyed you tonight. I think tomorrow is going to be another time we find more compatibility."

"Yes, I think so to. I like the idea of us having quiet time."

"So do I."

Angela pulled out her house key and unlocked her front door. "Well, this is it." She told Mark.

Mark grabbed her hand, kissed it, and looked into her eyes saying, "Yes, this is it. Have a good sleep and I'll see you tomorrow at 7." Mark returned to his car as Angela watched him drive off. "Ahh, it leaves her hanging for more." Mark thought.

Angela woke early afternoon after a morning of tossing and turning, sleepless as the thought of being with Mark lingered, connecting the subconscious battle to her reality. She again saw her mother crying in a dream. "Why on earth is Mom crying?" Angela asked, noticing the time. "I'll ask her." Without a second thought, Angela dialed her parents' number and thought how to break the ice about Mark. "Why is it important to tell Mom about Mark?" she asked, waiting for an answer, "It's not like we're getting married, or it's not like I need her permission. So why is it so prevailing I have to tell her?"

"Hello," Angela's mother answered.

"Hi, Mom," Angela said with excitement. Their relationship was very close. Angela grew up with her mother giving the right answer. Even when the answers were bad, Angela felt a serious connection to her mother. Her truths were validated as long as her mother understood her needs as a child. Not once did she make judgment or tell her of an experience where she didn't make sense.

"Hi Angela, how are you?"

"Mom, I'm doing well."

"What about money? Are you ok or are you physically hurt..?

"No Mom, I'm not hurt. I have a question though; I need to know something very important. I've seen you crying twice in my dreams."

"Crying? I haven't cried in ages. Well, not outside of sad movies," Mom responded.

"Well, I didn't explain why I think you were crying. I met this wonderful guy. He is full of spirit, great character, handsome, and smart. But there is one catch."

"He's married."

"No, not married. I don't think he is at least. I know he isn't."

"It's the usual answer or he's black."

"Wow Mom. How did you know?"

"I'm your mother. I know you and wondered if you'd ever cross the line. You see, you were young when we moved Midwest from the East coast. You played with kids of all races back then. I didn't think anything of it. You were so fond of this little girl you played with."

"You mean I had a black friend as a child?"

"She was your best friend. Partly the reason we moved was your father wanted you to be around Caucasian people."

"Why, Mother?"

"Because he wanted a better life for you, just as I want the best for you."

"So, you're saying if I decide to date Mark you'd not support me."

"I'm not saying any such thing. I dated a colored guy back in college before I met your dad."

"What?"

"Yes, it wasn't the same as now. He was charming, a real classy guy and the smartest man I'd ever known. He would have been the student body president had he been a different race."

"Why didn't you ever tell me this?"

"It wasn't important. I didn't want you to think ….well, hurt your father."

"Dad doesn't know about your college sweetheart?"

"No he doesn't. If he'd known, you wouldn't be here today."

"Is he really bad, mom?"

"No, not really, but some men in those days labeled you if you dated anyone but white men. And you know your father is a proud man."

"Then you'd not have a problem with me dating Mark."

"I'd never have a problem. But, we'll have to ease him to your dad when the time comes. How serious is it?"

"I like him a lot, but worried about you and dad. I felt there would be a fight or something between us if I totally went for it."

"I think you've fallen for him already."

"Why would you say so mom?"

"Why are you asking me about dating him? You've never asked me about dating someone since leaving college. And I only get to meet the guys you're serious with."

"You're right. Am I very obvious?"

"I'm your mother remember. Do what makes you happy and don't make the mistakes I made in the past. Sometimes I question my decision, so never let others influence yours."

"Thanks, Mom. Tell Dad hello for me and I'll call him later. I love you."

"Love you too."

# Chapter 11

Mark felt positive with Angela last night. He was confident his actions were right by not forcing the issue of being with her. If it were any other woman during his younger days, the two of them would have cooked breakfast this morning. In his gut, and with positive hopes for the future, his decision to sleep alone would turn into a fantastic time later today. "What can I take to her apartment?" he pondered while in the shower. This Sunday afternoon wasn't quite like any other where chores and planning kept him busy; nor was it like hanging with friends playing sports. This Sunday of all days made every thought prevalent on Angela. Mark dressed and wandered into his kitchen for a cup of coffee, grabbed a bagel, and sat for a spell. He lost concentration on eating while thinking of that gentle kiss on Angela's hand. His thought led to the desires he struggled with, to not be with her, giving her space, and not be aggressive. "Is this out of my character?" he asked. "What if I don't go forward with seeing her tonight, will it be safe to continue as friends?" Mark learned from history if you're too aggressive, it tends to scare off the women with most interest. "I can see her eyes, just as she looked at me last night. I can feel her body, as if she just left me. I can only imagine how tender her kiss will be. If I'd followed through, these wouldn't be questions. I'd know the answer and she'd be with me now. Right now; dang, what the hell was I thinking?"

Midday swept by like a burst of water during a summer rain shower in the desert. Angela heavily pondered her mother's conversation. It was as if the points her mother made lingered, replayed like a song repeating on the CD player… "…best friend… dated a black guy in college… and she kept it secret all these years." Angela moved around the room as if still in a haze. Even though the day was sunny and inviting, she could not get out of shock. "I've got to tell

Mark. No, why does it matter? I'll tell him nothing about my mother. I am happy she approved. I know she'll help with Dad if Mark and I get serious. I can see Mark without any flak from home. Awesome!" Angela smiled brushing her teeth in front of the bathroom mirror. "Awesome," she thought. Repeating the emotion was like lifting a burden off of her shoulders. "The weight of denial lifted and now I can open my mind to someone so dear, so pleasant, he's so damn sexy. It's going to be a fun day, I know it." Angela completed her dinner plan with Mark. She ran an errand to Kroger for a few items. The entire time walking through the store, she started noticing people with an open eye. She evaluated dress, the way people walked, the way they shopped, the various accents, and the differences as well as similarities. For the second time in her adult life, she actually paid attention to her surroundings. She gave attention to the intent of people. What she saw astonished her and surprised her like a door opened to learning. The entire trip to the local grocery was a college campus of education. On the road she noticed the various types of cars people drove, and wondered how people like the same things, even if they were different colors. She observed others being together, in an interracial group and laughing. It reminded her of spending time with Karen and Margo. It seemed like a new day for Angela. A new out look, and a fun territory to really explore.

Mark jumped in the shower, dressed, and headed to the local Wal-Mart Super Store. He purchased a flower, a light colored red rose with gold tip edging. He searched for dessert. He didn't know what she enjoyed, "ice cream is never a bad deal," he figured while walking the freezer aisle. Selecting ice cream created another challenge, as there were so many selections for him to choose. Instead of just grabbing any type, he stood in the middle of the aisle and pondered, "What did she say she enjoyed most? What fruit did she say she liked best? I can't remember." He decided to select the three safest flavors of all. "Every kid has eaten Neapolitan at one time or another." He smirked while looking at the rainbow selection, grabbed it and did not glance at another type. "This is going to be a nice dinner." Mark smiled at his thought as he paid the cashier and headed to his car. "Nothing can get me to Angela faster than….oh wait, it's too early." Mark headed back to his townhouse and placed the goods in storage; refrigerating the rose and freezing the ice cream. He settled in to watch a televised baseball game. Periodically, he gazed at the wall clock for time, and realized he'd lost track of an hour, somehow. "It's still too early." Time seemed slower as the arm on the second hand clicked in slow motion. His eyes focused on it as if a super power overwhelmed his vision and a tick closer to 12 was held against its will. "Time didn't just stand still, it froze in an eternity." Mark thought as he couldn't believe how time was moving so slowly. It was only 5:00 pm and two hours left before he could imagine leaving. Mark grabbed the cell phone and dialed nine of the ten numbers. He stopped dialing, and decided to wait instead of calling for an earlier arrival. "I don't want to seem too anxious."

Angela returned to her apartment with a greater enthusiasm of being open and wanting to explore social customs. "I get why mom wasn't so upset." Angela recalled as a pre-teen how she never asked much about race because in her town there weren't any people to identify being different. She barely remembered migrant workers passing through the city or seeing televised drama with people of color. It wasn't until college when she got distant exposure. Looking back on her history, Angela realized how much she'd missed in life. She could have attended so many festivals, art shows, diversity classes, and mingled with some people at those college parties where she didn't attend for long periods. "I'm so glad I met Margo and Karen," she smiled as her activities in the kitchen included storing her newly purchased groceries. Angela turned on music and got busy to prep the apartment for Mark's arrival. She set the table, placed a bottle of wine in the refrigerator, lit scented candles, and found herself being a host with particulars of making tonight fun and inviting. "I'm really looking forward to seeing Mark," she thought when her cell phone rang. "Hello." Angela answered.

"Hey. How are you?" Margo asked.

"I'm doing great. You aren't going to believe this. Mark is coming over and I'm looking forward to him being here."

"Are you serious? I knew you two would hit it off. I knew it," Margo laughed in delight.

"Yes, it's good. Last night we went to Londzell's and things sparked just as you suspected. I was hesitant about it, but oh my goodness, was it the experience. I never thought a man could have such an influence over me. I practically melted in his arms."

"Melted in his arms? You mean he…"

"No, he didn't but if he'd pushed it, I'm sure I would have. You know I don't kiss and tell," Angela sighed, "Right now after talking to Mom, I should have."

"You called your mother? You told her about Mark?" Margo surprisingly asked.

"Yes, I told her I was dating a black man."

"You must be serious. How can you be so serious after one date?"

"It's been more than one date; well we've had more than one encounter. Remember we went out before, but as friends."

"That's right. I forgot. Now you're ready to give him a try."

"Yes I am, and I have my mother to thank."

"It's so nice hearing you've crossed the bridge. Well you must be getting ready for tonight. What time is he coming over?"

"He should be here around 7:00."

"You'd better get moving. It's after 6:00. I'll talk to you tomorrow and do something I wouldn't."

"You wouldn't. What's that?"

"Enjoy!" Margo ended her call thinking, "It's about time she enjoyed life. She's such a nice girl and deserves a nice guy."

Mark arrived at 6:50 pm, and sat in the car debating if he should enter or wait the ten minutes. He scanned the parking lot for any activity for his entertainment. Nothing happening around the neighborhood but a few people moving from cars and others walking dogs. Mark noticed three minutes had passed and finally decided to head to the apartment. With a rose in one hand and ice cream in the other, he walked to the apartment door and knocked. Angela opened the door with a smile. "Right on time," she told Mark and smiled as she received the rose. "Just one! Are you kidding me?" Angela giggled as Mark had a confused expression on his face. "Just kidding, it's lovely," and returned to the kitchen for a vase.

"Oh and here's dessert." Mark lifted the bag holding ice cream. "I didn't know what to get, so I did the safe thing."

"Safe thing?" asked Angela.

"Neapolitan and you can't go wrong with three types when you don't know. Didn't you eat it as a kid?"

"As a matter of fact, I did. You are too sweet."

"Thank you." Mark moved to the kitchen. "Is there anything I can help with?"

"You can open the wine." Angela handed him the cork screw. "I hope you're hungry."

"Oh, I'm starved. It smells wonderful."

"You'll like my dish. I learned it at cooking class."

"Whatever it is, I'm excited for it."

"It's salmon and I hope you don't mind."

"Mind? I have a lovely woman cooking for me, wine, nice music, and on a day we can relax. I don't think a man can ask for much more."

"You men can imagine more things to ask for." Angela laughed at her comment as if he'd understand the inside joke.

"Oh I get it. You have jokes."

"Well we can't live without humor, now can we? Can you grab the plates from the table please?"

"Sure, no problem." Mark responded, performing the task. "I like a woman with humor. What other jokes do you have? Will the salmon explode?" Pointing to the table he asked, "Or is this a trick candle?"

"Don't be silly. I'm not quite that type of jokester. I enjoy a good laugh or two."

"It's all good. We should laugh whenever we can." Mark took one prepared plate and placed it at the end of the table as if he knew which seat Angela would sit. He waited for her to leave the kitchen or hand him the other plate. Angela quickly recognized his manners and without second thought passed him the plate she prepared for her. "I'd guess you're ready to pour the wine."

"I'll pour it, but can I have a glass of water first before you leave the kitchen, please?"

"Oh I'm sorry I didn't offer you anything earlier."

"But you did," Mark smiled while looking directly in her eyes.

Angela stopped in motion and returned the look, the gaze of intrigue, and lust beating them to the punch leading their minds into the physical attraction. Mark turned for a glass on the counter. "Is this one ok?" he asked and thought, "Too soon, I have to take it easy and build it. Dang, how much do I have to build? … Silly me."

"Yes. Do you prefer cold water with ice?" asked Angela.

"No, the tap is fine. It's not that I don't like wine; it's just I drink a glass of water to help my intake level. It looks good and I don't want to ruin my first dinner in your home by pigging out."

"Really?"

"Yes, really; I would eat every bit of this. I'm definitely hungry and you're a great cook. We can make great music together."

"You know what they use to say, "A way to a man's heart is through his stomach.""

"But this man has his heart wrapped for a special lady and he's waiting for her to take it as a gift."

Angela sat silent across from Mark and looked in his eyes to find truth in his comment. It's as if Angela remembered the eyes were the window to a person's soul and she searched for truth. Mark sat in silence after drinking the water, waiting for her to start eating, yet he nodded his head and said nothing, but cut his eye contact away from Angela. "God, don't let me blow this and bless this meal." he silently prayed. Angela broke silence asking, "Aren't you going to try these mixed vegetables? I seasoned them with a secret ingredient." Mark did as directed and tasted the veggies.

"Wow. These are good."

"I'm glad you like it. Some people do and others don't." Angela responded with a small bite. "It's the way the veggies take the spices as its own and builds such a unique flavor."

"Did you learn this in class too?"

"No, it's a family trick I learned as a kid."

"I love your family already," Mark smiled while taking another bite.

Angela sat back in her chair with a wine glass in hand thinking, "If he only knew." Then replied, "That's another story Mark." Angela sipped wine from the glass. Not knowing what to expect in the next minute, Mark changed the conversation. "What about last night wasn't the band awesome?"

"I enjoyed them. I thought they were good, and I'm surprised they aren't signed with a big label."

"Jazz is a little different. It's because the market doesn't support those artists right away. It's tough and of course, most teens don't listen to it."

"Good point." Angela sat forward giving the body signal of interest and attention. "What did you think of our dance?"

"You mean when we melted together? Can we do it again?" Mark smiled as he responded.

"I'd like too. I've never had such an experience. Am I telling you too much?"

Mark looked at Angela after a bite of salmon, pondered her comment and decided to direct the subject to something less serious. "This salmon is very delicious. I'd bet it's another family secret."

"No, remember I learned to cook this in class. The veggies are a home dish." Angela was surprised at his change of subject. "Why are you avoiding our attraction?"

"Me, avoiding our attraction is a funny question." Mark placed his fork on the table and grabbed his glass, then sat forward. "I've been attracted to you from the very beginning. When we talked day after day at the bookstore, when we went to dinner, when we passed each other in stores or parking lots, my attraction has been with you for weeks on end."

"You mean, if I hadn't pushed you away, you'd have pursued me?"

"Without a doubt in my mind or heart, you'd be my girl right now." Mark responded tipping his glass towards Angela. "And I'm sure you'd be happy with me as your guy."

"I wasn't sure of it then as I am now," Angela sighed as if she was willing to spill her discovery from her mother's conversation. "I talked to my mother earlier today. The conversation was amazing."

"I'm, um, don't think I'm ready – we're ready to meet parents just yet."

"I know, but this is different for me, Mark." Angela stressed her point on different. "The unusual thing to do between people of a different race is date or fall in love."

"Angela, your thought is right down my line, but why think of falling in love so quickly?"

"Because it's a big change for me. From now on I have to think of you being the last man I see. I don't think any man will ever want me if we don't make it. No white man anyway."

"Is this your thought?" Mark sat back in his chair with hands palms down flanking the dinner plate. A surprised look on his face as Angela stared at him for a euphoric response. "Dang, what kind of pressure is this?" he thought while gazing at Angela. "She is gorgeous, a great cook, easy to be with so far, fun really, intriguing to a point, and worth investigating more... What the hell, she's worth every bit of my attention." Mark paused a little longer, before responding, "Look, Angela." Mark slightly leaned to the right to have a clear view between them, "I really like you and actually excited about being here. I know there are sacrifices one makes to go against the grain, per se. But, if you're willing to walk with me and enjoy life, I'm willing to hold your hand along the way."

"I think I'm willing to walk." Angela responded but pondered, "I hope Mom takes care of Dad."

"Are you sure? I mean it's us going through this and you're going to learn a lot of American social culture. Some of it will be pretty and other times it can be nasty."

"I think I'm ready for the change. Because, first of all, it's not the average guy I'm walking the path with. You are funny, intelligent, gorgeous, fun, and totally a gentleman. I see all the things I want in a man and have seen it for sometime now. So, I'm ready to walk, but just don't let go when I don't understand."

"I'd never." Mark sat back in his seat. "But you have to promise me one thing."

"And that is?"

"Always be honest in your response. Good or bad, even if you think it will hurt my feelings, you have to be honest, brutally honest."

"I think…, no I know I can do it. I like honesty and I can be myself at all times."

"Good, I like you being yourself. I get to learn more about you, see more of your inner thoughts, and feel your ideas and affection. I like the idea or concept."

"Since you're asking me, you have to do the same thing. Total honesty and you can't let anything hold you back from telling me whatever it is on your mind."

"Good, we can do this. First thing on my mind right now is…" Angela leaned to her left getting a good view of Mark as he spoke. "And that is?" Angela asked.

"We start dessert. Are you ready for dessert?" Mark laughed.

"What a jokester!" Angela giggled but she's glad Mark lightened things up. Mark stood with his plate, retrieved Angela's dinner plate and headed for the kitchen. "I'll do the dishes after dessert. Is that ok?"

"No, you're my guest. You better enjoy it because as we do what we've discussed, you'll do lots of dishes in time." Angela pointed. "Just place them in the sink and I'll get them later."

"Where are your bowls?" Mark asked.

"I have a different idea for dessert"

"You do?"

"Why don't you open the other bottle of wine and come to the couch?"

Mark followed Angela's suggestions and in minutes joined Angela on the couch. Angela left the candles burning and added a couple while Mark opened the wine. She left the two glasses on the coffee table and changed her CDs to her classical collection. Nervous, Mark saw the set up and immediately stepped back in his mind as a football quarterback studying the field to call a play. "Should I go for the Hail Mary or a field goal?" he pondered while moving forward to the couch. "I can toss a Hail Mary, but I want this to have a foundation first. I want it right, as it might be our beginning. Sex can wait, but what if she's in the mood for sex?" Mark looked at Angela and added up the signs, remembered last night, recalled the nervous tension when he walked in the apartment and then concluded, "She's ready."

"Mark, I think we should continue our conversation." Angela opened the door so she could clear her mind and be honest about her earlier hesitation.

"I'm listening, what's on your mind?"

"I ah ...we just talked about honesty and being up front in thought. I want to clear a few things before we move forward."

"Is this a business agreement? Are there limitations I need to consider?" Mark jumped on the defensive recalling an earlier relationship where all activities were out of public view.

"No limitations. I just need to get this off my chest and open the air on how I got to this point."

"Whew, I'm glad you want to."

"Huh?"

"Go ahead, I'll explain later." Mark stopped the antics and gave her total attention.

"I've never dated a man of color and it makes me nervous. I like you, actually admire you, and secretly compared you to other men I dated since going to Café 290. You were sweet, kind, fun, and a total gentleman. You did all the right things, like including me in conversations with your friends, so I felt comfortable in a crowd of strangers; you impressed me with your social manners and table etiquette, and gave me total respect. I took it all for granted at first and didn't think of dating you because I listened to friends and feared relatives' thoughts."

"I understand. Does this mean it's not going to happen?" Mark knew the answer, but wanted validation.

"It's going to happen but I want you to know what I'm going through and went through to get me here. Earlier it was a fight just to admit I liked you. I had such an influence from others about people, I forgot about what was important. I started to do things against my better judgment and then fought to be myself along the way. Then I met Margo."

Mark's eyes showed concern as Angela mentioned Margo in the conversation. "I bet you had an interesting conversation. She's a lovely lady, that Margo," Mark added.

Angela smiled while responding, "Don't worry, she didn't tell me everything between you two. And if she had, I'd still be here."

Mark lifted his wine glass as giving a positive agreement of relief. "I hope she at least told you good things."

"She did. Besides I saw many of those things before meeting her. I knew you were educated, had a great job, enjoyed life, and loved to read. I wanted to learn so much more..."

Mark quickly agreed in response "...as I wish to learn more of you."

"I got so wrapped up in your being black, I called my mother. I had to discuss it with her because I dreamed of her crying when I thought of you in the night. I called her today before you came."

Mark braced himself for bad news. His experience led him down a path of conflict between daughter and mother when it came to him being with a first time woman stepping out of her roots. "Are you sure you want to do this? I mean I don't want to become a wedge between you and your family. It's not like we're committed to a serious relationship. Well, not yet anyway."

"No, it's nothing like you think. No wedges between my mother and me. Now my dad is different and mom said she'd handle him for me."

"Again, Angela you're an adult and family is always important. I don't want us moving forward if you aren't ready to have a bump in the road."

"I want us moving forward. But it has to be one step at a time. I mean this is new to me, totally new."

"Just be yourself. Please be yourself and don't do anything different because you think it's a black thing or change your conversation, style, or anything about you. I like you as you are, so please be yourself."

"I can. Why would I change into anything else?"

"Because some women do, as if it's a difference between our cultures. I mean, so many people buy into the hype. Yes there are differences, some subtle and some big, but you have to be you and don't worry about what people think we are."

"I've learned already. I didn't know people change when they date people of color."

"To some extent many do, but most don't because it's learning the differences and holding onto self identity."

"Oh, I love the idea. Anyway, I had to consider you in my decision process. When Margo and I talked she let me in on some horrifying history. She made it clear the risk you were taking by dating me. It was an eye opening conversation which brings me to your decision. Why me?"

Mark sipped wine from his glass, cradling it with both hands, as he thought of a way to explain his actions. He wanted to give an intellectual answer, helping her understand the root of his attractions. "To me you're like this beautiful soul, wandering the earth as if you have an entourage supporting your every step. I feel warmth in your presence; I feel excitement from your touch, and see potential of having a partner in life. I feel the envy of others whenever we're together. I saw the glow of reaction others gave you when they interacted with you. It's something I wanted as a part of my life. This is my motivation to be with you."

Not sure how to respond, Angela sat in silence next to the candle where Mark observed the flickering light on Angela's skin. The soft light accented her features, the little nose, the seductive lips, the oval shaped eyes, her soft structured chin, a perfect neck. Mark held his breath for a moment and sighed to relax as his temperament took him on a journey of desire for passion. Angela finally broke silence, "I've never had anyone in my life explain how they felt so clearly."

"I didn't mean it to seem like lines of poetry, it's my heart and the reason why. I don't think you'd like it if I told you a poem."

"No, I wouldn't. So where did you attend college?"

"We have never talked about it, have we?" Mark asked, as he recalled discussing other subjects, but never talked about their background or childhood. He responded with his birth date as if telling an autobiographer, and hour after hour the two exchanged their lives in a nutshell. It was as if Monday wasn't a work day, and the conversation lasted for hours on end. One a.m., two, three a.m. all came and still the conversation carried and the energy between the two never dropped to a lull. One after the other, they exchanged events bringing them into their identities, their personalities, and spoke openly on past relationships, including sexual experiences. They talked, and talked, and talked, touching everything of importance. They voiced on the number of children each thought of having, they spoke of countries they wish to live or visit, and what types of homes they would love to have. The conversation ran into the morning workday sunrise. Realizing the time, Mark rose from the couch, stretched and said, "My sweet Angela, we have to go to work. Why don't we finish this conversation tonight?"

"Yes, why don't we?" Angela agreed, standing.
Mark embraced Angela, holding her tight and placed his lips within a fraction of hers. He moved a little closer, and patiently waited for her response. Angela moved to connect for their consummating kiss, starting their new era in life, hand in hand taking the first step upon the journey.

Monday afternoon, Mark sat at his desk pondering last night's conversation. "I'm really into Angela. She is truly my match. How can I keep her interest and expose her to my world? I'll have to start planning, based on what she told me and those things I saw her excited over." With every intention of being in tune with Angela, Mark made a list of things she mentioned during last night's conversation. He surfed the internet for a local activity newspaper and created a chart of available events matching Angela's likes. The first one was Wednesday's Martinis and Imax Screen in midtown Atlanta. He carefully calculated the travel time from Alpharetta to midtown and the possibilities of leaving early to beat traffic. He made a time chart before finalizing his thoughts and invited her. Instead of writing Angela a text, Mark decided to talk to her about it later in the day. "After work or after the gym workout," which Mark didn't think he'd make since staying up all night. But his energy level took him by surprise from anxiety and excitement to get started on this sought-after relationship. "Hi Gorgeous, please call me." Mark texted Angela.

Angela's Monday morning at the office had co-workers seeing her smile. Her energy level provided them the picture of a focused person. It was her energy high from not sleeping, and a second wind playing with the body and mind. She moved from meeting to cubicle, completed reports, and made clear concise calls to her customers. In between activities, she recalled her conversation with Mark. ".....you're like this beautiful soul..... warmth in your presence...excitement from your touch...a partner in life." Lost in the moment, Angela finally heard her cell buzz from an incoming call. "Hello." she answered without looking at the caller ID.

"Hi, Angela." Margo thought she'd hear from Angela last night.

"Hey, I have got to tell you Mark is really a nice guy, full of life, and I bet a fantastic lover."

"Didn't you spend the night with him?" Margo asked, as if she knew Mark was an aggressive lover.

"Yes, but we talked all night."

"You mean pillow talk, right?"

"No, I mean actually talked and connected. We talked about everything and anything. I felt so comfortable with him; it was fun and the first time a guy actually listened to me. Totally listened."

"I guess you passed the bridge. I'm happy for you." Margo's voice reflected a smile, and a sense of adulation.

"Yes, I called my mother after you left and you aren't going to believe what she told me."

"Let me guess, it is ok" –"as if it weren't apparent she got approval," thought Margo.

"Yes, surprisingly so, but my dad is another story."

"Some fathers are and some aren't. Either he'll accept Mark in time or turn away from you both. There is no middle ground there."

"How do you know so much when you didn't get serious with Mark?" Angela's curiosity gave doubt to Margo's and Mark's earlier relationship.

"It was observation on a couple of girlfriends while growing up. I saw one father say yes it doesn't matter, because he wanted his daughter happy. The other was pushed away and hadn't been spoken to her since. It's been eight years...and the guy isn't African American, he's Asian."

"Wow. I guess it depends on how they see race all together."

"Remember, it's just as hard for them to change and accept, as it is for society."

"I'll have to work on him." Angela's excitement returned after realizing Mark's limited involvement, as Margo explained earlier.

"Yes, it's a work in progress. But, don't move so fast...unless..."

"Unless what?" Angela thought waiting for the hammer to fall.

"You're seriously in love."

"Oh, I'm not there, I like him, but love. I don't think I'm there at all."

"Then why worry about your dad? Go explore and enjoy life with Mark. I'm sure you'll have fun doing so."

"Good point, a very good point. But you know if he keeps going the way I think he will; we're practically there."

"Ok, fantasy girl. I've got to go. Karen and I are planning a Friday girls' night out. Are you interested?"

"Of course, let me know where and when. I'm there."

"What about Mark? Aren't you going to ask him if he has plans?"

"I'll let him know I have plans for then. Don't worry I'll be there."

"Great, see you Friday and I'll call you with the time and place. Bye."

"Bye." Angela snapped her phone and returned to work. Multi-tasking, she continued office chores with thought, "Why am I so worried about Dad? I didn't tell him about Eric, or Christopher, or my experience with Bill. Why must he know? Mark and I aren't serious, even though there is potential."

Late Monday afternoon Angela's phone chimed with a text message "Hi Gorgeous, please call me" with Mark's number. Excitedly she dialed him and wanted to hear his voice. "Hi, Gorgeous!" Mark answered.

"Hi, Mark. I got your text and couldn't wait to call." Angela admitted with excitement.

"I'm glad you did. I was thinking of Wednesday night. How do you feel about going out on a weeknight?"

"I'm ok with it. I mean look at us today, we haven't slept at all and I'm doing ok. I'm still going to the gym so my energy level is fine."

"Good, because I have an idea. We should go to midtown for Martinis and Imax Screen."

"I've heard of it but never attended. I'm game what time?"

"We have to leave the office around 4:30; do you think you can get off by then?"

"Sure. I'll mark my calendar and make adjustments."

"Great! I'll pick you up from your office. Let me know tomorrow or later today where it is, so we can make time before traffic hits."

"Sounds great. By the way, Friday night is my normal girls' night out. Did you have anything planned for then?"

"I remember your night out. I was there at the last one." Mark laughed.

"Yes, I remember it was such a scene."

"I don't mind, because it's your thing and friends are important. I'm sure I'll find something to do."

"I see this is going to work fine," Angela admitted without thought to a response.

"Yes, I do agree. I'll call you later. Have fun at the gym."

"I will. Talk to you soon." Angela ended the call and returned to work with a smile. Excitement ran through her mind and body as the energy high continued. Happy she agreed to Wednesday night, Mark started planning a place for dinner before arriving to the museum. He followed a simple guide from the weekly event paper and identified a couple of locations with quick service. "I'm planning way too much," he realized, as the hour to end his day neared. "Play dinner by ear, but have a place in mind just in case," Mark concluded, returning focus to the job.

Tuesday zipped in like lightning after they both went through the normal workday, workout, and skipped dinner and crashed for thirteen hours. Angela couldn't believe it was a full night and Mark woke with a new energy, reaching over for his cell, he checked to ensure he'd not missed a call. The last thing Mark wanted was giving doubt to Angela by missing a call. Mark dialed Angela. "Good Morning Angela, are we having coffee together this morning?"

"I'd like that." Angela responded, "I'll be there in thirty minutes."

"So will I." Mark ended the call and rushed to ensure he'd arrive at the bookstore coffee shop as planned. It was like clockwork as both Angela and Mark headed out to meet for coffee. It was their routine being in the Barnes and Noble months ago, but this time it was more than just sitting for a chat. It was the motivation starting the day with a view of each other. "Building a relationship one step at a time and the greater the exposure, the more time spent, the greater the foundation for a successful love," Mark pondered while driving to the bookstore. He arrived before Angela, entered the coffee shop, and ordered her specialty coffee. "One tall latte and one grande coffee of the day, room for cream," Mark told the attendant.

"Hey, Mark," Angela smiled with a greeting, as if the sun just rose to full brightness.

"Gorgeous," Mark replied while reaching with one hand, not to show an aggressive side, but showing affection, and kissed her on the cheek. "I ordered a latte for you. I think I'm right."

"It's been some time since we've shared coffee and you remembered? I'm impressed."

"How can I forget anything about you? You're my dream girl."

"Oh, stop it," Angela blushingly replied. "You're attentive, it's your nature."

"It may be so, but look who I'm attentive too."

"Good point." Angela smiled and pointed at him, "Good point."

The attendant shouted, "Mark - tall latte and a grande coffee of the day, room for cream," and placed the two cups on the counter. Mark reached for the coffee and passed the latte to Angela. "Are we sitting here or going into the bookstore?"

"I'd like to steal you to myself for a moment." Angela directed him to an open table on the secluded side of the coffee shop. "How was your night?" asked Angela, as the two sat next to each other.

"I slept like a log. I remember there was a time I could stay awake for days and not feel this way. Now, there is no way I can do it."

"It's not age; it's a healthy life style. Your body needs rest because it's part of your workout."

"I believe you. But you need to tell my mind that." Mark laughed. "I don't think it understands all I wanted to do was get to you. But my body didn't let me."

"Funny, I wanted the same but didn't think you were open to it."

"Are you kidding?"

"Yes, I'm kidding. I crashed too, like a log," Angela snickered, mimicking his comment. "You know, I'm open to you coming over after the job or the gym."

"Are you really? You don't think it's moving too fast?"

"No, for some reason I'm not worried at all."

"I'll keep your lack of worry in mind."

"Please do. Are you sure about Friday night?"

"You mean girls' night out?"

"Yes, I get to see Margo, Karen, and maybe Amy." Angela smiled thinking, "I get to tell them of my comfort with Mark."

"All you're going to do is talk about me, right?"

"No, not the entire time; I'll tell them how much I enjoyed talking to you Sunday night."

"I enjoyed you too. I'll never keep you from your friends, I promise you."

"And I'll promise the same, however you have to tell me if we cross the line and not receive support from those so-called friends."

"If my friends don't support us, they aren't my friends." Mark made the comment as rigid and sound as possible by tapping on the table.

"I get it. Oooh scary."

"No, not scary, but serious; a true friend may suggest things but accepts you as you are. As a matter of fact, a friend actually knows you to be a certain way and do certain things. If he or she is a true friend, they'll speak their piece and support your decision."

"I used to think I had a friend as such. I found out later it wasn't the case."

"It always happens when you open your eyes."

"Yes, it does." Angela admitted to Paula being so different than she thought earlier in life. She paused a moment and then said, "Yes, it does."

The two sat in the coffee shop for over an hour. Time flew and neither one noticed the environment, traffic, or noises around them. If Mark hadn't looked at the time on Angela's watch, the afternoon would have taken them by surprise. Quickly the two hustled to get to their office. "Oh by the way," Mark spoke as he walked Angela to her car, "tonight is Martini's and Imax Screen. Remember I'll pick you up at the office at 4:30 to beat traffic." Mark closed the car door.

Life continued with one major change, major interest from a person with compatible nature. Now they receive increased numbers of text messages and phone calls throughout their day. The focus surely made their day go much easier than usual. Any meeting or work challenge for either was now at a point in between a phone message or text. The added activity motivated them like school kids living through those adolescence years when finding new interest. Angela felt as if her life was really changing. The focus was amazing as she found self discovery with each text or call. "I've never had

the feeling of being able to freely say what's on my mind."
Angela thought as she ended her call from Mark. Angela
recognized her dynamics were becoming clear as moments
passed throughout the day. The office receptionist walked to
her cubicle with one red and two yellow roses, wrapped in
green paper. "These were delivered for you a few minutes
ago"

"Thank you," Angela smiled while responding. "Did they
leave a note or is there a card?"

"No, just a nicely dressed guy dropped them off."

"Thank you so much." Angela baffled at the arrival of her
roses, pondered who would send them, and immediately
assumed it was Mark. Without further hesitation, she text
Mark with, "Thank You, Affectionate Man." She placed the
flowers in a large plastic cup from the break room. Returning
to the cubicle, her phone had a new text, "Can't wait until I
see you again- Mark." Angela blushed, and looked at her
office clock. Her anxiety to leave now took over as the day
slowed to a crawl. She worked through lunch so her day
ended at 4:30 as planned. The day finally started moving as
she redirected focus on her current project. Within what
seemed minutes, 4:25 appeared like a zap of energy. Angela
shutdown her laptop, and gathered her things to leave for the
parking lot. As she entered the building elevator, a text
signal appeared, "out front -Mark." Without missing a step,
she scurried out to the front of the building, her blood
zooming; stopping only to seem less excited to see Mark
waiting in the car, and slowing her pace. Mark saw her and
quickly opened the passenger car door; waiting with a smile,
"Hello, Beautiful," he greeted Angela.

"Hi, Gorgeous man. Thank you so much for the flowers.
How did you know I liked colored roses?"

"Remember our all night conversation?"

"Of course I remember us talking all night."

"I actually listened and remembered everything you told
me about you."

Angela smiled while sitting in the car and thought, "He
actually listened. What a good thing!" Just as she snapped

the seat buckle, she leaned to Mark and placed a gentle kiss on his cheek. "Thank you."

"Wow, what a nice kiss. I'm not going to wash this side of my face forever. My face will have one side with a beard, the other side smooth, or just the patch of hair growing down to my shoulder."

"Don't be silly."

"No, really. My angel kissed my cheek when I least expected it."

"Your angel?"

"Yes, my angel. Isn't Angel the name origin for Angela?" Mark turned south on GA 400 while talking, making the time seem short to the distance traveled. "You know, it's a dream having you with me this evening. I always thought we'd do something special in life. Yes, it's a thought I had when we first met. I'm glad my dream is coming to a reality."

"You mean; this is a dream of yours. Just going to Martini and Imax Screen?"

"Yes, it's a dream come true. I wanted to explore this with you before. And now, it's real. Aren't I the lucky one?"

"No, you are the chosen one," Angela smiled in response. "Only a smart, intriguing, and cute guy would ever come on my court to play. I opened the door."

"You sound conceited," Mark laughed. "As gorgeous as you are, you have a right to."

"I'm not conceited, just confident," Angela remarked and asked, "Where are we going?"

"The Fernbank. I read there's a lot going on there and I've never visited the place."

"Neither have I. It's been on my list for quite sometime, but never had any of my friends wishing to go. You know, it's never ladylike to go to these things alone."

"That is so cliché, and untrue. It's not the lady factor; it's the fear of someone passing judgment on you. I've seen women go to places alone and have a ball."

"Well, I'm not one of those to go alone."

"I respect you for not going, I do. Do you worry about what other people think of you?"

"What do you mean?"

"People pass judgment on others all the time. Do you take their thoughts to heart?"

"Honestly, I used to. Well, actually I did but now I find myself more focused on how I think of things."

"Great answer." Mark smiled as her answer indicated a level of self-confidence needed to continue their relationship.

Entering the Fernbank Museum of Natural History was a moment of awe as dinosaur skeletons, plants, and other nature items of earlier eras were presented. The building was huge with high ceilings and a second floor with an open hallway. The place takes your attention to its setup and displays. Yet, Mark and Angela didn't miss one step as they held hands and walked to the Martini bar in the other section. There was a stage, multiple tables, and a long snack bar of delicate pastries, appetizers, and tapas. There were all sorts of people from every walk of life conversing in groups, some diverse, and everyone drinking. They arrived right at the beginning of the band's first set. Mark ordered an Apple Martini for Angela and decided not to take a chance on drinking and driving. He ordered tonic water with lime. Angela found a table and directed Mark there, just as she took her Martini. "I think this is a great spot," she said and moved in the direction. Mark followed right behind her, observing her fluid walk as if she were gliding upon the marbled floor, her buttocks swung as if moving in rhythm to an imaginary beat, her hair, flowing soft in the breeze of the air conditioning, and the figure excited him, as his imagination ran rampant in a room of nearly a hundred people. "Beautiful," Mark thought as he stopped to observe her stand in front of a table she chose. Angela looked at Mark and noticed a sparkle in his eye, the same gleam she saw the other night during their slow dance. She knew exactly how to connect to his thoughts, as if tuned in to smile in response. "Are you coming?" Angela asked.

"Yes, I'm nearly there," Mark answered as he snapped out of his daydream.

"This is nice," Angela commented.

"Yes it is. I have a question for you Angela."

"Yes?"

"Do you mind public affection? I mean, I know about the other night at Londzell's, but this is different. It's bright, a lot more people, and really public. Is there a chance I can…"

"Kiss me?" Angela quickly answered leaning closer to Mark. He stopped talking and seductively touched her lips with his. Gently touching her with his lips he explored the inner rim of her mouth with his tongue. The moist feeling surprised Angela as she felt the urge to pull him closer for a longing French kiss. Mark obliged just as he dreamed of doing long ago. The kiss was their connection and an introduction to the public they were indeed one couple. Now, sitting closer to each other, listening to the music, the two constantly stole moments of pleasure. A kiss here, a hug there, and a whisper of excitement at multiple moments. "Why didn't we just do this earlier?" asked Mark.

"I don't know. I didn't think we'd enjoy each other as much. I mean, I didn't have the open mind to try at the time we first met."

"It's ok. We all have to go through something to start dating people different than our parents. I mean, it was ok for me being a military brat. I didn't know there was a focus on race until college."

"I knew there was one, but not in my social circle. But I'm glad I opened my eyes to you. So far, you've been a true gentleman and I love the way you treat me. You are an impressive man."

"No, I'm a man who knows a lovely woman when I see one." Mark leaned and kissed Angela on the cheek as he finished his whisper. As the band completed their first full set, Mark inquired to Angela having another martini or an appetizer. She answered yes and instructed him to choose anything he'd like adding to the additional Martini, of course. He did as she directed and left her at the table to retrieve those items. Angela took in his actions of affection, and then took in the participants of the room. She noticed there were couples, singles, business men and women, also a group of people laughing, reminding her of Karen's dinner party. She finally noticed her table had additional people whom she didn't recall sitting there. "How long have you two been together?" One lady asked from the other side of the table.

"We," Angela stopped to think of her answer as she realized it's been quite a short time, "are just starting out actually."

"You look happy, really in love."

"I..." again Angela thought how to answer, realizing how wonderful it felt being with Mark. "Thank you for the observation. I can't say we are at the moment."

"If you keep this up, you'll be like my husband and I. We're still at it after fifteen years."

"So nice seeing it works. Do you two come here often?" Angela asked.

"Yes we do. We love the environment and it's nice listening to good music. This is where we met and it's a rekindle spontaneous event for us now. We just love coming here."

"I'm impressed with it myself. It's our first time."

"It won't be your last, if you two ever come up for air." The woman laughed.

"He is a very nice man and I think he's really a great catch."

"I'm sure you'll keep him. He's very attentive and those are great indicators to an affectionate and caring man. You'll keep him, trust me."

"I think you're right," Angela smiled as she confirmed the lady's advice. She noticed other couples in the museum. For the first time in her life, she really paid attention to the different ethnic groups as people walked passed her table or walked within her sight. She observed who they seemed to interact with and surprisingly, she saw a multitude of diversity in the room. Then in a flash, the lady's husband returned to the table and he was Caucasian and she was African American. "Wow, you'd have never known."

Angela thought. "Hi." Angela said to the gentleman. "Are you having a lovely night?"

"She's in love, darling," the wife answered.

"Nice, really nice, I told my wife you were lost in amazement there for a moment."

"Really?" Angela responded a little puzzled.

"You and your guy were here all alone. We didn't bother asking if we could sit with you because you'd never hear us. You being amazed with your guy told me you two were either newlyweds or just starting out."

"Well, you're right, I'm amazed with Mark. He's a wonderful guy."

Mark returned with drinks and appetizers. "Here, gorgeous."

The gentleman snickered, "I use to say the same thing to you doll, early in our time."

"Don't believe him, he still does and never stopped calling me those sweet names," the woman responded with a light laugh.

"I hope we continue our love like you two," Angela told them while Mark listened.

"You will," the gentleman added, "just keep doing what you two do now. It'll work out."

"But one piece of advice," the woman added, "do not let people tear you down or apart."

"Thank you so much for the advice," Angela responded to the couple and turned to Mark, "What did you get us?" Angela pondered the couple's comments. "I think I know what they're talking about. Like my father disapproves of Mark being in my life, so will others."

"We have, Santa Fe egg rolls, sautéed chicken pieces with almond sauce, fruit, and to finish - chocolate covered strawberries. Is this ok?" Mark asked.

"Yes, it's wonderful."

The rest of the show, the two continued just as their night began. They returned to being alone in a well populated place and before you knew it, the band stopped playing and the lights brightened. Many people left and they noticed a few tables with couples finishing their conversations and drinks. Angela and Mark never saw the couple at their table leave, nor did they realize how late the night became, as tomorrow was another work day. "I guess this is our cue to leave," Mark suggested as he finally increased his space from Angela.

"Yes it is. Where did the time go?" Angela remarked as she looked at her watch.

"Didn't you know it was true?"

"What was true?"

"Time flies when you're having fun."

"It seems so, doesn't it? We better head home. I have to work in the morning and this time I need to rest a little before going."

"I agree. We need to because the day we didn't sleep was so hard."

"You crashed and burned didn't you?"

"That night I didn't realize how much I crashed and burned. Wait, look who's talking, you did too."

"Yes I did," Angela giggled, "did I ever."

Mark and Angela rode to Alpharetta much closer than heading to the Fernbank. It seemed the night allowed them to show the world their interest in each other. Angela couldn't forget those words the woman table companion said about her and Mark being in love. The words resonated in her mind, as if a seed was planted. "Love," she thought as street lights flashed while Mark drove through town. "Love," she asked herself as if a questionnaire of doubt ran through her mind, like a checklist of events should have occurred before thinking such thoughts. "Love," she continually pondered and compared her past with how Mark treated her and how attentive, sweet, and fun he seemed to be. Not one point of Mark was negative or atrocious. Not even a fact of him being a well educated and a greatly read man, a man of precise words, a man of comfort and fashion. "It's just a thought," Angela admitted, "it was just a thought."

Mark drove with a smile and in comfort as he was feeling the light shine on his night. "I don't want to stop but we have to." He looked at Angela and observed a glimpse of street lights flashing on her beauty, her curves, and the contentment she was showing. "She's truly an angel."

The drive was pretty relaxed and the two talked about the night's events, the couple sitting on the table and small talk about their observations. Angela commented on the Martinis as a joke for Mark to take advantage. Mark joked about Angela telling the woman at the table his secrets and it was why they were so in-tuned with them during the night. Not that either paid attention to the environment, but they agreed it was a fun and classy night. "What was the name of the band?" Mark asked.

"I have no idea. They were good though."

"Yes, they were."

Mark exited off GA 400 near Angela's home. "I should take you home and pick you up in the morning. We make sure you have a ride to the office and I get to have coffee with you."

"Not a good idea." Angela told him.

"What do you have in mind?"

"Seeing you as the first thing I see when I open my eyes."

"I..." surprised at her suggestion, Mark paused in response as he smiled in his heart and embraced the idea. "We can do this. Do you want your place or mine?"

"I'd like to see your place."

Mark turned the car towards his townhouse without responding. He contemplated his actions "If we do this, what will it look like when I'm serious with her? Is it too soon, or is it not soon enough? I surely like this woman, a lot more than she realizes." He turned the car off and exited without a word to Angela until he opened her door. "We're here."

"I noticed," Angela replied with a smile. "Does that mean you're lifting me over the threshold into your place?"

"Like being married and you are coming home for the first time?"

"Yes, coming home for the first time."

"Isn't it bad luck for the future?" Mark asked while lifting Angela in his arms.

"No, it's not bad luck. Consider it practice."

Mark took those words to heart, as he knew if things went as he'd like the idea could be a reality. "As long as you don't get heavier..."

"...oh, is there a problem with my weight?"

"Not at all; I mean later if we get to do this a second time. I'm not good at carrying a larger woman over the threshold."

"I don't think you'll ever have to worry."

"Great." Mark thought he dodged a tough subject of conversation. "Here's my place." Mark allowed Angela to stand. "Make yourself at home. Can I get you anything?"

"Yes, a t-shirt because I'm tired and don't sleep nude."

"Not sleeping nude."

"I really don't, but you know, it depends on the action in the room. I usually don't sleep nude at home. And you said, "make myself at home.""

"I did. Why don't you come with me?" Mark led Angela to the bedroom and pulled a t-shirt from his drawer.

"I like the way you have your place. You have nice taste."

"Thank you." he responded while heading to the bathroom and then closed the door. Angela changed into the t-shirt and it was large as she suspected, and it fitted well as a night gown. She sat on his bed and looked at her reflection in the dresser mirror. "I'm doing the right thing. I want to feel him, indulge him, and make love to this gorgeous and sexy man."

"Do you need to come in here?" Mark asked.

"Yes I do." Angela opened the door and walked in the bathroom.

"I have a tooth brush for you if you want to use it." Mark passed it to Angela and left the bathroom. "Damn she's sexy. How the hell am I going to control this?"

"Thanks." Angela brushed her teeth and looked around his bathroom. She found nothing out of the ordinary and noticed no women items there; which she smiled and said, "Good, real good."

"What's good?"

"Good, it's really good brushing my teeth before bed."

"I thought it would be."

Angela crawled into bed next to Mark and found a comfortable spot. It was right under his arm and close to his chest. Mark lightly stroked her back while the other hand ran through her hair. "You know, this feels wonderful, having you next to me in bed. Allowing me to stroke your hair, caress your back and feel the warmth of your body."

"I feel good too. I feel really good and it's nice you're caressing my back and stroking my hair."

Mark kissed her forehead and pulled her tighter in his embrace, he felt the excitement build, and lay still where as not to offend Angela. Yet his power of control overtook his manhood, he became erect and it pressed against the triangle of affection, pushing the button of indulgence. Angela responded, kissing his neck and pressing her breasts upon his chest. She moved with little rhythmic motions next to his penetrating muscle. Mark grabbed her ass, and stopped moving as he deeply kissed her. "I want you, but not like this, not where our time is limited and tomorrow we have to rush. Our first time should be when we can truly explore and not worry about time, nor if we have to get up, if we can repeat the smiles we'll share, or the walk around the house and enjoy being spontaneous. I want us to have the freedom and not be limited to a quick session of making love."

"I..." Angela thought reluctantly because she was on fire for this man, yet she understood the moment as he explained, "...agree. I feel your power of desire for me, just as I have for you. I understand waiting can be good."

"Hey, it's easy for us to do this but it's harder for us to make it worth something more as the first time should be a wonderful experience. Not saying this wouldn't, but I'm not into kissing and running for a first time. I'm, as you'll learn a slow and patient lover. You'll see."

"I will see, for sure," Angela responded as she readjusted for slumber, finding her sleeping comfort zone with Mark.

# Chapter 12

Karen arrived just in time for the girls' night out. She entered the bar with small bags. "Hey," she spoke to Angela, Margo, and Amy.

"Hi." the three responded in unison. "What did you do?" asked Margo.

"Nothing serious I hope," Amy chimed in.

"No, I wanted you to have these." Karen gave a bag to each of the girls. "I found these on sale and they were so nice I had to share them."

"Thank you," Angela said as she opened the bag. "You didn't have to do this."

"I know I didn't, but I want my friends to have something nice."

"Oh wow! Designer wallets and a matching purse, oh my God."

"This must have cost you a fortune," Amy said while going through her purse.

"No, trust me, it was a steal. Phillip and I were traveling and we came across these and automatically I thought my best friends should have one."

"Thank you, it's way too much," Margo told Karen.

"Come on, you should be the last one talking about too much. Did you tell them of your art show?"

"What?" Angela asked.

"Yes, she's scheduled to show her art at the Art for Hire in Roswell."

"Are you kidding me?" asked Amy. "When did you plan it?"

"I didn't plan it, it happened. It was Karen. And I finally listened to her. It was funny as her contacts pushed for a show and the gallery became available. It's like everything fell into place," Margo explained.

"Well, I think it's awesome." Angela smiled in a congratulatory fashion.

"Yes it is." Karen admitted. "What's happening with you Angela? What about Mark?"

"I think it's exciting. We woke yesterday morning and as I went to the bathroom he made coffee and toasted bagels."

"Wait, you slept with him?" asked Margo.

"No, he insisted we wait. I wanted to, but he explained why he wanted more time. Like any man can endure an entire night."

"He's pretty close," Margo jokingly said. "I'm not the kiss and tell but, he's a serious lover."

"Phillip too, but who's asking me?" added Karen.

"Like Bill, well I think he's great. Don't you Angela?"

"I wouldn't know, Amy."

"Let him take time with you. Too many guys rush with the first opportunity or jump on you and hope for the best. I'd gather Mark wanted to really lay it on you."

"Like he did you?" Amy asked Margo.

"I don't kiss and tell, but he is surely a great lover. If you know what I mean."

"I guess it's the idea of being...well..."

"Excited," added Margo. "What else have you two done?"

"He sent me flowers to the office. I was impressed as he remembered my favorite colors and type of flowers."

"Flowers?" asked Amy.

"Wednesday, he sent one red and two yellow roses. I was so surprised," Angela smiled while explaining.

"He's putting on the charm," Karen commented.

"He is, but it's so enjoyable he knows how and doesn't seem to drown me in it. I mean, there is balance. He took me to Martini and Imax Screen the other night and it was awesome. I mean, what I recall. I seemed to have missed a few things here and there."

"He cornered you from everyone else?" asked Margo.

"No, not at all, he was the total gentleman. There were people sitting at our table and we didn't know they were there half the time."

"She's gone," Karen giggled.

"Oh, she is really gone," Margo laughed.

"And you spent the night with him, it was his idea right?"

"Actually he offered to take me home. And like I said before, I didn't sleep with him, well no sex."

"I can't believe you," Amy added. "There is no way a man can sleep next to a woman and not try. Were you nude?"

"No, I wasn't nude. I told you he didn't want to."

"Then something is wrong with him. He's not normal."

"He's very normal. Is it always for us to give up our bodies when we sleep next to a man?"

"No," Amy laughed, "Well, hell yeah."

"You're bad, really bad." Angela pointed out.

"At least she knows what she enjoys," Margo added. "Like another margarita." Margo waved for a waiter. "Are you two planning to come to my show? I'm planning to have a jazz trio with wine, cheese and fruit for the attendees."

"I'm going and I'll get Bill to come too," Amy added waiting for smart comments.

"Bill?" asked Karen.

"He's changing. You know, the power of a woman influences all." Amy laughed.

Karen raised her drink to toast, "Yes the power of women." The others raised their glasses and finished the drinks. The waiter arrived and asked, "What can I get you ladies?"

"Another round, please."

"Will do." The waiter left with haste.

"You have him running Karen. How did you do it?"

"I have no idea. Maybe he's a hustler," Karen commented as she watched the waiter move quickly amongst the crowd. "He's working on his tip."

"What are you going to do at Margo's art show?" asked Angela. "Are you catering?'

"I didn't think of it. I know wine, fruit and cheese isn't hard."

"Would you like more, Margo?" asked Angela.

"It's my first. Don't you two create something bigger than tapas?"

"I can't believe you're having Bill come. Wow. Will you have Paula and Ron come along?"

"You know, we don't hang out much together since the trip or like when we first met. I'm not sure what Paula is doing these days."

"Interesting. I thought for sure you four would be really active."

"No. Ron did tell me she has new friends keeping her busy."

"I can only imagine what they look like," Karen laughed.

"I wouldn't know for sure, but you're probably right." Amy agreed.

The girls talked for another hour as the night took on a new meaning. Karen stopped drinking with her second margarita as Margo and Amy followed suit. Margo answered Cedric's text and decided to meet him at a nearby pub. Amy decided to leave heading north to prepare Bill's habitual snack he enjoyed after playing billiards. Angela told Mark not to expect seeing her tonight. She decided to head home and finally read a book she's had for some time. On her way home, her phone received a text message from Mark. "I hope you're having fun. Miss talking to you." Smiling, Angela dialed Mark right away. "Hi, gorgeous man."

"My beautiful woman, I thought you'd be out all night with the girls."

"No, not tonight, we decided to call it quits. What are you up to?"

"I stayed in tonight. I decided to relax and hopefully get a chance to chat before going to bed."

"I'm happy you sent the text. I didn't think I'd hear from you until tomorrow."

"You know the phone works two ways."

"Yes I do. But you never said for me to use your number freely."

"Use my number freely, please." Mark, being the smart one, commented on the idea of Angela holding back her activities because of his not giving full permissions and freedom to interact. "You should know my door is open at anytime."

"I know, but we're just starting and I don't know how to take us. I mean, should I say we're an item?"

"Yes, please say we are. There is nothing in the world like an angel being the woman of your life. I'd like you being my angel."

"I don't know about angel, but a woman of interest, equal interest, will be just fine."

"Equal interest. Well, dear equally interested woman, what do you say we see each other tonight?"

"I'd love to. What do you have in mind?" Angela asked "How about I come to your place, since you slept here the other night?"

"You know," Angela paused in her answer as she recalled Margo's comment on Mark being a passionate lover. "Ok but under one circumstance, no funny stuff."

"No funny stuff?" Mark asked as if Angela's point was a twist.

"No, I mean no sex because I'm tired and want to wait as you suggested. We need our time to bond slowly."

"Tonight would have been perfect for me, but I agree. No sex. Cuddling is good."

"Yes, cuddling is good."

"I'm on my way. Be there in twenty minutes."

"Great. I'll see you soon." Angela ended the call, ran into the apartment, and placed her cell on the charger. She went into the bedroom and changed into something more seductive for the night. A laced teddy, red like the rose Mark sent to the office. It fitted perfectly like a glove to the curves of her body. She wore a robe over the teddy and waited for Mark's arrival. "I hope he enjoys me wearing this." Angela recalled conversations with Mark on their intimacy. "He wanted to wait, so let's see how serious he is about it. It's late Friday night and we have all day Saturday to relax, unless he has something else in mind."

Mark arrived and knocked on the door with anxiety. He desired spending the night with her from the very beginning, even when she wanted to attend girls' night out. With anticipation and before arriving, Mark prepared himself for the chance to indulge Angela with affection. He cleaned up with a quick shower, placed cologne in multiple hot spots, and changed into something quite presentable but not flashy. Though Mark agreed to no sex, he was prepared to impress and really get to know Angela intimately. Angela answered the door, greeting Mark, "Hi."

"Hello, beautiful."

"You want a glass of wine or tea?" Angela asked while walking into the kitchen for a glass.

"Wine, please. I'm not driving anywhere tonight so I can have a nice glass of wine." Mark answered while sitting on the couch. "What were you watching on television?"

"Not watching anything. I decided it's a quiet night for a book."

"What are you reading?"

"Something from an unknown author, <u>Good Guys Finish Last</u> is the title."

"Let me see it. Where is it?" asked Mark.

"It's in my bedroom on the nightstand."

"I'll wait for you to get it. I'm not going in there uninvited." Mark laughed.

"Please, you're being such a gentleman. Will you ever let your guard down?"

"I will. But it's not about being a gentleman, it's about being respectful."

"I don't mind you going into the bedroom," Angela said while heading to the couch with Mark's glass of wine. "I'll get it." Mark watched Angela walk away. He admired her body in the house coat, observing the way she floated in her stride, like a beauty queen on the walk way. He observed the coat sway with her hips, and admired how there was no effort or exaggeration as she headed further away. "Wow, she is really fine." Mark thought as she finally disappeared from his view. Angela returned with the book and sat next to

Mark on the couch. "Here, take a look," she said while passing it to Mark.

"Odd cover."

"Yes, it's why I looked at it in the beginning."

Mark read the back cover and suggested, "We should read this together." He opened the first page and read to Angela. Surprised, Angela grabbed the remote and selected classical music on her CD collection. Mark stopped reading because of her action. "No, don't stop." Angela ordered. Mark continued to read through the first chapter, periodically taking a sip of wine and observing Angela. She took in every word and admired the fact he was reading to her. "It's the first time a man outside of my father ever read to me, especially a romance novel."

"I think it's a sign of being interested and entertaining." Mark replied as he knew reading was pure pleasure and an escape.

"Yes, my turn." Angela took the book and read the second chapter. Mark settled in and listened along the way. He stopped her by touching her hand, "Hold that spot. What do you think the author had in mind?" he asked.

"I think he's trying to get us to believe there is goodness," she replied. The two ended up discussing the book as they exchanged reading along the way. She'd agree to disagree on some as he'd agree and countered on others. The book led them through the night as time faded into the wee hours of the morning. They drank two bottles of wine while reading and seemed to enjoy this type of interaction. They finally finished the book. "I'm pooped now." Angela said while looking at Mark. She rose and gestured for him to follow. Mark did exactly as directed. He followed and became mesmerized with her beauty and walk of royalty. Angela ensured he was close enough to watch her disrobe allowing the soft light to show her teddy. Mark stood at the door and observed Angela slowly drop her robe, starting with the shoulders, barely showing the lace. She inched the robe down to her waist and quickly dropped it to the floor, revealing all. Mark stood in awe as he tried to maintain his thoughts. "Why would she?" he pondered as he remembered his agreement. "You like?" asked Angela.

"Wow, I really like," Mark answered with excitement.

"You promised no funny business."

"I know, but you're making it really hard not to think of you as my angel, my opportunity to start a life of love and seduction."

"Intimate moments can be a number of things and making love is just one."

"You are really making this and me hard." Mark turned back to the living room, grabbed his wine glass and found another bottle. "We can continue this in the bedroom," he exclaimed as he grabbed the second glass and headed to Angela. "The wine made me do it. That's my excuse." Mark planned his comment as he returned. "Angela, I think we can drink to this. I've only dreamed of a woman so beautiful and your being with me, wow!"

"I'm glad you like it." Angela said while taking a wine glass and held it so Mark could pour. "I'm glad you enjoy my teddy. I have many and waited for the right man and time to wear them."

"I'm really happy you wore this red one. I'm impressed beyond your imagination."

"I can tell; you can't get out of those pants." Angela pointed to his crotch where Mark's excitement is like a car's beaming headlight. Mark managed to undress and crawl into the bed next to Angela with both the bottle of wine and wine glass. "You make it really difficult. Is this a test?"

"I'm not testing you, just following your words of waiting for the right time. I'm not forcing the issue, am I?"

"No, you aren't forcing the issue; you're making it very difficult. But no fear, I promised to follow your lead."

"My lead?" Angela responded with a second thought, "I didn't expect you to play dirty."

"Yes, I see what you're doing and it's nearly working, but you have to want this to be more than just a fling. Remember, sex is easy, but intimacy is much greater and challenging. I want the intimacy part to come along with the pleasure of loving you, passionately making love to you, and enjoying the bond of making love as one. You know what I mean, right?"

"Yes, I know the difference. I'm surprised you're not attacking me. But, I love you aren't attacking me, because I want the same as you, an everlasting love and no games. I'm so tired of games with my heart and emotions. Talk is one thing but actions are much greater." Angela embraced Mark and kissed him softly on the lips. Expecting Mark to respond with roaming hands, she moved closer, to feel the great touch and caress. Mark adjusted to Angela exactly as she moved and being excited, he lay on his back facing the ceiling and continued embracing Angela. He pulled her close in his arms and stroked her hair. His focus enabled him to ease the moment and fall into a slumber where they found comfort in being together.

The sun rose and moved quickly to late morning before the two opened their eyes. They found themselves in the same position as when they fell asleep. Neither jumped, breaking the embrace. Nor did one speak without first gently kissing as if they'd been together for years. "Good morning, beautiful," Mark spoke to Angela as he broke the silence.

"Hi." she softly responded.

"Did you sleep well?"

"You snore," Angela laughed.

"I do not."

"I know, I'm kidding. I slept great and I'm surprised, as it's the second time we've slept together and I'm very comfortable with you."

"A good thing, don't you think?"

"Yes, I do." Angela moved across the bed, and quickly ran into the bathroom, closing the door. Mark stood, put on his pants and made the bed. Angela yelled, "Mark."

"Yeah." Mark responded listening to Angela brushing her teeth.

"Wait a minute." Angela muffled in sound and Mark understood as he stood in the room. "We've talked a lot and spent time together. I enjoy you and I'm thinking of our conversations. I can't seem to put my finger on it."

"What do you want to know?" Mark asked, thinking of heading to the Aquarium today.

Angela opened the door so Mark could actually hear her question. She turned to the mirror and brushed her hair. Mark observed her beauty and smiled as she was still in the teddy. Without a break in brushing, Angela asked, "What is your dream girl?"

"Have you looked in the mirror?" Mark responded and then paused before continuing. "You see her smile, her joy through those beautiful eyes, and view how the world takes in her beauty."

"Nice, but really, how do you know it's your dream girl?"

"Because when you sit for coffee, you reflect the goodness and share it with all. I know because I've watched you so many times. Let me explain a little more. You see, my dream woman is one of love, full of kindness, adventurous, and she's a load of passion. Aren't you all those things wrapped in one?"

"I think so."

"Of course you are. So when you look in the mirror, you see my dream girl, especially when you smile."
Angela, moved by Mark's answer, ran into his arms. "I'm smiling."

"Yes, you are." Mark smiled holding her tight. "I'd love kissing you but, I have killer breath and it isn't fair you cleaned up. I should do the same. I have my gym bag in the car. I'll get it." Mark broke their embrace and began leaving the apartment saying, "Can you do me a favor and wear a bathing suit under your clothes? I have a surprise for you."

"I can do that," Angela replied and wondered of the surprise? She did exactly as asked and dressed without question, giving Mark total trust. Mark returned with his kit and cleaned up. He came out wearing swim trunks and a t-shirt. "How about brunch? Would you like me to cook or head out for a quick bite?"

"I think we can cook. I have lots of things available in the fridge."

"Since you cooked for me once, I think it's time I cook for you." Mark moved directly to the kitchen and prepared breakfast. He made coffee and his infamous French toast. "I hope you like cinnamon." Mark commented as he pulled spices from Angela's spice rack. "Do you like confectioner sugar?"

"I'm not a sugar fan so I doubt if you find any. Do you need it?"

"No, I'm glad you told me but it's no big deal on the sugar. I can still make the toast. Tell me how you like your eggs."

"Scrambled."

Mark worked on breakfast while Angela found entertainment in television news. She moved to the kitchen and poured a cup of coffee. "Do you want a cup?" asked Angela.

"Yes, please" Mark answered from the stove. Angela pulled out plates and silverware before returning with coffee to the living room.

"Breakfast is served," Mark announced and moved to the dining area with prepared plates. "I found fruit in the fridge."

"It looks great." Angela complimented Mark on the toast presentation.

"I'm glad you think so. I hope it tastes as good as it looks."

"I'm sure it will."


After breakfast, the two cleaned the kitchen like a team of workers attack painting a house. They completed the task in minutes and turned to each other, smiling at their accomplishment. "You know, you make this so easy. It's like we don't have to instruct or advise about anything. I'm so surprised," Angela said.

"Yes, it's amazing how we work together. I guess you can credit it to my being a bachelor."

"I don't think so. I've seen some bachelor apartments and you are not the usual bachelor."

"I can say I try to keep up with my place."

"I noticed."

"I hope you noticed my effort to enjoy us at every opportunity. And speaking of opportunity let me take you someplace really neat." Mark headed to the living room and waited for Angela to follow. "I know you'll enjoy this."

"Are you sure?" Angela responded as she followed.

"Yes, I heard what you said and remember I listen to you."

"Well, what else do I need? I assume I'll need a beach towel."

"Yes on the towel, but not necessarily a beach towel. And bring your hair dryer just in case we decide not to come back right away."

"I can no problem."


The Georgia Aquarium was nearly closed for noon feeding by the time they arrived. Mark called a friend who worked with the company and agreed to have Angela and Mark join him in his afternoon routine. "Hi, guys." Mark's friend Tim greeted them.

"Hi, Tim. This is Angela." Mark introduced Angela as she entered the door first.

"Nice to meet you. Are you better at snorkeling or are you a scuba diver?"

"What?"

"Oh, I didn't tell her what we're doing." Mark explained. "Remember you told me about enjoying snorkeling? Well the aquarium allows people to feed the fish and enjoy the largest tanks in the world. You can snorkel while feeding or if you were scuba qualified you can enjoy helping maintain the tanks while the fish are inside. It's just like being on the ocean reef. Since you chose snorkeling, we'll watch the feeding and cleaning, and snorkel with the fish."

"What about the sharks?" Angela asked concerned at the idea of an attack.

"They don't bother you," Tim explained, "It's different inside the tank and since they're fed consistently, there's no fear or anxiety for them to attack. If we didn't think it was safe, we would not open the doors to the general public to assist."

"I've done this before and it's a lot of fun. The experience is awesome and since you're a water lover I thought you'd enjoy this," Mark added as they walked towards the locker rooms.

"I like it. I have to warm up to it a little more. We're here, so let's do it."

"Great," Mark smiled and watched Angela disappear into the locker room.

"Dude, she's gorgeous," Tim told Mark.

"My dream girl and I'm serious about her. Remember I told you about the girl at the bookstore?"

"Yes, I do. That's her?"

"It's her."

"Now I understand."

"I'm glad you do. So let's make this fun for her and I'll owe you."

"No problem," Tim responded and did everything to make their experience an amazing memory.

Angela enjoyed the aquarium. She couldn't stop talking about it on the return ride to the apartment. "It was awesome." she commented, telling Mark of her brush with the shark, and stingray. "I was nervous, but then they were so calm and those guys cleaning the tank had a lot of the fish attention." Mark kept his focus on Angela as he drove North on GA 400. He repeatedly responded with excitement as Angela explained her experience in the tank. "Thank you, Mark. I would have never thought of swimming in the aquarium, the whales were fun. Thank you so much. I'll never forget the experience."

"I'm so glad because each time we do something; it builds our foundation for a long future. I'm banking on the idea of us growing together."

"I can see you're really dedicated to making it happen. You are the first man in my life who gives true focus on me. I think it's such a difference."

"I hope so. I don't think you'll ever see any other man cherish you the way I do."

"It's a new experience for me. I'm almost not sure how to take it."

"Just be you and do what's best for you. You'll be surprised how easy our relationship will build."

"I trust you."

"Good." Mark smiled and turned up the radio volume.

Tuesday morning coffee with Mark and Angela remained in a wonderful mood. For the first time, she felt involved, excited, and content with Mark being her guy. She found herself making more of an effort to spend time with him. The morning after not spending nights together, they'd meet at the bookstore coffee shop. This became their routine. The two would sit for coffee and then explore for new reading material. Strolling, aisle after aisle, either would comment on the number of books striking their interest. Today, Mark left Angela's side and found something interesting for them to share. He returned, showing Angela. Just as he arrived, Mark noticed some guy pointing his finger within two feet of Angela and then towards him. Angela turned beet red as she nearly broke into tears when Mark arrived. "You are not going to believe what that guy said to me," Angela told Mark.

"What did he say?"

"…Something to the effect of my being a disgrace to my race by being with you."

"Are you serious?"

"Yes, I didn't understand what the hell he was talking about until he pointed at you."

"Baby, if we are to be together, you'll have to get out of the fantasy world. I know we're quite happy right now and I expect it to last a life time, but don't think its going to be a cakewalk."

"I don't expect it to be a cakewalk, but my God, he doesn't know me from Adam!"

"His perception is you're betraying the white race."

"I guess it's a taste of my Dad."

"I guess so. Look at it this way. Being with me you're going to run across a number of cases where all people are against us. Most will not address us, but some will snarl with their eyes or make snide remarks. You are going to have to get thick skinned at times. And remember, it's going to come from all nationalities and ethnic groups."

"I expected some, but never this direct." Angela frowned as she realized her challenge being involved with a black man. "I don't like it. I find this wonderful man, and society wants me to please them? I don't get it."

"You will never get it. Just remember it's going to be challenging for you, as it's your first time."

"Why is it so difficult for them to believe love is blind?"

"Are you saying you're in love with me?" Mark asked taking her focus away from the guy's comments.

"I'm not saying I am, but I won't admit not being in love just yet," Angela responded as they walked to the exit.

"At least I'm not out."

"No, not at all, I think you're further in my heart than any man in my life."

"Keep that in mind today while at the office. I'll catch you later, sweetie." Mark kissed Angela just as she entered her car. He left for his office just after Angela drove off.

Margo and Karen sat at the table over breakfast. Margo found it interesting her career change was taking off. She took a leave of absence from her current job to focus on her art show. "Are you ready for this?" asked Margo.

"Ready for what?" Karen asked, not sure what 'this' happened to be.

"The chance I'm successful. Will you still present my art to your corporate clients?"

"Of course I will. It's better when you have success. This makes it easier to sell."

"I'm actually nervous because of the pressure."

"I wouldn't worry about pressure. I'd worry about continuing the creative blood and ideas flowing."

"You are so supportive. I love that about you, Karen."

"Thank you. It's what friends do. They support each other. Have you heard from Angela?"

"Not recently. I know she's getting deeper with Mark."

"They are a cute couple. I have faith they'll make it."

"I don't know. I hope they do," Margo subjected to the skepticism based on Angela being naïve to people in interracial relationships.

"Why are you skeptical?"

"She's new at being the general public's focus. You know, it's not easy for a woman who's stepping out of her norm to handle snarls against them." Margo spoke from experience.

"I agree. You should call her. Let her know we're here for her."

"Calling her is a wonderful idea. I will after we finish our breakfast and complete planning the art show." Margo and Karen continued working on the show and how to get the right people to attend. As Margo vacated the restaurant she called Angela for her availability. "Hey, Angela."

"Hi, Margo, what's up?" Angela answered.

"I hadn't heard from you in sometime and I wanted to know how things are going with Mark."

"Mark's wonderful. I can't believe we didn't get together sooner."

"Have you forgotten? You shut down the interest the first time you met."

"I remember, and I'm so glad I took the chance with him. He is really a great guy."

"What are you doing for lunch or can you get out early?"

"My schedule is pretty open today. What time are you thinking?"

"How about meeting in thirty minutes at the bookstore Starbucks?"

"I can. I'll see you there."

"Talk to you soon." Margo ended her call and immediately headed to the bookstore. She was happy Angela agreed to meet on such a short notice. "I wonder if she's fallen for Mark. It sounds like they are really hitting it off. I'm happy if they are," she thought while driving on her way.

Angela took off quickly after shutting her laptop down and decided she would work remote, if need be. She passed her boss and explained the work plan since the schedule was slow. Without restriction, the boss agreed to Angela's request. Within twenty minutes Angela arrived at the bookstore, ordered her favorite coffee, set up her laptop and waited for Margo. Margo arrived within five minutes. "Hey. I didn't think you'd be here so soon."

"I left right after you called. I checked out with my boss and she agreed to my working remote."

"A working break. I like your job." Margo smiled while making the comment. "So tell me, how is everything with Mark?"

"Like I told you on the phone, he's a remarkable guy and it's going great."

"Did you..." asked Margo leading to the intimate point of the conversation.

"No, not yet, but we've done a few things together which are great. He's really something to hold on to."

"I told you. I said he was a great guy." Margo silently waited while thinking of a way to address the interracial issue. "I know you're going through a radical change. I wanted to know if you're handling it well."

"Radical change?" Angela asked as if confused by the question. "I got it. Yes it is radical. Just this morning a guy cursed me in the bookstore. He even pointed a finger towards Mark, as if marking him." Angela frowned in disgust during her explanation. "The bastard has no right to even talk to me about Mark and my life."

"I'm afraid it isn't the way he or a number of people will see it," Margo explained. "Some will be threatened by it, ashamed of it, and feel you are decreasing their values."

"How the hell will I do something to those people by dating Mark?"

"It's their belief system. Believe me, white and black people are going to say things or do simple insulting things."

"I can't believe those types of people."

"I wanted to tell you this because it's your first time and to reinforce some of the challenges you'll face."

"How did you handle it?"

"I stayed focused on the reality and let them think as they may. I embraced my guy at the time and didn't let snide remarks or stupidities get to me."

"I can see my skin is going to get hard. But you know, so far it's only one incident."

"One now, but as soon as you learn the body languages of people, the number will grow. Or you'll become numb to their comments or actions."

"I don't worry about them now."

"Good, so remember you'll have to stay strong. I'm sure Mark can handle his own. But if you doubt it for a minute, just talk to him and never keep it to yourself. It's why mixed couples make it last. They find ways to battle the stupidity or make it a game to get through it. Mark will likely keep it realistic if he feels threatened."

"Threatened?"

"Well, think of the guy you encountered this morning. Back during the Klan's powerful influence, he'd call someone and there would be a gang of people after you. You would be placed in an asylum and he would more than likely be hung."

"I know but it's the year 2007. Why on earth would anyone think of such?"

"I can't say they will, but some people don't like the idea of you two being together. Black women will think he's a great guy that got away. White men will think you are not worth their time or you're now tainted, like diseased. I'm not saying all will, but there will be quite a few who would. I'm telling you things because you're going to get a whole slew of people and face a number of situations you're not going to believe. "

"I know many people will not support Mark and me, but he's worth it. I think he's really worth it and I don't mind the added pressures. I'll face them when it's time but enjoy him as much as possible. I can love a guy like him, I mean really fall in love with Mark."

"Since Mark's a great guy, I know you're in good hands. Remember, I told you he's a keeper and a really good guy. I knew you two would be a great match. I'm happy for you."

"Thanks Margo. I'm glad we had this talk."

"Me too. I'm off to finish my painting for the art show. You are coming right?"

"Wouldn't miss it for the world."

"Great. Make sure Mark is with you. I want to see how happy you two are together."

"We'll be there." Angela stood with Margo and gave her a loving hug. "I'm so thankful having a friend like you," Angela whispered.

"I'm happy for you. It's time you found true love."

# Chapter 13

Mark arrived at Angela's apartment just in time to attend the art show. With a long stem rose in hand, he tapped on her door and waited. Faintly he heard Angela calling, "I'll be right there."

"OK," Mark yelled in reply. Angela opened the door and stood in the center. "Wow!" Mark said while staring at Angela. "You look marvelous." Angela wore a bright green dress, form fitting showing her fine curves. As much as she worked out, she deserved looking great. She grabbed Mark, pulled him closer and seductively laid a deep kiss, long, soft, gentle, and loving upon his lips. "You smell good," Angela smiled while responding. She took the rose and sniffed it on the way to the kitchen. "Thank you for the lovely rose. You really know how to get to a girl."

"It's a reflection of how I see you, totally beautiful in every form. A rose simple and elegant, empowering and weak, yet it's the strongest symbol of affection and the most influential compliment a woman can ever receive. You are my rose. I can't wait to show the world how lovely you are. Believe me, the world will take notice."

Angela smiled as she poured water in the vase and dropped the rose in. "What can a woman say to that?"

"Just say what's on your mind."

"The rose is a rose and I'm happy to be yours."

"As I'm happy you are too," Mark replied as he moved closer for another kiss.

"Don't get carried away, we have a show to attend," said Angela.

"I hear you. I'm ready."

"Yes, you are," Angela said while grabbing her small purse.

"Your chariot awaits, lovely woman," Mark said while pulling the apartment door tight. They entered the car and took off for the show.

Karen and Phillip arrived at the art show before the general public. "Can you believe this is it?" Karen asked Phillip.

"I believe it. You've pushed it and supported Margo for sometime now. I'm glad she's finally following your advice."

"She's a talented artist. I loved her work from school. It's only gotten better over the years."

"Ok, baby. You have to promise. You are not going to purchase one painting tonight."

"Why?" Karen frowned.

"Because, you currently have three and there's no room for another. I'm not giving up my wall. Let someone else get a chance to buy one."

"I see your point."

"Karen…" Phillip called in a deep empowering voice, "…I mean it."

"Ok, you know she's my girl and I want her to succeed."

"She knows. Trust me, she knows." Phillip opened Karen's car door and gave her assistance exiting. She stood in a lovely maroon dress, loosely flowing in the wind, showing her curvaceous body. Enticing to Phillip, he grabbed her and deeply kissed her as if it were time to head home for more excitement.

Margo removed her hand from her face and adjusted the painting Cedric placed there minutes ago, and asked, "Why did you put this one next to the statue?" Walking by with another painting in hand, "It's where you told me to." Cedric replied.

"Oh, well I've changed my mind. I think the one in your hand is better here and this one can go where the light is softer. It gives a better presentation."

"Is this the last one?"

"Yes, I won't have you move anymore. We're set." Margo gave Cedric a gentle kiss on the lips. "Thank you for being so patient and helpful."

"Anything for my girl, even when I'm frustrated, you're still my heart. I can never stay frustrated with you."

"Thank you, darling."

Cedric moved the painting as Margo directed and headed to change clothes for the event. Karen and Phillip appeared at the entrance just as Cedric was exiting. "Hi." Cedric said, greeting the two.

"I see you've been busy." Karen noticed Cedric wasn't dressed for the show.

"Yes, but according to Margo we're ready. I hope you don't talk her into changing another thing. We've been at it for a few hours. I should have changed clothes over an hour ago."

"I get your point," Phillip added. "Did the caterers show?"

"I think so. Margo's instructing them now. I'll catch you two later." Cedric continued his journey with a quick step to his car.

"Later, dude." Phillip waved as he and Karen turned to enter the gallery. "My God, you are one fine woman," Phillip told Karen as he watched her from behind.

"You are so silly," Karen smiled with her response; then yelling, "Margo, where are you?"

"Over here," Margo answered just in front of the far corner bar. She walked toward Karen's voice to meet her. "Hi." Margo smiled as she saw Karen and Phillip.

"You look marvelous," Karen complimented Margo.

"Superb," Phillip added.

"Are you nervous?" asked Karen, feeling partially responsible for the art show.

"I am, but it's just butterflies. I want things to go well, really well."

"I'm sure they will," Phillip said as he looked around the gallery. "Everything looks great. You did a good job displaying your work."

"It's lovely and I'm so glad we got this gallery to work with. It's a great location and the RSVP list is nearly a hundred percent match to the invitations. Have you seen anyone else just yet?"

"No, Karen. You two are the first to arrive. Poor Cedric, I know he's tired of being here. I worked him so hard getting things here and displayed. I even left him to get dressed and relieved him so he could now change."

Phillip chuckled while saying, "We saw him on the way out. He told us to be careful as you may change your mind again and move something else around."

"You don't have to move the paintings. I think it's perfect."

"The eye of the beholder speaks well." Phillip smiled after his response. "You've done a great job, really a great job." Looking at Karen, he said, "Babe, let's buy it all."

"You can't be serious," Karen answered. "You told me not to even think about it."

"I know, but they look so nice. I can imagine them all around the house," Phillip commented as he moved to the next painting.

"I told you she's good."

"Margo, you're really good. Outstanding! I think every piece will sell tonight. I really do."

"Thank you Phillip. I hope at least three paintings move tonight. I'm happy for those three. I hope I didn't overprice them."

"I'm sure you didn't," Karen pointed out. "I've purchased this caliber of paintings for years, and I think you're under priced."

"Good, so people will not have sticker shock. I'll wait until the next set of paintings and price them higher. Being expensive makes me nervous."

"You can always strike a deal lower and make it seem like a sale."

"Isn't the concept tacky for a new artist?" asked Christopher as he entered the gallery.

"Hi, Chris. I'm glad you made it."

"I wouldn't miss it for the world." Chris gave Margo a friendly hug. "Where's your old man?"

"He's changing clothes. He should be here in a short time. Let me introduce you to Karen and Phillip." Margo made introductions and pointed Chris to the nearest bar. "You should break the house open with the first drink."

"I can and will. Would anyone like anything?" asked Chris.

"I'll get something just after one more round of checking things," Margo answered.

"We'll join you in a minute." Karen responded. Chris moved along to the far corner bar where the bartender was a young blonde, well figured, woman. "He hasn't changed." Margo said while he walked away.

"I think he has his mind set on more than the bar." Phillip commented.

"I'm afraid so," Karen giggled.

Angela and Mark arrived at the gallery, entered the building and quickly looked around. "Wow, I didn't think Margo was this good. I didn't mean good, but really good," Angela said, stopping in front of one particular painting. "This is really a great painting. What do you think Mark?"
Mark replied while gazing at the picture. "I knew Margo had talent, but not at this level. She's found her calling for sure. I love it and can see it on a wall in my townhouse."

"You know, I'm thinking the same thing. I can see it on a wall of anyplace I own."

"You are a woman with great taste, and after my heart."

"Now, think about it. I thought I had your heart." Angela winked.

"A confident woman knows."

"And I know." Angela pulled Mark closer and placed her arm around his waist, showing her affection. Mark responded just as she envisioned, not stepping away and together they displayed their union. The two fluidly moved around the gallery observing Margo's work. Angela heard her name and broke from Mark to investigate. "Hey, Angela," Margo called.

"Hi." Angela moved towards Margo meeting her en route. "You are awesome. I didn't know you were so talented."

"Thank you. I still don't think I'm really good, but modesty gets you nowhere in this business."

"I'd guess not, but you'll impress some people coming to the show."

"I hope so, but again it's a blessing just to have one painting sold."

"I'm not worried about your selling so many. I have one in mind, but I'll keep my fingers crossed it's still there when you start the sales part."

"Let me know which one and I'll set it aside, if you like." Margo smiled and said, "You don't have to do this, you know. I understand you're my friend and I have your support."

"Margo, Mark and I actually like the painting. It struck us as something either of us could display forever." Angela explained.

"The two of you are an item now. I'm happy for you. Let me tell you, Chris is here, so be careful."

"I have my guy. Why would I have to be careful with Chris?"

"You're right, you don't have to." Margo refrained from reminding her of Amy and Bill attending the show. "I'm glad you're here. You seem so happy."

"I am. I feel really good."

"Go enjoy the show and grab something to drink," Margo suggested.

Before Angela and Margo walked in different directions, Mark approached with three drinks. He passed one drink to each lady and kept the other for himself. "I couldn't let you two walk around empty-handed," Mark smiled, serving the drinks.

"Still the sweet man," Margo complimented Mark, recalling his actions.

"He really is. He surprises me all the time." Angela said.

"You two need to stop, you're making me blush."

"Truth is truth," Margo said while turning to observe Cedric entering the gallery. "I'll catch you two around. Excuse me, please." Margo moved toward Cedric to greet him.

"Sure thing," Angela responded as Margo left. "She's so formal tonight."

"Don't you think she has to be?" Mark responded just before sipping his drink. "This can make it for her. It's a new beginning."

"I wish her the best of luck."

"We can help. I looked at the price of the painting we like. It's kind of steep for one person, but not for two people."

"Are you asking me for a loan?"

"Of course not, I just want you to think of it as something to own."

"I can own it." Angela paused, "Were you thinking of....?"

"Now you get it," Mark smiled and lifted his glass to toast Angela. "Now you get it."

Karen and Phillip walked through the gallery observing the collection of paintings. Karen explained her selling points on Margo's artwork as they stepped from one to the other. Friends and work associates joined Karen's tour, moving about the gallery. It was as if Karen became the gallery's curator and guide. She moved the crowd in a direction in Margo's view where she smiled, observing the number of people following her. Margo, nearly in tears, realized how this couldn't be possible, if it were not for her best friend Karen. Cedric, standing next to her observed the touch of emotion she was fighting not to show. He placed his arm around her saying, "its ok baby, and you deserve this." Cedric held her close and gently kissed her forehead. "Look around, there are a lot of us who love and wish the best for you."

"I see. But I'm worried my paintings aren't good, and my friends are buying them for me."

"No darling, look around. We don't know all of these people."

"You're right, but it makes me nervous too. What should I tell them when I go out there?"

"Try telling them how you felt when you painted them. Just tell them what you saw in it as you let the brush move with your hand. Tell them how you start with blocking the background and fill the canvas as your ideas and colors appeared. Tell them how you painted with patience as you delayed the work, unless your heart gave your mind a vision to pursue. Tell them you paint with fervor, once you get going and finalize your vision. Show them how much you love painting."

"That's it! Thank you so much!" Margo smiled and ran to the back of the gallery.

Chris approached Cedric as Margo left and asked, "Why is she moving so fast?"

"I have no idea. She said she thought of something and ran off." Cedric replied.

"Dude, Angela looks great."

"She is lovely. Did you see someone with her?"

"No, I saw her near a painting on the far wall when I went to get another drink."

"She has a guy in her life."

"Bummer, I thought I'd get a chance to finally have sex with her. Damn, she looks good."

"You should forget her and work on the bartender."

"She can't do anything until the show is over. I expect to have one before then and why not Angela?"

"If I were you, I'd let her go. Didn't she diss you at the bar the last time you two saw each other?"

"It was bad timing, dude, bad timing." Chris pointed in the direction he was walking and said, "later, dude."

Cedric observed Chris mingling amongst the crowd and shook his head side to side. Cedric facially expressed, "that guy will never get it."

Mark stood near the corner bar waiting for drinks. He watched Angela chat with a couple about Margo's painting. He watched, as if Angela portrayed a magical ability to interact with others. "She is really a lovely woman." Mark thought as he listened as best he could to their conversation. "I wonder if they'll buy the painting because of her."

"It's a very nice piece." Chris spoke to Mark as he noticed him observing Angela.

"Excuse me?" Mark asked.

"She is hot. I saw you looking at her and I agree."

"She is drop dead gorgeous. I think she's top line too."

"I don't know if she's top line, but I'm going to find out. She wanted me too. I know she did."

"Really; she wanted you?" Mark looked at Chris as if he subconsciously told him something. Chris wasn't paying attention to Mark's body language but continued with his thought. "Yea bro, she was all over me. I was going to hit it once, but she became this bitch. I had to forgive her."

"You had to forgive her. Let me warn you before you go on. The woman you referring to as a bitch just so happens to be my girl. I'd appreciate you keeping your negative thoughts to yourself." Mark frowned and swelled; being defensive and preparing to thrash the living crap out of Chris.

"Are you kidding me? She couldn't have me so she settled for you? What a bitch!"

Mark grabbed Chris with one arm and with the other he pointed towards the back door. "You should come with me."

"What the hell are you doing? Let me go. I don't appreciate you touching me."

"Ok, I'll let you go but be careful what you say. I'll beat the crap out of you if you ever address Angela as a bitch again. As a matter of fact," from his coat, Mark pulled his business card and placed it in Chris's shirt pocket. "Call me whenever you feel like blasting my girl, so I can show you a thrashing of your life."

"Are you threatening me?"

Mark moved closer as to whisper, "That, my friend, is a freaking promise. Guaranteed and I need you to remember how dangerous it is when you are playing with fire."

Chris walked away, as if the promise was a joke. He laughed while moving toward Angela. Mark stood observing Chris while grabbing the two drinks. Chris asked Angela, "How could you fuck a black guy and not fuck me?"

"You're an ass, Chris. Leave me and never talk to me again," Angela retorted angrily.

"I deserve an answer, bitch," Chris sneered as he grabbed her arm pulling her outside.

"I suggest you let her go." Mark stood in Chris' path.

"This is not your business," Chris explained as he pulled Angela behind. Mark stood in front of Chris and said, "I suggest you let her go or I'll do as I promised." Cedric approached Chris and immediately addressed him, "What on earth are you doing?"

"This bitch screwed him and didn't touch me." Mark gave Cedric the two drinks "Hold these, Cedric."

"You don't want to do it, Mark. Chris, what the fuck are you doing? You'd better think about this before you cross that line."

"I'm not second to anyone and this bitch has to know."

"That's it, you dumb fuck." Mark jabbed Chris's nose as a boxer's set up for a knockout punch. Chris released Angela as he grabbed his nose. Mark pulled Chris outside.

"Mark, no!" Angela shouted.

"Babe, I got this, I'll be right back." Mark snarled as he pulled Chris. "I warned you, but you let your ass overtake your brain." Mark punched him in the stomach and Chris finally tried to fight back. Just as Chris swung, Cedric grabbed his arm as he came out to stop the nonsense. "You need to leave, Chris," Cedric instructed.

"You aren't going to help me?" Chris asked.

"Mark beat me to knocking the crap out of you. It's been long overdue but I hadn't the heart to beat you myself. Tonight you really deserved an ass whooping. Now leave!" Chris gathered his wit and did as instructed. "I'm sorry Mark." Cedric said.

"No problem, Cedric. It was bound to happen, but I can't let it happen with Angela. She doesn't deserve anyone treating her as such."

"No, she doesn't," Cedric agreed.

The crowd managed to return inside, as if nothing happened between the two guys before heading outside. Fortunately, the band picked up a hot tune and a few people danced in the aisle. Margo whispered to the band leader, "Thanks."

"Anytime," the band leader answered with a smile.

Amy and Bill arrived just as the music went to a livelier beat. Amy wore a fantastic flowered dress, nearly formal in length. Bill wore a sports coat, nice shirt, and jeans. He presented himself quite well. "Hi, Margo," Amy greeted her with a smile. "It's a nice crowd tonight."

"Yes, I'm surprised it is," Margo replied.

"This is Bill, my boyfriend."

Margo shook his hand. "Nice meeting you, Bill."

"I'm pleased. I've heard a lot about you," Bill told her.

"I hope it was all good."

"Well…"

"Bill, don't you dare make up anything." Amy stressed. "Your jokes aren't always funny."

"I wouldn't say anything she hadn't heard."

"I don't think he'd try to embarrass you, Amy," Margo suggested.

Amy smirked with her response, "Huh, you just don't know."

"Come on, lighten up. I'll get you a drink." Bill walked to the nearest bar and ordered Amy a drink. "Close call," Amy told Margo.

"Do you always prevent him from making snide comments?" Margo asked.

"No, not always, but here I'm trying to keep him within reason."

"Good luck."

"I don't think he's a bad guy. He'll be ok. I have to remind him. He's actually a sweet man."

"I'm happy for you. He doesn't seem bad, but I'm not with him, you are."

"I'm pretty happy with him. He can be a pain sometimes, but he can change. I know he can."

"Sure, all people can change. I just hope he changes enough without you making all the effort."

"It's going good since returning from Jamaica. He's been pretty cooperative with getting out to cultural events."

"Sometimes people do things for those they like. I hope it's his reason for you."

"I'm sure it is." Amy smiled as Margo confirmed her effort to change Bill.

"I'll catch you later. Let me get back to hosting." Margo headed to another guest observing one of the paintings. Amy headed to the bar with Bill. "Thank you." Amy said as Bill handed her a drink.

"No problem. I know it's your favorite."

"You are so sweet." Amy smiled just before taking a sip. "Are you enjoying this?"

"To be honest, it's a little fancy-smancy if I'd say so. I don't quite understand the paintings, but I like the colors."

"Abstract art is pretty much like that. Use your imagination when you look at the paintings. Try to see anything in it you recognize." Amy explained.

"I'll try," Bill responded as they stepped in the direction of Margo's largest painting on display. "I like this one," Bill said while pointing to the top. "It starts like a mountain waterfall and twists to the countryside behind what I think are blue rocks."

"I think you've got it. This one is titled 'Waterfall'." Amy read from the small placard. "See, you get it."

"Are you kidding me- $15,000.00 for this painting?!"

"Some art cost more. Fifteen grand isn't high priced, not for good art."

"Serious?"

"Yes, seriously. You have to think of what it adds to the location. Some of this goes in office buildings. It's why interior decorators do well when they get commissions on certain products."

"What a deal. Even as a carpenter we don't get but so much on material. I can't imagine one piece costing that much."

"It's not quite a home run, but it can be for some artist. I don't think Margo priced these. She had Karen's help, I'm sure."

"Karen? Where have I heard the name?"

"She's one of my friends I told you about."

"Oh, the black woman."

"Yes, the black woman."

"She was the one being smart with Paula."

"Not really. Paula did the smart thing herself. Besides, she's a sweet woman and one of my friends. So when you meet her, you'd best behave and get rid of the attitude." Amy frowned, scolding him.

"I'll think about it. Remember, just because she's your friend doesn't mean that woman is your equal."

"Don't go there, Bill. I thought we had an agreement. You have to look beyond color and see people."

"I'll think about it." Bill raised his drink for a sip just as Angela passed. "There is that snooty woman, Angela. Thank God she didn't call me back. I can't stand her."

"How can you say such thing about a woman just because you didn't hit it off?"

"Because I'm a great guy, isn't that what you said?"

"Yes, you're a great guy for me, not for every woman. You have qualities I like in a guy, but sometimes you are so out there. If I can get you around this race barrier you'd be better off."

"How do you figure? I don't mind them, as long as they don't disrespect my race." Bill observed Mark placing his arm around Angela and the two smiling together. "See that crap? They are God-forsaken wrong. Those two should not be together in any kind of fashion. It angers the crap out of me."

"You have no right getting angry, Bill." Amy blocked him as he tried to walk in Angela's direction. "It is none of your business who Angela dates or has interest in."

"It is my business when a black man gets greater interest from a white woman even if she is crazy or mentally ill."

"Mentally ill? Why on earth would you say mentally ill?"

"She has to be to like those people enough to sleep with one. I'd never date a woman who's ever been with a black."

"Watch what you're saying Bill." Amy stood defensive.

"You better watch your tongue or you'll learn something hurting to you."

"What? Are you saying?"

"I'm saying you better watch it, if you want me to stay around."

"I thought you were going to tell me you were with a black man." Bill sighed in relief but angered as he redirected his interest to Angela and Mark.

"You don't get it. I..." Amy hesitated to finish her sentence, "I am, aargh." Amy stormed towards the rear exit. Her frustration with Bill's prejudice took her to the time she first met her stepmother. It was her mother who stopped the child from visiting her dad. Why? Her step mother was Asian, a very beautiful Korean woman. Amy's father married Ki and moved in the neighborhood near her mother. Her mother was so furious she did everything in her power to keep Amy from Ki. From moving to a different state, creating multiple trumped molestation charges, to false accusations of kidnapping, Mom raised holy hell with Dad all because Ki was Korean. It made even less sense when Amy discovered as a teen it was her mom who walked out of the marriage. As a child, Amy never knew such hatred until then. It turned out; Ki was the nicest step-mother one could imagine. "Why do I date such jerks? It's time to tell him of my past. I'd hoped for him to open his mind to people being people," Amy thought. Bill walked out of the gallery and quickly observed Amy looking at the ground.

"What the heck is down there?" Bill asked.

"The truth," Amy snapped in response. "It's time I told you more about my past."

"I'd like the truth."

"You're an ass. I'm tired of you being such a jerk about people of color. What do I look like to you?"

"A very gorgeous white woman," Bill replied, "and a proud white woman too."

"Well I am a proud woman but not quite the way you see me. I'm one of those women who slept with black, Asian, and Hispanic men."

"Why didn't you tell me?"

"Like you, I didn't want to open past relationships. I didn't think it mattered. I like you for you, but you're such a fucking jerk. I don't know what the hell I was thinking by dating you. I had you looking outside of your world and things started looking good. But then you fall back to this crap. When will you open your eyes to the world? What makes you think by being white you're better than those men I dated?"

"How could you do this to me?" Bill asked in disgust. "How could you?"

"It was easy. I like you as a person even with one flaw. But here you are pushing that crap. And what did I do to you? Make you open your eyes to enjoying more in living life; show you there are things other than playing pool all weekend, and gave you a reason for excitement, while talking to your friends. I gave you boasting rights with your friends, while all the time you are having tainted love. Are you going to scrub your body, especially the scorned pecker?"

"You bitch, how dare you?"

"It is not how dare I, it's how dumb are you? You live in a well with your beliefs while the world passes you by. You should find a cave and move in for your tiny ego's security. You couldn't function anywhere other than your corner lot."

"You are a bitch traitor." Bill frowned in anger while pointing, "You will never be with a white man again. I promise you that."

"I'll be with any man I choose. All white men are nothing like you. Only those with small minds are even close to the Neanderthal likes of you, asshole."

Bill left in anger and cursed under his breath, "How dare the bitch trick me? I knew she wasn't worth two cents always going to those places with those people. I can't believe she screwed me like that. No wonder she didn't mind Jamaica, she probably screwed the whole beach when she wasn't with me. That bitch! Her crap is out of my house!" Bill drove to his place without Amy. He decided letting go was best, but keeping her past experience secret left him in good standing with his friends. "What they don't know won't hurt them."

Amy returned inside and grabbed another drink. She showed her anger with closed body language; crossed arms, frowning, and long stares. Angela approached her and asked, "Hey, what gives?"
    "The asshole just left."
    "You mean Bill?"
    "Yes, the asshole. I didn't think he'd hold long anyway. I'm a bit pissed for investing so much into him."
    "Let's face it, we invest in every relationship. We surely invest time and emotions."
    "I agree. I should have dropped the bastard long ago!"
    "It's easy looking back while you're angered. Just think of it as an opportunity for the right person to come. As long as you don't try to change a person, it will work."
    "You are so right, Angela. Changing a guy is ridiculous. I'm finished with such crap."
    "I know you are." Angela walked to Mark and grabbed his arm right at the elbow moving closer to him. Amy went into the gallery's office and slammed the door. "What's wrong with her?" asked Mark.
    "She broke up with Bill," Angela answered.
    "Isn't she a friend?"
    "Well, not a close friend, but I'd consider her a friend."

"Why not help her ease the pain. I'll be fine without you for a few."

"You are really a sweet man. I'll be right back." Angela kissed Mark on the cheek just before leaving for the office; within seconds she knocked on the door. "Can I come in?" asked Angela.

"Sure, it's not my office," Amy responded.
Angela entered and observed Amy with a drink in one hand and tissue in the other while sitting on the couch. "How are you?"

"I'm not bad. I'm just pissed," Amy replied before sipping her drink.

"I'd think you were hurting too."

"Pissed at the time I invested in him. It's a great thing I didn't move in with him. I was so close."

"My, you were serious."

"I was serious enough and had hopes for a future. My mother is going to be scared again. I'm thirty years old this year and not married. The pressures to do it right is there. My mother expects grandkids and to see me happily married. It's her dream of me being the soccer mom with the white picket fence."

"I know the pressures. I think all mothers want the best for their kids. Mine is no different when it comes to thinking of the kids "

"You know the bad thing?" Amy sighed while wiping a tear from her face. "I had an opportunity and it wasn't good enough." Amy looked at Angela as if sending a signal of importance. "You have a nice relationship now. You remind me of Michael and I. Please don't let anything get in the middle of it or you'll miss out on a sweet love."

"You and Michael?" Angela asked to further understand Amy's advice.

"Michael Martinez, a gorgeous guy with great family roots. He wasn't a Spaniard as mother wanted, he's Mexican-American. His family migrated to the States and he grew up in the Midwest. He lives here in Atlanta, a lawyer, does well, and a wonderful lover. Two years ago we were a hot item.

My mother liked him, as she knew him only as Mike. When she discovered he was Mexican, she blew her top and I wasn't strong enough to go against her. I thought of kids, family, society, and all of those crappy things most women fear."

"You gave him up for family?"

"I gave him up for the idea of a perfect union. The relationship society wants us to believe in having."

"It was a perfect relationship." Angela added, recalling the conversation with her mother. "I hope you find yourself doing the right thing again. Can you get him again?"

"No, he's married now. I don't want to even think about our love. It hurts too much to remember."

"You really loved him. You still do. Don't beat yourself up over it now. Let someone come to you without social or family influences."

"Angela, it is exactly what I'm telling you. Don't do what I did and lose the special love most people dream of having. Love and be loved, as life doesn't give you but so many gifts." Amy wiped another tear sniffling while remembering her loss. "I'm sure you won't let others take your love away."

"Love, I'm not in love, but I am excited about Mark."

"Is he showing you anything at all?"

"Yes, he's showing me more of what 'we' should be."

"You'll be in love trust me. It's going to happen and he seems like a great guy."

"Yes he is. I've never experienced such a great loving guy in my life." Angela smiled after telling Amy her thought. "One I've never crossed before." Angela repeated.

"See, I'm sure you're feeling those butterflies. Don't stop them and be happy with how you're feeling. Accept him and don't let him go."

"What about you? Are you going to be ok?" Angela redirected the focus.

"I'll be fine." Amy stood, right after placing her glass on the table. Angela followed and moved closer to hug Amy.

"Thank you for listening," Amy said while giving Angela a friendly hug.

"You are very welcome and thank you for the advice."

"You'll be fine. Now go out there and stick to your guy. I'll catch up with you in a minute."

Angela walked to the door and before leaving she said, "If you need anything, a place to stay, a ride home, just anything."

"Thanks Angela. I'll be fine. I have my place, so…"

"If you don't want to be alone for the night, please..?"

"I'll call you. Trust me, I'll call you."

Angela walked to Mark near the corner bar. When she arrived, she turned toward the office and observed Amy walking in the gallery. "Is she ok?" Mark asked.

"She's going to be fine. A little rough at the moment, but she'll get better."

"You're a good friend, Angela."

"And so is she." Angela smiled, "And so is she." Angela grabbed Mark and kissed him on the cheek.

"Why the kiss?" Mark asked.

"Advice from a friend," Angela answered with a seductive smile.

They roamed the gallery observing people and enjoying the music, then entertained conversations with couples, artist, and general observers. One couple complimented them on being newlyweds, which they quickly denied. Another gentleman complimented Mark on his ability to capture a lovely woman's heart. Again, they laughed with adolescent pride. "If one more tells us about being in love or a couple, I'm going to…"

"Scream or kiss me?" Angela finished Mark's statement.

"Kiss you is better."

"I think so too."

"Why don't we call it a night?" Mark suggested. "We can finish this later."

"My sentiments exactly..." Angela smiled as she grabbed Mark's arm and asked, "Should we say good night to Margo and Karen?"

"As a courtesy, you're right. Besides we have to tell Margo not to sell our painting."

"Our painting?" asked Angela in confusion.

"The painting we liked. I thought we'd purchase it with one stipulation."

"What's the stipulation?"

Mark explained his deal. "If we don't make it, you get to keep it as a reminder of our lives together. If you decide to get rid of it, I'll buy your half. This way I don't lose the painting if we lose each other."

"Well, Mark this is big for us."

"We're doing it already, Angela. Haven't you heard all the people complimenting us? They think we're together. I think we're together. I thought you were feeling the same as all these people observing us. No doubt to where my feelings and focus are."

"I know, but it's financial," Angela responded.

"If money is your concern, then let's not do it; but if it's emotion?"

"I...I'm falling for you Mark. Haven't you noticed?"

"Then we'll do this as our first step of binding our love." Mark hugged Angela and kissed her deeply as in sealing the deal. "Let's tell Margo about the painting and we'll head home."

"Home?" Angela asked. "My place or yours?"

"Whichever makes my girl comfortable. I'm happy wherever we end up. I'm happy as long as I am next to you where my body and heart can become yours to enjoy."

Without a response, Angela led Mark to another part of the gallery, searching for Margo. The two never broke contact as they weaved through the crowd and avoided dancers. "Margo," Angela called, as she finally spotted her at the other end of the gallery.

"Hey," Margo smiled.

"We are heading home. Save the first painting on the right for us, we'll get it later. Ok?"

"You mean the Star of Love?" Margo asked.

"If that's the name of it, it's fitting," Mark added, looking at Angela.

"It's the one." Angela answered. "Save it and I'll call you. Please save it for us."

"Sure thing. You two have fun and I'm glad you made it," Margo told Angela and kissed her on the cheek. "You too, Mark." Margo kissed Mark on the cheek also. The couple left the gallery. Margo headed to Karen, "Hey, you will never say again my matchmaking doesn't work."

"What?" Karen responded with interest.

"I'm a matchmaker. Angela and Mark are going to make it."

"I knew that. Tell me something else," Karen snickered.

"How did you know?" Margo placed her hands on her hips as if she were out of the loop.

"You didn't see them when they entered the gallery. It was obvious."

"You think we have a wedding coming up?"

"I'd place my money on it. If she does, we'll make it great with her."

"Knowing Mark, he's ready this time. He's got a great girl too. She deserves a good guy."

"Don't we all?"


Mark opened Angela's car door just after parking in front of his townhouse. Getting out of the car, he grabbed Angela and kissed her, deep and strong as Angela's back was against the car. Without a second thought, Mark scooped Angela into his arms, gave her the house key and carried her to the door. "Can you get it?" Mark asked as Angela tried to unlock the door while Mark cradled her in his arms.

"I got it," Angela said as the door opened. Mark kicked the door closed just as they cleared the threshold and ended up in his bedroom, placing her gently on the bed. He began kissing her neck, gentle as the wind before a hurricane. He caressed her like the rolling tides from the easy wind. One hand explored the body while disrobing her beautiful dress. His actions, smooth as the stingray gliding on the ocean's shelf. Step by step, Mark explored Angela. His lips were upon her, his hands, his muscular body and tough skin next to her. Angela responded with fainted breath, and quick grasps for air until she felt those lips of passion touch her like the petal of a flower. Like a hurricane changing its strength, Mark moved with actions guiding Angela into a position where she felt his excitement. As the outer band got closer to shore, so did his erection, pointing to the very entrance of tomorrow's dream. "I've waited for this moment. I so want this." Mark whispered.

"My love, it's ah…." Angela panted in excitement. "I want this too, but I'm afraid of one thing. I'm afraid of being hurt."

"Baby," Mark softly replied while penetrating with little movement. "I'm not going to hurt you, as I want your heart."

"Ooh, I feel your want. I feel.., oooh" Angela answered moving her hips grabbing for more. "I ah ah oooh."

Mark continued his slow build up, like the outer hurricane band pushed before the rain. His movement got stronger, like shore crashing waves surfers love to enjoy. Crash, and it was finally in, push-crash, push-crash. Mark moved as if he was the very strength of the ocean water. Moving in and out, hard, harder, harder, and soft with his multiple strokes he was now as rhythmic as dancing in the rain. Again like the storm bringing its wind and rain, he kissed and caressed, never stopping those rhythmic strokes. Her nerve endings stood and her breaths were faster pulling him closer, clutching his ass with her feet, pressing him deeper. "Oh oh oh," Angela moaned while using her arms, clamping him with all her might, as if squeezing for dear life. Mark never stopped, and while forcing his movement, he plunged for greater depth. "Yes baby, this is our first," he excitedly yelled. Their bodies shivered as if they were soaked by the rain and chilled as the wind increased with strength. They shivered, and didn't move, connected in time, and touch. Angela caught her breath and released her grasp saying, "I, I'm afraid Mark I have a wall protecting my heart as I've been hurt so many times."

"Keep your wall of protection," Mark replied. "Lower the wall when you're ready to trust me with your heart." Mark moved, shifting his weight off Angela but never losing the connection making them one. In another breath he said, "Your heart then becomes my responsibility. It becomes something I protect, I appreciate, and I treat as a gift. It becomes my best friend, my partner, and my lover. It becomes something I cherish and never take lightly." Mark moved like the hurricane's eye, pounding, pushing, shoving, engaging, then shifted her into his lap, still without losing connection; buried in the depths of Angela. His thrust was of the powerful storm, holding her close to him while they moved like a level 3 wind gusts, moving the entire bed. Just as thunder exploded the sky, Angela shrieked in pleasure. He held her tighter and never released the pulsing spot of enjoyment, they rode and Angela shuddered with passion. Again, she shrieked this time louder and her body beaded with sweat; reminiscent of running miles on the gym's treadmill. "Oh my Gawd," Angela panted, "It doesn't stop." Silent, Mark continued, he stood, holding her connected to him and turned her body over on the bed where she was now on all fours. Still connected he pulled her waist towards him, stronger ...the wind slammed the ocean water against any object...he stroked harder, and not letting go...pushing as deep as one could, he felt her rocking back for more. "Angela, this is for us...Let me take care of your heart."

"Ah hah," Angela replied as her body shivered again. She rocked and collapsed on her stomach, shivered as cold wind and water crashed through the window. Mark fell on her and never left her chamber of affection. He covered her body with his and moved as if being prodded. He moved gently with his standing muscle of youth. He caressed her back and nibbled on her shoulder and neck. Giving her warmth with his body, but not fading with effort, still stroked for dear life, for ecstasy, for future sake, he wanted this woman to keep his heart too. Mark never stopped stroking her, but this time gently pushed and massaged her back as he managed to maneuver to their side. He grazed her smooth skin; sweat soaked back, with his fingertips and never stopped being a part of her. He spoke, "My angel, what a dream you are. I can't believe we finally arrived."

"Me too," Angela answered while moving in rhythm with Mark. "It has taken us a long time to get here. Longer than any other man I've ever..."

Finishing her sentence, Mark jumped in, "...not here for comparison my love, just here for us, our first time being one."

"I know, but this is a first in so many ways."

"It won't be our last. I'm sure of it. I want this to be our connection, our peaceful storm."

"Peaceful storm," Angela repeated but thought "Some storm!"

Mark lost their connection by sliding out of Angela for a moment, turning her to face him. "You are truly gorgeous."

"I'm so lucky."

"We are lucky. We are really lucky." Mark kissed Angela deeply and started a second round. This time in a missionary position, kissing, caressing, moving and feeling the passion rebuild for the second hurricane band before the sun returned.

Margo, Cedric, Karen, and Phillip sat in the office after all the guest had finally left. "Coffee!" Margo called to the others.

"I'm game for a cup," Phillip answered.

"So am I," Cedric admitted.

"I think you two should run out and get us coffee," Karen suggested to Phillip and Cedric.

"That's our cue to leave, partner." Phillip tapped Cedric.

"Right behind you," Cedric followed Phillip to one of the gallery bars.

"You had a wonderful show tonight." Karen told Margo.

"I'm surprised it went well. Do you realize we've sold nearly every piece of art tonight?"

"As I thought you would."

"How were you so sure? I know my work is good, but wow. Most artists hardly move art during their first show. We must have made nearly $50 grand tonight. The biggest paintings left first. I am surprised."

"You shouldn't be surprised. You sold most of the art to corporate decorators. I introduced your work to a few people. I had no idea who most of the people were tonight." Karen admitted.

"I'm glad they came." Margo recalled Karen sending the guys out for coffee. "Why did you get rid of the guys?"

"I wanted to congratulate you first with this check." Karen pulled a check from her purse.

"OH MY GOD!" Margo summed up and shouted with excitement as she read the check for $100,000.00.

"What are you going to do with it?"

Panting with excitement, Margo sat on the couch, caught her breath and controlled her excitement. "Where did this come from Karen?"

"One of the guys approached me and wanted to know how much it would cost to paint murals in six of his major buildings. I told him this is his start."

"I can't take this." Margo stood, shaking her head handing the check to Karen.

"Sure you can," Karen said as she refused to take the check. "You did it, not me. I only gave a price and I hope its enough."

"It's too much and the expectation is so high."

"No, think – 'You can do this.' He will contact you Monday and work the details. This check is his way of saying he's seriously motivated."

"Are you sure?" Margo sat staring at the check.

"I'm sure. Talk to the guy Monday when he calls. I'll be there if you need me." Cedric and Phillip entered the room with coffee.

Phillip asked, "Need you for?"

"I told her about the deal," Karen answered.

"What deal?" Cedric asked with curiosity.

"Here," Margo passed the check to Cedric.

"Wow! Are you serious?"

"Yes. She's serious," Phillip answered.

"You knew," Margo said as she sipped coffee while seated on the couch. "How did you know?"

"I was in on the conversation. Heck it surprised me too. Just goes to show how talented you are."

"Darling, you are talented and I've told you this for as long as I can remember." Cedric smiled moving closer to Margo and kissed her on the cheek. "I kept my fingers crossed one day you'd be discovered."

"You were today." Karen smiled while enjoying the moment for her best friend. "It is your dream. Don't be afraid."

"I couldn't have done it without you," Margo teary, eyed admitted, "I couldn't."

"What are friends for?" Karen sat next to Margo and placed her arm around her, pulled her close for a one arm embrace. "What are friends for? You'd do the same for me."

"I would," Margo responded while hugging Karen, "You know I would."

Tuesday morning arrived with repeated smiles from the girls. Margo agreed to painting murals for six buildings over an eighteen month period. She left her job and pursued her dream to be a professional artist. Karen's company won a decorating contract for six new buildings in the city. It gave her enough work and money to extend her employee base, provided funding for direct marketing campaigns for new business, and ignited her business schedule for the next two years. Angela shared her love experience with Margo and Karen over Tuesday morning coffee. She cried while describing the lovemaking session with Mark and never fully explained it in detail. The first time she cried over making love, it was so powerful. It surely made her move with

349

emotions for Mark. Hearing her experience, Margo and Karen encouraged her to be happy and go with her heart. The three ladies set forth on their own paths that Tuesday.

Mark planned dinner with Angela for Wednesday night. He called the Sun Dial and made reservations. He coordinated with his head waiter buddy, for a special presentation during the dessert. He planned the timeline to drive Angela downtown Atlanta and detailed his events. He made special purchases, delivered the goods on Tuesday and anxiously waited for Wednesday night. He explained dinner ideas to Angela and without question she jumped on the idea of spending any time with Mark. After coordination, research and investment, Mark and Angela headed to dinner in the evening. Mark chose the restaurant at the top floor of the tallest hotel sky scraper in the city. The restaurant circled on axis where patrons viewed the city for miles around. Mark timed the dinner reservation with the sunset so the two could watch the change to darkness and street lights pattern like ocean waves, rippling out to sea.

At the hotel Mark guided Angela to the elevator entrance. The receptionist greeted them, "Welcome to the Sun Dial. Do you have reservations?"

"Yes, Mark Anderson party of two."

"Thank you," the receptionist responded and said, "I have it right here. Please take the elevator."

"Sure thing," Mark answered and pulled Angela close to him. He placed his arm around her and the entire lounge of people emptied. With the first elevator bell, he kissed Angela as if a snapshot of times to come.

"Why the kiss? I'm not complaining," Angela smiled as she inquired.

"I'm happy being with you. You look wonderful. I didn't want to lose the moment. I couldn't help it."

"I'm glad you couldn't." Angela smiled as they stood waiting arm in arm.

The elevator arrived with a few people and two other couples entered with Mark and Angela. They stood near the corner looking out the glass wall, watching the cars, trees, and building, diminish in size as they rose to the top. "You aren't afraid of heights are you?"

"Why do you ask?" Angela smirked.

"We're here on the top floor. Some people get nervous."

"I think its going to be beautiful."

"I'm sure it will."

The two met the waiter and followed him to their table observing the decorations. Mark noticed two paintings along the way. "Aren't those Margo's?" he asked as pointing to the wall.

"It sure looks like her work. If it isn't, it's pretty close."

With everything from earlier coordination, Mark winked at the waiter and passed him a note without Angela noticing. After the waiter explained the specialties, Angela decided to tell Mark her order instead of the waiter. It was the normal process she now enjoyed since dating Mark. "We'll have the specials," Mark winked as he told the waiter.

"Thank you sir, I'll be right back with your drinks."

"I didn't order the special." Angela said. "Why didn't you order what I told you?"

"I did." answered Mark. "I know you now and trust me with the order. Trust me, ok?"

"I do. Everything you've said you'd do is exactly as you've done."

"You are important to me, and life is now really fun and interesting."

"Interesting?" Angela asked while observing the city lights.

"Yes, very," Mark replied.

The waiter returned with drinks and placed them on the table. He quickly grabbed the extra silverware and left the right setting for dinner. "Your dinner will be served shortly," the waiter announced.

"Thank you," Mark responded. Nervous in thought, "I hope Angela takes my offer," Mark mused.

"Why are you making that face?" Angela asked as she noticed Mark's facial expression.

"Just nervous, thinking of how lucky I am being with you."

"Why on earth are you nervous?"

"I don't want us to lose anything we've gained. I mean, we've grown so fast and I want it to last. Wanting so much makes me nervous."

"You shouldn't be nervous." Angela smiled as she too felt the exact emotion, without fear.

"I'll hope for a positive future."

Dinner arrived right after a moment of silence. Mark tried not to give his thoughts away. He created small talk during the meal and made laughter over little things. It was if he was nervous before asking for her hand in marriage. "Nothing close to the marriage question, but surely asking her about the weekend away is nerve wrecking," Mark thought. He watched Angela complete her dinner and finish her wine. She looked at Mark noticing his behavior being different than usual. "Is there something wrong?" asked Angela.

"No, nothing's wrong. Are you ready for dessert?"

"I'm not sure I want dessert tonight," Angela responded while she observed Mark starting to sweat.

"I made a special order for our dessert tonight. Are you sure you don't want it?"

"Well, since you made a special order I would be honored to take it, only with one exception. We have to share."

"Done," Mark smiled and thought, "Close." He waved for the waiter and said, "Dessert, please." Mark poured wine in Angela's glass. "I know you're going to like the dessert. I noticed so many things while we were getting to know each other."

"You are so perceptive and attentive. Those are two things I love about you."

"Thank you so much. Hopefully you'll love this."

The waiter returned with, a red rose laid across the tray, a slice of chocolate mouse cheese cake, and two envelopes. With a big smile, Angela said, "What did you do?"

"Baby, I'm serious," Mark said while the waiter placed the dessert between them and sat the forks on each side. He placed the envelopes in front of Angela as Mark instructed. "Before you say anything, or open the envelopes, I have something to tell you."

Angela looked at Mark with curiosity and thought, "what on earth?"

"I don't want to sound cliché. I've thought of this moment for days. Since we developed such feelings for each other, I'm ready to move closer to you. My dream is the same since the day we met. My heart fluttered with every moment we spent together, and when we aren't, I thought of times when I could get back to you. When we spent the other night making love, it was the very first time I didn't want the session to end. It was the first time I wasn't on a triumphant journey. It was the first time I felt love and finally met someone as a partner." Mark waited as he cleared his thought, sipped a little wine, and said, "You are my dream girl, whenever I see your smile, I see your joy through those beautiful eyes. I view how the world takes in your beauty. You see, my dream woman is one of love, kind-ness, adventures, and passion. You are all those things wrapped in one."

"I'm speechless Mark. I...."

"...want us to move to a different level. Come with me." Mark lifted the first envelope and handed it to Angela. "Come with me on a journey to celebrate us, moving closer." Angela opened the envelope and saw airline tickets to Florida for the coming weekend.

"Wow, Mark. I've never had anyone surprise me with a trip." Angela left her chair and sat in Mark's lap, laying a deep seductive kiss. "I've never had anyone ..."

"...and I want us to share this. Open the other envelope." Mark handed it to her and observed her opening the envelope.

"Another set of tickets. We're going to a jazz festival on the beach for two days; sun, surf, and jazz. Perfect!"

"Yes, are you ready to enjoy the first of many to come?"

"Anywhere with you, I'll go anywhere with you!"